# BARBARA COPPERTHWAITE

# her last secret

bookouture

Published by Bookouture
An imprint of StoryFire Ltd.
23 Sussex Road, Ickenham, UB10 8PN
United Kingdom
www.bookouture.com

ISBN: 978-1-78681-260-5
eBook ISBN: 978-1-78681-259-9

To Ellen, my big sister. We used to argue over everything, now we just argue over who should buy the drinks.

# PROLOGUE

A lifetime can flash by in a moment. A moment can last a lifetime.

Right now, everything seemed cradled in the pause between breaths. It wasn't so much that the world was in slow motion, more that Dominique's senses were so heightened that she could note every detail: the look on her eldest daughter's face; the desperation that made her husband's voice hitch; the squeak of her youngest child when she got excited or scared. She thought of all those things, examining them. Wondering whether to smile or cry at their memory.

Dominique had spent most of her life hiding from herself, from others, from her past. Now, she felt secreted in a between-world, like the moment before waking. She needed to make a decision. Should she remain and carry on hiding, her life sliding away like water through cracks in the pavement; or should she act?

There were consequences to actions, though. Prices that must be paid.

She exhaled. Decision made.

The time had come to expose all the secrets, no matter what.

If only she had the courage to do so. If only the family was strong enough to survive it. If only she didn't do something stupid herself.

# CHAPTER 1

## CHRISTMAS DAY

Squad cars blocked the normally peaceful Burgh Road, in Black-heath, London. The blue lights were switched off but, had they been on, wouldn't have looked out of place among the festive illuminations strewn over trees in many front gardens, lighting up the dark hours pre-dawn. The handsome red-brick houses were all large, neat, detached, built for affluent Victorians during the heady decades before the First World War. The period properties were what kept Blackheath such a desirable address still.

Along the tree-lined street there were few net curtains to twitch at the gathering crowd of police officers. Instead, neighbours peered, bleary-eyed, around blinds, or pulled back wooden shutters that matched the original sash windows of their homes. Adults shooed their little ones away, but stayed rooted to the spot themselves, clinging to each other for safety behind the glass. The children probably didn't need much persuading to stay away, overjoyed at an excuse to unwrap their presents without their parents wearily trying to go back to bed just a little longer.

Christmas had indeed come early for them.

Chief Inspector Paul Ogundele checked his watch – 3.47 a.m. – and got out of his car to take charge of the scene. He noticed how some neighbours, bolder than their counterparts, edged to their front door and stood watching, poised to bolt at the first sign of trouble. He'd have to remind uniformed officers to send them back inside for their own safety.

According to a laminated poster still attached to a fence, Burgh Road had been closed a fortnight earlier, too; that time for a festive street party for neighbours to get to know one another and to allow youngsters to play in the road without fear. Cheery, multicoloured bunting still hung from lamppost to lamppost, dripping in the pouring rain. Below it, in swags, was yellow police tape.

Outside the cordon, paramedics hunched in their ambulance, steaming up their windows as they waited to be told when it was safe to do their jobs. They wouldn't be setting foot anywhere until the police's armed response unit had finished securing the place and given them the nod.

Chief Inspector Ogundele took it all in in a second. He ducked under the tape and strode over to a uniformed officer standing stoically, pretending she didn't notice the waterfall running in front of her face from her hat.

'Sergeant Hussain. What's the situation?'

'Gunshots were reported at 3.20 a.m. by a Mr Alan Jackman, of 17 Burgh Road. At least two shots fired within his neighbour's home at number fifteen. Mr Jackman told the control room during his 999 call that his neighbour has a shotgun and regularly goes clay pigeon shooting. He also says he heard "shouting and one hell of a row" which woke him immediately before he heard gunfire.'

As the officer spoke, she indicated over to a man in his early fifties whose pallor matched his prematurely grey hair. He was still in his blue towelling dressing gown and matching pyjamas, but stood defiantly to attention at his front door, as though afraid of showing weakness. Especially in his new, bright yellow Simpsons slippers.

'Residents have been warned to stay indoors, sir,' added Sergeant Hussain.

The chief inspector made a noise of impatience. People so rarely listened to orders, curiosity generally overcoming fear. Some residents even held up their mobile phones, filming the excitement and no doubt live-streaming it on Facebook, Twitter, and any other social media they could think of.

'What do we know about who lives in the building?'

'Number fifteen belongs to Mr Benjamin Thomas, forty-eight, and his wife Dominique, forty-four. According to the neighbour, they have two children, Amber, who is between seven and nine – the neighbour isn't sure, and Ruby, a teenager of about sixteen. Checks have confirmed that Mr Thomas has a licence for a shotgun, which is kept on the premises.'

Had Benjamin Thomas had an accident? Discovered burglars and taken a potshot? Or perhaps been shot at by armed thieves? Did the gun go off by mistake? Or had he gone crazy and killed or injured his wife, children and himself? Murder/suicide was a terrible thing, and rare, but not unheard of by any stretch of the imagination. At this time of year there was generally a spike in domestic abuse, due to people being in close proximity for longer periods than they would be at other times of the year.

Just what happened to the family inside number fifteen?

# CHAPTER 2

Mouse loved this time of the day best of all. Everyone she loved the most in the whole wide world were all together, happy and peaceful, and still in bed, sleepy tired. Outside, darkness paled, which made her brave, so that she knew the shadow of the monster terrifying her every time she woke at night was really her dressing gown hung on the back of her door. The house had even stopped making creaking noises like a ghost.

She loved first thing in the morning for all of those reasons – and also because she could read quietly for a little while before Mummy came to say it was time to get up.

With a contented sigh, she turned on her torch and pulled the duvet, with its Big Friendly Giant cover, over her head to read. She didn't really need to; if she had put her bedside light on it wouldn't have disturbed anyone. Not now she had a bedroom all to herself.

She hadn't wanted her own room. She had preferred it when she and Ruby shared. Mouse hadn't got so scared then when she woke, instead she had been able to prod her big sister awake and climb into bed with her. But since she got her own room Ruby had started locking her bedroom door, forcing Mouse to come up with a different solution. She would burrow under her duvet and make herself read, forcing herself to concentrate on the words really, really hard until she forgot about the scary dreams and imaginings and was whisked off to magical places. It didn't always work, but mostly it did.

And when things got really bad, she hid in the wardrobe.

But right now, she pulled the duvet over her head purely to enjoy the warmth, breathing in the comforting aroma a little like fresh-baked biscuits. She started to read her book, *The Lion, the Witch and the Wardrobe*, but more thoughts about her sister crept in around the edges of her mind.

She wished she could do something lovely for Ruby, to cheer her up. When they shared a room, Ruby used to smile all the time, a hidden gem gifted only to Mouse. But now Ruby kept everything but her scowl locked away.

Having an idea, Mouse threw back the covers and padded over to her desk. Pulled out a drawing pad and some crayons, and started to copy the cover of her book. A lion with a huge mane and sad eyes. His face seemed a lot wonkier than on the cover, but she was pleased with it anyway. She ran her fingers over the crayons, thinking. The picture needed something else. Red love hearts kissed the page. Much better.

Holding up her effort, she turned her head on one side as if to look at it from all angles.

A soft bubble and chug sounded from the water pipes. Daddy was up and having his shower. Mouse smiled and hugged herself tight, lulled by the sounds of everyday life.

Mummy's gentle knock came. The door opened.

'You up, Mouse?'

'Up and at 'em.' She jumped and did a kick in the air like Kung Fu Panda.

'Oh, you are raring to go. See you downstairs for breakfast in a minute, eh?'

Mouse grabbed up the drawing again and dodged past Mummy, scurried along the hallway, pausing for a moment to wriggle her toes in the thick cream carpet and enjoy the feeling. She slipped the drawing under her sister's bedroom door then ran into the bathroom they shared, as her mum rapped to wake Ruby.

'Wakey, wakey, rise and shine,' Mummy called. Silence. Another knock.

'All right. I'm awake.'

Ruby sounded grumpy. Of course.

Mouse carefully turned the knob of the shower – a hard task with her fingers crossed. She hoped her drawing did the trick with her big sister.

❖

Dominique stared, unseeing, at the steam rising from the kettle. Didn't hear the click as it switched itself off. While Mouse and Ruby got ready upstairs, it left her free to think about the state of her marriage.

She felt so alone. Benjamin had turned away from her last night when she tried to have sex with him. It had been months now, and it wasn't like him. He could deny it all he wanted, but something was on his mind. Something big.

When he wasn't working late, he hid in his study, only coming into the lounge after she had gone to bed, and waiting until she was asleep before joining her. When they were in a room together, there seemed to be nothing to say. If she asked about his plans for the day, he would give a noncommittal answer; ask how his day had been, she got a grunt.

His rejection of her efforts hurt more than a slap. What did she have to do to get her husband to notice her? What did she have to do to win him back?

Whatever it was, she wasn't sure she had the strength for it.

She rubbed at her right forearm fretfully. When she realised, she snatched her hand away. Pulled down the sleeve of her dressing gown.

The twin silvery scars that ran beneath the long sleeve were hidden now. Still, they shimmered in her mind's eye, taunting her. Reminding her of a past she would rather forget.

Trying to banish the thoughts, Dominique dived into the inexorable morning routine. Poured the scalding water into the cafetière, cracked eggs into a dish, put on the toast for everyone…

A howl of rage rang through the house.

Dominique ran.

On the landing stood Ruby, glaring down at her black jumper as though someone had murdered it. The fifteen-year-old's face screwed up in disgust as she gave another moan, and pointed at her little sister. *J'accuse.*

'Mouse, this is your bloody fault—'

'Don't swear at your little sister. Now, what on earth has happened?'

'Look. There's a hole in my brand-new top. I caught it on that nail—'

'Well, that's hardly your sister's fault, is it?'

Dominique looked at her youngest. Her eyes were wide with hurt and protest, but she didn't say a word. Despite being highly intelligent, and articulate when she wanted to be, she always came across as being both old before her time and younger than her eight years. Her name was Amber, but no one called her that; instead, she was known universally as Mouse, thanks to her habit of finding small spaces to squeeze into so she could read undisturbed.

Beside her, Ruby huffed. 'Why are you always taking her side? I hate you.'

*I hate you.*

The first time Ruby had flung those words at Dominique she had flinched as if struck. The verbal blows were no longer unexpected, but they still hurt, and she still wondered what on earth she had done to deserve them. From the outside, her family seemed perfect. She and Benjamin made a good-looking couple, they had two intelligent, beautiful children, Benjamin was a successful businessman, running his own accountancy firm, they had regular holidays both home and abroad, and lived in a lovely home. They enjoyed all the trappings of success.

But as she looked at Ruby's fury, she wondered if it were all starting to disappear, like a dream on waking.

❖

Benjamin's hand made a squeak as it swiped across the bathroom mirror, clearing the condensation. The extractor fan wasn't working properly, which was infuriating. He'd have to get someone in to look at it. At some point. He had enough on his plate for the time being.

Despite standing under a too-hot shower for ten minutes, trying to work up the courage to step out again, he still felt exhausted. Tired, bloodshot eyes stared back at him from the clearing he had created in the mirror. Puffy skin stretched as he shaved but didn't ping back the way it had when he was younger. Scattered here and there on his cheeks and beside his nose were broken veins, hiding beneath the sunbed tan that faked the fact he hadn't afforded as many holidays in the sun this year as success dictated. The red spider veins were tiny, almost invisible, but enough to taunt him every single day. *You're getting old. You're past it. You're not the man you were.*

Shoulders back, he strutted out of the bathroom, naked, dick swinging like a pendulum between his legs. Dominique wasn't there to see his act, though, so he let his posture slump. He could hear her arguing with their teenage daughter, Ruby. He ground his teeth and he yanked on a pair of boxers, then trousers, as the conversation grew louder.

'I hate you,' Ruby shouted.

Right, he wasn't putting up with that. He would have respect in this house. Not bothering to do himself up, he flung the bedroom door open and glared down the landing at the frozen tableau.

Ruby glowering. Jaw set, fists clenched as she leaned forward. Dom glancing at him apologetically. Hands open in a gesture of peace towards her daughter.

'What the hell is all this racket?' he growled.

'It's nothing. Ruby and I were discussing what she should wear to school today. It's sorted now.'

Ruby looked from one parent to the other, then flung up her hands.

'Fine.' With a huff, she shut the door so swiftly that she almost, but not quite, slammed it – close enough that Benjamin took a step out of his own doorway to tell her off.

'Leave it. Please,' begged Dom. 'It's too early to have a row.'

He didn't want to give in. It showed weakness, and he already felt fragile enough in the rest of his life. But he had other things he needed his energy for. With a dismissive wave of a hand, he too closed his door.

He was turning into his own dad, he knew. Being a complete boorish arse. It made him hate himself even more. He'd try to make it up with Ruby later, if he had time. But not right now. If he did it immediately, he'd look feeble.

# CHAPTER 3

The last thing Ruby wanted was to have breakfast with that bunch of hypocrites. But if she didn't, World War Three would break out, and it totally wasn't worth it. Dad was such a control freak.

It was Mouse's fault. If she hadn't darted in front of her as Ruby was about to go downstairs, she wouldn't have had to sidestep suddenly and catch her top on the nail that stuck out near Mouse's bedroom door. It had pulled a hole. And Mum had no sympathy. Of course. It wasn't fair. If it had been something of Mouse's, she'd have been all over the kid. But Ruby was, what, supposed to just take it? Just do like Mum and quietly accept everything? No way.

It was a new top, too. And now she couldn't wear it to school, not with a massive great hole in it.

She threw herself onto her bed and hot angry tears spilled, making the dove grey walls blur and the members of My Chemical Romance bleed into each other on the poster over her headboard. It was so unfair. Life totally had it in for her, and no one understood. No one, except Harry.

Thinking about him cheered her up. And made her dry her face and start getting ready for school. Actually, the top didn't look too bad. The hole looked kind of cool after she'd pulled at it a bit more to make it bigger, and caused several runs up the knitted fabric. Yeah, nice. If Dad saw it, he'd have a fit and never let her out of the house, but she could hide it under her coat easy enough.

❖

She traipsed through the streets, dragging her feet through clumps of sodden, rusty brown leaves that stuck together like congealed blood. Kicked them into the air and listened to the soft splat they made. Trying to kill time because she absolutely would rather die than go to school.

Her parents were determined to get her into a better one, closer to home, as soon as possible. At the time, though, they had just been glad that any school managed to squeeze her in in September – she had been a last-minute applicant after an incident got her booted out of the last. Now her parents were lobbying to get her into a different place again for the following academic year. Whatever. Ruby had every intention of dropping out as soon as she was legally allowed – if not sooner.

Clouds glowered from a metallic sky. Moisture in the heavy air plastered her dark blonde hair to her face as she walked. Her coat only covered her to mid-thigh, so from there downwards her damp skirt clung to her chapped legs, making her shiver despite her thick tights.

She should have gone to Blackheath station really; that was closer to her house. But the longer walk was worth it because Westcombe Park was on a different line. On this line, she got to meet up with Harry. As soon as she jumped on the train, in her usual carriage, she sat in her usual seat, then dug out her make-up bag in preparation. Caked foundation on her pale skin, blotted out freckles and imperfections, then drew on thick black eyeliner. Done.

She'd get another lecture off the teachers, of course. That put a smile on her face. It grew bigger when Harry jumped on.

It was weird to think that the first time she'd seen him, almost four months ago, she'd thought he was kind of funny-looking, with his braces, the green-framed spectacles, which stood out so bright against his dark skin, and crazily curly hair. They were what you saw before looking properly and seeing the real Harry.

At the time, she'd been stuffing her bag into the locker she had been allocated minutes earlier by some teacher who smelled strongly of onions. Ruby had been trying to decide if it was fried food or body odour that was causing it, when she'd received a tap on the shoulder and a cheerful 'hello' from this weird boy.

'All right? I'm Harry. Harry Porter – get your jokes in now. What's your name? You're new here, aren't you? Where you from?'

She screwed up her face at the barrage of questions, and decided he was taking the mick, because she hadn't made friends yet. But she had high hopes, and didn't want this geek ruining her chances. He looked the type who wasn't in with the in-crowd.

'Yeah? Well, my name's Voldemort, so sod off.'

'No, seriously. My mum was, like, a massive Harry Potter fan, so named me after him. She reckoned it was brilliant. I reckon it's awful, man,' he explained, with the patience of someone used to saying the same thing again and again to people. 'You named after anyone?'

His thumbs were stuck behind his rucksack straps, and he swung from side to side a bit as he spoke. But at least he was actually talking to her, which was a step up from what she was used to. He actually looked interested in making conversation. Ruby had found herself softening.

'No, think Mum just liked the name Ruby. Don't know where she got it from. Then when she had my little sister, she didn't have the imagination to come up with anything original and decided to name us both after precious stones, so called her Amber.' She rolled her eyes for emphasis. Harry chuckled.

'So how comes you've joined this school? You moved round here?'

'I got expelled from my last school.'

His friendly eyes widened. Impressed. 'Why?'

'I got drunk. Downed half a bottle of vodka. When the teacher found me, I vomited so badly I thought I'd bring up my guts.'

Ruby laughed at the memory, and Harry joined in so that they almost butted heads. Which made them laugh harder.

'My dad went, like, monu-mental when he heard. But I got my own way and came here.' Telling Harry about it, it sounded funny and impressive, and like she was master of her own destiny.

The two teenagers had drifted to class together and sat side by side. Ruby hadn't been able to believe her luck at making a friend already. That lunchtime, they shared headphones to listen to music, nodding in time to Royal Blood, Bad Religion, and NOFX, with some Arctic Monkeys and David Bowie thrown in for good measure. It was the perfect eclectic mix. Ruby felt close to him. The closest she had felt to anyone in as long as she could remember.

Within days they had become inseparable. Three-and-a-half months on, that still hadn't changed.

Now, she undid her coat and showed him the holes in her jumper.

'What do you think? Too much?'

'It looks wicked sik,' he smiled.

By the time she hopped off the train a few minutes later, she had gone the whole hog and torn a couple of holes in her tights, too. She got some funny looks when she got to school. Let them look.

❖

As she pulled a book from her locker, Ruby's phone vibrated. Her hand clapped over it before she could stop herself. She glanced at Harry. The light reflected on his glasses so that she couldn't see his eyes, but she knew he would have noticed.

A blush crept over her cheeks in spite of herself.

'Who is it?' Harry asked, his voice insistent. 'What do they say? Show me.'

'Come on, we'll be late for class.'

'Show me. Now.'

'Ruby Thomas.' A voice rang out, loud, clear and indignant. 'What on earth do you think you're wearing? Come with me.'

The teenager closed her locker, threw Harry a shrug, then trailed after Mrs Simpkiss, the geography teacher. A lecture and a new pair of tights no doubt awaited her.

When she glanced back, Harry looked seriously annoyed. She mustn't forget to delete the message after reading it.

# CHAPTER 4

'Leave him.'

Fiona's red face was caused by the passion of her venom more than the few sips of complimentary wine she and Dominique had drunk. She stared straight ahead, talking to Dominique's reflection as they sat side by side at their hairdresser's.

'You deserve better than him, Dom, you know you do. He's so cocky – he thinks he's Mr Big, but he'd be lost without you. You're worth ten times that man.'

'Thanks. Why not tell the whole world?' Dominique hissed.

She and Fiona had been friends since school. They had gone from sharing Sindy dolls, to Revlon lipsticks, to Louis Vuitton suitcases as their lives had experienced an upward trajectory. Fiona's had come thanks to a career as a successful divorce lawyer with the sort of celebrity clients she wasn't allowed to name; Dominique's courtesy of her marriage to Benjamin.

Fiona's vehement dislike of Benjamin could be traced back to a brief crush she had for him back when she was twelve and she had sent him a valentine he hadn't acknowledged. She denied it, of course, but from that moment Fiona had bristled every time he walked into a room. Which had been often, because they were friends with his younger sister, Krystal.

So, her urging Dom to walk out on Benjamin didn't come as a shock, but Dom would have preferred it if she weren't so loud about it.

'You worry too much about what other people think. No one's taking any notice. Are you?' Fiona asked Saul, the skinny man in skinny jeans and T-shirt, floating like a butterfly around her hair, primping it to perfection.

'Hmm? Sorry, I was a world away. What did you say, my love?' he asked with exaggerated care, putting his hands on her shoulders and leaning down to make a big show of listening intently.

'See, far too discreet here,' Fiona smiled, turning her head now. 'It's one of the reasons why we pay so much to come here.'

'And I thought it was because of their incredible ability to make my thin, mousey hair look thick and lustrous.' Dominique laughed in spite of herself.

'Look like you've been dragged through a hedge backwards? Go to John Robertelli and you'll be red-carpet ready in minutes.'

'Probably closer to four hours, once you've had the head massage, the deep conditioning treatment, the blow-dry…'

'Hmm, don't forget the massage chair. I love having my hair washed while that chair works its magic.'

'Ooh, get you two. You sound like an advert for us,' sighed Saul. 'Can I give you two ladies a top up before Samantha starts on your manicure?'

'Yes, please,' said Fiona – as Dominique said, 'No, thanks.'

Saul looked from one to the other. Dominique caved first, removing her hand from over her glass. Fiona smiled her approval.

'Perfect. You only live once, and you know this is my big treat to myself.'

Dominique knew Fiona had a point. She worked all hours, thought nothing of working until midnight, then being up at four in the morning, when there was a big case on. Dominique didn't know how she did it. It made the stay-at-home-mum feel inadequate, even though she knew her oldest friend would laugh if she were to tell her. It said a hell of a lot about their friendship that no matter what occurred in Fiona's life, she almost always made time to keep this weekly appointment they shared at the hairdresser's for a pamper, followed by lunch. Fiona often worked all the way through the weekend, so this truly was precious time to the lawyer.

When Dominique was younger she had wanted to be a West End star. She'd dreamed of being pampered constantly, of being the centre of attention. Weekly blow-dries were the closest she was ever going to get now. Besides, Benjamin wanted her to look good for him, and her hair was, she knew, her crowning glory. She multitasked by having a manicure too, so it was efficient use of time.

As Saul sashayed away, Dominique breathed a sigh of relief that his suggestion of more wine had stopped the conversation in its tracks. Gazing out of the window, she saw that the rain had turned to snow, tiny flakes gently zigzagging down to the ground on the breeze. She opened her mouth to point it out—

'Right, as I was saying before I was so rudely interrupted by your paranoia: you should leave Benjamin.'

She should have known Fiona wouldn't be so easily distracted from her train of thought. Typical lawyer.

'I haven't even told you what he's done yet.'

'Don't need to. I can tell you're upset.'

'You know I love you to bits but… can we change the subject, please? Benjamin is working really hard at the moment and I'm feeling a bit neglected, that's all.'

'Well, you know I'm here for you, no matter what.' Fiona reached across and squeezed Dominique's arm. 'We're the two musketeers, right? And I know something's wrong; I just wish you'd tell me what. Besides, you know I'll give you a mega discount if you do ever divorce him. I could take him to the cleaners for you.'

'Fiona!'

They giggled as Saul made his way back, brandishing the bottle of white wine.

Dominique wasn't going to tell Fiona that her husband no longer fancied her. She would pretend that everything was fine – and hope that eventually, it would be.

'So, how's your love life, anyway?' she asked, as the manicurist got to work, putting the first stripe of varnish onto the nail, and pausing for a moment until Dominique gave a single incline of the head to show she liked the deep berry colour.

'Ha, what love life?'

'I thought you went on a date on Wednesday night?'

'Disaster. Complete and utter disaster.' Fiona took a sip of wine, settling back to enjoy herself, the great raconteur. 'I met him straight after work, at that restaurant across the river from Tate Modern. You know the one? From the start, he didn't seem quite as entertaining as I remembered. Where were the amusing stories? Where was the man who had me laughing all night? Then I realised… I was the one who had been cracking all the jokes. I'd been so off my trolley that I'd thought he was funny, but it was me.'

They turned at the same time, to give each other the same awkward look they had been pulling since they were kids and had loved Dame Edna Everage. Lips skewed, perfect scarlet lipstick exaggerating the expression.

'You can take the girls out of Essex, but you can't take Essex out of the girls,' giggled Dominique.

But even as she laughed, Dominique felt a veil of sadness and panic settle over her. She didn't want to go back to the single life, and going on disastrous dates with strangers. Not after twenty-two years of partnership.

Fiona sighed. 'I don't know… I'm not sure I'll ever meet someone. And to be honest, I'm kind of fine with that. No, really, I'm not playing the sympathy card. Look at my life: I earn great money, I have an active social life, I love my job, I have a lovely home. Someone to share it with would be a bonus, but it's not the be all and end all, you know? My only regret is… well, you know my regret.'

Dominique nodded. Fiona had always wanted children, but had never found someone to settle down with. She had considered a sperm donor a few years ago, but had eventually decided against it.

'If I became a single mum by falling pregnant accidentally, that would be one thing, but to actively make that decision… It's too massive,' she had confessed at the time.

'Well, if anything ever happens to Benjamin and me, you get the kids,' Dominique had joked. But Fiona had filled up, and what had started as a flippant remark had ended with a legal document being drawn up. It was now official; in case of some catastrophic happening, Fiona would become the children's legal guardian.

It was such a shame Fiona had never met Mr Right, because she would have been a great mum. While her nails dried, Dominique tried to imagine what her life would be like if she hadn't become a mother. She couldn't. As a child, she had dreamed of a career on the stage and screen, hitting the big time to become a star. Instead, she was a full-time mum; without her children, she was nothing.

Without her husband, what was she?

❖

She still pondered this as she and Fiona linked arms, and left the hairdresser's to have a late lunch in their favourite restaurant nearby. One of the many things Dominique loved about living in Blackheath village was the plethora of vibrant independent shops and restaurants huddled around a triangle of roads that hugged the open heath. Living near such an expanse of green space, which virtually ran into Greenwich Park, was a gift.

Blackheath didn't feel like London, despite being a stone's throw from the Thames, and a hop away from the O2 Arena. The capital's marathon started in the village every year, and Dominique loved to watch everyone streaming by; it made her feel proud. But Blackheath had a unique personality apart from the city's hustle: from the expanse of green, where in summer families flew kites, to the pretty church which stood proud on the heath. In its shadow, the shops and restaurants began, spreading out to the pubs that edged the heath. Blackheath was unique.

It had a strong sense of community, too. Only the week before, Burgh Road, the street Dom lived on, had been closed off for a street party. They held one every couple of months, and it was always wonderful to see the children all playing together in the road, the neighbours wandering over to one another to speak, where usually they were hidden in their homes.

Every time she looked around the place she had made her home, Dominique felt content. Doubly so on a Friday. Arms still linked, she and Fiona waited for three red double decker buses to pass, while hard little snowflakes drifted onto their perfectly blow-dried hair, starting to undo hours of hard work. The two women ran across the road, dodging the busy traffic, glossy manes swinging like something from a shampoo advert. Seconds later, they disappeared inside their favourite French restaurant.

As she closed the door, Dominique paused to check.

No one was following her. Of course not. Yet for months now she often felt a prickling unease on the back of her neck, as if someone watched her.

# CHAPTER 5

Ruby's phone vibrated again, but she ignored it and tried to concentrate on the maths book in front of her. The text swayed in drunken fashion. The desk joined in. The classroom walls. She felt sick.

Harry stared at her, heating her skin like a laser beam. He suspected something. She licked her lips, told herself she was used to living with the constant fear of him discovering. But it didn't stop her worrying – if Harry's reaction was bad now, what would he say if she showed him? What would he do?

So, Ruby snubbed her phone and tried to think about her teacher's words. Tried to stare at the numbers and symbols on the page until they formed some kind of sense. They refused. All she could think of was the phone.

What does the message say? Would Harry notice if she checked it?

She glanced at him from under her eyelashes. At the desk beside hers he did the same thing. He turned his head. Gave her a look so intense it felt as though they were the only two people in the room. He burned everyone else away, his love whiting out the real world. In truth, Ruby had disappeared into him the day she met him. But she had no regrets.

Well, hardly any.

The phone shuddered in her hands like something alive. Ruby clutched it blindly, trying to concentrate on the teacher's gobble-dygook. When the hell would she ever have to use Pythagoras's theorem? What was she even going to do with her life when she left school? The only thing that mattered in the world right now was that message.

The teacher waffled on. He seemed really enthusiastic about this triangle business, though Ruby couldn't understand why. Although not exactly gifted academically, she was no slouch either. But grasping theorems proved difficult when all she could think about was not being caught by her boyfriend checking her phone. She didn't want him making a scene.

She had to know what the messages were.

She should wait until lunchtime. Only half an hour to go until then. She could get away from Harry's watchful eyes by slipping to the loo.

Each minute seemed agony, though. Ruby couldn't last another second, let alone thirty minutes. The phone itched for attention, but she knew if she scratched it her soul would bleed.

Harry bent over his notebook, starting to write. Everyone did the same. Ruby wondered if she had missed some instruction, but didn't let it worry her. Instead, she swiped a finger across the screen to unlock it, all without even looking down. It would be the downward glance that was the dodgy bit, the bit that might alert her teacher or Harry to what she was up to. Mobiles were, technically, banned in classrooms. But Ruby had bigger things than that to think about.

She risked a glance at the message.

Shivered.

Looked up, unseeing. Stared with blank eyes at the teacher – who met her gaze.

'Finished already, Ruby?' he asked.

She jumped. 'Just thinking, sir.' Grabbed her pen and leaned over as if to write.

The phone's screen glowed with the message, the words burning into Ruby's retinas.

# CHAPTER 6

Acting confident, that was the key to success. It didn't matter what rubbish you spouted as long as you said it with authority. Benjamin had learned that years ago, when first starting out, inspired by the Muhammad Ali quote that if you could back it up, it wasn't bragging. Benjamin always managed to back it up, somehow, some way.

Still, he felt nervous about this meeting. He dug out a couple of antacids and swallowed them down to try to ease his stomach.

The meeting had been all set up for later that afternoon, and there was a lot riding on it. He needed to come across as the man: The Man. There couldn't be so much as a hint of his feelings of inadequacy from the morning.

The antacids weren't going to get rid of his jitters. He needed something more active. Something he had become addicted to as a way of calming himself. Did he have time? He checked his diary. There was nothing important, nothing he couldn't rejig.

'I'm just nipping out for an hour or so,' he told his secretary. 'Hold all my calls until then.'

He didn't like to, but making sure he felt good for the meeting took precedence over everything else.

'Oh, Benjamin, I need to talk to you.' His business partner, Jazmine Bauer, stood in the doorway of her office with her hands on her hips.

'Sorry, can't stop.'

'Where are you going?'

'See a man about a dog,' he grinned. He barely slowed his step as he walked out, even though Jaz called after him, voice tight with frustration. Screw her, she needed to stop acting like some mother hen, and trust Benjamin. He'd never let his partner down yet and he never would.

But right now, he needed a hit of a very particular kind of drug.

# CHAPTER 7

'Cocktail?' asked Fiona, flourishing the menu.

'Umm…' Dominique already felt rosy from the glasses of wine they'd had at the hairdresser's.

'Go on, it's Christmas.'

'Why not? You're a bad influence.'

'Didn't take much, though, did it?' Fiona gave her best Sid James chortle, which set Dominique off.

'Well, I'll show my good side by insisting we have one as our dessert, rather than start lunch off this way. Anyway, don't you have clients to see this afternoon?'

Fiona pulled a face, shaking her head. 'Wading through paperwork. Got a celeb divorce going through; a biggie. It hasn't even hit the news yet, so we're trying to sort as much as we can before that happens. Because when it does, both sides will start getting stubborn in order to save face. There'll be tit-for-tat articles written in magazines; they'll start believing what's been printed… Eurgh, it'll get messy. But I'll do it tomorrow.'

Dominique knew better than to ask her discreet friend who she represented, even though curiosity prodded her. 'Working the weekend again.'

'As per.'

'And you talk about Benjamin…'

Fiona gave her a look that penetrated Dominique's humour and made it deflate gently. 'I do. Because he has a family and someone who loves him. I don't have to please anyone but myself, so I can be selfish without it impacting on anyone but me. If I did, I'd change my lifestyle.' She moved her side plate out of the way, and leaned forward on the table. 'So, are you going to tell me what he's done? Is he still working crazy hours?'

'Yes. But Benjamin owns his own business, and you know what that takes. I can hardly criticise him for that. He hasn't done anything wrong. Honestly—'

'When people say that they're always lying—'

'Honestly,' Dominique repeated.

Fiona's hawk eyes pounced on her friend's hand. Dominique was rubbing at her right forearm again, at the twin silver lines hidden beneath her sleeve. She stopped instantly. Sighed.

'It's Ruby, if you must know. She's so angry all the time.'

'Typical teenager. Remember what we were like?'

The mum's fingers twitched to dismiss the comment. 'We were never like this. The way she looks at me sometimes, it's pure loathing. And she's always telling me she hates me.'

'Oh, I must have said that to my mum a hundred times when I was a teen. I was a bloody nightmare.'

'I wasn't though.'

Fiona shrugged while laying her napkin across her lap. 'Maybe she takes after Benjamin more than you. Just a sec: hi, could we order drinks, please? A bottle of sparkling water, and two glasses, and… a bottle of the Cabernet Sauvignon? Yes, that one, please.'

After getting the go-ahead from Dominique, Fiona pointed to her choice on the menu, and the waiter made a note as she added that they weren't ready to order food quite yet. Dominique always let people order for her, she realised; whether Benjamin or her best friend, she deferred. People tended to think of her as aloof, but her ice queen act was strictly for those who didn't know her. Not that she let many people in; too scared to reveal the vulnerability behind the show of strength.

'Sorry, you were saying… You think Ruby's behaviour is worse?' Fiona checked.

Dominique toyed with the stem of her empty wine glass, twirling it between her fingers and staring at it rather than her friend.

'It's nothing major. Just rebellious. Sneaking out, not doing as she's told. Barely speaking to us, and when she does it's only to answer back or shout. She never smiles any more. Remember how good she used to be with Mouse? Now all she does is yell at her little sister. I've tried talking to her, suggested we go shopping together as a treat, but she's not interested.'

'Rolled her eyes?' Fiona did a good impression of a surly teenager.

'Spot on, that,' Dominique snorted, despite herself. 'It's like she's taken possession of your body.'

'God, I wouldn't go back to being a teenager for all the tea in China.'

'No, me neither…' Dominique trailed off awkwardly, and Fiona reached out and squeezed her hand.

'No, of course you wouldn't. You mentioned Ruby's been sneaking out. Do you know where to? Who with? I suppose, on the plus side, at least you know she's made friends at this new school. That's got to be a good sign.'

'If she has, we never see them or hear anything about them.' Dominique paused as the waiter appeared with their drinks. Only after he had poured for them and disappeared again did she continue. 'She has made one particular friend though. A boy – a boyfriend, in fact – called Harry.'

'Oh? From your tone, I take it you don't approve?'

'He's fine. He's absolutely fine. I've only met him a handful of times, but he's always very polite.'

Fiona didn't say a word, waiting for Dominique to continue. Silence stretched on. Dom picked up her menu and pretended to read it, even though she knew it off by heart. Fiona idly ran a finger up her glass of water, creating a stripe in the condensation.

Dom caved first, filling the silence.

'There's something about him I don't trust. I can't put my finger on it. Ruby is absolutely head over heels, though. Thinks he's the best thing since sliced bread.' It came out in a rush, and she knew she sounded unreasonable. Jealous even. Which was ridiculous. Why on earth would she be jealous of her teenage daughter?

She could remember when she and Benjamin had been young and in love, though. When each had been the centre of the other's world. When they were young and broke and didn't care a jot as long as they had each other; well before they had become ensnared by the trappings of success.

'I take it they go to the same school.'

Dominique nodded. Looked at the menu until she realised she had been staring at the words *parfait au foie de volaille* for two minutes. She put her menu down with a tut of impatience.

Time to admit the truth.

'Okay, I know I'm going to sound like a snob, but he's not the sort of person I want my daughter hanging around with. His family is on benefits, they live in a council flat – not that there's anything wrong with it, I simply want more for her than that.'

'Well, it's not like they're getting married.'

'You haven't seen the way she is around him,' Dom snapped. She stabbed her index finger repeatedly onto the table as she spoke, wrinkling the red tablecloth. 'It's as though the whole universe revolves around him. "Harry this, Harry that." It's like she's lost the ability to think for herself. It's – it's suffocating. That's what it is. Claustrophobic. They spend every second they can together, too.'

'Okay.' Fiona's tone was low, neutral, the voice of a lawyer. Her eyes darted left and she gave the tiniest shake of her head. Dom followed her gesture, and saw their waiter backing away.

'Forget it, I'm overreacting, I know. Honestly.'

That word again. Fiona blinked at it, the only sign that she knew her friend was lying.

'I just thought Ruby's behaviour would improve once she started at this new school; after all, she got what she wanted. And it did – for a short time she seemed happier, more relaxed, smiled again. Then she started dating this Harry, and suddenly she's worse than ever.'

'You mentioned something about where he lives…?'

'Woolwich.'

'Okay, I'm sure you've heard bad things about the area. Violence, knife crime, drugs – but bear in mind that it's changed a lot in the last couple of years. Half the horror stories come from people who've never set foot there. Having said that, some of the most deprived areas of the UK are in SE18. All I'm saying is, get to know the boy before making up your mind about him. Besides, he and Ruby are a phase, a teenage crush, that's all. This time next month it will have burned itself out.'

For all those reassuring words, the ones sticking out were the bad ones: violence, knife crime, drugs, deprived. Even the smallest chance Ruby was near that sort of thing was a risk too far for Dominique. Keen to change the uncomfortable subject, she gave a swift nod.

'Absolutely; they'll never last. Now then, what are you ordering?'

'Usual. You?'

'Usual.'

With a wave of her hand, Dominique caught the attention of the waiter. Within minutes, the two women were laughing again. Dominique was being paranoid about the influence her daughter's new boyfriend had over her. That was all. Like she was being paranoid about her husband hiding things, and that someone was following her.

# CHAPTER 8

Ten minutes after leaving the office, Benjamin pulled up outside a large Victorian house that had been converted into flats. Nerves jittered through his stomach, and his heart thundered, but he knew they would be settled soon. The thought gave him a tingle of excitement, knowing how close he was to scoring.

The road the property was on sloped down, giving a great view of the mercury ribbon of the distant Thames from where he stood. He pressed impatiently on the flat's bell to be let in, trying to hide his watch, in case anyone dodgy happened past, looking for someone to mug. He had remembered to lock his car, hadn't he? He turned and pressed the key fob, in case. The lights flashed twice, confirming he had, indeed, already locked the vehicle.

'Hello?' came a voice. Female. Young. Wary.

'It's me.'

The secure entry door buzzed, and Benjamin pushed it open and launched himself up the stairs in one swift move. He couldn't wait much longer to get his hands on what he needed.

When he reached flat four, the door was already open, a blonde woman waiting for him. Pale-skinned, large-eyed, she couldn't seem to take her eyes off him.

'You know why I'm here,' he growled.

As she stepped towards him, he grabbed her face between both hands and kissed her. Backed her up against the door jamb, pressing his body hard against her as his tongue thrust into her mouth. Already he was stirring, hips starting to grind. They tumbled through the door, breathless, never parting and slammed the door shut.

❖

Kendra curled up in the warmth left by Ben's body. Pulled the duvet a little tighter around herself and buried her nose into it to breathe in his scent, as if he were still with her. Turned a pillow sideways. Flung an arm and leg over it, trying to pretend it was Ben she snuggled.

She wasn't fooled.

When was he going to leave his wife for her?

They had been together for four years now. During that time all of her friends had got engaged or married, some were even pregnant, as the milestone age of thirty approached. Not Kendra. She had waited for Ben, too in love to break it off with him.

It had been an instant attraction when they met at an awards bash. Ben had been awarded Entrepreneur of the Year by the local paper. She had got chatting to him when she found herself standing beside him at the bar.

'Congratulations,' she had smiled. 'Show us your trophy.'

He handed it to her and… she broke it.

'Eek. The top's come off the base; I'm so sorry,' she gabbled, giving it back to him, the clear plastic 'scroll' separated from the black plastic base.

'That's okay. But can I have your number? – I might want to get in touch about compensation,' he smiled, eyes twinkling cheekily.

They had spent the rest of the evening flirting and exchanging banter. He was older than she, but that hadn't put her off one bit. The way he instantly caught the attention of the bar staff to get served, unlike her as she waved a tenner ineffectually in the air as they swept past her to someone else. The way his suit clung to his powerful build. The air of certainty he had as he spoke. He was a powerful, sexy, successful man – and he knew it. Not in a cocky way, but it screamed from every confident gesture and look. When he leaned on the bar and his jacket fell open, revealing a designer logo, she had known her instincts were correct. This was a man out of her league, a man of the world, far different from anyone she had ever met before.

When they had decided to share a cab to the tube station, both had known it wouldn't be the train they would be riding that night.

The sex had been explosive. Ben was fit for a man in his forties. She should have been suspicious, of course, when he made regretful excuses about not being able to spend the night. Something about having to get up early for work the next day.

'Besides, I need to go so I can contact my lawyer about that compensation claim against you,' he joked, giving her a lingering kiss.

It had been the first of many excuses. By the time he had told her the truth, that he was married, she was too much in love to walk away.

Sometimes she considered it, though. At moments like this, when she was left alone after they had made love, she felt so empty and rejected. Just when she should have felt closest to him, they were at their most distant. The emotional hurt so complete that it created a permanent physical pain in her solar plexus.

She ached with longing for the man who knew her inside out, who understood her and listened to her. But the last few months Ben had grown so distant, closing her off.

She was losing him. At the thought, she curled in on herself more tightly, trying to protect herself from the truth, the pillow a shield as much as a comfort. She had tried everything, everything to keep Ben interested.

There had to be something more she could do. But what?

She thought of what desperation had driven her to previously and guilt churned her stomach until bile burned her oesophagus.

But no. Why the hell should she feel guilty? She wasn't the one clinging to a dead relationship, sticking it out in a loveless marriage because she was blind to the truth. She was in love. No one should ever feel bad about that. All's fair in love and war, her old gran had always told her.

In which case, perhaps she should declare war. She sat up at the thought, the pillow dropping from her grasp.

Yes, it was time to step things up. This would be the last Christmas she spent alone, the last time she saw in New Year's Eve watching Jools Holland's sodding *Hootenanny* and crying into a glass of Prosecco, then pretending to be fine when she got a quick call from Ben from the toilets of some restaurant or other where he was with his wife. No more trying not to sound as though her nose was thick with tears; instead she would be kissing the New Year in with her man.

Spurred by the thought, she jumped from bed and quickly got dressed. Before she could change her mind, she was out the door.

# CHAPTER 9

Despite the knitted hat, Kendra's waist-length hair swirled around her as traffic breezed by, but she barely noticed it, her vision filled with the building she stared at. She glared past the red awning with its cream writing swirled across it. Past the window she couldn't see into because the low winter sun reflected on it blindingly. All she saw was the scene she imagined playing out inside. It blocked out the reality of people scurrying along the streets that then opened into twin lanes pulling away from each other to form the wedge of Blackheath village's hub. Heads down, hands in pockets, hunched against the cold, faces hidden by hats, leaving a contrail of breath, they swarmed by, taking as little notice of her as she took of them.

Her own cheeks felt as if someone pinched them, it was so cold. She didn't walk away, though, only tugged her scarf and coat collar higher around her neck, pulled the woollen hat closer down around her head.

Someone was coming out of the door. She twitched, one foot sliding forward on the pavement. No, it was a tall, thin man with a balding head and a full beard, pulling on his beanie hat. Definitely not her quarry.

She glanced at her watch. Ben's wife was running late; she was usually out of the restaurant by now. What was keeping her?

Kendra had been with Ben for about a year the first time she had set eyes on his wife. He had got into a routine of seeing her on a Friday afternoon, but hadn't been able to on that occasion. She had tortured herself that he was spending time with his wife, not in a business meeting as he claimed, and so she had slunk to his house like an urban fox sniffing around a bin. There had been no sign of her lover's car, only some vile yellow Smart car that must have been Dominique's. Then she had appeared, tall, slender, and elegant; she was one of those annoying people with natural grace. Bitch. Kendra's heart had sunk, buoyed only slightly when she noticed her rival walked with her feet slightly turned out, like Mary Poppins. It was good to know at least she had one flaw, though Kendra wondered if she had studied ballet as a youngster.

That day, so long ago now, Kendra had followed Dominique at a safe distance, unsure of what she was doing, or how it would end. Would Dominique turn on her suddenly, demanding to know who she was and what she was doing following her? Would she call the police? Worse, would she mention to her husband that she had been trailed by a mad woman, and when she described her stalker he would know instantly who it was?

Was it bad that she thought Ben knowing was worse than the police being called on her?

Ignoring the disturbing thoughts, Kendra had followed Dominique to the hairdresser's, and discovered the weekly routine.

Rather than being sated by that look at her rival, Kendra's curiosity had grown. The following week, she had her own locks cut and blow-dried at John Robertelli's Hair Designs. The eye-watering bill had meant it was a one-off that could never be repeated even for a special occasion. Then she had followed Dominique and her friend to this restaurant, where they lunched.

As Kendra now stood across the road, she could picture exactly what would be happening in the interior. She knew that Dominique was sitting at her usual table tucked near the back of the restaurant, with her lawyer friend, Fiona.

Kendra glanced at her watch again. Only a minute had passed since the last time she'd looked. The pair must be getting the bill now, surely. Her legs trembled with the adrenaline singing through her bloodstream. She was so keyed up, she barely felt the cold slapping her as if trying to get sense into her head.

There.

Dominique appeared, swathed in a full-length camel-coloured coat, and pulling on her brown leather gloves. Her friend gave her a kiss on either cheek then walked away, turning to give one last cheery wave. Dominique grinned as she waved back, her cheeks glowing with wine and the sharp chill in the air.

Tucking a stray piece of hair behind her ear, Dominique started back towards home, a spring in her step. Kendra self-consciously stroked her own slightly wild waist-length mane into place, then stepped out in front of her.

'Excuse me.'

Kendra cursed her trembling voice as she spoke to her lover's wife.

Dominique managed to both frown and give a smile at the same time, treading the line between wary and friendly.

'Yes? Are you lost?'

She must have picked up on Kendra's Edinburgh accent and taken the hesitation as shyness. Kendra almost nodded in relief at being given an out. But she shook her head and ploughed on.

'Are you married to Ben Thomas?'

'Yes? Why?' The smile disappeared.

'I'm Kendra; his mistress.'

It sounded so dramatic putting it like that. But Kendra didn't know how else to describe herself. She was lover, friend, confidante, partner, so much more than any single word conveyed, but mistress would do as shorthand for now. It had the desired effect, Dominique taking a step back, clearly horrified by what she had heard.

But then she pulled herself up, crossed her arms, and looked down her nose at Kendra.

'Really? When do you see my husband, exactly?'

'Umm, well, all the time,' Kendra flustered. 'Friday afternoons, I see him a lot.'

'Are you sure we're talking about the same Ben Thomas?' asked Dominique. 'Describe him for me.'

'Well, he's, he's, erm, five feet eleven. Dark hair. Stocky build. Handsome. Blue eyes, you know. Bit of a wonky nose because of the rugby—'

'What's his date of birth?'

'His birthday is 27 August. He's forty-eight.'

'Well, it seems we are talking about the same person.' Dominique gave a cold toss of her head, freshly curled hair bouncing. 'What exactly do you want?'

Kendra hadn't expected to be questioned. To have to prove she was telling the truth. This wasn't how it went in films. She had expected disbelief, sure, and even braced for a slap across the face. But a cold and calculating questioning? That was just weird. She found herself shrugging, hands open.

'What do I want? Well, to tell you... that – that I'm seeing your husband. We celebrated our fourth anniversary a couple of months ago. He wants to leave you and the kids, but he hasn't got the courage to tell you, not yet. But it's only a matter of time.'

The other woman blinked rapidly, twice; the only sign she gave of being hurt. 'You thought you'd give him a helping hand out of the door, is that it?'

'Continuing the charade isn't going to help anyone. You need to let him go.'

One perfectly arched eyebrow rose. 'Oh, I do? Well, thank you for the tip, but I'll decide what happens in my marriage.'

With that Dominique swept past her, imperious as an ice queen. Kendra watched her open-mouthed as she disappeared up the right-hand spur of the split road. It was only when Ben's wife went around the corner that Kendra allowed herself to sag.

'What the hell was that all about?' she asked herself out loud. The man who had been walking towards her crossed the road to avoid the obvious nutter.

She shoved her hands into her pockets and stomped off, furious with herself, eager to burn away the anger with a brief but breakneck walk to the train station. Her cosy Charlton flat was calling her.

Kendra had thought she was pulling the pin in a grenade that would blow Ben's marriage to smithereens. Now she worried it had badly misfired.

No; no matter how calm Dominique seemed, she would surely go ballistic once her husband got home. Then, finally, Ben would belong to Kendra and only her.

# CHAPTER 10

Dominique kept her head high as she walked away from her husband's tart, despite her legs feeling weak and strangely jointed. She should turn around and slap that Kendra woman. Give her a mouthful in the street. But she was already running late to collect Mouse. No way would her child suffer because her shit of a husband had been cheating on them all.

Already temperatures were plummeting as the sun raced towards a horizon hidden behind buildings. The handful of snowflakes that had fallen earlier were frozen in place, twinkling in the late-afternoon light like nature's jewellery.

It was cold enough to freeze Dominique's heart for ever.

Children streamed from the school building, many wearing paper crowns at jaunty angles. Of course, it had been the school party that afternoon. Mouse shouted goodbye to her friends and bounded over, face pink with excitement.

'Mummy, I've had the best day ever.'

Dom bent down and hugged her daughter tight. She was not the most demonstrative person in the world, struggled sometimes to show her children how much she loved them. But right now, her heart was so full of love it might explode. Her children deserved better than to come from a broken home.

That Benjamin had betrayed her, when he was all that she knew, hurt like hell, but she could cope with it. That he had betrayed their children was unfathomable.

Dominique felt a failure.

Mouse, so articulate and empathetic, would be scarred for ever if her parents split up. Ruby, insecure beneath her veneer of anger, was at such a vulnerable age that she could easily end up doing something silly as a reaction to her father's treachery.

Mouse jumped around Dominique as they walked home. Telling her about her day.

'And when the music stopped for the last time, it was me. I was really careful not to tear the paper...'

But Dom wasn't listening, too lost in the past...

Benjamin and she had known each other since they were teenagers; she and his sister, Krystal, had been schoolfriends. Back then, the two of them always had a laugh together, and he was loyal, hard-working, stuck up for his mates, and would do anything for anyone. Still, they hadn't got together until Dominique was twenty-two. One night a big group of them all, including Krystal and Dominique, had gone out together. Somehow, she and Benjamin had got separated from the crowd and got chatting, and... the rest was history. She had known from the beginning that he was a keeper, their transformation from friends to lovers so easy. And of course, he knew about her past—

'Then guess what, Mummy?' Mouse interrupted her thoughts.

'Erm, what, sweetheart?'

She didn't hear the answer...

Benjamin had an amazing body back then, sixteen stone of solid muscle. She had cheered him on from the rugby field's sidelines, watching him tackle people as a prop, and thought he was sex on legs. The two of them hadn't been able to keep their hands off each other, but they had always talked, too. About anything and everything, but mostly about their hopes and dreams. They had shared a vision of the future: he, building a business; she, looking after their family.

Where had it all started to go wrong? Almost as soon as they married the slow drift apart had seemed to begin, with Benjamin working to provide the life they had envisaged together...

Mouse danced around her, holding her hand. The tug, tug, tug on her arm made Dominique's shoulder socket ache as much as her head did. She was jabbering on about the school party, a stream of consciousness with barely a breath between words. Dom rubbed at her temples with her free hand.

'Calm down a bit, eh,' she said. 'Mummy has a lot on her mind.'

Mouse stilled only slightly, kept skipping along. But it gave Dom a tiny respite from the throbbing in her head.

She remembered Benjamin's glow of love when he proposed to her. It had been perfect. He'd taken her away for a weekend in Paris, and proposed to her in a restaurant, in front of everyone. When she said yes, the waiters had swept in with champagne. As the restaurant erupted in clapping, Benjamin had wiped tears of joy from his face, embarrassed.

He had taken that joy and shattered it into a million pieces.

Mouse's words distracted her. 'Do you want to see my prize, Mummy? I'll show you.'

'Wait until we get home, eh, sweetheart.'

'Okay – then I can show Ruby and Daddy at the same time.'

Perhaps Fiona was right. Perhaps she should make Benjamin pay. It might be fun to see him squirm. Take him to the cleaners, like Fiona was always joking about; really hit him where it hurt.

She imagined his face twisted in mea culpa, his body curled up as though beaten and bruised. But even as she saw it, it disintegrated. She could never be one of those people who deliberately hurt someone – not even when that person had hurt her. In fact, burying her emotions had caused Dominique problems in the past. Confrontation never had been her strong suit. But her frozen heart twitched in rebellion, reminding her that perhaps it was time for her to try.

# CHAPTER 11

History, geography, English… all the lessons crawled past Ruby.
All the time, she thought of that last text message she had received.
The clear, precise instruction. The terror it had instilled.

The second the bell rang for the end of school, she walked from
the classroom as quickly as she could without rousing suspicion.
Generally, she hung back and was one of the last to leave, but
today was different. Today she had a plan and she was looking
forward to putting it into action.

Weaving through crowds of pupils flurrying around her like
snowflakes in a storm, she finally made it to her locker. Harry
was already leaning against it, ready and waiting. Smirking, she
stalked towards him – and swept by until she reached the girl
behind him: Jayne Seward.

Wham.

Jayne's head snapped back, bounced off the locker and lolled
forward again. She stumbled, knees almost giving way. Then she
straightened, hand to her face. Blood leaked between fingers,
like scarlet scarves flowing from a magician's sleeve. A scream was
Ruby's applause.

Ruby's mouth twisted into a smile of satisfaction. She stepped
forward, braced, swung with her whole body not just her fist, like
Harry had taught her. Jayne didn't have time to dodge, too busy
looking in horror at her bloodied hands. Ruby's blow sent her to
the floor. No noise escaped this time. She was out cold.

'Finished?' Harry asked.

Ruby turned and nodded. He handed her the things from her locker as if it were a normal day, while around them girls screamed. The boys looked on, stunned, not sure if they should get involved in a catfight or if it would somehow lessen their standing.

'Better get moving. Someone's bound to grass this to a teacher,' Harry added.

'Good plan. That felt bloody brilliant, by the way,' Ruby observed. The pair started walking towards the main exit. 'What do you fancy doing now? Home, or shall we hang out together?'

As he opened his mouth to reply, a piercing screech rang out.

'Jayne's come round, then,' he chuckled.

'Screw her. Screw them all. I'd burn this whole building down and them inside, given half a chance.'

Harry and Ruby high-fived as they pushed open the doors. Their joy was short-lived, though. A hand landed heavily on Ruby's shoulder, and she turned to look up into the narrow eyes and pursed, pale lips of the headteacher, Mrs Margaret Dudgeon.

# CHAPTER 12

Benjamin straightened his tie, then ran his hands over his hair. Pulled at his crotch, adjusting his trousers to better accommodate himself. He was still a bit tender after the going over he'd given Kendra. He had to hand it to her, though, she was definitely better at calming his nerves than just a quick hand shandy in the office loos.

This meeting was a big deal. He needed to land this account. But he could do it. Why? Because he was The Man. *Comprendez?* He only had to remember Kendra's desperate cries of ecstasy to know that.

*Yeah, you've still got it Ben, my boy.*

Benjamin had it all: the incredible career, the trophy wife and gorgeous kids, an impressive home. Inevitably, he also had the mistress. She was a good kid; he was fond of her. And thanks to her, he felt young and invigorated again, ready for his meeting with Vladimir Tarkovsky.

All he had to do was get the Russian businessman to sign on the dotted line, and Ben would be able to get away with everything. No one would ever find out the truth.

The internal line on his phone rang. It was his PA, announcing that Mr Tarkovsky had arrived. Benjamin crunched a couple of Rennies antacid tablets, rolled his seat back, so he could stand easily. Wait for it, wait for it…

In came the Russian. Benjamin counted a beat before looking up from what he was pretending to peer at on his computer screen.

Gave a slow but wide smile of welcome that he had practised enough in the mirror to know it oozed confidence and charm.

Tarkovsky was an intimidatingly large man, with a waistline that had to be equal to his height. His black hair was dead straight, and looked strangely solid on his head, like Lego hair. He sported a moustache that reminded Benjamin of a 1970s porn star, though it was handy to disguise the fact he constantly breathed through his mouth. He may not have film star looks but, from the cut and cloth of his suit to the watch he wore, he dripped wealth. Benjamin was determined to show Tarkovsky that he was at that level, too.

After pleasantries came the pitch. Benjamin's accountancy company was small enough to guarantee personal services and complete discretion, but big enough and experienced enough to be able to handle all of Tarkovsky's business ventures, from oil to rail.

As he spoke, Benjamin leaned back, gesturing expansively. He was a man in control.

Tarkovsky gave a rumbling laugh that set the apron of flesh tucked into his trousers jiggling. Even the best tailors in the world can only disguise so much.

'You want to represent all my businesses? No, no, no, Mr Thomas, you have misunderstood me. You are pitching only for you to take on my building company here in the UK.'

'Pitching? I thought you'd made up your mind you wanted us,' he said disingenuously.

The Russian gave the tiniest of gestures with one hand, turning it palm upwards. 'There are no decisions made yet. The building industry here can be a colourful affair sometimes, and I need to know that my accountant has creative flair as well as efficiency. You understand me?'

Benjamin moved slightly, feeling the sands of his confidence shifting beneath him. He fiddled briefly with the cuff of his shirt. Adjusted it until his watch was visible. That was better.

'I understand exactly the kind of business you could put our way, and I can assure you that Thomas & Bauer are more than up to the job. Another benefit of this company is that we can move swiftly when required, and I'm sure you would find our flexibility an asset. Let me grab a pen and make some notes on what you want,' he added, and looked around. 'Oh, it's over by you, just let me get it.'

'I am out of time – or rather you are,' Tarkovsky said. Despite his words, the Russian picked up the silver fountain pen and passed it over.

Benjamin prayed he knew quality when he saw it; that he would realise it was a Montblanc. He reached for the pen with his left hand, his eyes never leaving Tarkovsky's as he thanked him. The men broke eye contact at the exact same moment, and glanced down together to make sure their fingers didn't brush awkwardly. Benjamin saw the man's glance linger briefly on his Rolex Datejust II; that was seven grand well spent.

Oh, yeah, he knew how the big boys rolled.

A watch like that spoke for itself, and for its owner – it screamed taste and money. It yelled that Benjamin was a winner.

Nothing attracted success more than success.

'If you have to leave, Mr Tarkovsky, then I won't detain you. But… if I may extend an invitation to you…'

Minutes later, the Russian swept from the building. But not before arrangements had been made for he and Benjamin to go clay pigeon shooting together that Sunday. It was a typical British country sporting event that Benjamin hoped would impress him. After the door had closed, he let out a huge breath and nodded to himself. It had been touch and go, but his charm had won out in the end. He was getting there. He gave a delighted chuckle. He really was going to pull this off – and get away scot free.

# CHAPTER 13

Mummy's face was going a funny colour as she listened to the other person on the phone, which had been ringing when they got home. She looked like Mouse had looked that time she had drunk a bottle of pop too fast then gone on the trampoline, bounce, bounce, bounce, until her belly had bounced right out of her mouth and Mouse had had to have a sit down for the rest of the afternoon while Mummy stroked her forehead and watched *Paddington* with her.

The little girl watched as her mum ended the phone call but continued to stare into space, not moving.

'I think you need to watch *Paddington*,' Mouse decided.

Mummy's eyes came into focus as she returned from the place her mind had been hiding. She looked at the eight-year-old as if seeing her for the first time.

'What was that? No, we can't watch a film right now. We have to get Ruby from school.'

Mouse wrinkled her nose. 'But why? She always walks.'

Instead of answering, Mummy told her to put her coat on. She used her angry voice, but like the anger was in the distance, not close by, not at Mouse.

So, the girl shrugged and did as she was told, grabbing her rucksack, too. Jumped into the back of the car and did her seatbelt up, hating that she still needed the stupid baby booster cushion.

The traffic was terrible. It moved slower than her school pet, Tony the tortoise. Mouse tried to show Mummy the prize she had won in pass the parcel at the school party, but she said she was too busy. She spent a lot of time hunched over the wheel muttering what Mouse was sure were bad words. Sometimes she hit the steering wheel. Sometimes she slumped back in the seat as if she didn't know what to do.

Mouse jiffled uncomfortably. She had a bad feeling that Ruby was in Big Trouble. What had she done this time? Ruby was always in Big Trouble. Mouse only got into small trouble, thank goodness.

'Come on, quick, quick,' Mummy said the second they parked.

Mouse scurried along, taking two steps and sometimes a hop for each one of her mummy's long strides. She felt as though she was streaming out behind her like a cartoon character, feet off the ground. If she let go of her mum's hand she would be lost in a speed cloud and a pinging noise.

Ruby's school was loads bigger than her own. The corridors seemed to stretch on and on as if they had no end, and Mouse's legs were starting to ache from all the hurrying. But suddenly her mum stopped in front of a desk and said: 'I'm here to see Margaret Dudgeon. I'm Ruby Thomas's mother.'

The lady pulled a face. She tried to mask it, but she looked like she'd found a sprout hidden underneath her mashed potato and accidentally eaten it. Yucky. From her gritted teeth, she was still trying to swallow it as she told Mummy to go in.

'You sit there, and wait for me, okay?' Mummy told Mouse.

She nodded back, sitting up straight to show what a good girl she was going to be.

She soon got bored, though. The school smelled strange, not like the Playdoh smell of her own school, which was much smaller and prettier and friendlier somehow. There were bubbles under the paint on a couple of the walls, and the corners looked dusty. She didn't like it here. But she pulled her book out and started to read, glad she had thought to grab it before they left. As long as she had a book, she didn't mind waiting, even if she was in a yucky place. Besides, the words helped to block out the raised voices coming from the door, across which was emblazoned a single word: Headteacher.

'Absolutely no proof, Mrs Dudgeon. You didn't see my daughter do anything wrong, and no one else has said it was Ruby—'

'It's clear exactly what she did. Everyone is too frightened to come forward. Mrs Thomas, your daughter's reputation…'

The voices faded to a murmur.

Ruby was definitely in Great Big Trouble.

# CHAPTER 14

'Relax. You're like an old woman.'

Benjamin stuck his feet up on his desk and put his hands behind his head, while Jazmine glared at him. He wasn't worried, though; he knew how to handle her. They might be business partners on paper, but it was he who was really in charge, making all the key decisions Jazmine lacked the balls to take.

Ha, she literally lacked the balls. Benjamin smirked inwardly at his joke.

Jazmine was his sensible, steadying influence, but she sweat the small stuff and didn't have the Midas touch that Benjamin had because he was all about the big picture. That was why they made the perfect business partners, balancing each other out. Most of the time.

They were an odd coupling at first sight. People had been surprised he had gone into business with a hairy-legged lesbian from Dagenham. That's what his rugger bugger pals had said, anyway, when they first found out, even though there was nothing butch about the brown-haired accountant, with her elfin features, glossy pixie crop, and fitted suits. Sometimes, he was willing to admit, his friends could be complete idiots.

Jazmine stopped pacing in front of him and pulled up a chair instead, leaning her elbows on his desk and pushing her glasses up her nose slightly before doling out a glare that skewered him.

'I really don't like this, Ben. We don't need this Russian's business—'

'Since when is it about need? We land this, and we'll make a fortune. It's called expansion, it's called good business practice.'

'Not if we lose clients because they don't want to be tarnished by his reputation.' She smacked his foot. 'Oy, I mean it. We've taken years to build up a list of decent, reliable people who run totally legitimate businesses. You know Tarkovsky's reputation – don't bloody play the innocent, Ben, I'm not falling for your "butter wouldn't melt" look.'

He opened his arms wide. 'Who? Me? Never. Seriously, you're worrying about nothing. I'll admit that Vladimir does have a certain… reputation, shall we say. But his operations in the UK are totally legit – or don't you trust me to have done my homework on this?'

'You don't have the contacts to have done the right kind of homework on this sort of man.'

'Unlike you.'

Jazmine jerked away from him as if he'd poked her with a cattle prod. She didn't like to be reminded about her past, the dodgy estate she had grown up on, surrounded by thieves and drug dealers. Most of whom she was related to.

'All right, yeah; I know what I'm talking about when it comes to dodgy geezers,' she conceded after a pause. 'This guy makes me twitchy. If you're determined to get into bed with him then maybe I should ask around a bit, check he is legit. I've fought hard to get where I am, to leave all that crap behind, Ben. I'm not going to be dragged back into it because you want to become the next Rockefeller.'

'Actually, he was mainly in oil but—'

'Don't change the subject.' Her words were loud and sharp. Her cockney accent sounded rough beside Benjamin's softer, more gentrified tones. But then, she hadn't been pulled up constantly by her father about 'speaking properly'. Not a day of Benjamin's childhood had passed without some comment about 'the common

Essex accent' he had apparently been developing, and that must
be stopped at all costs.

'I mean it, Ben. I want you to listen to me on this. He beats
people up if they cross him – maybe he even does worse.'

'That fat bastard? Couldn't if he tried.'

'People like that don't have to lift a finger. They give an order
to someone lower down the food chain.'

'Seriously? You've been watching too many Bond films. You're
going to let us lose money because of rumours? I'm not walking
away from a brilliant deal, unless you've got some kind of proof
of your allegations. Well, have you?'

'No, but—'

He took his feet off the desk and leaned forward so he could
meet her gaze. Said softly, sincerely: 'Come on, Jaz. When have
I ever steered you wrong? I swear on my life, this is a great move
for us. It will take us to the next level.'

She didn't say a word. Didn't look away, either. Benjamin did
what he always did best: took a gamble.

'Look, I'm feeling on top of the world here, and you're bursting
my bubble. If it really means that much to you, though, I'll let
this go, even though it goes against everything I think. It seems a
shame when I've virtually landed him, is all. Especially as he really
is all above board. But I'll give his PA a call.' He lifted his phone
up for good measure. 'Tell her that I'm cancelling our shoot on
Sunday. He'll think we're a bit rude, but so what.'

Jazmine's hand rested on his, stopping him from dialling. She
peered over her glasses at him. Scrutinising.

'You really have checked him out.'

'I really have checked him out. Honest.'

He gave a grin. His cheeky chappy one, he called it.

'Hey, a bloke like this, giving up his time at a weekend; he
wouldn't do that unless he was definitely going to come with us.

That's a massive coup. Just imagine the looks on our rivals' faces when they hear.'

She gave a smile. It was reluctant, but it was there.

'It could be nice to rub Watson & Co's nose in it. Cheeky buggers have been crowing ever since they nicked that café chain account from us.'

'Yeah. So, you going to let me do what I do best? Schmooze this whale?'

She laughed. 'Okay. As long as you can guarantee me he really is legit.'

'Cross my heart and hope to die.'

# CHAPTER 15

Dominique rubbed at her temples, trying to dislodge the buzzing swarm of bees in her head that were forming a furious headache.

In front of her stood Ruby, arms folded, face defiant. Leaning against the kitchen counter and rocking back and forth in a cocky manner that reminder Dominique of her husband.

Her cheating shit of a husband, she reminded herself.

'You did hit this Jayne Seward, though. Didn't you? I know it, the headmistress knows it, the entire school knows it even though all the pupils seem to have been temporarily struck blind. If just one of them confirms the head's suspicions, you'll be expelled.'

'Big deal.'

'It is, actually, Ruby. Why did you hit that poor girl? Why won't you even apologise?'

'I'm not sorry. And I'm not going to lie and pretend I am. I'm not like you, Mother; I'm not a doormat, saying what I think people want to hear and letting everyone walk all over me just to keep the peace.'

Ruby had always been the funny one. The smart one, ready with a quip, or an interesting question. Sometimes it was annoying, especially when, around the age of four, it had felt as though every other word out of her mouth was 'why'? But it proved what a sharp, enquiring mind she had. She had been known for her smile and was followed around by a flock of friends, but everything had changed when she started at that private school.

Dom had hated her going there, and was ashamed she had crumbled to Benjamin's snobbery about sending her to boarding school. Although in front of Ruby she had seemed to back Benjamin, behind closed doors she had fought hard that Ruby be allowed to go to the local comprehensive as she had asked.

In the end, when Ruby was booted out, it had been something of a relief. Dominique had been convinced that her daughter would go back to her real self now that she'd got what she'd asked for. She hadn't. Dom was slowly realising this nightmare child before her, full of hatred and disdain, might be the real Ruby. She wanted to ask her daughter what had happened. She wanted to get back her little girl, full of smiles and sunshine and constant questions. But she didn't have a clue where to start.

Perhaps Ruby was right.

'I'm not a doormat,' Dominique said, ignoring the doubt in her mind. 'I only want to know why you hit that girl. We're lucky no one is pressing charges. Do you realise how close you came to expulsion? It's only because none of the pupils will admit who did what, and because it's so close to Christmas, that you've got away with this.'

'Worried what people will think? I could tell you a thing or two, if you're really interested. Things that would make your hair curl, Mother.'

The bees in Dominique's head seemed to be stinging her brain repeatedly, the jabbing, stabbing pain and agony that made her jaw clench until words were hard-pressed to escape.

'Oh, Ruby…'

She needed to lie down, not argue. She needed to clear her head. Even her vision seemed misty. Benjamin's mistress, his betrayal of his family, what was she going to do? And now Ruby in trouble again, for beating someone up.

'Look at you. You can't even be bothered to listen to me. Then you expect me to talk to you. You're pathetic.' Ruby spat the venomous words then stomped from the room.

Dom watched but didn't have the strength to go after her. Instead, she pulled out a chair from the kitchen table, and slumped into it. Folded over the table and pressed her forehead against the cool wood, trying desperately to marshal her thoughts.

She could only deal with one thing at a time, she decided. She would talk to Ben about Ruby, but she would hold off doing anything about Kendra. She refused to have her hand forced by some little tart; the mechanics of how to end her marriage was too big a choice to be rushed into. Decisions must be made first, things put into place and set in motion before she could give Benjamin a heads-up.

She looked at the large black-and-white photo on the kitchen wall. It was her family before Ruby started withdrawing and attacking everyone. Mouse had her arms wound around her mum's neck, legs wrapped monkey-like around her waist, as she waved at the camera. Ruby was on Benjamin's shoulders, a big grin on her face. They had been lost in Barcelona, and Benjamin had made locals laugh with his appalling attempts at Spanish. Ruby had taken charge at one point, confidently announcing that she knew the way, but would only show them if they all did the conga – that had caused a few funny looks being thrown their way. They hadn't cared. Getting back to the hotel had taken for ever, but they had loved every second of their adventure.

If the scene were re-enacted today, it would descend into squabbles and screams of hatred within minutes. What had happened to her family?

❖

Ruby hadn't thanked Mouse for her drawing. That hurt. And was annoying. If that was her attitude, Mouse would take it back. She was starting to feel seriously grumpy. Mummy hadn't listened to her about the party, and now Ruby was in Super Duper Trouble, a whole new category Mouse had been forced to create. Mouse had never seen Mummy or Ruby so mad before. No one was interested at all in seeing the prize she had won in pass the parcel.

When Daddy got home there was bound to be fireworks – an expression Mouse was particularly fond of because she always thought it sounded pretty.

She sneaked into Ruby's room to see what her sister had done with the drawing, but couldn't see it anywhere. Then she realised: it must have slid underneath the doormat Ruby had put down inside her room. The one with the naughty words on it that Mouse wasn't allowed to say. Mouse had argued that 'off' wasn't a bad word, so she could say one of them out loud, but Mummy had screwed her lips up like she was eating sours sweeties, so Mouse hadn't said anything else. She wanted to make sure she got her presents, and she wasn't going to miss out because Ruby had bought a rude mat – it wasn't her fault her sister was bad. Everyone was so mean lately.

Mouse was walking back to the mat when Ruby appeared.

'What are you doing sneaking into my room?'

'I was only—'

'I don't care, Mouse. Fuck off.'

'You said the bad words.' Mouse pointed down to the mat, to emphasise her point. 'I'm telling Mummy and Daddy.'

The sound of the front door opening and closing, and Daddy shouting 'hello' paused their furious words. They heard Mummy speaking soft and low, then the door of Daddy's study close. Ruby's eyes were big and round as a Pokémon's, but not friendly like theirs. She looked fearful and tense, her fists balled by her sides, arms straight as a ruler, as she listened to the prickling silence.

A huge bellow. Bigger than the one the rhino gave that time the family all went to a safari park.

Mouse whipped around to look at Ruby, scared.

Her sister didn't look worried any more. Her hands unclenched. She grabbed Mouse by the hair and pulled her close. Mouse shrieked as pain shot across her scalp.

'You bit me,' she yelped.

'Yep. That's for coming in my room without permission. Bad people do bad things, squirt; it's about time you realised and toughened up. Best of all, you can't go snitching on me because no one can see the marks in your hair. Now get out.'

Mouse grabbed her big sister's hand and sank her teeth into it. Ruby's shriek of pain and annoyance was deeply satisfying. Even better was seeing an imprint of her teeth in her sister's flesh. Before Ruby could lash out, Mouse scurried out to her own room, picked up Ted, and climbed into the wardrobe. As soon as she closed the door, her anxiety lessened. Curled into a corner, in the darkness, she pulled clothes over her head by touch alone. It muffled the shouting from downstairs. The warm air under the clothes made her feel protected.

'It's safe here, Ted,' she whispered. 'You don't have to be afraid any more.'

She hugged him tight and that made him feel much better, too. If she concentrated hard on the sound of her own breathing she could pretend she and Ted were the only things in the world. Her scalp tingled and throbbed, and she rubbed at it, burying her face into Ted's fur for comfort. Why had Ruby hurt her? What had she done this time that had made her sister so mad?

Her parents' arguing moved to Ruby's room. Mouse made out the odd word, but not enough to understand what was really happening. Curiosity was making her fidgety. She jiffled under the clothes mountain, as the temperature beneath reached oven-hot. Cautious as her nickname implied, she crept out from under it and opened the door of her built-in wardrobe. Listened. The shouting was definitely coming from Ruby's room. Creeping to her bedroom door, she opened it a crack. Darted into the bathroom. Locked the door behind her, then pulled everything out of the bottom of the airing cupboard and crawled inside, knees under chin, pressing her eye against the wall.

There was a little crack right near the skirting board, which Ruby didn't know about. Mouse knew all the hidey holes in the house, and all the best listening places, too. Despite people's best efforts, there were never any secrets kept from her – apart from what Father Christmas was going to bring her. She hadn't managed to find that out yet, but there wasn't too long to go until the big day arrived. Only eight sleeps.

But Daddy's voice dragged her away from thoughts of piles of gifts in sparkling paper, and back to the present. To his tanned skin paling as he spoke, and the trembling of his finger as he pointed it centimetres from Ruby's nose. Ruby glared past it, meeting his eyes without flinching.

'Don't answer back; I'm not interested. Your time for explaining is long gone. You will apologise to that girl's family, otherwise they are going to press charges. And—' he raised his voice over Ruby's shriek of protest, 'and you are grounded for the foreseeable.'

'It's Christmas.'

'You should have thought of that before you were so irresponsible,' Mummy said. 'You can't see Harry Porter again, either, Ruby. Even in the New Year. You're too young to be in a relationship.'

'No, Mum. No, please.' Ruby's voice sounded different. Shocked, wounded, small… and more like her old self before she got so grumpy.

'Your mother's right. He's a no-good, got no future ahead of him but signing on like the rest of his family. I've seen his kind a hundred times before, and he'll drag you down with him.'

'What? Because his family is skint? Because he's black? You racist, Dad.'

Daddy pulled at his tie viciously, like it was strangling him. 'It's not his colour, it's his type. And I'm not arguing about this – this is the way things are, end of story.'

'This is stupid. I can't NOT see him, can I – not when we go to the same school.'

'You will not spend time with Harry; you will not speak to him. Are we clear?' said Daddy.

'I love him.'

'You've only been with him a few months, Ruby. I know it probably feels as though you love him but you don't.'

Mouse couldn't see Mummy, but her voice sounded much calmer than Daddy's.

'What do you know about love? You and Dad can't stand each other. You don't even speak when you're in the same room. What I've got with Harry is real.'

'Well, real or not, you're not seeing him anymore. The fact is… well, we didn't want to say, but we've heard things about Harry. He has a certain reputation for dabbling with drugs, and his mother is a drunkard, by all accounts.'

'Oh God, Mother, are you going to listen to a load of crap rather than your own daughter? Harry does not do drugs.'

'For goodness' sake – you are not having any more to do with that lad. End of conversation,' Daddy bellowed.

'I wish you were dead. I hate you. I hate you both.'

Daddy took no notice, just left the room, ushering Mummy in front of him, and closed the door. But before the door shut completely, Mouse was sure she heard him mutter under his breath: 'Yeah? Well, sometimes I hate you, too.'

# CHAPTER 16

Chief Inspector Ogundele knew it was decision time. No one had answered repeated phone calls to the house, so the next move was to go in. The lives of his officers as well as the people inside the property depended on him making the right call.

On his orders, ten members of an armed response unit slipped into place, ducking out of sight of anyone who might be looking from 15 Burgh Road. They wore black protective clothing: body armour, crash helmets, safety goggles. Gloved hands held sidearms, or the occasional automatic rifle. They were ready for whoever had fired the shotgun inside that quiet family home.

An eerie, rattling cry came from above. Ogundele looked up. A magpie, its black, blue, and white feathers a mimicry of the uniforms below it, peered down from the roof of the besieged suburban house, from which light blazed in one bedroom, and a single ground floor room at the side of the property. It cocked its head on one side, and crackled its call again, as if asking him what he was waiting for.

It had a point. Situations such as this were a delicate balance between moving quickly, in order to save lives, and taking the time to assess the situation and ensure it was safe for the team to go into the building. Bystanders filming everything would be quick enough to go to the press to criticise if civilian lives were lost due to waiting too long – but rushing in and potentially triggering a gun battle was a possibility. Hindsight is a wonderful thing.

But all was quiet inside the family home. No one shouting or shooting. No one to benefit from the negotiation training Ogundele had. And there may well be people inside the house who needed immediate medical care. Every second of delay could be a life lost

'We move now,' he decided. The magpie bobbed up and down in excitement.

Sergeant Hussain nodded, causing a deluge from her hat, and added: 'The dog unit will be arriving any minute, sir. They're still a few minutes away.'

'No time to wait. We're going in now.'

A moment to confirm everyone was ready, then: 'Go, go, go,' Ogundele ordered.

Thump.

An expert swing of the Enforcer battering ram on the red front door. It burst open, sending to the floor the holly wreath that had been pinned to it.

The chief inspector held his breath and prayed for his team as they raised their weapons and swarmed into the darkness of the house.

# CHAPTER 17

Dominique blinked in confusion. Swayed slightly. Blinked again. Screwed her eyes shut for a count of three before opening them.

She was in the hall. How had she got here?

She lifted her bare feet then stamped them down again. They made a gentle slapping sound against the wooden parquet flooring in which she was reflected. This was real then. Not a dream.

Okay, okay, okay. Her heart ratcheted up a few more beats per minute, even as she tried to talk herself down.

It was happening again. It had been years. She had thought she was over it.

Maybe if she kept quiet and made herself calm down she would be all right. This time no one would get hurt.

Could she really risk it?

She looked guiltily around to make sure there were no witnesses to her shame, then scurried up the stairs, silk nightdress billowing around her ankles. She concentrated on feeling the material. On the sensation of her toes sinking into the deep pile of the carpet, reminding herself of the weeks of intensive searching it had taken to find the exact shade of golden cream she required. How important it had been to her to get something thick and luxurious so that the children could wander around barefoot without being cold or uncomfortable. It had cost a lot but it had been worth it. Losing herself in those details grounded Dominique.

She took comfort in the material things of life because they were real and solid, and would never let someone down. Because when she had gone through a terrible experience before, all those years ago, it had taken a lot to make her separate the dream from reality – and there had been terrible consequences.

Remembering the past made her shiver in fear. A conviction grew, making her heart pound. Something had happened to her children. She needed to see them – now.

Worried, she quietly opened Ruby's bedroom door first. She was fast asleep, her face squashed into the pillow, lips pushed to one side, allowing her to breathe. She looked as if her face had been put on sideways. She wrinkled her nose in her dream and turned over, making Dominique retreat hurriedly in fear she might wake.

She crept into Mouse's room. The little girl lay on her back, her slender face pale and angular like a medieval knight's effigy on a tomb.

Her babies were safe.

Taking in every detail of her surroundings, Dominique climbed into her own empty bed. Crisp cotton sheets beneath her, the slight warmth still emanating from where she had lain previously; the soft pillow, comfortingly cool. All of it helped bring her back to reality and calm her.

But no sign of her husband.

She was grateful Benjamin wasn't there to see what she had been reduced to. Almost. Despite everything, part of her longed for him to hold her tight and whisper that everything would be okay.

He was probably with his mistress, though.

Ice crystals formed on her heart, stabbing her painfully. Too scared to go back to sleep, in case she went walkabout again, all she could do was lie awake and accept the torment.

❖

Finally, at around four, the bedroom door gave a guilty creak. Dominique kept her eyes closed and her breathing steady as Benjamin eased into bed beside her.

Out with his mistress, cuddling up to her, before slipping home like a guilty dog, to keep up appearances.

All Benjamin really cared about was the look of the thing, and she knew how perfect their lives looked from the outside. He would probably be happy to go on living a double life. But she wouldn't let him. Despite what Ruby thought, Dom was no hypocrite.

But she kept the anger balled up inside. She wasn't ready for a confrontation. Not yet. Almost, but not quite. Instead, she concentrated on the feeling of the light duvet over her body, the smell of the fabric conditioner on the fresh pillow cases.

I'm here. I'm awake. This is real, she told herself, silently, again and again. She fought the heaviness of exhaustion, scared of sleep – and what horror waking might bring. But in the end, it smothered her.

❖

Kendra tapped on her teeth, as she always did when deep in thought.

It was three a.m. and there had been no calls, no texts, nothing from Benjamin. She hadn't been able to settle all evening. Had eaten her body weight in chocolate to try to distract herself, flicked through television channels trying to find something to watch, jumped on Facebook. She couldn't stand doing anything more than a few minutes before checking her phone again.

No messages. Full service.

Ben must have chosen his wife and kids. Fresh tears followed the tracks of old ones. She should walk away, start a new life. Perhaps move back to Edinburgh. That would show him.

Kendra missed her family, and her home city with its clean air, stunning architecture, and friendly residents. She had moved five years earlier, feeling she simply had to get away and have a change of scene. She had thought it would be for a year or so, tops, doing a spot of waitressing, bar work, whatever she could pick up. She had only been at that awards ceremony because her friend, Kim, was working behind the bar that night and had said it would be fun. She and Kim had arranged to go out on the pull after, but Kendra hadn't made it that far. Because that night she had met the love of her life. The fact Kim no longer spoke to her because she felt 'dumped' by her friend didn't bother Kendra at all – it showed how petty Kim was not to understand.

She couldn't go home, though, and couldn't give up on Ben. She would show him that she was a winner, exactly like him. That she would do whatever it took to get what she wanted, because she wasn't a quitter. Only that way could she prove she was worthy of being his partner.

And she had to be. Because every time she considered life without him she felt panicky, as though someone was suffocating her with a pillow.

She might lose this gamble, though. The thought made her wrap her arms around herself, rubbing at the goosebumps blooming on her skin. Pushing things had been a long shot – she'd known it would be – but part of her had wanted to press the self-destruct button, because at least then something would change and she would finally know where she stood.

It had become increasingly clear, after four long years together, that Ben would never choose her unless given a nudge. That was all she was doing, she reasoned, as she once again had a moment's panic over her actions. Nothing she was doing was that big a deal. It wasn't evil. It was just a nudge.

A nudge for the greater good, she reminded herself.

Ben would be happy once he was with her. He was miserable at home, which meant he was also making his family miserable. They would be hurt, at first, when he moved out, but they would recover – it was like ripping a plaster off, they would gasp when the moment came but then it would all be over.

She had thought that moment would have come by now though. She had thought telling Dominique about them would tear their marriage to pieces.

A noise sounded outside her door. She jumped up. Was that Ben, turning up with his bags, ready to move in? No, it was her neighbour, Dawn Seward, by the sound of it, going into her own flat. She must have finished her nursing shift. Kendra considered nipping across the landing and seeing if she fancied a chat, but what if Ben tried her landline and she wasn't in? Better if she waited here for news, even if it was killing her.

Was the landline still working? She picked the receiver up. Yes. Of course, it was.

Okay, okay, she just had to calm down and think rationally. Dominique wouldn't confront Ben until he came home. Say six p.m.? There would be one hell of a row. Hours of shouting and recriminations. That would take them up to right about now, so it wasn't necessarily a bad sign she hadn't heard anything yet.

After the screaming, the two of them might even start working out the terms of their split. Ben was very practical and Dominique was clearly a cold fish, so it made sense that they would start thrashing things out immediately. Splitting their assets, working out access to the children, there was a lot to consider. It could potentially go on way past the small hours.

Kendra needed to be more patient; she would hear something soon. She gave herself a hug, poured a large glass of gin and tonic and settled down to watch *P.S. I Love You.*

And checked her phone every now and again.

# CHAPTER 18

Ruby's pen flew over the pages, vitriol spewing so fast it weaved over the lines. No chance of sleep – there never was lately, so she put the time to good use. On the front of the black cover she had scrubbed out the word 'Diary', stuck a red rectangle of paper over it. 'Book of Hate' now adorned it, in spikey black lettering.

*Mouse is such an interfering little brat. Sneaking around in my room, trying to get me into even more trouble with Mum and Dad. Like I give a stuff what they say anyway. I wish they was dead. I wish I was dead,* she wrote.

Now she was banned from seeing Harry. No way. Meeting Harry had been like seeing the stars and the moon up close and being blinded by them. She felt as if the secrets of the universe had been revealed to her. Being without him now would be leaving her in the dark once again, and the thought of going back to that made her shiver.

Never in her life had she felt so close to anyone; at the moment she had felt most alone, he had appeared. They had so much in common.

*Nobody else liked him because he was annoying. Until he came along no one ever listened to me,* she scribbled.

She surrounded the statement with love hearts, then realised how dorky that was and turned them into stars instead, which was slightly better.

Behind the goofy smile, Harry was clever. Maybe not academically, his grades were poor, but he was really quick and sharp. He seemed to know what was going on in her head better than she did. Which was why trying to keep the texts hidden from him was proving such a major pain in the backside.

Her parents were completely oblivious to the messages – and determined to ruin her life. They were the ones who had insisted on sending her to that expensive private school when she was eleven: Tennyson's Exclusive School for Girls. It had almost destroyed her. She felt she was being rejected by her parents, especially as she didn't even need to board overnight, because it was only a mile or so down the road. Father had been adamant it 'added to the experience and made her a more rounded character'.

After three years, Ruby felt so rounded she wanted to roll under a stone and die.

Finally, she screwed up her courage, and confessed to her parents how she hated being away from her family at night, even though she was home every weekend. That she missed her little sister most of all. She had been four when Ruby went away, and starting school herself. Almost every weekend when Ruby came home, she could discern a change in Mouse: she had grown a little taller, learned something new, found a different game to play together, there was always something. Ruby was happy that she was happy at school, but worried, too. She needed to be home more, to keep an eye on things.

All of that was true. But it wasn't the main reason why she was desperate to leave. She would never tell them the real reason.

Instead, she had begged and pleaded until her father had offered a deal. If Ruby got her grades up from Ds and Cs to Bs, she could attend a different school.

The relief.

It would be a challenge. Ruby wasn't the most gifted person in the world academically, and knew it would be a miracle if she did it. But she had worked her socks off, sometimes doing homework until past midnight, spurred on by her dad's promise. And she had done it. She'd got Bs in all of her subjects. All except maths. She was really, really bad at maths, but through sheer determination and a lot of tutoring, she managed to get a C and was overjoyed.

When she had given her parents her report card, she had been full of hope that her efforts would be worth it. That they would see how hard she had tried. That she had done everything that had been asked of her.

'What about this C in maths?' her dad asked.

He hadn't even commented on the other grades, apparently blind to the huge improvement she had made.

In his eyes, she would always be a failure.

He had stood his ground and refused to let her leave the private school because he said she hadn't kept her side of the bargain. She felt utterly betrayed by him.

To 'encourage' her to try harder, he had even persuaded the school to no longer allow her to be captain of the netball team.

'To teach you that you can't always get what you want,' he had said.

She knew that for sure. Ruby never, ever got what she wanted, even when she did as she was told.

If her dad hoped that no longer doing the one thing she loved would concentrate her mind academically, he failed miserably. Ruby gave up trying. Why bother, when she couldn't win no matter what she did?

She had got herself expelled in the end, thanks to getting drunk one night. When she first met Harry she'd told him about it, all full of bravado and making it sound dead cool. Only later had she told him the full story. A gang of the cool girls, led by Poppy Flintock, had been drinking and Ruby had been so desperate to impress them that she had joined in. She'd been delighted when they let her, thinking they were finally going to be her friend. But they'd got her to drink loads. Cheering and egging her on, telling her she had to finish a bottle of vodka as an initiation – that would prove she was good enough to hang out with them.

She'd done as they asked, not noticing that they were barely sipping their own alcohol. Once she was off her face, the giggling gaggle of bitches had then dobbed her in to a teacher. Led one right to her as she lay face down in the toilets, in a pool of her own vomit. Of course, they had only called a teacher once they had taken some video footage of her and a ton of photos to post online.

Father had been furious, but at least Ruby had got what she wanted – to leave all of her troubles behind and enjoy a fresh start at a local state school.

What a joke.

She should have realised that there is no clean slate in cyberspace. Videos do not disappear simply because you move away. There is nowhere to run and hide, no matter how far you go. Beginning at the new school in September had been the starter gun for matters getting even worse.

Beside her, her phone buzzed silently with a message, as if confirming her thoughts. She stiffened. Turned it over, to lessen the temptation to look at it. Carried on writing in her 'Book of Hate'.

*Thank goodness I have Harry. He has taught me how to cope. He tells me the way things really are, and makes everything so clear. Just a week or so after meeting, our first attack took place. That was the real turning point of our friendship. The point where we fell in love.*

*Bloodshed tends to bond people. One way or another.*

She drew some love hearts around that sentence.

# CHAPTER 19

The rattling cry of the magpie sounded outside. Like it did every morning. Benjamin clenched his teeth, and turned over to stare at the alarm clock. He had been wide awake already but that didn't stop him from wanting to shoot that bloody bird. Its call was the precursor to the alarm going off, and another day officially starting. He couldn't face having to get up and try all over again. It being a Saturday made it all the harder somehow, thinking that the rest of the world was relaxing and having fun while he slogged it out.

Another guttural call came from outside. No light was seeping around the edges of the curtain. It was dark still outside, too early to get up yet. Why did the bird sit on the roof above his window every morning anyway? It was like a harbinger of doom. If he believed in that kind of thing. Which, of course, he didn't. Successful people made their own luck.

As the clock's digital read-out edged towards seven a.m., Benjamin turned the alarm off by touch alone. No point in waking Dominique yet. He gently pulled back the duvet and got up slowly so that the movement wouldn't stir his wife. He couldn't face her. Not yet. He needed time to gird himself for it.

Pausing as he scratched himself, he looked down at her face in the gloom. Smooth forehead, one hand resting on the pillow and slightly tangled in her long auburn hair, cupid's bow mouth open the tiniest amount. She looked so peaceful.

Hate soured his blood.

The bitch didn't have a care in the world.

Finding the energy to drag himself out of bed every morning was getting harder and harder for Benjamin. All he wanted was to curl up in a ball and cry. Crying was for wimps, though. Real men didn't do that. So instead he got angry. Anger was a great force to power him. That and the fact that he didn't want anyone to discover his lies. If people found out, everything would be lost.

As if Benjamin didn't have enough on his plate, bloody Ruby was playing up again, too. He was sick of it. Why couldn't she behave?

He put his shoulders back and didn't shuffle to the bathroom; he strode, knowing that it would wake his wife. Good. He wanted her to realise he was still the virile, powerful man she had married.

He heard her sigh as she woke. The rustle of the duvet as she moved.

'Good morning,' she murmured sleepily.

Benjamin shut the door to the en-suite bathroom, pretending he hadn't heard her. When he looked in the mirror, he fought to convince himself it was her he hated, and not himself.

As he did up his trousers, Benjamin had to breathe in, hoisting his gut up and in. Back in the good old days he had been something of a star on the rugby pitch, tackling people as a prop. He'd been solid muscle back then. Powerful and impressive. Now he had run to fat. Too many nights working late and scoffing dinner quickly before going to bed, exhausted. Too many corporate lunches with clients, eating rich food that gave him indigestion and heartburn so that he had to permanently live with a packet of Rennies in his jacket pocket.

With an audible huff, Benjamin let his breath out and his stomach sag. He slapped his hand on it, contemplating how his life had all gone wrong. He'd had it all worked out when he was a go-getting twenty-something, still lighting up the rugby field. When he had caught Dominique's eye and swept her off her feet with his talk of how he was going to take over the world. By the time he was forty, he had told her, he would be a millionaire several times over. He would retire aged fifty-six, when all of his annuities were due to come to fruition, by which time the children he planned on having (a boy and a girl) would have both turned eighteen and be at university themselves, living independently, though still coming to their dad for advice because he would be their best friend.

The first disappointment had come, in fact, when Dominique gave birth to Ruby. He had wanted his son and heir born first, and hadn't been entirely sure how he would connect with a daughter. But he'd convinced himself that she would, obviously, adore him, and that his son would come along soon.

It had been a long wait until Dom had fallen pregnant again. There had been talk of IVF, of mucking about with tests, and he hadn't approved of that at all. If there was a problem, he didn't want people finding out about it. Certainly, he didn't want anyone thinking that it was he who had the problem. Benjamin was all man.

Not that he felt it lately.

After six long years of waiting, along had come Amber; their little Mouse. She was a strange one. He liked her more than Ruby, he admitted grudgingly to himself, then hastily reminded himself that he did love both his daughters very much – of course he did.

The truth was, his children were an enigma. Before fatherhood he had assumed he would automatically love his kids, and they would love and respect him. But they didn't listen to a thing he said. They questioned things. They answered back, even when he gave them the simplest of instructions to follow. It was infuriating.

Benjamin had tried over the years to bond with his children. Neighbours would often have seen him in the park, when they were younger. He had tried to teach them how to throw and catch a rugby ball, but although Ruby had been keen at first, she didn't have the sticking power and gumption to put in the hard work needed to be good. Such a shame, as she'd been fast and fleet with the ball. He had looked forward to those games in Greenwich Park, throwing the ball long to her; her face a picture of concentration as she followed it in the air, sprinting to get into place below it. Jumping and catching it, the elation in her eyes clear as the wind whipped her hair around her face. Dominique clapping her hands and calling encouragement, standing on the sidelines with Amber in her pram.

Afterwards, they would sit together with a little family picnic. Tired but happy, they'd look down the hill towards the Thames, sparkling in the distance, as they chatted and ate. Those had been wonderful days.

Then puberty had hit, and Ruby stopped wanting to play with her old dad. At first Benjamin had been disappointed – felt rejected, even – but he realised it was a waste of his valuable time teaching her. A girl would never become a great player and represent her country. And people might think it was odd if she got too good at it anyway – he didn't want to be known to everyone as the bloke with the butch daughter.

Benjamin didn't like to be different, he wanted to be exactly like everyone else. Only better.

Still, he had tried to be there for Ruby. Done his best to encourage her. When she had been struggling academically at school, instead of giving in to her demands to leave, he had insisted she stick it out. He had faith in her, knew that with enough carrot and stick she would get there. The worst possible thing for her long-term would be to give in, because then she would learn that failure was rewarded. He wanted her to realise that if she applied herself, she was capable of realising her dreams. So, he had made her stay at that private school, told her that she could leave only if she got good enough grades.

But she had let herself down.

Bad enough she had failed to get her grades, but to be thrown out for drunken behaviour was unforgiveable.

She was getting worse and worse, and he had no idea how to help her. Benjamin didn't have time to pander to her, she needed to pull herself up by the bootstraps and get real.

He looked at himself once more in the mirror as he did his jacket up. The Savile Row suit fitted him perfectly, hiding the worst of his stomach and giving the impression of broad shoulders and slim-ish hips still. The blue tie exactly matched his eyes – which was the reason why he wore it.

He'd still got it, baby. He was still a winner.

If he played his cards right, no one would ever know what he had done…

# CHAPTER 20

'It's an angel, playing a harp,' cried Mouse, excitement making her shout, her slippered feet dancing. She moved to the next advent calendar, eyes darting around the picture of Santa and his reindeer pixellated by smaller images peering through windows. Where was today's number?

Dominique smiled as she watched, and could see the tension of her daughter's body as the hunter found her prey. Sharp nails picked at the edge of the cardboard door...

'A beautiful snowflake! It's all sparkly with glitter,' she gasped. 'And look, only seven days to go.' She pointed to the inside of the door, which contained a countdown. Mouse was almost beside herself. 'This time next week it will be Christmas.'

Unable to contain her glee, she curled up her fists and jumped up and down in her baggy-bottomed sleep suit.

Dom's stomach dropped at the sight. What would Christmas be like, knowing Benjamin was carrying on with another woman? Even if she were ready to confront him, she would have to keep quiet for the children's sake, so they could have one last festive season all together as a family. Even if it was a charade. Once Christmas ended she would tell Benjamin that she wanted a divorce.

Did she though?

Between worrying about her marriage and Ruby playing up, no wonder she had started sleepwalking again. Dominique felt better for having warned Ruby off Harry, though. Dominique hadn't had the chance to really get to know the other parents of children at the school, but she'd chatted with a handful who had been eager to fill her in on rumours about Harry and his no-good mother. They lived on a rough estate, Harry's father had disappeared long since, and his mum had fallen apart and turned to drink – maybe even drugs. One mum had gleefully told her about a time a few years ago when Harry's mum had been sacked from her job in a supermarket because she was slurring and clearly the worse for wear. It was disgraceful. The estate they lived on was well known as a drug den, too; it was always in the news. So, it was all too likely that Harry himself was dabbling. How could he not, raised the way he had been. The conversation she'd had with Fiona, far from soothing her fears, had added to them. Dom only hoped her rebellious daughter listened to her for once.

Still, part of her felt guilty. If she and Benjamin split up, then the teen was going to need all the support she could get. But the relationship with Harry was so intense it was almost claustrophobic.

No, it was the right thing to give her daughter some enforced breathing space. She was too young to get involved in a serious relationship, and when it inevitably fell apart, she would be devastated. Just like her mum felt. Better Dominique stepped in now and saved Ruby further pain in the future.

Right now, though, Dominique was going to enjoy Saturday with her youngest girl, who had now opened all her advent calendars.

'Do you want to help me put up the decorations?' she asked.

'Yes.' Mouse's mouth formed a perfect circle of elation.

'Breakfast first, then get dressed. Hopefully Daddy and Ruby will help, too.'

It was boiled eggs for breakfast. Dominique followed the 5:2 diet religiously, keeping her figure slender at a point in time when she had started to naturally thicken slightly around the waist. Surely forty-four was too young to start middle-age spread?

One of the eggs in the roiling water cracked, its contents spilling forth and solidifying until it looked like intestines. Dominique shuddered at the thought, wondering where such a dark image had come from. She was letting things get to her.

Well, she would have to eat the cracked egg, because Mouse certainly wouldn't.

Mouse already sat at the kitchen table, her legs almost but not quite long enough to reach the floor. She was growing up fast.

She pointed, wrinkling her nose. 'Eurgh! Your egg is trying to escape,' she giggled.

'I know, the shell cracked.'

'You're not very lucky with boiled eggs, are you, Mummy? Yours always cracks and mine never does. Why is that?'

Dominique tilted her head and gave her daughter a smile that glowed. 'You must just be a very, very lucky girl.'

Then they both dived into their breakfast, and the only sound was of happy munching.

⚜

That was the highlight of the day for Dominique. Once the Christmas tree was delivered, it quickly became clear that Benjamin would not be coming home early from the office to help, and that Ruby would not be appearing from her bedroom. Even Mouse quickly bored of decorating, frustrated because she wasn't allowed to do it the way she wanted, with everything messily everywhere.

Dominique was not a fan of the decorations, either, if she were honest. They were too desperate to be chic, the white colour scheme too cold and corporate. A bowl of lemons was not Christmassy, no matter how tasteful it may look. It was all too considered, which automatically sucked the joy out of it. Christmas should be about laughter, really bad decorations made by the children, and making an arse of yourself in charades.

When she and Benjamin had first moved in together, they had such a laugh at Christmas. They'd had no money at all. Dom's parents owned a dance studio, which they'd set up after retiring from professional ballroom dancing, so although comfortable, didn't have much money going spare to help the young couple set up. Not that Dom would have accepted anyway, particularly after Benjamin had so generously given his share of his inheritance from his father to his mother and sister. So, they had lived in a draughty flat, cheap as chips, with dreadful storage heaters that couldn't cope with the cold snap that made Jack Frost patterns on their windows. But they had kept warm making love, or cuddling up on the sofa under a blanket watching *It's a Wonderful Life*. On Christmas night, after spending time with each of their families, the pair had come home to discover the heating had packed up altogether. Instead of despairing, they had put their music on full blast and jumped around to their own private disco, singing and laughing helplessly.

Dom had spent all her money that Christmas, about £40, on a Sekonda watch she had had engraved for him.

*Time for love*

A play on something Benjamin had whispered to her not long after he had told her he loved her for the first time. As he had laid out all his hopes and dreams for the future, and launched his business with Jazmine Bauer, he had said he would work hard every single day to give Dominique the life she deserved.

'No more draughty flat, no more rusty cars. We're going to have a wonderful life together. But I promise, no matter how hard I work, I will always make time for you.'

Benjamin had worn the gift for years, but stopped suddenly when he bought his fancy timepieces. The latest in his ever-increasing snobbery.

Fatherhood had wrought the initial change in Benjamin, Dominique realised now. When she and Ruby had come home, he had been a bundle of nerves. When he held Ruby, the newborn cried.

'She just needs her nappy changing. Can you do that, please, while I take a nap?'

'What? No, I – I can't.' The panic on his face.

'Benjamin, you look like I've asked you to disarm a bomb.'

'I can't. You do it.'

'Don't be ridiculous.' She folded her arms as he proffered their baby, eyes beseeching.

He'd burst into tears. Actually broken down, hunching over Ruby as he held her away from his body.

'I'm just scared I'll break something,' he confessed. 'Look at my massive rugby player hands. Look how tiny she is.'

Ruby's skin wrinkled ever so slightly where he held her. Dominique smiled. 'And look at how you're holding her as though she is the single most precious thing in the world. You would never do anything to hurt her – I know that, you know that. Come on, I'll watch while you do it.'

And he had, marvelling at Ruby's perpetual motion once she was on her back, little arms and legs wiggling. So careful with her soft skin as he wiped her, then did up the new nappy.

But Benjamin had never really conquered that fear. Overwhelmed by the responsibility of a little life depending on him, he had become more and more uptight. More convinced that his role was to provide the money and hers the love; traditional roles, and she had nothing against that, but she didn't understand why he had thrown himself into it quite so much. Or when material things had begun to outweigh the love his family gave him.

Benjamin would, Dominique already knew, spend this Christmas Day lounging in bespoke cotton Charvet pyjamas. Even his bloody pyjamas had to be mega expensive. She wished he'd just grab some velour leisure wear, extract the poker from up his backside, and chill out.

Was he the same with his mistress? Was he as grumpy, or did they laugh, talk, have wild sex without fear of being overheard by the children?

Did they dance around to their own private disco?

# CHAPTER 21

Bloodshed tends to bond people, one way or another. Ruby sat on her bed and looked at the words she had written in her 'Book of Hate' earlier that day. Sucked on the end of her blue Biro, remembering the exact moment when she had realised she was falling in love with Harry. From the moment they had got chatting in the school corridor, on her first day, they had clicked and started hanging around together. Deciding to meet up on a Saturday night the following week hadn't felt like a big deal at all.

Ruby and Harry had walked along, heads bent together so they could share the same set of headphones. It was a hot, sticky early September evening that still felt like summer. Neither teen had wanted to go home, even though it was approaching ten p.m., Ruby's curfew. The day so hot the roads released their tarmac smell and metal railings had been almost untouchable, had turned into a stifling night.

They wandered through the skatepark, nodding their heads in time to the beat and swapping smiles at the really good bits that made them want to air guitar it out. It was dark, but the skate park was well lit, and even though it was late the roar of the boards' wheels over concrete could still be heard as dedicated boarders practised on halfpipes.

As they came out of the brightly lit oval, through the other side of the skatepark, and entered the twilight area before they reached the orange-lit street, they noticed the people standing in front of them.

A group of teenagers.

A group of teenagers from Ruby's old school, Tennyson's Exclusive School for Girls. The girls who she had desperately tried to befriend – and who had made her life a misery. Poppy Flintock's head tilted like a cat that had spotted something interesting to toy with.

No, not here, not when she was with Harry.

Ruby groaned inwardly for letting her guard down and allowing herself to think, even for a moment, that she could be happy. She had forgotten momentarily that she was the carcass on which all carrion fed.

'Hey, shithead.' Poppy's drawling call was unmistakeable.

'Hey, shithead.' Poppy's devoted followers echoed her, a choir led by their conductor.

'Got yourself a little friend? Found another shithead? Wow, well done, who'd have thought there would be another one?'

Poppy wrinkled her nose and put her head on one side as she studied Harry. 'Doesn't the smell put you off? I mean, she stinks like shit. She's got piles. Doesn't the cloud of flies buzzing round her bother you?'

Her brow smoothed, as if realisation had dawned. How she loved to put on a show for her audience. 'Oh, no, I get it,' Poppy sniffed theatrically. 'Yeah, you smell of shit, too. So you don't even notice it. How sweet.'

Her followers snuffled like eager piglets. Giggling, nudging each other, some going the extra mile to impress their leader by pretending to choke on the imaginary stench of Ruby and her friend.

'Oh my God, I just thought.' Poppy's hand flew to cover her mouth as if to hide the smile behind the mock horror. 'You… you're not going to have sex and give birth to a load of tiny little shitheads, are you? Oh my God, Ruby, are you up the duff? You are. Look at you blushing.'

The followers didn't need any further instruction. They took their cue, chanting.

'Ruby's up the du-uff, Ruby's up the du-uff.'

Harry looked at Ruby. Disgust, anger, even pity – that was what she expected to see. He rolled his eyes and laughed.

Not at her. At them.

Taking her hand, he walked through the crowd. There was no choice of going around them, the only means of escape to carry on forwards, or go backwards – and Harry clearly realised as well as Ruby that doing that meant turning their backs on her enemies. Not a good idea.

Ruby gripped Harry's hand and let his strength flow through her. It wasn't an act this time as she stood that little bit taller, walked that bit more confidently. She had Harry by her side, she could conquer anything.

And she did.

The mob parted for the couple, in shock.

Closed around them.

Poppy turned – and spat in Ruby's face. The shock of the gobbet sliding down her cheek froze Ruby in place. Until she spat right back, and all hell broke loose.

Harry tried to push a lad off him. Even as Ruby was punched in the ribs, she saw her boyfriend yank at his enemy's top, pulling it over his head to try to stop him being able to hit out.

Ruby lashed out, trying to stop herself from falling to the floor.

Where was Harry? Was he all right?

There. Poppy's boyfriend had shoved Harry's glasses up and put his fingers right under Harry's eyelids. She'd never seen anything like it. He screamed. Ruby lurch forward – she had to help him. A fist smashed into her stomach. She doubled over, gasping, unable to breathe.

Fury wouldn't let her give up.

Head still down, she ran full tilt at the lad, just like she'd learned when playing rugby with her dad. Butting him in the side and causing him to stumble and let go of Harry.

Harry didn't need a second chance. He punched his opponent hard in the face, while he was still down. Once, twice, three times.

Ruby could barely breath, she was so badly winded. Harry turned to grab her hand, and the urge to run died on his lips as he saw her wheezing.

If they didn't get out of here soon, they were done for.

# CHAPTER 22

More blows rained down on Ruby and Harry. More screams.

'Get her!'

'Kill her!'

'Slag!'

'Shithead!'

She kept her eyes on Harry as he pushed people away. But there were too many of them.

'Oy! What the…? Come on, quick, a couple of moshers are getting banged up bad,' came a yell.

Running feet. The mob scarpered, scattering like marbles spilled from a pocket, and disappearing into the shadows. Skateboarders appeared, surrounding Ruby and Harry, but this time with gentle hands, soft voices.

'Woah, man, are you okay?'

'We're fine. Thanks, though,' Harry mumbled through a lip already swelling, his beautiful skin split and dripping blood.

With well wishes from the skateboarders, the couple limped away. It took several streets before Ruby realised Harry's fingers were entwined with hers. It had been so natural, so right, that it hadn't seemed a big deal. They were bonded for ever, thanks to those troublemakers.

❖

Ruby's parents were still out when they got back to her place, thank goodness. She hated to think of the drama they'd create if they saw her. No way was she going to tell them.

Harry looked like crap. As well as a thick lip, one eye was black. Ruby tried to mask it behind heavy black eyeliner, telling him he looked like a gorgeous goth, but nothing could disguise the swelling.

'Aren't your parents going to ask questions?' she asked anxiously.

He gave her a look that told her she had inadvertently asked an exceptionally stupid question.

'How are you doing?' His face was tender now. He ran a thumb along her jaw, giving her goosebumps.

'My bruises are mostly hidden,' she replied. 'Look.'

She lifted her top, almost wincing as her arms rose to shoulder level – her muscles were stiff from the pounding they had received. Harry flinched when he saw the storm cloud bruises billowing across Ruby's ivory flesh. He reached out, hesitant, but Ruby didn't move away. His fingers landed on her ribs like the wings of a butterfly. His digits kissed her skin as they traced the outline of her injuries with only the lightest of touches, making her shiver when he arrived at the tenderest spots.

'You might have a cracked rib,' he said, as she took a shuddering intake of breath.

'I'm fine,' she lied. Because she knew her breathing was down to more than simply her injuries. Finally, she had found where she belonged, she realised. Nothing else mattered. People could do what they wanted to her, as long as she had Harry.

'Who were those people, anyway?' he asked.

Ruby's eyes darted round, trying to flee the conversation. Harry took both her hands and rested his forehead against hers. They breathed in one another's breath, until Ruby's pounding heart had slowed to match Harry's. No one else existed apart from them. Ruby stared at Harry's eyes, noticing the deep brown flecks that made them look almost black, the amber around the pupil that made them glow like fire.

Then she told him everything. How hard she had tried to fit in at her old school. How badly she had failed. And her hopes for a fresh start at her new school.

'Everyone hated me at that posh school. They made my life a misery,' she revealed. 'All I wanted was to go to a normal school. But Dad simply had to make me attend that place, trying to impress the neighbours or his partner or whatever. Who cared if his own daughter was miserable as long as everyone knew how much money he was chucking at me?'

'It's over now. All that's in the past. Everyone at school likes you so far, so screw these others. Bumping into them was just bad luck.'

The bitter betrayal and constant fear of the last few years melted away at his words.

They fell asleep together, exhausted. Holding hands, still facing each other, curled up on their sides.

❖

The front door closing woke Ruby. Her eyes flew open, and she prodded Harry awake. His eyebrows shot up in confusion that was rapidly blinked away at her urgency.

'You've got to hide. Quick. Into the cupboard.'

Without a word, he hurried over, and the second he pulled the door closed, she entombed herself in the duvet and closed her eyes. Turned away from the door and forced her pounding chest to rise and fall slowly.

The bedroom door opened quietly, the only giveaway was the hushing sound of it brushing over the thick carpet. A pause, then the same hushing and a click.

'She's fast asleep,' Ruby heard her mum say out on the landing.

She waited for a minute, heart still threatening to give her away with its thumping beat. It could be a trick. Her parents may have realised she wasn't asleep and wanted to catch her out.

But they hadn't.

After five minutes, she crept over to the wardrobe, wincing at the movement.

'You okay?' she checked.

Harry gave her a soft smile of reply. 'Am I all right to go now?'

'Should be. Come here.' She opened the window and leaned out. 'See that ledge? Immediately below it is a trellis and, look, that fancy bit of stonework. Think you can climb down using them? Don't look so worried, Mouse did it all summer. She thinks no one knows, but I've heard her during the day, when she wants to get something from her room and doesn't want to get told off by Father for "traipsing through the house every five minutes".'

'Yeah, I can do that. No problem.'

He hesitated, then leaned forward and kissed her. Gentle; all the more so because of his split lip, but it made something inside Ruby come alive.

Her first kiss.

❖

By the Monday, everyone had known about the attack.

*'Two skanky moshers get what's coming at the skateboard park – what a mess.'*

That was the message that flashed across Ruby's phone. There was a video of her. Blurry, but still discernible, as she had momentarily curled up into a ball, feet kicking at her.

From that moment, her fate had been sealed at her new school. Somehow, a girl called Jayne Seward had spotted the footage on Facebook or something. Recognising the new girl, Jayne had made sure the video was shared far and wide.

Jayne had continued what Poppy had started at Ruby's previous school, for no reason other than it was fun. People sniggered, pointed, whispered comments.

So much for a fresh start.

Ruby's family were the only ones who had no clue. The teen hid her war wounds beneath long-sleeved tops and a mask of thick make-up. Before, she had tried everything to be like everyone else. That changed after being beaten up. Ruby realised she would never fit in – and she decided to embrace it. Her make-up got thicker and darker, her clothes blacker and more extreme. People were going to stare and hate anyway, so she gave them something to stare at and focus their hatred on.

Her father shouted at her for what she wore, of course. He was such a loser. As for her mother, she was predictably mute as a statue. If Ruby stabbed her, she wouldn't be surprised if the blade broke on her stone exterior.

Now Ruby's parents wanted to ban her from seeing the only person in the world who understood her, and who cared about her. Why were they so determined to do everything in their power to make her life a misery? She wished they could leave her alone, disappear without a trace. They expected her to play happy families when it suited them, but they despised her.

And she loathed them.

That was why she had stayed in her room all day while the decorations were put up. She'd used to love that, until she had been sidelined and forgotten by her own family.

A yell came from downstairs. Mouse was calling her name.

Across the other side of the room, Ruby's phone vibrated angrily. She had received a message. She stood, gave a resigned sigh, wiped on her jumper the sweat that had suddenly bloomed on her palms. Then read the text.

*'You're dead meat.'*

# CHAPTER 23

'Ruby, do you want to help me switch the lights on?' called Mouse at the top of her voice.

She stood on the bottom step of the staircase and swung on the bannister as she waited for a reply.

'Ruby? Come on!'

She counted to ten, but got no reaction. She ran back towards the living room, deliberately skidding along the hallway first.

'She doesn't want to join in, Mummy.'

'Okay, well, it's the two of us, then. Ready?'

'Yeah, yeah, yeah.' Mouse put her hand on the switch, Mummy put a hand on hers, then she put her other one on top of that and Mummy's hand last of all. Layers of hands like a sandwich.

'Ten,' called Mummy.

'Nine,' grinned Mouse.

'Eight.'

'Seven.'

Mouse spotted Ruby lurking just outside the room, arms folded. She looked like she wanted to join in but didn't dare, and Mouse didn't understand why. She didn't mind sharing the moment with her big sister – though she definitely wanted to be the one who actually did the switching on. She remembered last Christmas, when she had fallen over and scabbed her knee when she fell off her new bike. It had still been hurting that night when she went to bed, and Ruby had found her crying. So, Ruby had grabbed a balloon from downstairs, then rubbed it over her hair. The sight of her big sister with her hair standing on end had had Mouse in fits of giggles. She'd soon forgotten all about the aching knee. She'd begged to have a go herself, and Ruby had obliged, then carried Mouse to the mirror so she could see the halo effect.

If she hurt herself now, would her big sister still comfort her, she wondered.

'One… Lift off! Woo hoo!'

The tree lit up so sparkly and bright that it was impossible not to feel filled up with the lightness of it. Mouse felt it spread out to her fingers and toes until they tingled and her whole body seemed to be smiling.

She grinned and turned to the doorway. But Ruby had gone. Oh, well. Instead, she looked at her mummy.

'What shall we play now?'

'Oh. Umm, I don't know. What do you want to play? I thought you might like to spend some time watching television.'

'Not in the mood. Let's play Spot the Difference.'

She ran and grabbed her pens and some sheets of paper from her room, pausing only to do more skids along the hallway. She loved sliding. The bottoms of her sheepskin slippers had worn glass smooth, and were perfect for skidding on the shiny wooden floor, although Mummy got annoyed when she caught her.

Deciding she didn't want to push her luck, she skipped quickly into the room, before Mummy could guess what she had been doing, and carefully drew two pictures while Mummy watched. She spent ages making sure the Christmas tree was good and spiky. Getting the details right was very important in Spot the Difference.

'What's the difference?' Mouse asked, finally.

'Umm, oh, I know. The tinsel goes around the opposite way in that one.'

'Yes!'

'And the bucket under the tree is different.'

'That's not a difference.'

'Isn't it? It looks like one.'

'No, that's just my rubbishy drawing,' Mouse giggled.

# CHAPTER 24

'Ta-da!' Kendra held up the bottle of white wine and grinned as the door opened. 'Fancy a drink?'

After a largely sleepless night, and a day of once again checking her phone every five minutes, and not daring to leave the flat in case Ben turned up – which he hadn't – she was going out of her mind. So, she had sent a text to her neighbour, Dawn, and arranged to pop over for a Saturday night together.

'I've already got one chilling,' laughed Dawn. 'Come in, come in. The kids are in bed and Jayne's hiding in her room pretending to do homework, but probably texting people she shouldn't, or whatever it is she does on that bloody phone.'

Dawn closed the door behind Kendra, who automatically went straight through to the living room without having to be shown. 'If she says she's doing homework on a Saturday night then she's almost certainly texting people she shouldn't,' Kendra giggled over her shoulder.

'Hey, well, she can do what she wants this weekend, cos you'll never guess what happened to her.'

Dawn sounded so outraged that Kendra stopped in her tracks and turned to face her friend. 'Sounds serious.'

'Some little bugger punched her. Honest, I thought her nose had been broken when I first saw it.'

'It was that bad? Who was it? What happened? A mugging?'

Dawn shook her head and chivvied her on towards the kitchen. Clearly booze was called for to finish the story. 'It happened at school.'

'No. Right, where's your corkscrew?' asked Kendra.

'Like you don't know. Anyway, I get a call from the head saying our Jayne's been hit and can I come straight away. I had to run out on the ward mid-shift; that took some organising to cover, I can tell you, but that's a different story. So, of course, all sorts are going through my head, and when I get there… well, she looked almost as bad as I'd been imagining.'

Kendra gasped to show her appreciation of a good story. 'Was it one of the other kids, then? She being bullied?'

Dawn nodded, lips a grim line.

'Some jumped-up little rich girl who started there in September. She's been giving Jayne loads of trouble; thinks she's too good to be at an academy cos she used to attend some private school until she got chucked out.'

'Oh, yeah?' asked Kendra, premonition prickling.

'Hmm, Ruby Thomas is her name. Now poor Jayne is probably hiding in her room because her nose is purple. She's lucky not to have a couple of black eyes.'

'Have you been to the police?'

'I want to, but Jayne's refusing to say who did it to her—'

'But you just said—'

'Oh, I know who did it, believe me. But Jayne's staying quiet, and so are all the other kids. You know what it's like at that age, no one wants to be a grass. Everyone went temporarily blind when she got hit. But Jayne's mentioned this girl before, and I'm sure it's her. Jayne should get the mad cow locked up for attacking her. Ooh, come here, I can open that faster,' added Dawn, snatching the bottle away impatiently.

Kendra didn't argue. She was too busy trying to process what her lover's daughter may have done. There was no way she was going to tell Dawn who the thug was; it could impact on their friendship – and goodness knew, Kendra didn't have many friends close by. She just thanked her lucky stars she'd been discreet enough to never mention Ben's surname, or named his children. Paranoia had always made her careful with facts that could identify her lover.

When Dawn Seward had moved in across the hall from Kendra the previous year, Kendra had been in a good place emotionally. She had felt secure in her position as Ben's true love.

She and Dawn had bumped into each other as each was carrying groaning bags of groceries up the stairs. Despite their lives being so different, they had clicked. Dawn was bright, bubbly and kind. Kendra had liked her instantly, so invited Dawn inside for a cuppa.

Not only was Dawn trying to recover from heartbreak, she was also coming to terms with being a single mum to her three children, Jayne, fifteen, Faye, thirteen, and Oliver, ten.

'Can't be easy starting again,' Kendra had soothed, popping the kettle on. 'I've been through my own share of bad break-ups, a fresh start was one of the reasons I moved down here, so I feel for you. If you ever need to talk…'

She had felt rather smug that her own love life was so perfect.

Soon, though, it hadn't been her helping Dawn, but Dawn giving her a shoulder to cry on. The mistress and the single mum had become unlikely but firm friends. Dawn never judged Kendra because her own marriage had crumbled after her husband discovered she had had a drunken one-night stand with his brother. Messy, but meant she was on morally shaky ground if she tried to look down her nose at Kendra.

Another point in her favour was she had as little social life as Kendra. The pair were constantly popping over the hallway to have a chat over a cuppa, or something a bit stronger. It meant that Dawn could stay in with her kids while still socialising with a pal, and Kendra could have fun too, while still being available to drop everything if Ben texted to say he wanted to come round. All she had to do was nip across the hall and get herself ready for him. Perfect, everyone was happy with the arrangement.

Dawn filled a large wine glass almost to the brim.

'I can't drink all that,' Kendra gasped.

'I need it after yesterday. And it sounds like you do, too, from the tone of your text. So, what's the latest?'

Kendra's eyes filled with tears, so she looked at the floor to hide it. 'There is no latest. I know Ben will be with me eventually… I must be the only woman in the world who has had an affair and the man hasn't left his wife for her. What's wrong with me?'

'Hey, there's nothing wrong with you. And if he can't choose then maybe it's crunch time.'

'That's why I went to see his wife. But nothing seems to have changed,' Kendra wailed, telling the whole sorry story.

Dawn listened, sipping wine and not interrupting. When Kendra finished, her pal looked thoughtful, opened her mouth, then jumped.

'Bugger. The food; it'll be sticking to the bottom,' she said, stirring at a pan furiously.

'So, what are we having for dinner? Smells good.'

'Just spag bol. Hope you don't mind, but I'm too knackered to do anything fancy. I'm not like you, don't get time to *MasterChef* it up in the kitchen.'

Kendra laughed through her tears. 'Well, I have all the time in the world, that's the only reason I do it.'

Without a job to distract her, it killed the hours when she was rattling around her flat alone, feeling as though she was going out of her mind with boredom. Ben was always impressed with her culinary efforts – it made her feel as though she was really looking after him, and gave her a feeling that she was better than her rival at something.

*See, I could look after you like this every single day*, that was the subliminal message she was trying to convey through her cookery.

'Caught it just in time,' said Dawn, stopping her stirring and turning to Kendra once more. 'Look, I know you don't want to hear it, but how long are you going to put your life on hold for Ben? I mean, don't you want marriage yourself? Kids of your own?'

Kendra blushed. She hadn't wanted kids. When younger, she had announced to anyone who would listen that children were an expensive way to ruin her figure, and she was too selfish for them. On meeting Ben, she had thought that eventually becoming a stepmum to his children was the perfect compromise; that way, she could be maternal when she wanted, but hand them back when any real problems arose.

But lately second thoughts had crept in. A desire grew inside her, one she had never expected to experience.

'I want to have Ben's child,' she admitted, taking only the smallest sip of wine. The sharp, crisp liquid tasted good. 'Which is why I've done something a bit sneaky. I've come off the pill without telling him.'

'Blimey, Kendra. Are you sure? What if you get pregnant and he still doesn't leave his wife? What then?'

She gave a small shrug.

'He will leave her, because he loves me.' Her voice was as diminutive as the shrug. 'He'll choose me and the baby that will come along, eventually, I'm sure of it.'

Fairly sure of it.

Hopeful, at the very least.

It was all part of her Big Plan to give Ben a push in the right direction. But she wasn't going to tell anyone the details of that plan. Not even Dawn would understand if she knew the truth.

'Anyway, are you all set for Christmas?' she asked, desperate to change the subject.

'Eurgh, don't ask. It's Tony's turn to have the kids this year, so I'm dreading it.'

'What will you do?' Kendra was genuinely curious, and not only for her friend's sake. She was trying to imagine what Dominique's life would one day be like. 'Maybe you could go to a spa, treat yourself.'

Yes, that would be the kind of thing the soon-to-be ex-Mrs Thomas would do, probably with that friend of hers she always spent so much time with.

'A spa? You're joking. I'm a single mum, love, I'm permanently boracic.'

'What's that?' Kendra frowned in confusion.

'Ah, you poor wee Scots girl, it's cockney rhyming slang. Boracic lint, skint.' She gave Kendra a penetrating look over the top of her wine glass, before taking a massive slurp. 'And if you go ahead with your plan, you might end up like me.'

'Okay, okay, message received and understood.'

Kendra held her hands up in surrender and smiled despite the niggling annoyance she felt.

Soon, Dawn was dishing up and the friends carried on talking until Kendra finally called it a night at midnight. Despite her exhaustion when she fell into bed, her mind whirled. Dawn hadn't approved of what she was doing – if she knew the whole truth, what on earth would her pal make of her then?

# CHAPTER 25

Dominique woke in a panic. She'd gone blind. No, it was just pitch-black in the bedroom. The duvet felt clammy, her body running with sweat. She flung back the covers and welcomed the cooling air that rushed over her skin.

Another vivid nightmare had chased her rest away. Blood bathing her skin, dripping from the ceiling of her bedroom. It had seemed so real.

Her eyes adjusting to the darkness, she saw the outline of the lamp and turned it on. No sign of Benjamin. He must be out with his tart. The pair of them were probably laughing at her for being so pathetic and staying quiet. Actually, they were probably too busy planning their wonderful new life together and having oodles of sex to worry much about how Dominique was reacting.

There was a scraping sound of someone pushing a chair back on the wooden floor of the study downstairs. Dominique gripped the bedsheet in fear. Someone was in the house. She needed a knife, a gun, something to protect herself and her family.

A familiar cough sounded. Ah, it was Benjamin. In, but not yet come to bed. He must be avoiding her.

The scars on her arm prickled as she padded to the bathroom, sweat making her nightdress cling. She turned on the shower.

She was going to have to get help before someone got hurt, like they had last time.

# CHAPTER 26

Armed police swarmed into the house, shouting at the top of their voices. Shock and awe, that was the name of their game; to visually and aurally overwhelm through a confusion of shouting and lights, as much as through firepower.

Chief Inspector Ogundele kept his hands firmly in his pockets, to avoid the temptation to touch anything and contaminate the scene, as he walked through the house, while ahead of him armed officers checked each room. Somewhere inside this home a gun had gone off. Yet no concerned owner had come running at the sound of their door being knocked in. Which meant whoever was inside was dead, injured, or hiding – with a shotgun.

Despite this, the chief inspector trusted his team to keep him safe as they swept through the building. As he walked through the property, his keen eyes cast around, but spotted nothing out of place downstairs. The large Victorian house boasted many original features. The front door had stained glass in it, and an old-fashioned brass knocker in the shape of a lion's head, formerly framed by a large holly wreath that now lay severely trampled on the ground. The crushed red berries looked like blood. Parquet herringboned across the hallway floor, the lacquer highly polished to reflect the oak bannister running up the staircase. A jumble of coats hung on pegs, shoes placed neatly on a rack below. At the bottom of the hallway Ogundele could see what looked like the dining room, and through it a large kitchen. Before them were two doors to the left.

The entire ground floor was, apparently, clear.

The chief inspector liked coming to crime scenes, but climbing the ranks was moving him further away from that. He had never joined the force for the politics and management opportunities, but because he wanted to make the world a better place. Even after everything he had seen during his career, that still held true – although some days were tough. Today was probably going to be a tough one.

He took the first door on the left.

No signs of any disturbance sullied the peace of the sitting room, dominated by two large sofas at right angles to each other. The impressive open fireplace looked as though it might be the original mahogany, and had a large mirror integrated above it. Either side of the chimney breast were floor to ceiling bookcases. Beside the bay window stood a Christmas tree, filling the room with the fresh scent of pine, and so tall that the star on top almost scraped the ten-foot-high ceiling. Frosted white baubles bedecked it; it looked like something from the window display of a very expensive department store. Perfectly wrapped presents fixed with white ribbons rested beneath the tree.

The next room was equally neat and tidy. A large wooden desk, with red leather writing pad, sat beneath the window; the executive leather swivel chair facing towards the door. Beside a laptop, an empty low-ball glass sat on the desk. Ogundele hovered over it and sniffed. Years of experience at crime scenes had long ago counteracted the instinct to pick up such things. He could smell whisky. Expensive, good-quality Scotch, from the smoothness of the aroma. In a wastepaper basket lay what looked to be an expensive watch. Everything was perfectly tidy, like a film set rather than a home. Ogundele got a tingling sensation. Even if he hadn't been called here because shots were fired, he would have known, instinctively, that something wasn't right in this house.

Where was everyone? And what had happened here?

# CHAPTER 27

SUNDAY 19 DECEMBER
SIX DAYS TO GO

Ruby's bedroom door was open, but she held the doorknob like her life depended on it. Leaning out at an almost forty-five-degree angle, she tried to get closer to the stairs so she could listen more easily, but refused to let go of the handle, in case she had to bolt back inside her room.

Despite it being ridiculously early on a Sunday – nine a.m. – she was wide awake and fully dressed.

Her parents were below, hissing snakes having an argument that they thought their children weren't aware of. They did that a lot, as though whispered words hurt less than ones that were screamed. In Ruby's experience, whether the ugly words were quiet or loud, whether people let you down easy or stuck the knife in, it still hurt the same. Even if the pain wasn't immediate, it would slowly spread through the body to immobilise, if you waited long enough.

Generally, she didn't care what her parents rowed about. This time she had a vested interest – Mum and Dad were supposed to be going out today. She needed them to. They were supposed to be going shooting together, with some stuck-up businessman that Dad wanted to impress. As usual he was trying to trot the family out like some kind of prize, all shiny, bright, perfect. Screw that. It was a load of fakery that Ruby didn't want anything to do with.

Luckily, Dad didn't like her and Mouse going shooting, said they were too young. So, Ruby was meant to be babysitting Mouse while Dad showed off his trophy wife. Result.

But now it looked like her stupid parents were about to scupper her plans. She frowned, listening hard to make out the words among the sibilance.

'Please stop your stressing. I'm too tired to go out today. I was busy decorating the house all day yesterday – not that you've noticed.'

Unbelievable. Mum had spent an entire day wafting around making sure glass baubles were in the perfect position, and was offended because no one cared? Ruby had assumed she'd done it for her own gratification; she had certainly seemed happy enough, humming along to Aled Jones singing carols, then switching to Band Aid's 'Feed the World'.

Dad's reply was a grunt. 'Christmas is your thing. I've more important things to think about than if you've tied the perfect bow,' he spat. 'Such as landing this deal so that I can keep this very expensive roof over our heads, pay for the presents under the tree, the new carpets, everything that you take for granted. That iPhone for Mouse wasn't cheap—'

Ruby stiffened when she heard about the expensive gift her sister would be receiving.

'Come off it, you do it for yourself, Benjamin. You do it because you love business. You love it more than you love me, or the kids, or anything else in this world.'

'Yeah? Well, your only job is to look after the kids and keep the house going, sweetheart. But you'd rather hang out with your mate, Fiona, and get drunk. Not exactly parent-of-the-year material yourself, are you?'

'Be careful, Benjamin. You're on thin ice. And nothing you're saying is improving my headache or making me more inclined to go shooting with you.'

'Fine.' Ruby could imagine her dad throwing his arms up in the air, like a child, the way he always did when he knew he was losing. 'I'm going. I don't know what time I'll be back.'

Ruby crept back into her bedroom and slowly, quietly, eased the door closed so that she wouldn't be heard.

Typical. Usually, her mum was utterly pathetic. She always went along with anything and everything that Dad wanted. Ruby often despaired at her lack of backbone and wondered what the explosive consequences would be if she ever stood up to him. Finally, today of all days, she had decided to make a stand. Not a very honest stand, though. The truth was, her mum hated shooting, even though it was only clay pigeons, not actual living things. But, of course, she didn't have the guts to tell Dad that.

Mum's newly grown courage was totally annoying, though. Ruby needed both of her parents out of the house. She had arranged to sneak out and meet up with Harry. Yeah, she was supposed to be babysitting Mouse, but the kid could look after herself; all she ever did was find places to hide so she could read in peace. That and spy on people.

Now all Ruby's plans had been slashed to pieces because of her stupid parents. Was there a way she could breathe life into them? She really wanted to see Harry. She needed to see him. She was ready now; had put her black skinny jeans on, cute pixie boots, and a black cropped jumper that showed off a glimpse of her flat stomach – she'd inherited her mum's figure, thank goodness. The jeans were high-waisted enough to hide the thin scars criss-crossing the skin below her belly button.

She really, really wanted to see Harry. Despite the ban.

Screw it, she'd go anyway. Her mum might come up and check on her, find out, but what was she going to do? She never shouted, never did anything.

Throwing open her bedroom window, Ruby hung out, looked down the trellis. They had only moved into the house in June, and although Mouse had quickly discovered this alternate route into the bedrooms, Ruby herself hadn't tried it yet. It couldn't be that hard if the squirt used it, though. She chucked her Puffa jacket down to the ground first, then hauled herself over the sill. Balanced on the ledge, which was wide enough for her to stand on, on tiptoes, then felt blindly with one foot for the solid wooden trellis that would act like a ladder. There it was. It was a little awkward, but she was soon down on the concrete slabs of their patio. No sign of her mum. She nipped around the side and was out of the gate in seconds as she pulled on her coat, on her way to her date.

# CHAPTER 28

Dominique wasn't sure that she had convinced Benjamin her headache was real, but she was equally unsure she cared. She didn't feel like being the trophy wife, looking the right way, saying the right things. She hated shooting, anyway. Even with ear defenders on, it might actually set off one of her buzzing headaches. Benjamin had started shooting a year earlier, and it had been a relief when he'd quickly bored of it. But apparently it had been resurrected.

As soon as she heard Benjamin's car pull away, she went to check on the children. Mouse was curled up on her bed with Ted, reading. She barely glanced up when her mum entered the room.

'You okay there? Do you want anything to drink? Or eat?'

'No, thanks.' A flash of a grin, then Mouse's eyes buried themselves back in *The Worst Witch*. She had won it in pass the parcel on Friday, and been so proud showing it off. Dominique spotted something else…

'Have you been helping yourself to the mince pies, Amber?' Her mouth twitched into a smile.

'No, Mummy.' Mouse looked horrified. The drift of crumbs and icing sugar down her top told a different story.

Dominique backed out, closing the door behind her. As she turned to Ruby's room, she felt a tug at her jumper. Damn. With a gentle tut, she unhooked her cashmere and silk garment carefully from the nail beside the door. Eased at the fibres until the slight hole it had stretched disappeared. She would have to speak with

Benjamin about getting rid of it. She would do it herself, but she knew he would only complain about the tiny hole it would leave in the wood… She sighed, shaking her head. She had learned a long time ago that life was easier if Benjamin got his own way.

She hesitated outside Ruby's room, then knocked. There was no reply. Another knock.

'Ruby? Are you okay? May I come in?'

No reply. Of course. Dominique already knew what she'd find before she opened the door, but she still felt her stomach sink when she took in the empty room.

'I'll kill her.'

She must have sneaked out to see Harry. If Benjamin found out, Dominique dreaded to think what his reaction would be. At the very least, Ruby would be grounded for the foreseeable future. Which guaranteed a grumpy Christmas for everyone, despite Dom's own efforts to make this last one together special. She prayed Ruby would be home before Benjamin, then perhaps she could give her daughter a talking to herself, make her see the error of her ways. The thought cheered her. A calm conversation was bound to have more impact than Benjamin's favoured 'ton of bricks' approach – plus, it would make her feel better over his criticism of her own parenting. That comment of his that she 'wasn't exactly parent-of-the-year material' had stung.

Everything seemed to be piling up around her, a mist she could find no way through.

Resisting the temptation to sink to the floor and curl up in a ball, Dominique meandered downstairs, grabbed the landline and dialled.

'Ruby Thomas, call me as soon as you get this message. At least have the courtesy to let me know where you are and that you're safe – and what time you'll be home.' She hesitated. Wanted to tell her daughter she loved her. But knew she would look weak. 'I mean it,' was all she said before hanging up.

Exhaustion really was giving her a pounding headache. She didn't know what to do with herself. She loaded the dishwasher. Then went upstairs to grab a book.

There was a knife on her pillow.

Who on earth had put that there? Mouse wouldn't… which left only herself.

She had wanted one last night, but knew better than to give in to that urge. She knew first-hand the damage a blade did sliding effortlessly into flesh.

Yet there it was, shining in the winter sun angling through the large sash window. She must have put it on her pillow.

A low whimper escaped her lips as she edged towards it, head pounding in time with the beat of her heart. She didn't remember taking it upstairs. But she must have done. Picking it up gingerly between forefinger and thumb, she held it in front of her as she took it downstairs.

After putting it away, she tried to make herself forget by reading her novel. She didn't take in a single word.

She checked her emails. Lots of offers from different shops, but nothing interesting. She was even so desperate she nipped onto Facebook, but didn't stay on for long. It really wasn't her thing at all; she rarely posted because she couldn't imagine anyone being interested in her life.

After an hour, she was bored stupid with only having the gentle gurgle of the central heating and the glow of the gas fire for company. She kept thinking about finding the knife. She kept thinking about waking in the hallway. Worrying about the implications. Rubbing at the scar on her arm, as if trying to erase it.

She knew that she needed to talk to somebody. Last time, Fiona had been there for her every step of the way. Benjamin hadn't been on the scene back then; she had been away at university – until forced to give it up after the incident…

When she and Benjamin had got together, she had confessed everything. Although he had been supportive, he hadn't really understood because he hadn't seen it himself and it was all in the past.

Now it was spilling into the present again.

Dominique knew that if she didn't speak to somebody then danger lay ahead for her and her loved ones.

There was only one person in the world she truly trusted right now with her deepest fears. Fiona. She quickly called her best friend.

'It's happening again,' she said.

'What's happening again?' Fiona's voice was confused but sharp.

'You know.'

'What?' An intake of breath. 'The sleepwalking?'

'Yes, the sleepwalking.' As soon as she said it she burst into tears.

'Okay, hey, it's all right. You're sure this is happening?'

'Of course I'm sure.'

'Has, has anyone been hurt?'

'No, no. Not yet.'

# CHAPTER 29

Not yet. The phrase hung in the air, teasing Dominique with how quickly that situation could change.

She swallowed down the fear blocking her words, and forced herself to continue.

'I woke Friday night and I was in the hallway and I didn't know how I'd got there. Last night I had another nightmare.'

She stopped short of confessing to finding a knife on her pillow. She didn't want to sound completely mad. Exhaustion and worry was playing tricks on her.

'Okay.' Fiona's voice was gentle but probing, persistent. Her solicitor's hat was on, and Dominique was soothed by her calm approach.

'Can you remember the dream that led you to sleepwalk?'

Dominique gave an involuntary shudder. 'Yes, I... Oh, but there's something that you need to know first, Fiona. A woman came me up to me on Friday, after you and I had enjoyed our lunch, and she said that she's having an affair with Benjamin.'

'Right. I see. How are you doing? Bloody stupid question. You're not doing well, clearly. Why didn't you tell me?' There was no hint of 'I told you so' in her tone.

'I was too embarrassed, and I needed to try and process it myself.'

'The thing is though, Dom, you're clearly not processing it, are you? You're not dealing with it, otherwise we wouldn't be having this conversation about you sleepwalking again.'

Dominique rubbed at her forehead and closed her eyes. 'I know. That's why I'm calling you now,' she offered to her friend.

And she told Fiona all about the horrible confrontation with Kendra.

'The stupid thing is, I think I've sort of suspected for a while now. But when I was confronted by his mistress, it was still a shock. I've spent a long time imagining what my rival might look like, but I wasn't prepared at all. I was just so shocked by how young she was. She doesn't even look thirty.'

'What a cliché. He's a fool, I've always said that. What did she look like, anyway?'

'Pretty. Dirty blonde. Big boobs and a tiny waist. Your basic nightmare. She's so different from me – I mean, I'm straight up and down—'

'Er, you've got an amazing figure,' Fiona interrupted. 'You've had two kids and your stomach's flat as a pancake. Bitch.'

'Not enough, though, is it? Maybe I should stop with all the yoga and jogging and dieting, and try to get myself some curves.'

'Don't be silly. Anyway, what did you do? Did you slap her one? As your solicitor, I'd advise against it; as your friend, I actively encourage it.'

'I should have done. Or walk away with some dignity. But I was so shocked I found myself wondering if she'd got the right person. Oh, Fiona, I started asking her questions; I even asked what Benjamin's date of birth was. I think I was hoping that she'd give the wrong answer and then realise I wasn't married to her Benjamin Thomas. I'm such an idiot.'

'I bet she had no idea you felt like an idiot. I bet she thought you were an absolute ice maiden, so super cool. I've seen you in action, remember? You always come across as in control, though I know the truth of it. You shut down, don't you, love?'

'I do. I wish I didn't but I do.'

'Hard shell on the outside, mushy slush on the inside.'

'Yes, sometimes I think all my strength is pretend. I just wish some of it were real. When I got home I couldn't even confront

Benjamin. I don't know what to say to him yet. How can I have a go at him when I don't even know what I want from the conversation? I don't know whether I want to end it; I don't know if I want us to try to fix things; I don't know if I want to bloody kill him for what he's done. Or if I want to say to him "I still love you".'

'And do you still love him?'

'I don't know! But it's Christmas, so I have to pretend for the kids' sake.' Dominique groaned, kneading at her temples with the knuckles of her balled hands. Trying to figure out the answer. Talking about things seemed to be making everything worse rather than better.

Fiona gave a small sigh down the phone.

'All of this stress is causing the sleepwalking now, isn't it?'

'You're right. I should have spoken to you or Benjamin or somebody, or I should have done something. But instead I've done my usual thing and just locked it away in a box, hidden it inside me rather than dealing with it. Now it's triggered my old problem. I don't want to hurt anyone. I don't want to end up in court like before.'

'So tell me about the dream.'

'Oh, God, it was horrible. It was the children… oh God, the children.' Dominique's voice was a frightened whisper. 'Someone had broken into the house, and they were coming for my babies. They wanted to hurt them. To tear my family apart. I picked up Benjamin's gun, ran downstairs, and it was only as I heard the noise and shot blindly into the dark that I woke up, terrified, this horrible sick feeling in my stomach.'

Dom clutched at her belly, the memory bringing the feeling back. 'My heart was pounding. When I looked at my hands I couldn't understand where the gun had gone – and then I thought I might be awake, but because I was in the hallway I wasn't sure.

'Fiona, I had to really concentrate on everything to convince myself it was real. I think I felt even worse when I realised it was…' Her voice climbed an octave as she fought tears again.

'It's okay, it's okay,' Fiona soothed. 'The thing is, you were safe and so was everyone else.'

'Yes. Yes.'

'So that's good then. And, you know, you're recognising that you've got a problem and now you're tackling it by talking to me.'

'Yes,' said Dominique again, and a horrible knot of tension inside her unclenched the tiniest amount.

'There you go. It's good to talk to me. Really, really good. But, as you know, it's not enough. You need to speak to an expert again. You need to speak to someone who can really help you, because we don't want a repeat performance of last time, do we?'

'I know.' Dominique's answer was no more than a whisper.

'I know you know. It just helps to state the obvious sometimes. After all, we lawyers get paid by the hour so it's an easy habit to fall into. Tomorrow you'll make that call, won't you? I know you can't do anything on a Sunday, but today you've taken your first step, and tomorrow you can make the phone call. You still got his number?'

'Dr Madden? I'll call him tomorrow, promise. Sorry for phoning you in such a state.'

'It's okay. Let's not let things reach the stage they reached before, though, you know?'

Dominique brought her hand down finally from her face and looked at the silvery scars on her arm. A permanent reminder. 'No, I definitely don't want a repeat performance of last time.'

'Will you be okay now?'

'Yeah, I feel so much better. Thanks again for listening.'

'Hey, any time. And I mean that. Any time. Even if it's in the middle of the night; no matter what, you call me. We're the two musketeers, remember?'

'Yeah, all right, d'Artagnan, I'm off. I'll see you soon.'

'Love you, mate. Bye.'

# CHAPTER 30

Benjamin was knackered. It had been a really full-on day the day before, and not the success he'd hoped for. He had cleared out the history of his computer at work though, to ensure Jazmine wouldn't find out anything, and Dominique would never dream of suspecting him. The last thing he had needed this morning was a row with Dominique. He'd no idea why she had been in such a mood. Why couldn't she have come along with him? The row about baubles was pathetic – didn't she realise how important this meeting with Vladimir Tarkovsky was? Of course not, he reminded himself. But even so, it wasn't much to expect her to support him in his business dealings.

Too late to worry now, though. The Russian would just have to put up with him on his own. Maybe it was for the best; he wasn't sure introducing his wife and kids to someone of Vladimir's fierce reputation was the best idea, even if it did help land the deal of his life. No, better that it was only him, schmoozing the way he did best.

Ben hid behind his easy charm when he left the house, pretending everything was fine. The smile in place as always. As he put the shotgun in the boot, he displayed it to full effect to his neighbour, Mr Jackman, who seemed to be having a fight with a string of lights he was attempting to put round a tree.

'Need a hand, Alan?' Ben called.

'No, I'll be all right, thanks. How come you're not on festive duty? I've been given a list as long as my arm of things I need to do in preparation for Christmas.'

'Ah, the women do like to fuss, don't they? But Dominique is great, she's taking charge of everything while I go shooting. I go all the time. Hey, look at this beauty.'

He couldn't help showing off the gun. It made him feel manly beside his emasculated neighbour. When Alan asked if he could hold it, Ben shook his head in fake regret.

'Go to, er, shoot off, sorry.'

⟡

He was still chuckling to himself as he pulled into the shooting club's car park, which was full. Clearly everyone was desperate to shoot something and get rid of their frustrations before being locked up with their families for the festive season.

Where the hell was Vladimir? Benjamin checked his watch.

As he was going to be doing something sporty, he wasn't wearing his Rolex. It was perfect for fitting under the cuff of a dress shirt, but would look out of place in his current country gentleman outfit, complete with padded waxed jacket. So instead he chose his Audemars Piguet Royal Oak Offshore, because the rubber strap looked more sporty – plus, it had cost almost as much as his car, and was bound to make the Russian green with envy.

Benjamin had been blind to luxury timepieces until chatting to someone in the business class lounge of Heathrow one day. He and the man had been laughing at the poor suckers who had to fly cattle class and get deep-vein thrombosis due to lack of legroom. The other man had suddenly pushed back his sleeve and brandished his watch at Benjamin.

'You want to get yourself one of these,' he'd said. 'This will guarantee you get treated right no matter where you are.'

'Is it magic?' Benjamin joked.

'Might as well be. People take one look and they give you an upgrade because they know the sort of life you're used to. Seriously, I checked into a hotel in Vegas the other week, and as soon as the receptionist clocked the watch I was upgraded to a suite. Bet you've got a nice car, haven't you?'

'Yeah, a Merc.'

'People look at you a certain way when you get out of it, don't they? They know the type of person you are and the life you lead purely from the wheels you have.'

True – it was one of the things that Benjamin loved about his car.

'Well, unlike a car, a watch is noticeable wherever you are, at all times, in all public and private spaces, night or day, whether you're at meetings or going out with friends and family at night. It's the best investment you can make if you want to be taken seriously by people who matter.'

Benjamin hadn't been able to stop thinking about that conversation during his entire business trip, wondering what people made of him wearing the Sekonda Dominique had bought him years before. He'd quickly treated himself to a Rolex while away. He had reaped the benefits of his investment a few days later, when he had decided to upgrade his car. He had been chatting with one of the salespeople when the manager had come over, complimented him on his watch, and insisted on dealing with him personally. It had also got him the best table in a restaurant many times, when he had forgotten to book something. The watch was a lifesaver, and Benjamin had got used to receiving a certain reaction from people; they looked at it, and knew he was a serious man with serious money.

Looking at it gave him comfort and confidence as he waited for Vladimir. He glanced up at the sky expectantly. The clouds were the colour of concrete. So heavy and low it looked as if he could reach out and touch them. The helicopter the shooting club had arranged to pick the Russian up in should be landing in about five minutes. All these little touches added up, making Benjamin certain Vladimir Tarkovsky would be impressed and convinced that his company could handle his business. All of his business.

He smiled as he buffed his shotgun, making sure the dust that had gathered on it had gone. Finally, it was going to get some use, instead of sitting in his study like an ornament. He was looking forward to firing it.

# CHAPTER 31

Rather than spend yet another day wallowing, getting angry and doing stupid things she only regretted, such as drunk texting, Kendra decided to distract herself. She nipped across the hallway.

She felt both a dread curiosity about Jayne being hit, and a sense of responsibility: one day she would be Ruby's stepmum, after all. When Dawn answered her knock, she found herself gabbling with guilt.

'Just thought I'd see how you're feeling. Hungover? How's Jayne's face? I keep thinking about her.'

'She still won't come out of her room,' Dawn sighed. 'Want a coffee?'

'I'd love one, but I came over because… I wondered if you thought it might be worth me speaking to her, and trying to get the truth out?'

Dawn hesitated, the relief writ large on her face. 'Oh, would you? She won't listen to me or her father. But she thinks a lot of you.'

Kendra warmed at the compliment.

Dawn's kids were similar ages to Ben's two, and so Kendra always made an extra effort with them – with an ulterior motive. She wanted to be a good friend to Ruby and Amber. Hoped they would all bond and grow to love each other eventually. It would take time, naturally, but in the meantime, helping Dawn out gave Kendra the opportunity to get used to being around kids of that age. To discover what they were into, because it was all a mystery to her.

In her bid to become a good stepmum, Kendra had become fond of Jayne. Sometimes, when she knew Dawn was at work, Kendra would pop over to check on the teenager, and they would sit and chat. Hearing school gossip, giving advice to the youngster, even doling out make-up tips. Kendra had learned so much.

Now, she hoped she would be able to use her influence. Fingers crossed.

'Jayne. Come here a minute,' Dawn yelled.

A door opened and Dawn's daughter peered out from her bedroom. She had yellow shadows under her eyes, the bruising spreading from a swollen nose that was purple on the end. Kendra winced.

'See!' said her mum unnecessarily.

'I do… Gosh, Jayne, are you all right?'

The teenager gave a surly shrug. Jayne was built like her mum, sturdy and pear-shaped. But while her mum's eyes were blue sparklers that sang of kindness, Jayne's were a dirge of muddy brown.

'You poor thing,' Kendra tutted, surging forward with a hug. Jayne squeezed back. Dawn discreetly wandered away, closing the lounge door behind her.

'Now Jayne…' Kendra kept her hands on the teen's shoulders. 'What on earth is going on? Your mum says you won't say who did this.'

Kendra's hands rose and fell with the teen's shoulders.

'It's not worth saying. Thing is, it is that Ruby Thomas, Mum's right, but…'

'But she's a bit of a nutter, isn't she? I remember you telling me about her before.'

Jayne had told a couple of tales about Ruby, saying she was a troublemaker, stuck-up, didn't want to make friends with anyone, and all sorts of other things. Sadly, it was all things Ben himself had said about his daughter, the rare times he talked about his family. No wonder he was so stressed out all the time. And no wonder he didn't feel he could leave. If only he would realise that if he left home he would be happier, which would mean he would be in a better frame of mind to support his clearly troubled daughter. Kendra would help him as much as she could, too. Hell, perhaps her friendship and mentoring could even bring Ruby to her senses.

All Kendra wanted to do was make life better for her lover. Which was why she was talking to Jayne at that moment. She took Jayne's hand.

'You know, I understand why your mum thinks you should tell the police who hurt you… but you're right to keep it to yourself. They're not going to do anything, are they? And if this Ruby is as nuts as you say, well, it's best not to antagonise her – who knows what she might do next, otherwise.'

They talked back and forth for a few minutes, as Jayne filled her friend in on everything that had been said and done. Finally, she frowned, thinking. 'You're right. I should deal with this myself.'

'I think it's for the best.' Kendra gave Jayne's square hand a squeeze. 'But if your mum asks what I said, I tried to get you to tell all, yeah?'

'I won't drop you in it.'

'Thanks. Oh, I almost forgot, I brought this lipstick for you. I bought it the other day and it's really not my shade. Want it?'

Jayne's face lit up. 'Cool, thanks.'

The pink shade would currently only accentuate the purple of the teenager's nose, but Kendra kept that opinion to herself.

Mission accomplished, she was feeling rather pleased with herself as she nipped out to do some food shopping. She even spotted Jayne leaving the building, so had clearly made her feel better. More importantly, she had managed to ensure her silence. Benjamin would be so pleased with her when she told him.

She had tried several times to get Ben to open up about his children, but he rarely did. Kendra needed to show him she wasn't only with him for sex, or to be looked after, she actually cared about his life. By winning this small victory for him, and making sure Ruby stayed out of trouble, he would see more clearly how she and the kids would be able to get along once he and Kendra were officially a couple.

# CHAPTER 32

A comforting smell of grease basted the air. The fast food joint in Charlton was heaving. Ruby revelled in the total anonymity only achieved when a large group of people who don't give a toss about one another are crunched into the same space. She didn't bother looking at the menu lit up on the board in front of her; she always had the same thing: a burger and fries.

When it arrived, shoved into her hand by a teenager around two years older than her and with eyes that seemed dead, Ruby looked around for two seats, and finally found a free table.

She and Harry moved as one as they unwrapped their food, tossed the thin paper to one side, then took the top off their burgers and removed the gherkins. They could, of course, have ordered minus the gherkins, but both of them never did, and Ruby liked the sense of closeness it gave her that they shared this routine. As if they were one half of the same person. Soulmates.

They often met in Charlton. Harry lived on the western out-skirts, edging towards Woolwich, while she lived in Blackheath, so Charlton was halfway for them both. It was only five or so minutes for them to travel to. Plus, it was way nicer than Woolwich, but not so posh as Blackheath, where Harry joked people stared at him, worried he might be a mugger.

As they ate, they bitched about their lives, the people they knew, the stupid bullies at school, their pathetic parents.

'Well, Jayne and her cronies aren't going to bother you no more,' Harry grinned. 'Not after you clocked her one in front of everyone. That was a brilliant punch.'

'Thanks for teaching me,' she beamed, tearing at her burger with gusto.

'Yeah, but what made you do it now?'

Before she could answer, the stink of stale sweat and the sickly aroma of unwashed clothes suddenly assaulted Ruby's nose. She turned. A man who looked homeless wandered past, up to the counter. Sensing entertainment, she twisted in her seat for a better view, elbowing Harry.

''Scuse, mate, could I have a cup of tap water, please?'

The dead-eyed server's reply was short and to the point. 'No.'

'Come on, it's just a glass of water. I'm parched.'

'Tough,' she shrugged. 'Next.'

The man was shoved out of the way by someone desperate for a chicken burger, fries, and an extra-large Coke.

Unwatched, uncared for, the beggar shuffled over to a seat in a corner, and appeared to be making himself comfortable. Staff came over, told him to move on. But he refused.

A few people tutted, some at him, some at the staff. But no one got involved. Ruby and Harry watched, nudging one another and laughing. A trio of police officers arrived.

'Come on, sir, we've had a complaint so you're going to have to come with us…'

Harry jumped up. 'What you arresting him for?'

'Breach of the peace.'

'How has he breached the peace? Are you arresting him for trying to sleep here? There's nowhere else for him to go.'

'Don't be silly, son. You're not seeing the whole picture.'

Ruby leaped in, feeling a thrill of glee at baiting authority. 'What whole picture? Is he breaching the peace by being homeless?'

'You've really got a lot of learning to do, haven't you?' the officer sighed. He walked past them both, trying and failing to ignore the phone Harry was almost shoving in his face. 'Sir, don't come any closer with that camera, okay? You can record me, but please record me at a distance.'

'There's nowhere for that geezer to stay. He just wants some water and somewhere to sleep. This system is broken,' Ruby shouted.

'Yeah, man. Let anarchy rule. Screw the system,' Harry joined. 'Look at you, Mr Policeman, strutting about, fiddling the crime statistics.'

The policeman went red. 'Fiddling…? That's it, record all you want, but I'm not fiddling any statistics. If anyone is doing that, it's the government.'

'No, it's not. It's you. You claim to be protecting people but it's a lie. The whole system is a lie. It needs to be brought down.'

'Really.'

'You should arrest the real criminals. The bankers. The business-men. The dodgy accountants.' Ruby was particularly thinking of her father as she said this. 'MPs, and people stealing from taxpayers. Yeah? They're the real criminals.'

'Really.' Again, that same tired tone, an adult talking to a child. 'I think you need to get an education.' He started to walk away.

'Yeah? So do you,' shouted Harry.

The officer turned, pursing his lips. Trying to keep his temper. 'What organisation do you represent? You don't, do you, you're just a couple of kids…'

Ruby's heart jumped. It was impossible not to feel slightly intimidated by the black and neon figure bristling in muscles and a stab vest.

'Journalist,' she shrugged.

'You're a journalist? Really? Who for? Do you have a press pass?'

She sniggered. Beside her, Harry's shoulders shook, and she grew even braver. 'Yeah, right. I'm not here on official business. I'm here in my downtime.' She shoved her hands in her pockets and looked back at him, cocky and confident. 'We don't need a press pass here, we're in a restaurant. There's CCTV everywhere, we're already being recorded. We're just joining in.'

'Freedom of speech, man,' Harry added.

The officer folded his arms across his neon vest. 'Okay. Well, we received a report that someone was being aggressive, so we've responded to that. It doesn't help the situation to hear immature, petty comments from you, stirring it up. If you have an issue, if you have a complaint, I can tell you who my inspector is and you can make that complaint through the proper channels.'

'You're arresting him for no reason,' Ruby repeated.

'He's drunk.'

'Oh, now he's drunk?'

As if on cue, the bemused homeless man vomited a Technicolor rainbow. The only reason he stayed upright was the firm grip of the other police officers.

'Well, I'd be drunk if I had to sleep on the streets,' Ruby rallied.

'Here's some advice, kids: grow up, okay?'

'Grow up? You grow up,' Harry laughed. He grabbed Ruby's hand and ran from the building before the officer could say any more.

As they raced down the street, Ruby's blood was pumping. She kept laughing, wanting to leap. She felt alive.

'The system is screwed, man. What's the point of following rules that are meaningless and corrupt? If you want something, take it and screw everyone else. That's the only law that matters. Don't ever let anyone get in your way,' ranted Harry.

'Take the law into your own hands.'

'Yeah.'

'Yeah!'

The thought was exhilarating, liberating, like a thousand small explosions going off beneath the surface of Ruby's skin.

'World would be a better place if all the idiots died. Someone should kill them all,' she shouted.

'Everyone who has ever been awful to us. Anarchy!'

Harry's grin was so wide that Ruby couldn't resist. She stopped short, pulling Harry towards her. Snogged him, right there, right then. He drew her even closer, ignoring the tutting passers-by who barged into them on the crammed pavement.

Inside her pocket, her phone vibrated.

Harry pulled away. Gave her a penetrating look, serious brown eyes framed by the brilliant green of his glasses, which brought out the fire flecks around his pupils. She held her breath. Hoping, praying that he hadn't felt the buzz. That he wouldn't want to check her phone.

'I'm gonna have a whizz down this alley, yeah? Won't be a minute,' he said.

She tried not to show her relief. Simply nodded.

As Harry walked away, she turned her back and slipped her mobile from her inside pocket. Slid a finger across the screen to unlock it… as Harry snatched the phone from her fingers.

'What the hell? I thought this was over,' he shouted.

Her secret was out – and Harry was furious.

# CHAPTER 33

Benjamin and Vladimir Tarkovsky stood side by side on the rough grass. The weather was turning. What had been an overcast and mild day had begun to weep at Benjamin's attempts to woo the Russian businessman. Under the too-warm coat, he was sweating, but he couldn't take it off because then he'd get soaked. This was not a good impression to make on Tarkovsky, who appeared to be coated in Teflon from the efficient way his lightweight waterproof and flat cap dealt with the damp air.

'You both have your own guns?' asked one of the staff at the gun club. They nodded.

'Fibre or plas wads?'

Benjamin nodded. 'Yep, definitely.'

'Which?'

'Eight or nine. Twelve?' He couldn't remember. Had no idea if it mattered.

The man looked confused. 'Are you talking about shot sizes? Maximum size here is six, sir. We'll sort you out with some fibre wads, if you're not sure whether you want plas or fibre. Let's just go over some basics…'

What was a wad? Was it the same as a cartridge? It didn't matter, Benjamin itched to have a proper go at shooting, and listened impatiently as the man assigned to look after him went through the safety instructions. He was being shown up needlessly in front of his business prospect. He knew he'd be good at this. He had good hand-eye coordination thanks to his sporting days – and how hard could it be, anyway?

A year earlier, Benjamin had had the idea of going shooting, in the hopes of making some business contacts. Several of his old school pals were members of gun clubs. The idea of blasting something to smithereens appealed. It was manly, wasn't it? Guns, ammo, destruction.

But the people he met had not been businessmen on the whole. Nor had they been particularly macho. In fact, they seemed to dislike any gung-ho comments he made. Which was a bugger, because he'd bought all the kit by then. Right down to a shotgun and bullets, or whatever.

After attending gun club a handful of times, Benjamin had grown bored. The gun languished in the corner of his study untouched for months on end, looking like a rather cool ornament thanks to some pretty metalwork on its side. According to the terms of his firearms certificate it was supposed to be kept in the secure cabinet he'd had to buy specially, but he wouldn't have been able to see it then. He would never have admitted it, but the engraved metal had been the reason why he had bought it. It looked fancy.

Benjamin had a bad feeling that the staff at the club were realising how little he knew about his gun. Vladimir looked completely at home with his own shotgun broken over his arm as he stood casually to one side while Benjamin was shown the ropes.

Just point and shoot, right, how hard could it be?

'Yep, yep, got it,' he nodded, the movement so curt it was almost a karate chop. He slid the ear defenders in place.

'Pull,' came the shout.

The clay pigeon flew free.

Bang!

Benjamin was almost overwhelmed with disappointment. He'd missed it – by a country mile.

'Damn gun must be shooting wonky or something,' he muttered. His right shoulder throbbed from the kickback.

'Don't worry. Most untrained users aren't accurate with firearms. Particularly if they've never held one or used one before,' his helper said. Bastard. 'So, that scene in films where the utterly untrained user picks up a pistol and puts a blooming rose right between the eyes of the assailant fifty yards away – that's lottery-winner lucky.'

A deep chuckle came from beside him.

'Pull,' came the heavily accented instruction. A blast, and the target shattered. Vladimir was a perfect shot.

'Great. Well done.' Benjamin smiled through slightly clenched teeth. He felt a useless idiot, but at least the Russian was going to have fun… laughing at his expense.

But that was okay, because Benjamin would have the last laugh.

# CHAPTER 34

Harry's yell of fury ricocheted off the buildings as he glared at Ruby's phone. Ruby couldn't look at him, eyes glued to the floor in shame. She couldn't believe how stupid she had been, letting him get hold of it. There would be no more hiding, the truth would come out and that was the last thing she wanted. She couldn't handle the shame.

She risked a glance up. Several people hurrying by looked their way, but no one slowed down, no one wanted to get involved in a domestic.

Harry thrust the phone at her, the message leering at her.

'*I can see your rolls of fat in that outfit. Ugly bitch.*'

The words made her flinch, check over her shoulder…

'Is this Jayne?' Harry demanded. Looked around, expecting to see the bully lurking a few feet away, or across the road.

'I don't know who it is. Not for sure.'

'Yeah, right. We both know who's responsible. How long has this been going on?'

She shrugged. 'Ever since we got beat on.'

'Man.' He hung his head. Looked like he wanted to throw her phone away. 'Why didn't you tell me, Ruby? I thought people had got bored of all that. I knew you'd been given a hard time initially, but thought it had all died down. You've been so weird about your phone, though, I kinda started suspecting something was happening. That, and you punching Jayne's lights out. It's why I tricked you – sorry.'

It was her turn to hang her head. She toe-kicked at a piece of chewing gum stuck to the pavement. 'I didn't want you to think I was a loser…'

'Never.' He took her face in his hands and stared into her soul. 'I love you, Rubes. Love the bones of you. It's me and you against the world, right? Thought you knew that.'

'You and me against the world. No matter what.'

Harry pushed one side of her mouth up into a wonky smile. She fought to keep the miserable look on her face, but Harry's giggling made her laugh, too.

'Prat,' she sniggered.

'Too right – but I'm your prat. Now let's go somewhere quiet and you can tell me all about the text and stuff. You hear me?'

Under Harry's arm, Ruby felt safe and protected as they walked along. No one could ever hurt her, not truly, while she was with him.

# CHAPTER 35

Ruby's misery had started from the very moment she had begun at Tennyson's Exclusive School for Girls. She had always been popular at her junior school, with a gang of friends to choose from. When her father had insisted she attend this expensive private school, she hadn't minded one way or another. She wouldn't know anyone there, but then neither would anyone else in her year, so they would all be in the same boat, she reasoned.

Many of the girls did know each other, though, from their previous private educations. That had come as a bit of a shock. All the other girls there seemed to have so much more money. It was a strange sensation for Ruby to be the 'poor' child, and she had struggled to fit in.

At first Ruby had tried talking to her parents about it. Her mum had made soothing noises, not bothering to actually understand, instead simply offering platitudes. Her father had given her a rousing lecture in bucking up and sticking with things. He had, she realised, wanted her to hang out with all these people so she could become a pawn in his social climbing. She had become more desperate to fit in as those first months passed.

The bullying was subtle at first. Ruby was never invited to trips to the cinema, parties, or shopping. She often sat on her own in lessons, because everyone else naturally fell in with their friends, and she had none. Not really.

Her fellow peers were always vying for recognition for having the trendiest clothes, the best holidays, the latest phone. Ruby was made to feel a second-class citizen, but she tried harder to fit in, pushed herself to join conversations. When she spoke, no one seemed to hear her.

One day a gang of the girls, headed by Poppy Flintock, the most popular girl in the year, were talking about their holiday plans. Lots of them, it seemed, were going to the same place with their families and were arranging to meet up.

'The skiing at Courchevel is wonderful,' drawled Poppy, flicking her glossy, almost black hair over her shoulder. 'It will be such fun that we can all hang out together.'

Everyone agreed. Ruby felt twitchy, desperate to join in the conversation and prove that she was exactly like them.

'It's such a shame we're not going this year,' she said.

All eyes turned in her direction. Gulp. They all seemed to have heard her this time.

'You've been to Courchevel? Really? It's quite exclusive...' Poppy gave a cynical laugh.

'Oh, we've been a lot. In fact, Father says he's bored of it, so that's why we're not going this winter,' Ruby bluffed.

'Right... So have you spotted any of the celebrity regulars?'

Ruby could feel her face getting hot. 'Um, some, yeah. Who have you spotted?'

'Well, it's vulgar to name drop, but put it this way: we had a delightful lunch with a lovely couple called William and Kate.'

'Wow.' It was a collective exhalation of awe. Apart from on Ruby's part. William and Kate? William and Kate who? Her mind raced through celebrities and discarded them just as quickly. Then... good grief, did she mean Prince William and the Duchess of Cambridge? When Poppy had said the resort was exclusive she hadn't been kidding. Ruby was starting to regret her little white lie, but it was too late to back out. At eleven years old, she didn't know any better than to keep going with the fib.

The minute she was alone – which didn't take long – she googled the ski resort. Discovered the pretty Alpine village in the Alps was a firm favourite of A-list film stars and celebrities such as Victoria and David Beckham. And William and Kate, of course. She had a bad feeling about her lie, but she was desperate to try anything.

Still, she stuck to her guns, using the information online to answer Poppy's and her pals' repeated questions. Ruby had hoped she might just get away with it. The girls were starting to thaw a little towards her.

A few days later, Ruby had captained the netball team for the first time. If she could lead the team to victory, she was sure everyone would like her then. Her parents came to watch, and she tried to swallow down her nerves.

At half-time, her team were ahead, and things were going well. Some team members gave her encouraging smiles. Ruby's soul soared. As she ran back onto the court, her dad gave her a thumbs-up. But her heart stuttered as Poppy wandered over to her parents.

She was being silly, worrying over nothing. Poppy chatting to her family was a good sign.

Still, Ruby felt scared. She hurried over herself, as Poppy called her goodbyes to Benjamin and Dominique over her shoulder – and cast a sly grin at Ruby, raising a knowing eyebrow in her direction as they passed each other.

'Lovely girl,' observed Dad. 'Very polite. Perfect elocution.'

'Er, yeah, so what did she want?'

'She was pointing out some of your friends,' smiled Dominique. 'She was saying how a lot of them are going skiing next month, during half-term, and that it's a shame you're not going. I couldn't help laughing. The idea of us going skiing – you know how I hate the cold.'

'S-so you told her we've never been skiing.'

'Of course. Are you okay? You've gone terribly pale. Perhaps you should sit out this half…'

Ruby's mum wittered on, clueless about the damage she had done. That was the turning point; when isolation at school turned to name-calling, until she faced a daily barrage of abuse.

The people who mattered in her year had decided she was to be shunned at all cost – and so everyone else followed.

Still Ruby tried to fit in. But the more she tried, the more her bullies spurned her for being a pathetic lying loser.

If they didn't like her the way she was, she was willing to change, do whatever it took to make friends. The eleven-year-old altered her hair, styling it the way the other girls wore theirs. They mocked her for trying to be popular. She wore the sort of clothes they wore; they accused her of trying too hard to make herself look cool. She pretended to like the same things as them, researching whatever music, TV series, films – you name it – they were into, so that she could join in their conversations. Ruby was always experimenting to find the tiniest crack in which she could slip into the clique. She became a chameleon, attempting almost on a daily basis to become a version of herself that people would like.

They never did.

She started to dread entering a room. When she did, people would shout: 'There's Ruby – run!' and sprint away, giggling. To them it was a game. To Ruby, it was devastating.

There were times when she felt hope, though. Over the years, new people started at school. They would instantly click with Ruby and her friendly personality. Quickly they twigged that she was a social pariah, though, and that by befriending her they risked not only becoming an outcast themselves, but an active target of the bullies. Eventually, everyone always deserted her.

Sometimes, though, an olive branch would be extended her way.

'We've permission from school to go out tonight for a few hours. Nothing special, just hanging out at a café. Fancy coming?' Poppy asked one time.

Poppy's smile melted Ruby's fear-frozen heart, making her feel hope.

'I'd love to.'

'We're all meeting by the bike shed at four p.m. See you there.'

Brilliant. For the rest of the afternoon, she had felt as though she were floating along, buoyed up with joy.

Only to be slashed with disappointment when, after waiting for an hour, it became apparent everyone had left without her. Whether they had ever intended for her to join them then changed their minds, or it had been a cruel wind-up from the start, she couldn't be sure. All she knew was that daring to feel hope then have it crushed hurt more than not having it at all.

Yet she couldn't stop herself from trying to fit in.

Her parents had no idea of what she was going through. For her thirteenth birthday, her mum had offered to throw her a party to celebrate her becoming a teenager.

'It's a big deal. You can invite all of your friends. They could even sleep over. It'll be fun.'

Ruby had panicked then. She hadn't shared anything of what she had been going through with her parents. Not after the skiing debacle and the platitudes dished out by them. Rather than explaining what was happening, and facing up to the embarrassing emotions of constant rejection, she'd had a tantrum. An explosion of rage the likes of which her parents had never seen before.

The subject of a party was dropped.

Ruby's feelings towards her parents were complex. At first, her decision not to tell them about the bullying was a bid to protect herself from their reaction. Their involvement would, she was convinced, only make things worse. Later, she kept quiet because she wanted to shield them from her nightmare; and shield herself from their disappointment. What if they heard the ugly things thrown at her and started to believe them, too? Everyone else did.

Finally, the helplessness of her situation had turned to rage. She hated her parents for not realising what was going on. She was stunned they could be fooled by her acting for so long, and didn't bother peering behind the mask she wore. If they really cared they'd be able to see the truth, but they weren't bothered enough to try. When her father went back on their deal for her to leave Tennyson's Exclusive School for Girls, it finished their relationship for good.

Dreams of a fresh start at the academy had been shattered a couple of weeks into the first term. Once again, everyone thought she was a loser. Then there were the anonymous text messages.

Everyone let her down.

Except Harry.

He knew exactly what it was like to be picked on. People called him a black rat. The bullies couldn't hurt them any more though – together they were far stronger than apart. So, her parents' idea of separating them was an impossibility. Ruby would rather die than let Harry go.

The pair of them had vowed not to take anything lying down any more. They had been belittled and beaten for the last time. That was why she had punched Jayne, who had started the bitchy comments at this school, and was almost certainly behind the text messages, too.

❖

As Ruby explained all of this to Harry, he rubbed her shoulders, helping her to keep the shivering at bay. They sat on a bench in Greenwich Park, facing the famous observatory. Ignoring the cold and fine rain penetrating their bones.

'You're still getting texts, then? All the time?' he asked.

Ruby nodded miserably.

'I'm so sick of that cow, Jayne, pushing me around, telling me I stink, or that the world would be a better place if I didn't exist.

I know she's the one behind the horrible anonymous messages. She's been smirking in my face for too long.

'I thought smacking her one would have stopped her, but it's just carried on. It was great watching her nose split, feeling it crack under my knuckles and watching the blood. If I had my way, she'd bleed a lot more. I'd like to stick her like the fat pig she is.'

Harry snorted with laughter, pulling her closer. 'That's my girl. And if that hasn't stopped her, we'll have to step things up somehow. Time to hit back at them arseholes who are picking on us.'

'Yeah, and I won't be fighting fire with fire. I'll use napalm.'

'We'll go nuclear.'

She looked at him and her heart expanded with the love she felt for him. 'And what about my parents?'

'Like we're going to take any notice of them or anyone. They can't stop us from seeing each other. No one can.'

# CHAPTER 36

The notepad was full of random words jotted down. Dominique's talk with Fiona had really helped, clearing the tension headache that had plagued her since she woke in the early hours. 'Fiona the Miracle Worker' was her new title in Dominique's eyes. Still, if she let her guard down, there was a chance bad thoughts would come whirling back, like a tornado, to sweep away her well-being once again. The best way of avoiding that? Keeping busy, of course. Dominique had started a list.

She found herself staring at the words in desperation, trying to create some sense of order.

Cranberry sauce.
Stuffing.
Sprouts.

Was it all a bit old hat? Was turkey for Christmas dinner naff? She blamed Instagram. Everyone felt the need to outperform one another. It used to be with snaps of ever more glorious dishes in ever more expensive restaurants, and now it was 'look at me' food cooked at home. Bloody Nigella and other celebrity chefs were to blame, too. Looking all sexy and coquettish while cooking, when Dominique went red-faced and frizzy-haired, and usually needed several glasses of wine to really get into it when she was cooking for guests. If anyone whipped their phone out to take a snap she felt a burst of anxiety, in case the lighting didn't do it justice or the sauce didn't have a high enough shine. Couldn't people just eat the meal and not look at their phone for a few hours?

Oh, yes, because that was absolutely what she should be worrying about while her family fell apart, she reminded herself viciously. Maybe Benjamin had a point. Maybe she did neglect her family, casually putting herself first. She was often guilty of not listening to Mouse – perhaps that was why Mouse was the way she was. Perhaps Dom should be trying to bring her out of herself more; turn her into Amber rather than her nickname. What did it say about her daughter that everyone knew her as Mouse?

As for Ruby, Dom had given up trying to coax her eldest to talk to her. They had been quite close once, but since she hit puberty that had all changed. It was only to be expected, she supposed, so she tried not to be too hurt by it or kick up too much of a fuss. But she knew so little about Ruby's life now: her likes and dislikes, her friends, how she spent her time.

Perhaps she should suggest a last-minute, pre-Christmas shopping and bonding session. The decorations had done nothing to inject the family home with festive spirit, but perhaps cold, hard cash could.

❖

The sound of the front door opening and closing dragged Dominique away from thoughts of buying filial affection. From where Dom was standing in the kitchen she could see straight along the hallway to the front door. Talk of the devil and she appeared, slouching along as though she didn't have a care in the world. Ruby caught her mum's eye, and didn't even have the good grace to look abashed as she started towards the stairs.

'Just a minute, young lady. I'd like a word, please.'

Ruby's blue eyes harpooned Dominique with derision from their kohl cages. As Dom clicked across the parquet towards her,

Ruby crossed her arms, leaning back as if to get a better view. Her mum took a breath in an attempt not to get riled.

'I assume you've been with Harry, despite our asking you not to see him.'

'Ten out of ten, Sherlock.'

'I'm talking to you in a civil manner, Ruby. Could you please do me the same courtesy?'

She received a tut and impressive eye-roll as an answer.

'Fine. Look, either I tell your father about your little stunt today, and you get grounded for all eternity, or... Ah-ah, hear me out before you start shouting "it's not fair"... or you and I reach a compromise.'

The black-rimmed eyes narrowed. Suspicious but curious. Dominique ploughed on, mildly encouraged.

'How about you and Harry stop seeing each other over Christmas and January? At the start of February, if your behaviour has improved – and that includes no sneaking out – then you can see him again. If you love him as much as you say you do, it will be tough but worth it.'

She felt pleased with herself. And impressed that Ruby had done as requested and managed to button it long enough to hear her out. That was a good sign. A very good sign.

'Finished?' her daughter checked.

Dominique smiled. 'Yes – what do you think?'

'You've got to be bloody kidding me. You think you can con me into giving my boyfriend up? It'll be like improving my grades all over again: I'll deliver my part of the deal and then you and Dad will move the goalposts.'

'That's... no. Don't talk to me like that.'

'Don't talk to me like I'm stupid.'

'The world doesn't orbit around you, Ruby.'

'Oh, I'm well aware of that, thanks, Mother. No point coming crying to anyone, because no one gives a toss.'

'Is that what you really think?'

'It's easy to ignore trouble when you're living in a bubble, Mother. You never come out of your bubble. Because you don't want to deal with reality. You're too weak.'

Dominique blinked furiously as Ruby stomped up the stairs. The bedroom door slamming shut made the whole house shake, and the first tear spill down the shocked mum's cheek.

# CHAPTER 37

Ben was not a happy bunny after the shoot. Not only had he failed to hit a single clay pigeon, he had been taken to one side and given a lecture by the club about how he needed to take better care of his gun to avoid a danger of jamming and misfiring. He had felt like a naughty schoolboy. Vladimir had pretended not to notice, but his moustache had twitched as though hiding a smile.

Then Vladimir had announced he had decided to take his business elsewhere. Which left Benjamin officially up a very smelly creek with no paddle in sight. He pulled off his coat, feeling claustrophobic and sweaty.

What was he going to do? He needed the stupid fat bastard to give him money. Without that, his plan wasn't going to work.

He couldn't cover his tracks for much longer.

Time was running out. Benjamin felt like he was sinking into quicksand, helpless. It was pressing on his chest and he couldn't break free.

He was losing it.

He couldn't give up now, though. Muhammad Ali had always advised people to make their days count. His dad had thrown that quote at him a lot, and a shared love of the charismatic world heavyweight champion had been the only thing they had shared. Benjamin thought of it and knew he must make every single day he had left count to the max. He needed to get control again. He could do this – as long as he held his nerve. His hand reached automatically for the packet in his pocket, and he popped a couple of antacids as he came to a decision.

He'd go see Kendra; shag her brains out. That would make him feel like a man again. Then he'd see a new way forward with his problems.

When he had met Kendra, four years earlier, chatting her up had been a spur of the moment decision. Dominique hadn't been able to come with him to the awards ceremony because the babysitter had called in sick with a vomiting bug at the last possible minute. They had tried all of their friends, but no one was able to drop everything and be there with only an hour's notice. Benjamin had been pretty annoyed, because the award had been a big deal, and Jazmine had been away on holiday. He had felt quite lonely as he stood there with the stupid prize, no one to share his moment of glory with.

As soon as Kendra had asked to see his trophy, he hadn't been able to resist flirting, but felt certain she wouldn't respond. She was so young and fresh-faced. It had been more about testing his luck than actually thinking anything would happen. One thing had led to another though. At each stage of flirtation he hadn't felt guilty because he knew it wouldn't go any further; any minute she would knock him back and make it clear she was simply passing time until someone her own age came on her radar.

But that hadn't happened. They had shared a taxi. He had made a move, expecting a slap. The second their lips touched, he knew he had to have her. Simple as that.

What a buzz. Men half his age would love to be with Kendra, and he'd stolen her away from them all.

He hadn't thought further than wondering how long he could get away with it. He did feel bad about Dominique, but it was only sex. There was no betrayal of the heart, and that's what mattered.

Buying an apartment in Charlton and putting his mistress into it had been a smart investment on his part. Charlton was cut off from Blackheath by a ravine of concrete and carbon monoxide better known as the A120, creating two very different London villages. On one side was verdant Blackheath, where he lived, with its wide-open spaces, stratospheric house prices and trendy, middle-class buzz. On the other side was Charlton – with considerably cheaper house prices and more down-to-earth residents, who probably wouldn't hold their hands up in horror if a shop ran out of hummus.

Having Kendra in the flat meant he had someone he could trust looking after the place. Plus, she was pathetically grateful to him, thinking he was paying her rent – she didn't have a clue the place belonged to him. Technically, he should have rented it out to make some money, but playing sugar daddy had been an irresistible lure.

After four years together, he was fond of the kid. She was a sweet-hearted young woman, and being with her was a welcome escape from his life. She made him feel youthful himself – a sensation that had him more addicted than any junkie to heroin. After a disastrous day like today, he needed a hit urgently.

He sped to the flat, pressed impatiently on the buzzer, and leaned into the intercom when she answered.

'Hello, my gorgeous girl. Let me up, I'm freezing my nuts off down here. And I want you to warm them up,' he quipped.

A squeal of delight. The buzz of the door being remotely unlocked. He bounded up the two flights of stairs, three-quarter-length coat flying out behind him like a hero's cape. That made him feel good. By the time he rapped smartly on flat four, he had a genuine grin of anticipation on his face.

The door flew open, there was a blonde blur, and a shriek in his ear as Kendra threw herself into his arms, then covered him with kisses. This was what he loved about her; she was always as grateful as a puppy to see him.

He wrapped his arms around her slender waist and kissed her desperately, as though trying to suck the life force out of her so he could once again be her age.

He was tempted to get her to put the corset on for him, but he didn't have time. He tore at her clothes, pushing her back onto the sofa. Her grey eyes smouldered as she reached up and pulled him on top of her. She was as greedy as he was.

Yeah, he was still the man. Balls deep in a gorgeous young woman with soft puppy flesh. How many men his age fantasised about shagging someone her age – and how many could actually do it?

❖

Afterwards, she seemed a bit weird, though. Like she was working up to saying something. She looked pale, too. He kissed her, about to ask her if something was wrong. She got there first.

'So, everything okay? Anything interesting happened over the weekend? What have the kids been up to?' she gabbled.

He tensed. Could she tell something was wrong? He'd been feeling kind of all right again and now she'd gone and ruined it. He glanced at his watch, and not so he could revel in the expense of it.

'Just the usual. Nothing interesting. Anyway, I better get going.'

'Oh, right… See you tomorrow?'

'Maybe. We'll see.'

A swift peck on the cheek and he was out of there, closing the door on her kicked puppy expression.

# CHAPTER 38

Ruby pulled the duvet over her head, balled her body up tight as a fist. Screw everyone. Screw everything. She didn't care.

Sometimes, when she shouted at her parents, she absolutely didn't really feel the complete opposite, and want a hug more than anything else in the world. Definitely not. Of course she wasn't rejecting love rather than risking being rejected herself. That would be ridiculous.

She wiped a tear from her face and told herself once again that she absolutely did not care. She would fight fire with war. She was tougher and stronger than her bullies, and in her boyfriend she had the only ally she would ever need.

But her lying heart pounded. Traitorous tears leaked from the sides of her eyes. Her mobile buzzed again, and she gave an involuntary shiver. It was ten p.m., but the hounding was oblivious to the time of day or night.

Punching Jayne had made things ten times worse. The texts and social media abuse had become a storm over the last few days.

Ruby's trembling hand reached from beneath the Hades of her duvet, and wrapped reluctantly around her mobile. Once unlocked, the light from the phone was bright as a torch in the darkness of her hiding place. It made her think momentarily of Mouse, of when they had shared a room, and her heart gave a funny stutter of affection: little weirdo. Just as well they didn't share a room now, though. Ruby barely slept. When she did, she had nightmares: the fear of being beaten up again; the misery of her everyday life and her isolation from the rest of the world chasing her even in her dreams.

She should delete this new text. Not bother reading it. Reading it was stupid.

But she needed to know what was being said about her, what people were thinking. She had to attempt to understand. Why didn't people like her? She had tried and tried. There was nothing more she could have done and yet every single advance had been rejected and mocked.

Almost of its own volition, her thumb pressed on the message icon.

*'Why are you still here? Do the world a favour and disappear.'*

Ruby let the anger burn away her tears.

*'What do you want of me?'* she tapped out furiously. *'Would it finally make you happy if I killed myself?'*

Her whole body seemed to pound with her pulse as she waited for a reply. Minutes passed. Perhaps replying, confronting Jayne or whoever it was with words instead of fists, had done the trick. Scared her off. Made her realise things had gone too far.

Ruby unclenched her toes, allowed herself to relax, just the tiniest bit.

A vibration. The phone lit up. Ruby reached out a finger, let it hover for a heartbeat, then opened up the message.

A single word blazed up at her.

*'Yes.'*

Pushing the phone away as if it were on fire, she curled in on herself again. Bit on her fist to muffle her terrified yelps. Her bullies wanted her dead.

Outside, she heard her father's car pull up. Listened to the sounds of him coming inside then going into his study, which was immediately below her room. She threw the duvet back, wanting to run to him and feel protected like she had when she was little. When he had taught her to play rugby. She had loved that, had only stopped because the girls at school had found out about it.

They made all kinds of comments about her being butch, accusing her of being a lesbian. The girls had hidden themselves from her in mock horror when in the changing rooms getting ready for PE, sneering and sniggering that she was leering at them because she fancied them, when in reality she hadn't even dared cast a glance their way. So what if she had been a lesbian, anyway, it was nothing to be ashamed of. The comments were pathetic, but it had been enough for her to stop the rugby sessions with her dad in the park. When she had lost those, she felt as though part of her had been lost with it. She had only been eleven at the time, but she had somehow known even then that she would never get back her childhood happiness.

Since then, she and her father had grown increasingly distant. Would things have been different had she explained to him why she had stopped playing? Almost certainly not, she decided. He was a complete wanker these days. No, she wouldn't show weakness by telling him what she was going through. Instead, she forced herself to pick up her phone again and dial.

It rang four times before a sleepy voice answered.

'Harry, it's me. Can you come over, please? I've had some more texts. They're horrible... I'm sorry, I shouldn't bother you, but you said to tell you.'

'Hey, hey. I'll be right over.'

'Don't come to the front door. Climb up to my window.'

'No worries. See you soon.'

Ruby sat up, wrapped her thin arms around her knees and waited, rocking slightly. Eyes closed, trying to calm herself down.

She heard murmuring coming from Mouse's room, and slipped from her own bed to see if something was wrong. When she opened her little sister's door, a sliver of gentle light from the landing sliced through the darkness and cut dark shadows onto Mouse's peaceful face.

The kid must have been talking in her sleep. She giggled, turned without opening her eyes, face snuggled into Ted.

Ruby remembered one time when Mouse was about three and hadn't been able to sleep, so she had made up a story for her little sister. Each of her cuddly toys had had a part, and Ruby had never felt so content as she had watching Mouse's rapt attention sliding into yawns and heavy sighs and finally sleep.

Now, she took a step towards her, envious of the peace. Furious that she couldn't find some herself. Another step. Another.

She bent down. Felt her sister's breath warming her chilled cheek.

Ruby glanced over her shoulder. There was no one around to witness what she was about to do.

Closer she leaned. Kissed her on the forehead.

'Sleep tight.'

She stole back into her bedroom, in time to hear a gentle tap on her window.

❖

Once inside, Harry held her tight, listened to her fears, checked the messages and looked so angry that, for a moment, Ruby was afraid. She thanked her lucky stars he was on her side. When he dialled the number, there was no answer. There never had been when she had tried, either.

'Come here,' he said, lying down and pulling her down beside him. 'I'll stay with you until you go to sleep. You're safe with me.'

She put her head on his chest. This time when she curled up, it was in pleasure. Harry smelled of chicken in batter and chips, and the sharp, clean deodorant he always used, and the distinctive smell of cold air that still clung to him. Comforting things. She snuggled in closer, gave a deep sigh of contentment, as he talked gently about playing Xbox games, arguing with his little brothers, and getting shopping in because his mum was too out of it to do it. A lullaby of grit that soon had her drifting to sleep.

# CHAPTER 39

## CHRISTMAS DAY

Despite the officers storming through the building, their body cams recording everything at the scene, Chief Inspector Ogundele walked cautiously. Slowly. He stuck to one side of the staircase as he climbed, hands still in pockets, trying to minimise scene contamination as much as possible.

The second he got high enough to see through the balustrades on the landing, the calm perfection of the house shattered.

On the floor were two male bodies. A teenage boy lay on his back, one lens of his green-framed glasses smashed. Blood from a wound on the back of his head soaked into his black hair and the thick, soft pile of the creamy golden carpet, beginning to coagulate. He was only wearing one boot, the other stood upright in one corner. His big toe poked through a hole in his exposed sock. The officer noticed the grazes on the boy's slightly swollen knuckles, and several cuts to his left cheekbone. Discarded beside him was an ornate lamp, the stained-glass shade smashed, and the embossed base boasting a clot of blood and several tightly curled strands of jet hair.

A man in his forties sprawled face down a few feet away, frozen in the throes of crawling to one of the bedrooms. One hand stretched out towards the door, as if fighting to reach his family.

'He must have discovered the intruder, fought with him, overpowered him and then…?' pondered Ogundele quietly.

Then what? Ogundele frowned, peering closer. Although he had clearly been in a scrap, there were no serious injuries. Possibly the stress had brought on a heart attack?

But what about the two shots reported? There was no sign of a gun so far, and neither man had bullet wounds.

Nothing at this crime scene was adding up properly.

# CHAPTER 40

Panic was overwhelming Dominique. Her breathing so fast she was dizzy from hyperventilating. Where was Benjamin? He wasn't there. He was never there. And now she could hear the noise again and knew that someone was in the house. Getting closer.

She picked up the shotgun that was standing in the corner of her bedroom and edged towards the door. There was the noise again.

'Who is it?' she shouted.

No reply. Just a shuffling sound. A gurgling noise like the central heating made sometimes, but meatier, more guttural.

Her hands shook with the weight of the gun, the muzzle bounding around as she pulled the butt against her shoulder and fought to balance it with one hand. The butt's wood felt smooth and silky against her sweaty palms as the bedroom door opened.

*No. Oh God, no.* She gagged at the sight before her.

Ruby lay in a scarlet pool of blood that oozed across the golden carpet.

Dominique was too late to save her little girl. Who had done this? Why?

She dropped to her knees, the shotgun cast aside, and hauled her daughter's rag doll body into her arms. Rocked her against her chest, crying a river of tears that joined the scarlet puddle. There was so much blood. It covered her skin, gloved her hands, coated her fingernails until they looked like talons.

*No, not my baby. Not my little girl.*

Dominique held Ruby the way she was no longer allowed to, tight and fierce and protective. Bursting with love for her firstborn.

Where was Benjamin? She threw her head back and screamed for him.

Ruby twitched. Gave a jerk of life. Her hand flew up around her mum's neck and patted her back like a thumping heartbeat. Ba-boom, ba-boom, ba-boom.

With a gasp, Dominique's eyes flew open. Ruby's body disappeared. She was hugging thin air, sobbing on the landing over nothing. Benjamin knelt beside her, tapping her back, trying to wake her. Lit by the Tiffany lamp that stood on a circular occasional table, his eyes were wide with concern.

'Are you awake? Are you okay?' he demanded. He sounded so full of love that she flopped against him in relief as reality flooded back. Her daughter was alive, her family was safe, everything was okay.

It was only as Benjamin tenderly helped her to her feet, one arm around her waist, the other holding her hand, that she remembered with another jolt that everything wasn't fine. That her husband's love was an act.

Despite herself, she felt a connection with him, though, and allowed herself to be put to bed, docile as a baby. He pulled the duvet over her, got in beside her. She put her head on his chest and let herself be comforted as she keened. His heartbeat sounded reassuringly real, strong, true. He whispered nonsense as he stroked her hair and promised she was safe now.

Thank God he was there.

Her anger twisted inwards from him to herself, because she still didn't have the guts to call him out on his lies. She needed him.

They lie together, in every sense of the phrase, until seven a.m. Time to get up and put the mask of normality back on.

# CHAPTER 41

The shower pummelled Benjamin awake, whether he wanted to be or not. He was so tired of fighting, of trying to stay one step ahead all the time. Some other way of solving his problem must be found. The Russian would have been perfect, and there was still a slight chance he would land him. But not in time. Benjamin needed something fast.

He leaned against the tiles, still cool enough that he twitched away before angling back fully. Hung his head and tried to let the water wash away his troubles. Fat chance.

Benjamin had imagined that by this stage of his life, he would be living on easy street. The sheer slog and sacrifice he had put in for the past twenty years should have been worth it. By now he had imagined he'd be holidaying in Mauritius, jetting off whenever he fancied, own a couple of Mercs, have a mansion somewhere impressive. Instead, he had a decent-sized but not terribly impressive house in Blackheath. He only had one Mercedes, rather than one for every day of the week, and his wife drove a bright yellow Smart car which she referred to as the Canary. He hated it, but she insisted it was perfect for nipping around town and he pretended to agree because he couldn't afford to get her anything else.

But neither his car nor hers was paid for. The house, which they had only moved into six months earlier, was now security for a huge loan, which he had forged Dom's signature to get. He had already borrowed up to the hilt against Kendra's flat. He owed the tax man. And the business itself had massive debts, accrued after he had taken a few risks. When things had started to go wrong he had convinced himself it was an unlucky streak he'd soon get over. But the streak had turned into a monsoon of never-ending crap. It was too late for his luck to turn. Too late for him to save himself or his business.

He was too ashamed to admit what he had done, because it was caused entirely by his own arrogance and stupidity.

What were people going to say when the truth came out?

How would the kids cope? Dom?

They would hate him.

Dominique wouldn't survive the stress of it. She couldn't cope with losing everything. With her husband being sent to jail. The strain of organising Christmas was making her sleepwalk, for goodness' sake. All he wanted was to protect her. The urge so strong that sometimes he hated her for it with a passion that seemed to outstrip his love.

He thought of how he had found her sobbing the night before, on the landing, and led her to bed. He'd wiped her tears away with the sleeve of his stupidly expensive shirt, kissed her and tasted the salt on her lips. He loved her so much.

The consequences of discovery did not bear thinking about.

Unpleasant flashes of the future spun through his mind, as though he were standing in a giant zoetrope. His stomach contracted, bile licked his throat. He clung onto the tiled walls of his shower to keep upright, even as panic tried to drive him to his knees.

He would simply have to find a way to get some breathing space, and then everything would be fine.

If he didn't his life was going to follow his shower water straight down the plughole.

# CHAPTER 42

Tendrils of the night's terrible dream still clung to Dominique, making her shiver. Until she saw Ruby with her own eyes, she wouldn't fully shake the conviction that something bad had really happened to her. She sat at the kitchen table twitchy with anticipation, clutching her glass of orange juice so hard it might shatter. Her yoghurt was untouched.

Benjamin sipped his own coffee, watching her from the corner of his eye. Cleared his throat.

'Are you all right then? After last night?' he asked finally. Gruff, like he always was when nervous. Benjamin didn't do nerves well, preferring to bulldoze over them until they were squashed. A habit he had picked up from his own father.

'Fine. Just a bad dream.' She didn't take her eyes off the door. Why wasn't Ruby up yet? Maybe she should knock on the door again. She had received the usual grumpy response to her morning knock on her eldest daughter's door, and that had made her feel a bit better, but she needed to see her.

'Right. Yes. Obviously. But come on, babe, it was bad. When you had those funny dreams before you said it was—'

She threw a glance his way. 'It's the stress of getting everything ready for Christmas.'

It showed a lot about the state of their marriage that he was so easily fobbed off.

'Are you coming to Mouse's—'

'Amber's—'

'Nativity play later?'

'No, I'm too busy with work. Have fun without me.'

Footsteps made Dom turn her head.

'Ruby. You're up.' Dominique pushed her chair back with a screech across the terracotta tiles. Her daughter rubbed her eyes.

'Well, you woke me, so of course I'm up. Or don't you think I'm even capable of getting out of bed?'

Dominique clenched her hands to her sides, fighting the urge to hug Ruby and tell her she loved her. Goodness knows the reaction that would get. Instead she did the teenager some toast with marmalade, and drank her in through stolen glances.

It was just a horrible dream. No need to be scared.

# CHAPTER 43

Wow, there had been one weird atmos between Mum and Dad at breakfast. Even Mouse had picked up on it, appearing from behind her book to study them, roll her eyes, and return to her make-believe world. Ruby couldn't wait to get away; didn't want them ruining her buoyant mood. She felt happier after her decent night's sleep, and even though her parents were probably cooking up some fresh hell for her, she went to school feeling good because she couldn't wait to see Harry again. Lying in bed together the night before, with no attempt at funny business, had been such a wonderful moment. She felt it was yet another step to their path of love. Every time she thought they couldn't possibly get any closer, they did.

She pulled on her school clothes. In her hurry, she barely flinched in disgust at the scars at the top of her thighs as she pulled her thick black tights on. She almost skipped to the station.

But Harry didn't get on the train.

❖

When she hopped off at Charlton, every step she sent hopeful glances ahead, but never spied him. She hid around the corner to put her make-up on, the heavy eyeliner a mask behind which she felt safe enough to march into school alone. Shoulders artfully slouched, head at an angle carefully calculated to convey bored insolence to anyone who looked at her. Definitely not giving away any nerves.

She made her way to the lockers, passing easily through the crowds of pupils of varying ages who parted to let her through. She caught snatches of conversation, whispers on the air that floated to her and made her smirk.

'… punched her lights out…'

'… totally mental…'

'… for no reason…'

Only the slightest flare of Ruby's nostrils might have given away her disappointment when she rounded the corner to her locker and saw… no sign of Harry. He must be wagging school. Which meant things must be really bad at home for him.

Ruby didn't even bother putting on a show of staying for her lessons. She did a one-eighty and walked straight back the way she'd come, pulling out her phone as she went.

❖

Harry's arms were burning with the weight of the shopping bags he was carrying. Any minute now his fingers were going to be cut off by the plastic handles of the bags; he could see the tips turning a weird purple-blue. He tottered straight past his mum, who was out for the count on the grubby sofa, sprawled like a drunk across a park bench. A little snore escaped. He threw a glance her way and clocked the drool glistening on her chin, but he didn't slow.

Ow, ow, ow! Fingers!

He just managed to get to the kitchen in time, dumping the heavily laden bags on the floor then hopping around shaking his hands, trying to get blood flow back to his dangerously deprived digits. Once the pain subsided, he got to work.

Baked beans, tinned soups, a ton of Pot Noodles, a loaf of white bread, a couple of litres of milk. That was one bag of shopping emptied. Harry dived into the rest.

Biscuits, pop and crisps…

Frozen burgers, fish fingers, oven chips and stuff he could shove in the microwave.

Finally, it was all put away. Harry sighed, leaned against the counter in the tiny kitchen in which only one person could fit at a time, closed his eyes, and daydreamed. He loved to remember the first time he had seen Ruby, recognising something lost in the new girl that peeked out from behind the tough act. Before they had even spoken, he had felt drawn to her.

Thinking about seeing her for the first time had been his favourite memory, but now it had been supplanted by the previous night. He replayed looking down at her, her head on his chest, and his heart expanded until he pure might float, man. That soft, gentle smile that had tweaked the ends of her lips, it made him melt.

Imagining Ruby was Harry's escape from his crappy life. His home was a council flat full of city clichés, from the often-broken lifts and stairwells that stank of urine to the drug dealers who lived next door and had a constant flow of visitors, day and night. He'd heard they had a crystal meth lab there, too, so he was permanently braced for an explosion if that went wrong, *Breaking Bad*-style.

Reluctantly, he opened his eyes on reality again. He needed to do the washing-up.

The flat was cramped, and not the cleanest, because his mum didn't do housework. She couldn't, not in her state. It was Harry who kept it all together, looking after his two kid brothers, and clearing up after his mum when she couldn't make it to the loo in time, or holding her when she got the crazy shakes.

'That you, son?' she called now.

His heart sank. He could hear the slur of her voice, the way her lips struggled and slid over the 's'. Too much effort in her state. He glanced at the clock. It was only 9.30 a.m.; it was going to be a long day.

'Son? Come here.'

Harry turned and crept from the flat, clamping down on his lip to distract from the prickling threat of tears. Closed the door slowly, silently, then ran, his guilt lending him wings so that he could get far, far away. He couldn't cope with looking after his mum. Not right now. The thought of having to get a damp cloth to wipe the drool from her chin, or clean up the vomit that would almost inevitably follow… He pumped his arms harder, drove his legs faster, sent the pushers and bikers scattering around him.

He only slowed when Ruby called his mobile.

# CHAPTER 44

For once, neither Ruby nor Mouse found anything to argue about, which was a minor miracle. Benjamin and Ruby left the house at the same time, and Dominique breathed a sigh of relief when she got home after the school run with Amber and was finally alone.

It took a few minutes to search out her old address book and find the number she needed. Dr Madden's secretary answered almost immediately, and expertly fielded Dominique's request to speak with him.

'I can pass on a message and he can call you back, if necessary,' she said smoothly. 'Or I can make an appointment for you to see him. There is a three-month waiting list at present.'

Three months? She couldn't possibly wait that long.

'I'm a previous client of Dr Madden's. Please ask him to call me as a matter of urgency, as I'm having a recurrence of my previous problem.'

'Which was?'

'He'll know.' Dominique could be equally smooth, when required.

For the rest of the morning she rearranged the Christmas decorations to kill time while waiting for the phone to ring, and hoping it did so before she had to go to Mouse's nativity play. Several cold callers got short shrift, Dominique taking her disappointment that it wasn't Dr Madden out on them. It was particularly maddening when she was up a ladder, balancing precariously in order to hang the heavy swags of greenery and berries up around the rooms. She raced down as the phone rang out; breathlessly, answered it.

'May I speak with Dominique?' asked a familiar voice with the faintest Liverpudlian lilt.

Instantly, she was transported back twenty-five years to when she was nineteen. To the time when she had woken from yet another night terror, but the blood hadn't disappeared as her eyes opened. The warm liquid running down her arms, dripping down her fingers, and pooling by her feet, as Fiona wrestled the carving knife away from her and screamed and screamed and screamed...

Her dream had turned into a waking nightmare. She couldn't risk that ever happening again. Luckily, Dr Madden agreed she was an urgent case.

'I'm closing the practice over the festive period for a few days,' he explained. 'But in light of the seriousness of your previous episodes, I'd like to see you on Thursday for an emergency appointment. Hopefully, we can get some coping mechanisms in place to tide you over until we can start proper sessions in the new year.'

'That would be wonderful,' sighed Dominique, letting out a long slow breath of relief.

'In the meantime, try to adhere to good "sleep hygiene", which will help prevent the sleep deprivation that can bring on nightmares in adults. Be calm and avoid stress,' he advised. 'Go to bed at a regular time, and maybe try some yoga and meditation; both can be helpful. Also, be cautious about the use of alcohol, caffeine and nicotine – they can remain in your system for up to twelve hours after consumption and disrupt sleep patterns.'

'Yes, gosh, yes. I've got into bad habits over the years, but I'll start your suggestions again straight away.'

'Excellent. Until Thursday, then, Dominique. Take care.'

As the line went dead, she couldn't help thinking his departing comment sounded more like a dire warning than a fond farewell.

# CHAPTER 45

'James, you old bugger. How are you? You still shooting?'

Benjamin put his feet on his desk as he chatted. He felt loads better than he had first thing – because he'd had another idea. This was the solution. How could he not have come up with it earlier?

'Good to hear from you. It's been a few months since I last went, actually. Why, you fancy getting together?' replied James.

'We went on Sunday. That's what made me think of you. Dominique and I were saying how long it's been since we saw you and your charming wife.'

Good old James. Benjamin could imagine his piggy blue eyes crinkling with a smile, those ruddy cheeks of his pinking in delight at hearing from him.

Benjamin rolled the pen between his palms as he talked. Threw it up into the air and caught it. Laughed in all the right places, only half-listening, as his old rugby pal yattered on about some big business deal he had just landed.

James was a good man. They had met when they both attended London Metropolitan University, and had a lot of great connections. He also wasn't averse to lending a friend a whole stack of cash, and had once bailed out a pal who would have had to pay an exorbitant fee on a bridging loan when buying a new café for his chain.

'Well, listen, listen, we don't need to do all our catching up now. I'm calling with an ulterior motive, of course, James. We wondered if you and Heidi would like to come over for dinner on Wednesday?

I know it's short notice, but between you and me, Dominique is planning to experiment on the two of you – yeah, she's got some recipe or other she wants to give a dry run on before Christmas.'

'Sounds great. I'll have to run it past Heidi first.'

'Of course, mate. Drop me a text.'

'Will do. Lovely to hear from you.'

As soon as the phone went dead, Benjamin pumped his fist.

# CHAPTER 46

Bookcase, sofa, coffee table. Turn. Coffee table, sofa, bookcase. Turn. Bookcase…

The furniture blurred past the side of Kendra's eye as she paced in her living room. Round and round she went, mimicking her thoughts.

Of all the scenarios she had run through over her torturous weekend, the only one that hadn't entered her head was the very one that was now playing out. Dominique had clearly said nothing to Ben.

The selfish, cold, calculating cow.

What was Kendra supposed to do now? She had thought that Ben and Dominique would have split as a result of her revelation. At the least, she had hoped her own torture would be over. Instead, it just went on and on and on.

She should have known. She knew her lover's wife well enough by now to realise she was a cold fish, but Kendra had massively underestimated how far the permafrost penetrated.

Curiosity had started Kendra down the road of stalking. Like any red-blooded woman, she had wanted to check out her competition as soon as she had found out that Ben was married.

She'd taken a sneaky peek on Facebook, pouring over the photographs of Ben with his glamorous wife. Snorting in derision because Dom was the same age as Ben, so Kendra had youth on her side. But intimidated by her beauty. Dominique looked like an older version of the Duchess of Cambridge, for goodness' sake, though with olive skin and slightly (and only slightly) more meat on her bones. Her hair (or should that be 'magnificent mane') was the colour of mahogany, the sort of glossy shade only achieved in an expensive salon, and never from a home dye kit. Not that that had stopped Kendra from experimenting. She had wound up with hair that looked like a sunset, her blonde locks too pale for the dye, resulting in a strange pinkish orange hue that had taken several weeks to fade. Ben had thought it hilarious, although he had refused to be seen in public with her.

Those had been the days when he used to laugh. He never laughed now.

He had clearly laughed with his family back then, too. There were photos on their Facebook page of the smiling parents sitting on a log, grinning at each other, while the children gambolled (it was the only word for it, even though it made Kendra shudder). They gleefully threw golden leaves into the air, fingers outstretched, their faces upturned in delight at the soft sunshine slanting through tree trunks.

The perfection of the snap was, frankly, stomach-churning.

It was a scab Kendra couldn't help picking at though, luxuriating in the pain it caused her. She eagerly hoovered up every titbit of information she could from the social media site. Ultimately, though, she had discovered little about the family's actual day-to-day lives, or what their relationship was like. Either Dominique only posted around once a year, or her privacy settings were tight; but either way, there wasn't much for Kendra to glean.

Still, that had been enough to satisfy her. Why torture herself with what Ben's family was like when he clearly wasn't happy with them – if he were he wouldn't have taken up with her, would he? And she and Ben were perfect together in those first years.

When he had grown tired of not being able to see her because of her late nights as a barmaid, he had insisted on renting her a nice little flat in Charlton that was fairly close to his office and home.

But far enough away that he felt comfortable. He had taken on all of her outgoings, in fact, so she had given up work.

'You don't need to worry about money when you're with me, I'll take care of you. I don't want anything taking away my time with you, nothing getting in the way of us being together,' Ben had said. She had felt so special.

Being a kept woman was a wonderful feeling, luxurious.

It wasn't only the practicalities Ben took care of either. He lavished her with expensive jewellery.

'I've got to buy you beautiful things because everything looks dowdy compared to you,' he used to say.

Once, he had even jetted her to New York for a long weekend, and bought her a necklace from Tiffany's. He had taken a snap of her outside the famous jewellers, striking an Audrey Hepburn pose. It was now in a frame by her bed. She had never been able to share it on Facebook or tell friends about it because then she would have had to field awkward questions about who she had gone with.

So much of her life was secret, she thought with a sad sigh, slowing the manic pacing slightly. Friends she had once been close to had drifted away, either tired of her secrecy or judgemental of the life she chose to lead as a kept mistress. Her family knew nothing of her lifestyle and all thought she was terminally single.

'I don't understand it. You're a beautiful lass,' her mum constantly told her.

She couldn't wait for the day she could finally show her man off to the world. But over the past twelve months Ben's interest had waned. He was distant and distracted. When she spoke, he nodded and made the right noises, but she could tell he hadn't been listening.

She was terrified he was going to end things with her. That he had finally made his decision over who he loved more – and she had come a poor second.

At first, she had fought back by going to the gym more, losing the weight she had put on with all the meals they had together. Jogging, free weights, swimming, and yoga. There wasn't a bit of her that didn't ache every single day, but it had paid off. By their fourth anniversary at the end of July, she looked great.

Ben had lamented the loss of her curves. That was the only comment he had made about it. Said he liked having something to grab hold of. She had smiled a bright, shiny smile, then turned away to blink back the tears tickling to break through, while cutting herself a large slice of the cake she had bought for them from Patisserie Valerie, and viciously shoving a strawberry into her champagne flute.

That had also been the first time Ben had forgotten their anniversary. To make up for it, the next day he had presented her with one-carat diamond stud earrings in a platinum claw setting. She had been warring with herself ever since over whether to be mollified by the beautiful earrings (she had looked online to see how much they cost) or to be infuriated that he thought he could get around her simply by throwing money at the problem.

In the end, she had kept quiet because she didn't want to rock the boat too much. Not when her grip on him was slipping, and without him she felt she would drown.

Instead, she had got her curves back – which had been disturbingly easy – and splashed out on Agent Provocateur lingerie in order to spice things up in the bedroom. They had never had any problems in that department, but lately Ben had problems rising to the occasion. He often blamed her and it caused rows. Her already fragile self-esteem chipped away further. He fancied his wife more than her, clearly.

That was when Kendra had moved from checking out Dominique on Facebook to following her in real life. She had remembered that Friday years before, when she had followed Dominique to the hairdresser's and then lunch, and wondered if she still went there.

On the off-chance, she had tried – and there Dominique was, in all her slender, expensive perfection.

Following her was a one-off, Kendra told herself. But it's amazing how quickly a one-off can slide into a habit. And habit was only one step away from addiction.

Kendra often sat beside Dominique, and the stupid woman had no idea her rival was within touching distance of her. Instead, she sat gossiping with her friend, while Kendra listened in, unmolested. It had given her such a thrill of excitement knowing that, at least, in some ways, she had the upper hand over Dominique.

She often pretended to read a book as she ate alone, while all the time listening in on the pair's conversations. She had learned an awful lot about Fiona's love life and her intense dislike of Ben – which had almost made Kendra slap the annoying, loud-mouthed bitch. She made herself stay still, clenching her thighs together to keep them in place, fighting the urge to march to their table, swallowing down the words that leapt into her mouth to defend poor Ben.

It had been worth it. Dominique was discreet, but she dropped enough hints to show she was unhappy in her marriage – and that she knew Ben was, too.

That titbit had been enough to keep Kendra going and make her heart soar. It had been the sustenance that had fed her strength, keeping her going when she had doubts about whether or not she was doing the right thing. She was so close to getting what she wanted that to give up now would be ridiculous.

It was always darkest before the dawn, her old gran had always told her, and so she knew that the toughest moments were immediately before the breakthrough occurred. She was at her darkest moment, and felt ashamed of what desperation was driving her to. But she would keep on, and soon she would be in the light; she and Ben would no longer have to be a deep, dark secret. What she was doing was for the greater good, so how could there possibly be any harm in that?

She tapped at her teeth, deep in thought, and started pacing again.

Bookcase, sofa, coffee table. Turn. Coffee table, sofa, bookcase. Turn. Bookcase…

# CHAPTER 47

The small school hall was full of parents, smartphones held aloft to video their darlings in their acting debuts. Dominique was no different. She always looked forward to the school's show, and every time her daughter came on stage she leaned forward in her seat, pride shining, trying to get a better shot for the video.

Not that Mouse was on stage often. Amber did not like to be the centre of attention, hence her nickname. But she stood patiently with the rest of the children, at one point dressed as a cloud, though Dominique wasn't entirely sure why.

The storyline seemed to be something to do with a talent show. From what Dominique could glean, the judging panel comprised King Herod, a wise king, and Darcey Bussell. It was slightly confusing, but definitely entertaining and everyone got their lines right. One of the younger ones, who must have been only five, believed in shouting the words rather than singing, which made everyone giggle. Guilty parents hid their smiles behind hands and fake coughs.

Finally, it was Mouse's big moment. She stepped forward with her schoolmates and started to line dance, jigging around in perfect timing. Dominique was impressed; it was certainly a whole lot slicker than when she had been practising in the kitchen over and over again.

Finally, another child wearing a cloud costume floated into the middle of the stage.

'The end,' he announced, in an incredibly loud voice.

The place erupted. Everyone stood, clapping wildly. The children mainly beamed, a couple looked bewildered and blinked rapidly, and one of the little ones burst into tears and had to be swept off stage by her father because she had wet herself. On the whole, it was a resounding success.

Mouse ran over to her mum and launched herself into her arms. They hugged each other tight.

'You were brilliant,' whispered Dom. 'The best one there by far.'

'Really?' Mouse's eyes were wide with amazement. 'I'm just glad it's over.'

'Well, I could watch you all over again,' Dom decided. Then laughed at the look of horror on her daughter's face.

It was true, though. The fact was, Mouse was growing up fast, and all too soon she would be in big school. Dom knew she must cherish these moments, before they disappeared for ever.

'Hi, Dom. I haven't missed it, have I?' called a voice.

'Aunty Fiona,' cried Mouse, throwing herself at the lawyer.

'This is a surprise,' smiled Dominique.

'Surprise? You asked me if I wanted to come, remember?' replied Fiona.

Dominique didn't, but forced a laugh. 'Of course I do. But I must have got the time muddled up, sorry.'

As the three of them walked home, Dominique wondered if she was losing her mind.

❖

Benjamin reached for his phone the second it beeped with a message.

*'Looking forward to being your gourmet guinea pigs on Wednesday. Best, James.'*

Yes!

Right, he'd better let Dominique know she would be catering for guests in two days' time.

⁂

Ruby and Harry sat in the crowded fast food joint once again. Even though it was well past lunch, a constant storm of people flurried past them and piled up in a drift at the counter.

Ruby nudged her boyfriend. 'I'm sorry you're having such a crappy day.'

He shrugged. 'Thinking about you helped. And last night.'

Ruby hadn't been able to stop thinking about it either. It had been the most loving and intimate thing to ever happen in her life. She knew some other girls were desperate to take things further with their boyfriends, to get physical, but Ruby didn't understand why when what she and Harry had transcended everything.

'Reckon they'll miss us at school?' Harry asked, changing the subject.

'Reckon they'll be relieved we aren't there,' she laughed.

'They'll all feel safer knowing they can slag us off in peace and not have to worry about the consequences. Anyway, tomorrow's the last day at school before we break up, so it's not worth going in.'

'If I never have to see that place and all the stupid idiots inside it again, it will be too soon,' said Ruby, through a mouthful of burger.

'Someone should Columbine them,' quipped Harry.

Ruby swallowed. Looked at Harry and shook her head to convey she was clueless.

'Come on, you've heard about the Columbine killings, right?'

'Er, no.'

'Ah, man, I can't believe it. You've got to have heard of them. These two boys, right, they took out all their enemies at school. All the people who had bullied them and made their lives a misery for years. Revenge is sweet, man. If things had gone according to plan, the death count would have been massive. I mean… massive.'

He held his hands as far apart as he could, as if to demonstrate. 'They had bombs and all kinds of stuff. And why did they do it? Cos the people at school were asking for it, I'm telling you. You should take out some of those bitches who are ragging on you.'

She laughed. 'Yeah, it would be great to see the looks on their faces.'

'And be free of them once and for all.' He wiped his hands against each other as though getting rid of enemies was as easy as shedding crumbs on his palm.

Ruby shivered at the thought of it. The idea made her feel scared and feverish and hot with excitement; everything that was at odds with the cheery music playing softly around them.

'Wouldn't it be great, though,' she breathed. 'Imagine, if everyone who made our lives a misery were dead. If it were just you and me, and we didn't have to worry about anyone else ever again.'

'We could be together for ever. Get a little place to live. Yeah… One day, man.'

A pop song from before either of them were born gave a tinkle of jingle bells and a chorus of angelic oohing.

'I don't know if I can wait,' she said.

She took his hand and stared into a distant future where every night could be like last night. Where she could sleep peacefully, without fear, and be wrapped up in love. Surely it was too far away to ever reach. Surely her enemies would have won by then.

# CHAPTER 48

There was a tiny noise outside the window. So tiny that it would have been missed if Ruby hadn't been listening out for it. It was eleven p.m.; bang on time. She yanked the sash window up, letting in a rush of freezing air, and a cold and panting Harry. He helped her close the window quickly, quietly, then gave her a kiss with icicle lips.

'Come on, get into bed and warm up,' she urged.

He shed his jacket and pulled his boots off before clambering in alongside her and pulling the duvet over them both. She pretended to protest when he pulled her tight against him, insisting he needed her to warm him up. Through the winceyette cloth of her pyjamas his freezing body sent a jolt through her and she pushed him away, laughing.

'Come on, I'm nearly freezing to death for you,' he whispered, grinning.

'I'm worth it,' she smiled back, hoping desperately that it was true.

Harry's body seemed naturally set to hot, so it didn't take long for the pair of them to feel more comfortable.

For years Ruby's sleep had been disturbed. After she and Harry had been attacked, she had expected it to get worse, and been surprised when it hadn't. She reckoned that was thanks to her realising that she finally had someone firmly in her corner. But when the taunting text messages had started just a week or so later, that's when the nightmares had really kicked in. The flashbacks to being beaten up. Explosions of terror more painful even than the original punches and kicks. The feeling of helplessness suffocating her.

After long months, she had finally found a solution. This. With Harry, she would sleep well. She snuggled into his arms and let the warmth of his body pressed against hers ease the knots of tension away.

Ruby thought of the time when she was about seven, just before Mouse was born, when her parents had taken her to a festival. Dad had gone off in search of strawberry fizzy water for her, because she wouldn't shut up about how she wanted some. Someone nearby had lit a fire, and Ruby had been mesmerised by the sight of the orange glow in the dimming light. She had asked if she could light one. Mum had been scared of being told off, at first, but the two of them had gathered rubbish from nearby – and there had been a lot of it – and set fire to the towering pile. It had looked beautiful, and drawn people in to warm their hands and say hello, and chat, and Ruby had been warmed by her own inner fire, feeling as if she belonged somehow. She and Mum had sat side by side, Mum's arm looped over her shoulders, Ruby's hand on her mum's pregnant belly. Dad had come and sat on the other side of them, a group hug as they stared at the dancing flames.

With Harry, she had that same sense of comfort and belonging. Ruby thought of that as she drifted to sleep.

❖

When she woke in the morning, Harry had gone. Only two things gave away that he had ever been there: the window being open just a crack at the bottom, and the fact that Ruby felt well-rested and couldn't remember a single dream from the night before.

# CHAPTER 49

Two people had been found inside the house so far. Chief Inspector Ogundele looked past the officers kneeling beside the prone forms, and beyond the claret stain soaking through the golden carpet. Instead, he peered through the open bedroom door they lay beside. A teenager's room, by the look of it.

That was where the real carnage was.

The dove grey walls, white ceiling, and a couple of posters of depressed-looking pop groups dressed in black were decorated with blood spatters.

# CHAPTER 50

TUESDAY 21 DECEMBER
FOUR DAYS TO GO

The rattling cry of the magpies sounded again, waking Benjamin. It was six a.m. He was going to get his gun and shoot those buggers. He was sick of them waking him, their noise clear through the original sash windows that he was going to have replaced with double-glazing soon.

The house was falling apart. He should never have bought it. The latch on the downstairs loo needed fixing; maybe he could do that himself. He could definitely remove that nail sticking out by Mouse's door.

Was that what he was going to be reduced to? Odd-job man around his home, because he could no longer afford to get someone in to do it for him.

As his dad had always predicted for him.

No, this meeting with James would work. He'd get money to tide him over; it would be fine.

That's what he told himself in the shower; as he dressed; while he forced down breakfast. His family whirled around him like biological mist to be waded through. They made noises, tried to engage with him, but he couldn't pull himself out of the despair that seemed to be clinging to him. He had a bad feeling about today, but kept giving himself mental slaps, reminding himself of all he had achieved in his life: the awards his business had won, the huge amount of clients he had attracted, the high standing with which people regarded him. He had a beautiful wife, too. Although, she didn't quite seem herself lately; she seemed sort of absent most of the time, and the last few days she had an almost haunted look on her face. He needed to speak to her, see if she was okay after the sleepwalking business. But not right now; right now, he didn't have the strength to surface from the sea of stress he was drowning in.

⚜

By the time he arrived at work, he had slid on his bombastic mask. Spoke in his booming, cocky way, playing the big man. But it was tiring, and as he flirted outrageously with his secretary – enough to make her giggle and feel pampered, not enough to make her want to file a sexual harassment complaint – he contemplated chucking it all in.

'I'm not the man you think I am. I'm out of here,' he'd announce, and let everyone see the empty soul behind the façade. He could almost hear the gasps of horror, see the staff backing away from him, and Jazmine… Poor Jazmine, she hadn't asked for any of this.

He had no choice but to keep going, because it wasn't only him who would suffer if he didn't pull this off. He could not let anyone see through the cracks forming in his mask. He must refuse to give in to chronic fatigue and self-pity. Losers did that.

What was it Muhammad Ali always said? Those who don't have the courage to take risks won't get anywhere in life – or something like that. Just like Ali, Benjamin was the greatest, he was The Man, he would—

'Here's this morning's post.' His PA handed the bundle of envelopes over to him, shocking him out of his internal motivational speech.

'Great, thanks,' he said, giving her one of his best, most dazzling smiles. Act confident and he'd be confident.

He sauntered into his office, whistling as he went, and sifted through the letters, mainly cards from his clients and—

Oh, crap.

It couldn't be. Not yet. He had been sure he had until the new year to sort something.

His good mood nuked, Benjamin closed his office door, slumped into his chair and stared at the brown envelope.

At his name peering through the plastic window at him.

At the berating black lettering of the organisation which had sent it.

HMRC.

Coughing, he swallowed down the bitter taste of sick. Forced himself to tear the letter open.

The words blurred because the paper trembled so much. Benjamin grabbed at his right wrist with his left hand to try to steady it, but it was futile. Instead, he crumpled the paper into a ball and threw it into the bin. Only to retrieve it instantly, for fear of his secretary or the cleaner discovering it.

He could tear it up. He could set fire to it.

It wouldn't stop what he had read burning through his mind. His life was over. Nothing left but ashes and shame. He might as well be dead.

# CHAPTER 51

'Hello, Mrs P. You all right today?' Ruby spoke politely but slightly more accentuated and slowly than was usual. Just in case. Sometimes Harry's mum had trouble concentrating.

Looking at her always made Ruby a bit uncomfortable. She knew she shouldn't stare at the shaking, the dribbling, the slurring words, but it was easier said than done.

Mrs Porter nodded at her, head trembling and bouncing like one of those nodding dogs people had in cars and claimed were ironic.

'Why aren't you in school?'

Harry jumped in. 'I told you earlier, Mum, remember? We've finished for Christmas.'

'Oh, I thought that was tomorrow.'

'No, it's today. The twins finish tomorrow cos it's a different school,' Harry assured her. Chucked a quick look Ruby's way to make sure she didn't say anything she shouldn't. She and Harry had walked the boys to junior school together before deciding to bunk off again themselves.

'Almost Christmas already, eh, Mrs P. You all set?' she said, to change the subject.

'Aw, Harry's a good boy, he's put the decorations up.'

A plastic tree, so small it was more a twig, was sagging arthritically under the weight of cheap baubles, and home-made decorations clearly made by Harry and his brothers when they were younger. It was swathed, mummy-like, in tinsel, presumably to support it. At the top was a glitter-ridden fairy with a torn wing and a surprised expression as she gazed at her pink fluffy wand. The present pile beneath was tragically small, and the bright wrapping paper was the cut-price kind that was see-through unless you used twenty layers, and even then it tore if you looked at it too hard. Ruby thought of the huge amount of presents beneath the gargantuan tree in her own home, and shifted uncomfortably. All those expensive trinkets she would receive, which she didn't even give a stuff about.

'Do you fancy going for a walk? We could take you,' Ruby offered.

'No, no, I'd rather stay here,' Mrs Porter replied. Her voice was slurring with the effort, and her hands trembled.

With a nod, Ruby and Harry left his mum to it. She was already starting to slide down the sofa as they left the room, and Harry nipped back to lift her a little higher and arrange the cushions as makeshift scaffolding.

Although Harry only lived a bus ride away from Ruby's Blackheath home, it felt like a different world. He lived between Charlton and Woolwich, in an area of high unemployment, and headline-grabbing crimes. Low points included the racially motivated murder of teenager, Stephen Lawrence, a murder so well known that even though it happened before Ruby was born, she knew all about it. Another was that the town had been a major flare point during the 2011 riots – several buildings had been attacked, and the landmark Great Harry pub left a burnt-out shell. More recently, that soldier, Lee Rigby, had been run over then stabbed to death by Islamic extremists near Woolwich barracks in 2013. Her father would have had a blue fit if he knew she was in Woolwich; he thought it was far too dangerous. But it wasn't that bad, you just had to know where to avoid – and who.

'Woolwich boys don't mess about when it comes to business,' Harry had told her the first time she had visited him. 'Most people raised here end up in gangs. I know a few people in them, so I'm safe. Which means you're safe. Drug dealers hang around on the estates and sell cocaine and heroin, but they reckon they give money to the families that the government has forgotten. Woolwich's only problem is poverty, man. Get rid of the poverty and you get rid of the problem. They don't call it Britain's poorest postcode for nothing.'

Harry's home was a flat in a high-rise near a busy road, where the rumbling roar of traffic never seemed to cease, and the exhaust fumes choked even when the windows were closed. The living room was reasonably warm, thanks to an electric heater which only ever had one bar lit. The rest of the flat was chilled, as though haunted, but this particular ghost's name was 'being skint'.

She and Harry spent most of the day holed up in his bedroom, listening to music and talking, cuddled up to one another to keep the cold at bay. Every now and again Ruby huffed a breath into the air, and watched it cloud faintly in front of her.

'I've never seen that happen inside before,' she said, fascinated.

'Well, I know how we can warm up,' Harry said, giving that wonky smile of his that always made her heart hurt in a good way.

Kissing Harry seemed to open up a wormhole in space and time so that hours flashed by in the blink of an eye. But the persistent buzzing of her phone made her pull away finally, curious and full of dread, all at once.

Harry wrapped his hand around hers and the mobile it clutched. 'Leave it,' he urged.

She could feel the tears balancing on the bottom rim of her eyes as she looked up at him and shook her head. 'You know I can't.'

Looking was an addiction, a compulsion she was too weak to resist. She had to know what people were saying about her, then she could be prepared, and harden herself to the insults.

Harry sighed. In frustration, in sympathy, all of the above, she wasn't sure, but he prised the phone from her fingers firmly but gently. 'Then we look together. All right?'

She nodded, making one of the tears lose its balance. Harry wiped it from her cheek with his thumb pad.

'Ready? Three.'

She felt sick. Maybe she should just leave it.

'Two.'

If she left it, she'd only imagine the worst anyway. But the toast she had eaten for breakfast was threatening to reappear.

'One.'

Harry unlocked her phone. Alert after alert scrolled across the screen. Her eyes ran over them. They didn't make sense.

*'I wouldn't if you paid me. Looks like you could drive a lorry up her.'*

*'What a whore.'*

*'Nice tits. I would.'*

A couple of clicks, and all was made clear. There was Ruby, lying on a bed, naked, legs wide open, clutching her breasts together.

'Bloody hell.' Harry sprang up, dropped the phone. Glared down at it and then at her. His eyes burned. She'd never seen an expression like that on his face before.

'I – I don't understand… It's not me,' she begged.

He glared at her again, fists balled. Was he going to hit her?

'Do you think I don't know that, Rubes? I'll bloody kill Jayne and her crew for this.'

She snatched up her phone, had to look closer. The picture had been cobbled together badly. Her head, taken from the video of her being hit, was clearly pasted onto the top of a body nicked from a porn site. Angle and skin tone were all wrong.

The words typed under the image were brief but to the point:

*'Free sex. Give it to me, big boys, I'm desperate.'*

Below was Ruby's mobile number and email address.

There were already over fifty comments on it, and her phone was buzzing as if possessed with more notifications.

'They're never going to leave me alone,' she whispered. 'I wish I were dead. Honest, Harry, I just want to die and this all to be over.'

# CHAPTER 52

Benjamin had started out as straight as a die. Young, ambitious, keen, he had been a hard worker – still was. A few years into his partnership with Jazmine, he had dealt with an account where the taxman had made a mistake with one of his clients. It was nothing major, so he'd got the client to fill in a form enabling him to act on their behalf, and asked HMRC for a consolatory payment of £45 in recognition of the mistake, not in recompense – it took a hell of a lot more than a bit of provable inconvenience to make the taxman cough up compensation. A cheque for the amount was quickly sent, made payable to Thomas & Bauer's account, and Benjamin immediately transferred it into the client's account.

As he did so, he had a thought: HMRC never bothered checking such low payments. They were paid automatically if the amount was under £50, because it wasn't worth the man-hours.

Wow, it would be so easy for someone dodgy to take advantage of that.

The idea had amused him. One day, a bit bored, and with the devil in him, he decided to test the theory. Exactly like before, he filed a complaint on behalf of a client – only this time he did it without the client's knowledge, and without any mistake being made on HMRC's part to justify the claim.

Within weeks, £48.50 was paid by cheque to the company account, and Benjamin transferred it immediately into his own.

He waited a few days, keyed up for someone to notice and raise a query. No one did.

Unbelievable – he'd got away with it. It made him feel all tingly inside, sort of excited. It might only have been forty-odd quid, but it was the best money Benjamin had ever got his hands on because it was illicit. It showed how cunning he was. It was free money, not earned and not really stolen – after all, it didn't belong to a client or his own business, and in comparison to the billions of pounds the taxman dealt with every year, it wasn't even a drop in the ocean.

Still, there would be no repeat performance, because he wasn't a thief.

After a few months, though, Benjamin got bored again, and thought: *why not?* He would do it one more time, to check whether the first time had been a fluke, or if he was as clever as he suspected he was.

This time he tried for £20. It wasn't like he needed the money, it was purely for the thrill.

It worked.

After that, whenever Benjamin got bored and needed a buzz, he did the scam. At first he was cautious. Not because he thought he was doing anything particularly wrong – it was only a little tax fiddle, everyone did it to some extent – but because he didn't like the thought of being sloppy enough for people to realise what he was doing. He was better than that, cleverer than that.

It was only every few months. Not enough for people to cotton on. The gaps grew smaller though.

He made sure he hit different tax offices, spreading the spurious claims around the whole HMRC network to lessen the likelihood of anyone catching on. Four a month was only £180, so it was nothing to write home about, but there was something extra sweet about buying a treat with that money.

After a year or so he was growing tired of the game, and considering quitting. Why push his luck?

Although…

If it were that easy to get away with ripping off HMRC, then maybe he should make it a bit more worthwhile.

Not only was it easy money, it was a victimless crime. He was robbing the greedy, grasping government and giving to the – well, not poor, he definitely wasn't poor, but he was certainly worthier than most of the scroungers on benefits who got money chucked at them for sitting on their backsides all day, doing nothing. At least he had spent years paying his taxes. In fact, technically this was his money he was taking back anyway; he'd a right to it.

That was how Benjamin justified fiddling his own expenses and the company's when he came to doing the business accounts that year. He reduced taxable profit by a significant amount, and so the company paid a lot less tax than they were supposed to. As he was the one who had managed that, he figured it was only fair he gave himself a hefty bonus to compensate himself for the time and trouble – a bonus he did not share with Jazmine, but instead hid with yet more crafty and imaginative accounting.

He did feel a tad guilty about not telling his partner. But he figured the less she knew, the less could hurt her if his chickens did ever come home to roost.

Bolstered by his continuing success, the following year Benjamin did the same… plus, another cheeky little swerve he'd thought of.

He supressed Thomas & Bauer's turnover figures by not including all of their invoices. Fewer invoices declared made it look like they were making less money… which meant their tax bill was significantly lower yet again.

Again, he figured he was due a bonus equivalent to the amount he had saved the company. Fair's fair.

After that, he decided it would be wise to run two sets of books. The official ones were for HMRC and Jazmine – who totally trusted him, and was happy with the arrangement that he look after their accounts, while she undertook personnel matters. The real books were for his eyes only, so that he could efficiently keep track of exactly what he was doing.

The money had become a nice little earner. They meant he could afford a bigger house, a better car, to send his children to private school, to have the best suits. Hell, to pay for his wife to have a blow-dry every single week. He had to keep up appearances because clients had expectations, so really he had to spend a fortune on all those things. In which case, it was totally justified that it all be funded by the business. Besides, he had never borrowed more than he could pay back immediately if caught.

Not at first anyway.

But as the years had gone on and no one had twigged, he had found himself taking more and more. Needing more and more.

Life was sweet. Until it turned sour.

❖

The nightmare had started with a letter, eighteen months earlier. Benjamin had felt blasé as he opened it, despite the bold black print on the envelope, announcing it was from Her Majesty's Revenue & Customs.

*Dear Mr Thomas,*
*We wish to conduct an investigation into your account, under the…*

Benjamin's eyes had flown over the catalogue of various legislation they were using as an excuse to put him under the microscope. There was a huge list of paperwork they demanded from him, too. And a date by which he must provide it, along with a warning that if he failed to comply the issue would be sent straight to tribunal.

It was signed, 'sincerely', by a Mr Bernard Bairden.

For a moment, Benjamin felt as if all the world were suddenly glaring at him. Sirens going off, the searchlights trained on him. He perceived the whispered judgements of others that might come.

But he hadn't panicked. He was proud of himself for that. He had forced himself to sit down and unclench every muscle in his body until his mind relaxed enough for him to be able to think. He was clever. He could delay until he was in a position to breeze into the tax office and brandish all the correct – or at least correctly forged, if needs be – paperwork, laughing, and demanding to know what all the fuss was about.

The first task was to buy some time. He focused all his attention on the letter, refusing to let his mind wander into blind panic at what would happen to him if he were investigated, if the truth were uncovered, if his family found out, if his friends and colleagues knew.

He grabbed a notepad and pen, and started jotting down ideas as they came to him, ignited by the information in Mr Bernard Bairden's letter. Inspiration flew like sparks, took flight like embers drifting on the breeze.

As his notes grew, so did Benjamin's confidence. He was going to be okay. He could fix everything, come out unscathed, and with no one any the wiser. Of course he could. He was Benjamin fucking Thomas, accountant supremo: faster, cleverer, and more cunning than anyone else.

Benjamin tap-danced faster than Billy Flynn; only he was trying to save his own neck not some murderous broad from Chicago.

After a spot of double-checking on Google and reference books, he was satisfied with his draft letter. He even typed it up himself, as he didn't want his secretary getting wind of this – or even worse, his business partner.

His plan was simple. If HMRC wanted paperwork, he'd give them paperwork. He'd bury the bastards in it.

*Dear Mr Bairden, Despite the whole concept of the investigation being ill-founded, I am keen to help in every way possible to prove my innocence.*

Benjamin's reply went on to cover three sides of A4 paper.

He cited numerous pieces of legislation, not so much answering the points raised by HMRC, but answering his own questions instead, much like a cornered politician. Distraction techniques reigned supreme over actual facts. It was expertly done.

Even though he was trying to make Bernard Bairden join up dots that weren't even on the same page, HMRC were duty bound to reply to each and every one of the points that he made. Mr Bairden had to scotch every single issue he mentioned, no matter how irrelevant. Meanwhile he could reply with whatever he wanted, ignoring Mr Bairden's own valid points while raising yet more utterly irrelevant ones that suited him.

The letters flew backwards and forwards.

Benjamin really enjoyed himself. He loved the idea of making that cocky, missive-obsessed tax inspector squirm; making him scratch his head in consternation as he had to plough through all kinds of information in order to reply properly to him. If he didn't reply correctly, then Benjamin could launch a complaint against him, a serious thing indeed, as the body that would investigate was the same as the one that inspected the police. Fun.

The businessman stalled so successfully that he convinced himself everything was going to be fine. That no one would ever discover his shame.

He bought enough time to embezzle more money from the company, and this time he visited a casino. A winner like Benjamin would have no trouble at least doubling the stake; he'd always done well at these places, and when playing poker with mates. With his winnings, he would be able to cover his tracks and pay back the stolen money.

In one horrifying night, he lost £60,000.

That hadn't stopped him trying it again, because one should only ever quit while ahead. He still had time, he told himself.

Then he was asked in for a meeting.

❖

During the interview that felt more like an interrogation with the HMRC inspector, Benjamin had been furious. Who the hell did this Bernard Bairden bloke think he was dealing with? He wasn't some idiot off the street. He knew the inspector thought he was an arrogant wanker, but he didn't care. If he showed fear now, he was done for, and the best form of defence was attack.

Mr Bairden leaned forward. Put his elbows on the table and steepled his fingers together. Benjamin wanted to punch him right in his clever, baggy eyes.

'Mr Thomas, you know what a Business Economics Exercise is, don't you?'

'Of course I do, I'm not an idiot. I'm an accountant, for goodness' sake.'

'Good, of course. So, you'll understand that when we ran the Business Economics Exercise we created a model of the way your business must be working, by looking at your bank accounts, outgoings, withdrawals, your house, the car you drive... You know the kind of thing.'

Something cold was snaking its way down Benjamin's back. Sweat. But he continued to glare, refusing to acknowledge the fear. He waved his hand, regal in his dismissal.

'Yes, yes, basic stuff. Everything stacks up; I've got nothing to hide.'

'That's good. You'll know, then, that even when financial records are unreliable, HMRC can estimate business based on what we've found, and calculate your actual turnover. Our numbers are so accurate that they are accepted by HMRC Tribunals – effectively tax courts. A judge will then order the business to pay up what is owed.'

'Look, if all you've done is drag me down here to teach me how to suck eggs, I really do have better things to do with my time.' Benjamin started to stand.

'I really would appreciate it if you could stay here a little longer,' the tax inspector said, his voice remaining calm and level. 'You see, Mr Thomas, we ran a Business Economics Exercise with you and the figures it threw up were... unexpected.'

'This is absolute nonsense. You're going to feel very silly when you're forced to apologise to me.'

'A similar exercise can be run on personal finances, Mr Thomas. We start with what people are known to have spent, and work backwards to calculate income. You will know, then, that if someone's expenditure is a certain amount then their income must therefore be at least level with it. It's basic economics, yes? In the case of a millionaire, for example, we can work out down to the nearest £5,000 or so how much he or she is earning, purely by looking at his or her outgoings.'

'Well, this is, it's, you've got no right.'

'I do, Mr Thomas. I have compared what I know your expenditure to be over the past year, with the details you provided me with during our correspondence. Your expenditure exceeds your declared income. Can you explain this discrepancy?'

'Right, I've had enough of this. I'm not talking to you a moment longer. I want to see your boss. Right now. I'm a managing director, I'm not talking to some lackey who is clearly incapable of adding two and two together.'

'I can assure—'

'And I can assure you, pal, that I want someone a bit higher up the food chain than you. *Comprendez?*'

The two stared at each other across the table, and for a frightening second Benjamin was sure he could see a glint of steel within Bernard Bairden. But then his opponent gave a slow nod, stood and offered to get his boss. Who had turned out to be not only equally as stupid as Bernard, but had also insisted on backing up his inferior because 'he doesn't seem to have done anything wrong'.

By the end of the interview Benjamin felt very hot and very flustered, and more than a little worried.

Rightly so.

The money HMRC was demanding was huge. Unreasonably gargantuan. Accumulated over years of robbing Peter to pay Paul, aka robbing Her Majesty's Revenue & Customs to pay for a lifestyle Benjamin felt entitled to, it had built up to a sum that didn't simply make his eyes water, it made him want to fall to his knees and weep.

# CHAPTER 53

Benjamin looked at the crumpled letter he had just rescued from the bin and couldn't control his shaking. Involuntarily, as if they had a life of their own and refused to listen to his screaming brain, his eyes sought out the sum.

*Two million pounds. Payable immediately.*

The letter included a 'Statement of Means', which listed all his income and outgoings, and from which Mr Bernard Bairden had calculated how much Benjamin could afford to pay back. HMRC had decided £2 million was an amount Benjamin could reasonably pay while still affording a roof over his head – though not his current home, which was deemed 'excessive to his needs'.

They had not, of course, included his other debts, though. Gambling debts built up in secret while trying to dig himself out of this hole.

He reread the letter, trying to stay calm, trying not to sob like a child. Through eyes blurred with tears, he made out that HMRC had now passed the matter on to a Debt Collection Agency. If payment were not made, enforcement action against him would be pursued to recover the amount owed.

There would be no more stalling and letter-sending. Time was up, and Benjamin felt crushed beneath the huge machinery of the tax office.

He would be ruined. So would everyone he knew. His wife, his kids, his business partner, even his mistress. Innocent parties, all, but no one would be left untouched.

No, he couldn't let that happen. He could still pull things back with a big enough win, somehow. He just needed a loan from James to pay off the taxman, and he could deal with the other debts himself. Eventually.

# CHAPTER 54

Ruby sat on Harry's bed, clinging to him, trying to cry quietly so his mum in the living room next door wouldn't hear. A damp patch formed on Harry's hoody, right over his heart, where she was resting her head. She was the strongest person he knew, the funniest, too, and so clever. Everything about her made him feel awe, and walking down the street with her he genuinely could not believe his luck that she loved him. It was like his walk got an extra bounce when they were together, and the world got a bit of a polish, because the colours seemed cleaner and brighter. How could other people miss how amazing she was?

And how dare they reduce her to this?

The fury ripping through Harry was like nothing he'd ever experienced. People had thrown insults at him like rocks for years; he barely noticed now. They said he smelled, because he didn't always have time to shower before school, too busy getting the rest of his family ready. Or they laughed because his shirt was crumpled, if he hadn't had the chance to iron it. Hell, some people had hated him from the second he was born, purely because of the mocha colour of his skin. Stuff them. They couldn't hurt him unless he let them. He simply rose above it. But he couldn't rise above this pain. He couldn't ignore this fury. People hurting Ruby made him feel like the Incredible Hulk was trying to get out from inside him. If he saw any of her bullies, he'd tear them apart with his bare hands.

But right here, right now, that wasn't going to help his girl.

He stroked her hair and leaned down to croon in her ear.

'Hey, hey, baby girl, it's okay. Long as we've got each other, it doesn't matter.'

'But I haven't got you. My stupid parents won't even let me see you. They're so clueless they think you're the one who is a bad influence on me.'

'Maybe... I dunno, maybe it's time to 'fess up about what's going on, Rubes.'

The soggy snort she gave was muffled by his top, as she buried her face back into it, a mouse burrowing for safety. He thought he could make out the word 'useless' but he wasn't certain if it was only a cough.

'Ruby?' he probed.

She looked up at him. Red, puffy eyes, swollen lips and runny nose. He hated seeing her so vulnerable – but loved that he was the only person in the world privileged to witness it.

'What's the point? Even if they listened – which they totally won't – they'll just tell me to stop using social media. Yeah, because that will make it all go away. They're clueless about real life. Whether I'm checking or not, the posts are still there. Everyone laughing at me. Everyone hating me.'

Harry rubbed her arm up and down, helpless, trying somehow to erase her pain.

'I've never... I couldn't... telling them would be like... I don't know, they already think I'm such a loser, they'd probably agree with what everyone's saying anyway.'

'They're not going to agree to someone setting up a prozzie site for you, are they? Maybe it's worth talking to them about this so they can, I dunno, maybe go to the police. It might be worth seeing if your parents are as useless as we think – or if they can step up. What you got to lose, Rubes?' He could see the war going on inside her.

She threw her hands up in despair.

'When I try to talk about it, though, I get all bunged up. The words stick together in clumps and I can't spit them out. I can't even breathe with them there. It's just easier not to say anything.'

She was so pale, as white as the pristine trainers some of the crew wore.

'I get it. The stuff you've been put through… no one should have to put up with that, man. And I wish I could do something to make it better. Believe me. But, maybe once you tell your parents about this they'll go to the police, report that sick shit. This new stuff, making out like you're offering sex to any takers, it's off the scale. The police will see your parents, all nice and neat and middle class, and they'll jump. They'll investigate, they'll do their little technological magic to find out who did this and nail them. Job done. I can't do that for you. Wish I could.'

'I wish you could, too.' She pulled close to him again and they kissed. 'I wish it could just be you and me for ever. Screw the rest of the world.'

'Amen to that. Whole world could explode for all I care, long as we got each other. When people hurt you, I want to kill them all, Rubes. Swear. Hearing you say you wish you was dead… Well, if that happened you'd have to take me with you; I can't live without you, girl.'

He fell into her eyes, onto her lips. Even with all this talk of death, Harry's blood thrummed and he'd never felt more alive.

# CHAPTER 55

Mouse hung onto the back of the kitchen chair as she did a little dance. Turned her head to one side and grinned at Aunt Fiona. The little girl was glad her aunt had come home with her and Mummy after the school play. They always had fun together.

'Shall I eat a toffee penny? They're really, really, really hard. Do you dare me? But if I break one of my teeth, I'm blaming you.'

'I'm feeling lucky.' Mummy's friend grinned back from her seat at the table. 'In fact, I'm feeling so lucky that I'm going to dare you to have a competition with me – whoever can make their sweet last the longest, wins. S, by the way.'

They were playing hangman, and Mouse pulled a face before grudgingly writing an 'S' down at the start of the second word. Then considered Aunt Fiona's challenge.

'All right, let's see if at ten to five, in fifteen minutes, I've got some toffee sweetie left. Bits will still be stuck in my teeth in about three hours' time, so I'll win.'

'Deal,' nodded Aunt Fiona. 'Oh, an M, please.'

Mouse did a jumping jack and shouted the letter out with a laugh. Then she drew a circle for the man's face.

'No M? Well, I wonder what on earth this can be? First word has seven letters, second word starts with an S, something, double E, something. I wonder…?'

Aunt Fiona seemed to glance over at the tin of Quality Street chocolates, and Mouse decided to use distraction techniques.

'I want a mobile phone for Christmas. Mummy says they're expensive, but I've said the only other things I want are books, and they don't cost that much.'

'Well, you'll have to be good and see what Santa brings.' Aunt Fiona looked around to make sure Mummy wasn't looking, then stuck her tongue out. 'We've been sucking these toffees for five minutes, and I've still got mine. I rule – I'm definitely going to beat you.'

'You will not. You can't even beat me at hangman.'

'Have you got yours?'

Mouse giggled as she stuck her tongue out too. 'Is mine bigger?'

They shuffled over to a mirror and opened their mouths again, both cackling.

'You're winning.'

'I always win,' nodded Mouse.

'You should be in the *Guinness World Records*.'

'There's a world record for everything. There's a record for how long you can be silly for.'

'Really?'

'I don't know!'

Mummy walked in then, saying she could hear them laughing from down the hallway.

'What are you two up to?' She pulled a face like she was pretending to be suspicious, but Mouse could tell from her eyes and the twitch of her mouth that she was dying to join in.

'Just playing hangman,' Mouse replied innocently.

⟡

Watching Fiona and Mouse messing around for hours made Dom feel a surprise pang of jealousy. She wished she were so natural with her daughter, but despite being desperate for children, she worried that she was a little stiff with them. She had to try with game-playing, silliness didn't come naturally to her. Fiona could switch it on, though. No one looking at her with Mouse would guess for a second that she was a hard-nosed divorce lawyer capable of making grown men cry.

The pair of them could talk about books for hours, and Fiona had an ability to play make-believe with Mouse's teddy bear that made Dominique quite envious. Mouse couldn't get enough of her. But, finally, she was persuaded to go upstairs and watch television. She had started to protest loudly and vigorously, looking dangerously close to kicking off a tantrum, until she'd been reminded that Santa would put her on the naughty list if she didn't watch it. This would probably be the last year she would fall for that ploy, Dom thought sadly, as she poured herself and Fiona each a large glass of Cabernet Sauvignon.

'So...' Fiona trailed off meaningfully, and took a mouthful of the red wine. 'We all right to talk now? You're sure Benjamin isn't due back?'

Dom swallowed, shook her head. 'He won't be back for hours. I'm lucky if I see him before I go to bed, most nights.'

'Lucky? Unlucky?' Fiona pretended to ponder, making a flip flop motion with her hand. 'What about Ruby?'

'She sent me a text message saying she's out with friends. Some impromptu thing organised at school. She won't be back until nine. I replied back reminding her she was grounded and haven't heard from her since.'

'It really is all piling up, isn't it? How on earth are you coping?'

'I've had more dreams, if that's what you mean... But I've got an appointment for Thursday.'

'Great news.'

'If anything happens to me, you will be okay to have the children, won't you?'

'What are you talking about?'

'I don't know, if I'm sectioned or something. Benjamin's always too busy, so I need to know the kids will be looked after.'

'Hey, there is no way it's going to come to that. But if it makes you worry less then I will say the words: of course I'll have Ruby and Amber. You know I love them to bits, they're like my own children. Thanks for putting the hard work in giving birth and raising them so far, by the way. Don't think I don't appreciate your input with my children.'

Dominique laughed despite herself. Fiona could always cheer her up. 'Yes, that's no problem. They'd probably prefer to be with you anyway. You know how much they adore you.'

'What a load of rot. They know they've got an easy ride with me, that's all. I'm only ever around for the fun stuff, I don't have to actually raise them and make sure they turn into decent human beings. Left to me, they'd probably turn feral.'

'Oh, good grief.'

'You. Are. A. Brilliant. Mum. Believe it. Which is why you would be able to cope just fine alone, if you had to.'

Dom took a significant swig of her wine to show her scorn. Fiona ploughed on regardless.

'It's entirely up to you. Whether you kick him into touch or make a go of it, I'm here for you. But, to my mind, Benjamin doesn't deserve you. Juggling you and this mistress? Well, he can't even claim it was a moment of madness.'

'I know; he must have feelings for her. Four years of lies and deceit. I feel like I don't know him at all.'

'If he's capable of lying about this for so long, what else is he willing to lie about?' Fiona nodded. 'He's been having his cake and eating it. Time to make sure you get your slice, my love.'

Dom bit her lip, unable to reply.

The fairy lights winked at her, taunting that this was meant to be a time for happy families, for fun outings and cosy times indoors. Not a time for discussing breaking up the family, the fissures cracking open before her eyes.

Pretty soon she knew she was going to have to confront Benjamin. Tell him that she knew everything. But not right now. Not today. At least the festive season gave her an excuse to put off the inevitable.

For now, she was more worried about doing something terrible to her family herself, than the damage Benjamin was inflicting on it. That night, before she went to bed, she ignored Dr Madden's advice, and swallowed a couple of sleeping tablets. Hoped they would knock her out.

# CHAPTER 56

## CHRISTMAS DAY

Keeping to the side of the landing, the chief inspector stepped carefully into the bedroom. And stopped. A woman lay with her head blasted away. A teenager slumped over the body. An officer bent over her, moving a shotgun out of the way. The constellation of blood spatters, tissue, and bone fragments would tell their own story to experts: impact, direction, volume, would reveal who had done what, where, and perhaps even why.

Open on the bedside table, illuminated handily by the lamp, as though for dramatic impact, lay a diary. Ogundele peered at it.

*Today's the day. I'm going to kill them all. I hate them. I hate them. I hate them.*

The words had been underscored so many times the paper was almost torn.

# CHAPTER 57

Hair tumbled across the pillow and Ruby's face. Harry reached down and gently stroked the strands to one side. Ruby smiled in her sleep and it took all the strength he had to pull his hand back. With Rubes, he felt safe and comforted in a way he never did at home. Knowing that he made her feel the same, made him transform into a man, no longer a boy.

He didn't want to go, but it was late – no, early, he corrected, checking the time on his phone. Four in the morning. Despite the time, he wanted to stay with Ruby. With her, he felt complete in a way he hadn't been aware was possible, not when he hadn't even known he wasn't whole.

Once she had stopped crying this afternoon, he had persuaded her to switch off her phone while she was with him. They had both managed to calm down a little, talk and listen to music.

She hadn't left until about half eight; it was definitely after he'd had to put the twins to bed, because she'd helped him. His mum had been out for the count again. Every move he'd made, he'd wished Ruby was by his side, making smart comments, rolling her eyes, making him see things in a whole fresh way, and smelling so sweet that he felt like one of those old cartoons where people float on the scent. Funny, the more time they spent together, the more he wanted to. He never got bored of her. After spending a whole day together at his place, parting had been harder not easier.

But they hadn't been apart for long. By eleven p.m., as arranged, he'd climbed up the trellis below her window. It had been a bit hairy, because about a minute after he'd hauled his arse into her room, her dad had pulled up. But they'd got away with it. Her mum had gone to bed at ten p.m., according to Rubes, drunk after a night talking to some mate or other.

Both parents too wrapped up in their own worlds to notice Ruby had sneaked a boy into her room. Thank goodness.

He really, really didn't want to go. But it was four a.m. and he was shattered. It felt like he was being torn in two as he got up.

Holding his breath, he crept to the sash window, then glanced back. The cold might wake Rubes when he opened and shut the window. He slipped into the chilly air in double quick time, the original wooden windows sliding back into place easily, leaving only the tiniest gap beneath that he couldn't quite shut from outside.

The warmth of Ruby's body clung to Harry's skin as he jogged along the streets. It was a comfort. He didn't want to leave her but he knew he had to get out before the rest of the house stirred. They couldn't risk discovery. Besides, he needed to be there for when his brothers and mum woke. They relied on him.

❖

A long luxurious stretch, limbs extending, toes curling in the soft morning light peeking around the edges of her curtains. For a moment everything was bliss.

Naked body. Porno pose. Lurid messages.

The memories hit Ruby like a boxer's rally, left, right, left. The last a knockout punch. She closed her eyes, forced herself to breathe, made Harry's soothing words come back to her. They had talked about the fake prostitute web page set up in her name all night. Finally, she had agreed with him that she had nothing to lose and possibly everything to gain by telling her parents. As soon as they saw the photo and read the messages, they were bound to take action.

It would take a lot of courage, though. And more than a little swallowing of her rage, suspicion and pride. They stuck in her throat, but she remembered Harry's own pained face and decided to do it for him. Pulling her dressing gown over her pyjamas, she rushed downstairs.

❖

Her parents were in the kitchen, sharing a silent breakfast, both of them with their noses buried in their tablets. Dad would be reading his newspaper online and Mum would be reading whatever the hell it was she was interested in.

Ruby brushed aside her irritation, tried to ignore the staccato beat of her heart.

Mum looked at her first. Her eyes were red, dark marks beneath them, and her skin was pale, but she gave a tight smile.

'You're up early. What are you going to do with your first day of the holidays?'

'I, um, need to talk to you both…'

Dad put his tablet down with a theatrical sigh. 'What have you done now?'

'I – nothing. I haven't done anything.' Her voice was louder, more whiney than expected. 'No, I just—'

'You need to calm down, and stop shouting. You're in enough trouble already without coming down here and starting first thing.'

How was it all going so wrong so quickly?

'I am calm, I'm just trying to tell you something and you're not listening.'

'You better behave tonight. We have friends over and it's a very important night, okay, so we don't need you in one of your moods.

Best behaviour, young lady.' Dad gave her a long, hard stare then picked up his tablet again. End of discussion.

The rage inside Ruby was building up again. Blood thumping, body thrumming. Still, she tried to ball the anger up in her fists and hold it clenched there, but it seemed to be seeping through her fingers.

'Why don't you ever listen to me? There's something you need to know—'

Mum threw a glance over at Dad, and of course took his side, cutting her off.

'I don't think now is the best time, Ruby. Why don't you come back later and tell me about it then, eh?'

Later? Later?! Why was she always so low in their priorities? Why did they never try to listen to her? Ruby didn't have hold of the anger any more. It had her in its iron fist. Shook her like a rag doll. She screamed in rage, picked up her father's glass of orange juice and hurled it against the wall.

The room exploded with the glass. Shrieks, yells, her parents leaping to their feet. Finally, she had their attention.

'I hate you.' It wasn't a shout, it was a poison-laden whisper. She let it drip into her parents' ears then ran from the room, up the stairs and into her bedroom, which she locked.

The floor shook with Dad's stomping steps coming after her. He hammered on her door, told her to 'open the door immediately'. But she didn't. Didn't see why she should do anything to make life easier for those two cretins she called parents. They weren't interested in her or her life or her pain. They definitely weren't interested in stepping in and protecting her.

She wasn't only angry with them though – she was furious with herself for even trying.

Finally, Dad bogged off. She heard his car drive away.

A gentle tap on the door…

'Ruby? Look, what's going on? Do you want to talk about it?'

She unlocked the door and skewered her mum with a look of pure venom. When she spoke, she sounded calm. 'I don't ever want to speak to you again.'

Then she closed the door. Sat on her bed and hugged her knees as her rage took flight and her thoughts soared.

Who did they think they were? Even though it was first thing, Dad stank of whisky and had bloodshot eyes. Yet he had the audacity to lecture her on morals and good behaviour. Hypocrite.

And her mum was such a pushover. She let Dad get away with anything. What a doormat. She barely seemed with it these days, with her watery, pink eyes and distracted looks.

If no one was going to protect her, she would protect herself. She would make everyone pay. She would lay waste to them.

# CHAPTER 58

The sign glared back at Dom: *Ruby's Room, Keep Out.* It even had a pair of beetling eyebrows drawn over the two 'o's in 'room', which had been made into eyes. She tried one last time, knowing it was futile even before she tapped on the door.

Ruby was such a drama queen. 'I don't ever want to speak to you again,' she had said.

Dominique remembered telling her own mum that a couple of times, but not with the regularity of her eldest daughter. Still, it was just a teenage temper tantrum. She was probably making up for skipping the terrible twos everyone always went on about. Dom had thought she'd got the perfect child back then, little Ruby always laughing and coming out with the funniest things. She had such a gorgeous smile; why didn't she show it?

Dominique got the sudden urge to hold her little girl again. She pressed her face to the crack of the door, lips kissing varnished wood as she spoke.

'Ruby? Come on, talk to me. Hey, maybe you, me and Mouse could go shopping together later, eh? You might even get an early present, if I'm feeling generous…'

Silence.

She'd have to find out what was wrong with Ruby, but she suspected she knew what this morning's little performance was about. No doubt she had a protest speech prepared about the unfairness of being banned from seeing her boyfriend at Christmas, and was frustrated she and Benjamin hadn't made time to listen.

While Dom had a certain amount of sympathy, it didn't change that her daughter was far too wrapped up in that Harry boy. If anything, her behaviour this morning proved that.

Ever the diplomat, Dom had tried to step in between her daughter and husband to prevent an explosion. The mood Benjamin was in, he'd have erupted if Ruby pushed things any further. Dom had wanted to avoid a row over breakfast, but Ruby being Ruby, that wasn't good enough. Everything had to be her way all the time, or she lost her temper. She was so furious all the time, her face a constant scowl, her mouth drawn small and mean. Smashing things was not a new trick, it was a boring old one, and Dom was sick of it.

'Ruby?' she tried one last time.

What else could she do? Nothing. If Ruby chose to get angry instead of communicating, that wasn't her mum's fault. Actually, it was her grandfather's. Benjamin's father's temper had been the stuff of many whispered conversations between herself and his sister Krystal when they were kids at school. Gordon Thomas had never been violent, he had not needed to be, the imminent threat was enough. Dominique had hated going around to her friend's house because of the brooding atmosphere of control. Gordon had died when Benjamin was seventeen, and was mourned only briefly by his wife, who had made the most of her new freedom by moving to Spain as soon as her youngest hit eighteen. Benjamin spoke rarely about him, but Krystal had got tipsy one year and described to Dominique how every Christmas Gordon would make her and Benjamin line up in front of him so he could critique their gifts. No matter what Benjamin gave him, from a drawing when he was four to the gold tiepin that was the final gift, he was always singled out for particular criticism.

The thought of Ruby taking after that man was depressing.

Dom decided to leave her to calm down and see sense, then she would try again later. But right now, Dom had other things to worry about: whether she was a danger to her family, for example; especially after yet another vivid nightmare last night; whether she should leave Benjamin and destroy the family for ever (which she knew was actually Benjamin's fault, and yet somehow, she felt guilty about. So much for her being an ice queen). But most pressing right at that moment was: what on earth was she going to cook for this bloody meal tonight?

She had tried to persuade Benjamin to cancel the meal but he was adamant. Dominique got the feeling there was more to it than a simple get together, but Benjamin had only said he was trying to pull together a new business deal and it would be good to have James onside.

With a heavy sigh, she trudged down the stairs.

# CHAPTER 59

Apart from a couple of sexy text messages in reply to over-the-top lovey ones she had sent after a few too many, Kendra hadn't heard from Ben in the three days since he'd come over on Sunday. He didn't even know that she had saved his daughter's bacon by stopping Jayne Seward from reporting her to the police. She wanted to tell him face to face, so she could enjoy his look of relief and gratitude. And the incredible 'thank you' sex that was bound to follow.

When he'd visited, he'd said nothing about her confronting Dominique and, as far as she knew, he was still clueless about her conversation with his wife.

Perhaps she should tell him herself?

She wasn't sure she had the courage.

She was certain – certain-ish – that once Dominique confronted him, he would let her know – for good or ill. So what the hell was going on? It had been five days since she'd dropped her adulterous bombshell. Why hadn't Ben's wife confronted him yet? Why hadn't she torn a strip off him? No wonder he sought passion elsewhere, Dominique was a doormat. There was no fire in her belly; she must be awful in bed.

Fine. In that case, Kendra would have to take things up a notch. She wasn't going to be second fiddle any more. She didn't want to be a mistress. She wanted to be the wife.

She clicked a perfect shellac nail against her front teeth as she pondered.

Time for the next phase in her plan. It was a gamble. But, to quote Ben, if you didn't bet big, you didn't win big.

His positive attitude was one of the things she adored about him. He was always so flash. She loved the sharp, expensive suits, the designer shades he insisted on wearing most of the time outdoors. When she had spotted the brochure for Bentleys in his Mercedes the other week, she had felt so turned on. Not by the material things, although obviously that was an attraction and she wasn't going to be fake enough to deny it; no, it was the power that went with those material things. Her man had the status to take on his competitors and destroy them – and the car, the sunglasses, the suits, were the outward trappings of that. The proof of his power. He was a gladiator, slaying business deals rather than lions.

Come on, what woman wouldn't get turned on by that?

The telltale tingle between her legs made Kendra stop her pacing and sit on the edge of the sofa.

She and Ben were made for each other. That was why she had confronted Dominique. Kendra had imagined the wife would break down in front of her; perhaps Kendra ending up putting her arm around her and comforting her. One day in the future, after the inevitable anger and betrayal had faded, Dominique would remember how kind Kendra had been in her victory, and that would become the seed from which forgiveness and eventual harmony would blossom.

Kendra let herself dream about the day when Ruby was all straightened out, and she and Amber would run to Kendra when they visited for weekends, giving her a huge hug. She and Dominique would talk in friendly fashion – she wasn't silly enough to imagine they would ever be best friends, but they would be able to like each other. Ben would be so happy with Kendra that she wouldn't view Dominique as a threat. Besides, Dominique would have found herself the right man by then, thus realising that things had all worked out for the best. She wouldn't blame

Ben and Kendra for falling in love, because everyone was happy, whereas before, no one had been.

Kendra smiled as she imagined the scene. She and Dominique air-kissing either cheek, just like Dominique did with her friend, Fiona. Yes, it was time to drive home the killer blow to Ben's marriage with the final part of her plan.

She picked up her phone and sent a text to her lover.

# CHAPTER 60

The 'Book of Hate' was filling up nicely. Ruby poured all her emotions into it. It didn't quite shut properly any more, the ink had seeped into the pages, making them swell, so that when she touched them she was touching her own fury given physical form.

All the people who had hurt her and betrayed her. Every slight she had received; each sidelong glance that stung and brought tears to her eyes; every shouted insult; every time she had been pushed around, or something of hers stolen, and each time her parents had failed her. It was all contained in the thick notebook, with its spiky title. Bits of paper had been stuck into it, too, making it a scrapbook of pain, in order to accommodate all her words. She needed a new one really, but she was starting to think there would be no point in purchasing one. She'd stick with this to the end.

The last entry glared out at her.

*I'll make them pay.*

But how? She thought of the Columbine shootings that Harry had told her about and wished she had the courage to do the same thing. The looks on everyone's faces if she marched into school and blasted them all to hell. She'd leave Jayne for last, so her rival could see the trouble she had caused. Jayne could watch her cronies suffer, and feel the terror of inevitability building inside her as Ruby got closer and closer with her gun, until… BOOM… she fell backwards like a straw doll, arms windmilling like they always did in Hollywood films. Her stupid mouth sagging open in shock and awe, eyes begging as she realised she had made a terrible mistake in underestimating Ruby.

But that wasn't really an option currently. For starters, school had broken up until next term.

Besides, right now, it was Ruby's family she was most angry with. They had totally betrayed her.

All Dad cared about was making money and what other people thought. He hadn't even tried to listen to her. Ha, he'd be mortified if he knew people thought his daughter was a prostitute and were offering to have sex with her. Maybe that's what she should have led with when she'd tried to open up to him: that his own reputation was in peril. That would have made him sit up and listen.

Well, screw him. She wasn't going to help him out. Let people write all the vile comments they wanted about her. As long as she had Harry, she could face anything.

Almost anything. When Harry was there, she was strong enough to stay away from social media. Without him, she was weak. Unable to stop her compulsion to know exactly what was happening. She put her 'Book of Hate' to one side and got out her phone. Checked ASKfm, Facebook, Twitter. She was called an ugly *C-U-Next-Tuesday* by someone every single day. Today was no different. The texts had piled up, too.

*'Ugly'*

*'Stupid'*

*'Smelly'*

She knew the words were true. Even Harry's love didn't change her own self-loathing.

Ruby opened her bedside cabinet drawer and stared at the hairdressing scissors she kept there for emergencies. She opened them up as wide as they would go. Pulled up her skirt, yanked down her red-and-black striped tights, and pressed the blade to her flesh. The pale skin went paper-white under the pressure. She held it and held it… a jerk of her wrist and the scissors were free. A satisfying line of blood formed, held, spilled.

She rolled her head back. Gave a deep sigh of release. That was better. So much better. But it wasn't enough, and now she had an idea that would make her feel loads better, and also really infuriate her parents. A win-win situation.

Ruby looked herself square in the eye as she held a safety pin against the outside of her nostril. Her self-loathing burned through her as she counted down.

*Three, two, one…*

She shoved it through her flesh. The pain made her glare harder, but she didn't cry out, didn't shed a tear. Instead, she twisted the pin slightly, grimacing, to make sure it was all the way through and the hole was big enough. Her nostril distorted as she pulled it out with a meaty tug.

Smearing the haematic flow away to find the hole created, she eased in place a large silver stud, shaped like a rivet, that stood proud from her skin. Blood flowed down to the crease of her mouth and she licked at it experimentally. It tasted gross, but she did it again, to prove a point. Then grabbed a handful of loo roll and dabbed at herself until she was no longer bleeding. She stared at the wad of scarlet paper. Wiped it down her T-shirt, leaving a smear on the picture of the upside-down cross that adorned it.

She couldn't wait for the guests to arrive for Dad's dinner party.

# CHAPTER 61

Benjamin pulled into the drive at 6.30 p.m.; earlier than necessary due to nerves about the night's dinner party with James and Heidi. If he was there he could oversee things, make sure it all went smoothly and Dominique didn't forget anything. Not that she ever did. Always fabulous at this sort of thing, she knew just the right tone to hit; whether to be more relaxed or more formal.

As soon as Benjamin got through the door a heady aroma of herbs and spices caressed his senses and made his mouth water. Instantly he calmed. He was worrying over nothing; everything would be fine.

Down the hall, Dom was in the kitchen, already changed into a stunning grey jersey dress with elegant scooped back. Simple but classy, it showed her figure off to perfection. It was complemented with one-carat diamond stud earrings in a platinum claw setting, and matching necklace he had bought her in July, to celebrate their move to the house.

As she turned the oven down, he kissed the back of her neck. She twisted round, and he planted his lips on her, long and lingering. It was their first proper kiss in months, he realised. Lately they had become close-mouthed and perfunctory.

Why had he let things get so bad between them?

Why was he sleeping with another woman?

His phone buzzed, making him jump away guiltily from Dominique.

'Better get changed,' he said, backing away.

The message was Kendra saying she needed to see him tomorrow. His reply would have to wait.

⚜

Upstairs, his wife had laid a suit out on the bed for him. He smiled. She had always done that since they first moved in together. Dom always seemed to know, even without him saying, when an event meant a lot to him. Knew, too, that choosing his clothes when he was like this stressed him out. So, she chose for him.

For tonight she had picked the trousers of one of his made-to-measure Savile Row suits, the one in blue fabric a shade above navy, which lifted it from sombre to informal. A pale blue shirt lay beside it on the bed, along with a pair of platinum cufflinks that oozed timeless class. He and she would mirror each other without looking too matching.

His grey brogues were on the floor, and she had chosen a grey leather belt.

Perfect. Everything was going to be just perfect.

Hmm, there was always the Ruby factor. He felt bad about their confrontation that morning. Perhaps he should have a quiet word, see what had actually been bothering her. Even if it was that boy, Benjamin ought to make some time for his children. It had been a long time since he had been able to think of anything but getting out of trouble with the taxman, but once James came through for him everything would be fine. He'd be able to spend a bit of quality time with his wife and kids, give them all the attention they deserved.

And he couldn't wait to see the look on that smug bastard of a tax inspector's face when he paid up in full.

As he stepped into the shower, Benjamin whistled while he lathered shampoo onto his hair, wondering why he hadn't gone to James in the first place.

❖

Once he was spruced up, he felt really good. Powerful. Confident. The Man.

Passing Ruby's bedroom, he slowed. Knocked on her door.

'Are you ready to come down?' he called.

'In a minute.'

'Okay. Well, the guests will be here soon, so—'

'Don't worry, I'll be there.'

Ah well, hopefully she knew he was sorry about earlier, and they'd get the chance to chat tomorrow or something.

# CHAPTER 62

It was almost seven p.m. Ruby had left it as long as she could; now she stole from her bedroom, fiddled with her nose stud, turning it and enjoying the discomfort. There were only minutes left before the guests arrived, so it was the perfect time to unveil her new look.

Her smile grew wider with each step down the stairs.

'Ah, good, you're ready,' said Dad, who was standing in the hallway.

Blinked.

Looked closer.

Detonated.

Arms waving, spittle flying from red face. One day he might literally explode, Ruby thought. The veins in his neck bulged, and she watched one particularly large one in fascination as he ranted at her, not hearing a word. It would fill up, getting bigger and bigger, and bigger, until… KABOOM. His head erupted into tiny pieces, the debris flung outwards, covering everything in blood and tiny clots of flesh. Slow-mo, like in films.

'What are you sniggering at? What the hell is wrong with you, young lady?' he yelled. The vein bulged further.

'You're going to die soon, if you carry on like this,' she warned.

Dad blinked several times, as if punched, then shoved his face further forward as it turned puce.

'Watch what you're saying. I am sick of your cheek. Right, I'm taking away your presents.'

'Big whoop. I'm not bothered anyway. You're doing me a favour.'

'Oh! Oh, I'm doing you a favour, am I?' he spluttered impotently. 'Well, I'll have to come up with a better punishment, won't I?'

His head was ticking up and down. As if he wanted to punch something. He wanted to punch her.

'How dare you? You little shit,' he exploded.

The doorbell rang.

# CHAPTER 63

Benjamin froze. There was no way that James and Heidi wouldn't have heard that. Benjamin could feel his heart pounding painfully. He was going to have a heart attack or a stroke or something. That bloody child was going to be the death of him.

He took a shuddering breath in a bid to calm himself, as Dominique hurried from the kitchen, pale-faced.

'Get her upstairs before I kill her,' he hissed, jabbing a finger towards his daughter. Ruby smirked. His hand flew up before he knew what he was doing.

Mouse started to cry.

Shaking, he brought his hand down slowly. Ruby hadn't even flinched.

'Benjamin. Get the door, now. Let me take care of Ruby.'

Dominique's cool, commanding tone brought him back to his senses. He was close to the edge, so close to the edge now, and if Ruby ballsed this up for him everyone would lose everything. Why couldn't she just be a normal child, for goodness' sake?

But there was no time to think. He smoothed his hair, glanced at Dom as she led Ruby and a howling Amber up the stairs, then threw open the door with a big fake smile plastered over his face.

❖

James and Heidi huddled warily on the doormat, spot-lit by the security light, and half turned away from the door. They looked like they had been discovered trying to sneak away.

'Welcome to the mad house,' Benjamin chuckled. It had a hollow ring even to him. 'Come in, come in. Let me take your coats. Sorry about this; you've caught Ruby having a bit of a meltdown about what to wear, of all things. She's refusing to come downstairs. Teenagers, eh?'

James and Heidi smiled and nodded as if they understood. Which, of course, they didn't because they had no children. Lucky bastards.

As he ushered them into the living room, he was reeling. He thought of when Ruby used to run at him when they were outside together playing, when she had enough room to build up some serious momentum. He would stand sideways on, feet braced for impact, shoulder leaning slightly forward and she would careen into him at speed, trying to knock him down. At the very least she would send him reeling and stumbling twenty feet backwards. Now she had done that to him again, spiritually.

He quickly poured everyone drinks and played the good host by changing the subject onto his guests. He was surprised to see Dominique emerge only a few minutes later. Behind her, literally clinging to her dress, trailed Amber, whose red nose and eyes could not betray that she had been crying. Benjamin lifted her up and gave her a cuddle.

'What's wrong, eh? Overexcited about Father Christmas coming?'

She looked at him, confused. 'No, Daddy. I'm upset about you shouting.'

Benjamin's heart sank a little lower but he hid it by chortling. 'Children say the funniest things, don't they? What book are you reading at the moment, Amber? Why don't you tell James and Heidi all about it?'

Luckily, Mouse was much better behaved than her sister and soon won the crowd over.

'Do you like school? What's your favourite lesson?' asked Heidi. Benjamin could tell she wasn't a natural around kids. Mouse gave an exaggerated shrug.

'Umm, I like them all, really,' she said. 'Probably English best, because then I can make up stories. I hate sports. I don't like running. Or swimming. Swimming is the worst, running is the best of all the sports but I still hate it. Swimming, then football, they're the worst.'

'Right.'

She was an adorable mix of cheeky and intelligent, and kept the conversation going single-handed and without controversy. By the time she went to bed, giving everyone a polite goodnight kiss, the strained atmosphere had dissipated.

'Dinner is served,' smiled Dominique.

❖

Benjamin was overwhelmed with gratitude towards his wife. She really was working overtime. Thanks to her hosting skills and brilliant cookery, everyone was soon relaxed, bathed in a warm glow of just the right amount of alcohol, soft lighting, and neutral conversation.

Benjamin drew James out about what he was up to and was pleased to hear that things were going well. His pal had made a few impressive investments lately and they were looking to pan out very profitably.

Finally, Benjamin managed to get him alone on the pretext of having a cigar together in the study. 'We don't want to pollute your air, ladies, so we'll withdraw,' he said, bowing in mock grandeur.

The women rolled their eyes, laughing, and got back to their conversation about an amazing new local designer who had apparently opened a boutique and stocked dresses 'to die for'.

❖

The men went to the study.

Benjamin's stomach gave a little flip, but he steadied himself with a sip of brandy, and offered James a cigar.

'Not for me, thanks. Just thought I'd keep you company.'

'Sure? Huh, that's a shame. I was hoping it would soften you up a bit.' He grinned at his pal, knowing that the best way with James was not to beat about the bush.

'Ah, okay. Out with it then – you know I'm always keen to help.'

'Well, it's not help, it's an investment.' Benjamin puffed on his cigar, the end glowing like a glimmer of hope. 'I'm looking to expand the business. Got some exciting opportunities heading my way. But it's going to cost. I need an investor, James, and, well, I thought I'd give you first dibs.'

'Hmm, it does sound interesting.'

*Yes.*

'But now is not a good time for me.'

*No.*

Benjamin tried to play it cool. To ignore the sweat he could suddenly feel blooming. 'Oh? Why's that? Be a real shame for you to miss out, you know my place is a little gold mine.'

'Oh, I know. I only have to see the way you live to know that,' James assured. 'It's just… those investments I mentioned to you earlier? They're not going to pay dividends for me until at least six months, possibly a year. Anything else investment-wise would leave me a tad overexposed. I can't risk it – not even on a solid prospect like yourself.'

Benjamin fought to keep the relaxed smile on his face. It felt stiff as cardboard.

'There no way? Come on, surely you've a bit of spare going…?'

James pondered. Picked up a cigar and sniffed it like people did in films, then put it back again. Then smiled as he looked up.

'All right, you've caught me. I do have a little bit of leeway for something really good. How much are we talking?'

'Two mill.' Benjamin didn't so much as blink as he said it like it was nothing.

'Two million pounds? No, I'm sorry, mate, but that's too rich for me. Half a mill, maybe, but no more.'

'That's no use to me. I need the whole investment. Come on, for an old friend.'

James backed away, fingers spread in front of him. 'I can't, mate. Sorry. I really am.'

Benjamin's shirt was sticking to his back. Maybe he could take the £500,000 and gamble. If he won, he could easily turn it into the full amount, maybe more.

'Okay, you know what. I'm feeling generous, so I'm going to let you in with that pittance and find other investors to come up with the rest,' he smiled. Rubbed a hand over his mouth to hide the trembling he felt in his lips.

'Cool. We'll get the lawyers to draw up the paperwork in the new year. Right, shall we get back to the ladies?'

Lawyers? Paperwork? He'd assumed it would be an informal loan between friends.

Benjamin fell in step behind James, until pain made him look down. He had scrunched the burning cigar up in his clenched fist.

# CHAPTER 64

Everyone was so busy and in such a bad mood. Christmas was supposed to make people happy. Mouse frowned as she snuggled into bed, one arm looped around Ted, the other hand holding her book.

Downstairs she could hear the murmur of her parents with their friends. There was a funny atmosphere down there, like they were all pretending to have fun but weren't.

She tried to read all about a magical faraway land, but instead stared at the page, wishing there really were magic, just like in stories. Then she could magic everyone happy, and solve all their problems.

Sometimes she believed in magic. Sometimes she thought it was for babies. She had spent a really long time looking for fairies at the bottom of the garden in the old house, and had never seen one. She had also lost count of the times she had jumped into her wardrobe, closed her eyes tight, and felt around, hoping, hoping, hoping that instead of her fingers brushing the wooden back, they would find prickly fir trees and the snowy landscape of Narnia.

She sucked her thumb as she pondered, removing it only long enough to whisper to her best friend.

'Don't tell anyone, Ted. Mummy will lecture me about making my teeth go bucky. She says I'll end up looking like Goofy.'

Satisfied he wouldn't breathe a word, she put her thumb back in, and started to read.

❖

With a ring like a bell being struck, the last of the crystal glasses slotted into the dishwasher. Dominique turned it on, then wiped down the countertops.

What a thoroughly horrendous evening. She had worried constantly about what on earth Ruby had done to herself, and Benjamin's violent reaction to it. It had taken every ounce of self-control to appear calm for her guests' sake. They hadn't been fooled. There was something going on with Benjamin far beyond his affair, and she wanted to find out what. He was so volatile lately. This evening alone he had gone from being a bag of nerves to a screaming bully in front of the kids. She had never seen him like that and it was unforgiveable. Then he had sleazed around James and Heidi, like some kind of Lothario trying to woo them. It was embarrassing. By the end of the night he had drunk far too much and sunk into such a dark mood that he had barely said goodbye to his friends.

She twisted her wedding ring round and round. When she first met him, he had been so different. She missed the man who threw his head back laughing so hard. Who quoted Muhammad Ali to inspire her. Who used to buy her flowers, or hire a favourite film, or even, one Tuesday, set off fireworks bought from the corner shop, just because he knew it was her least favourite day of the week.

But that had all been a long time ago. People change. Now Benjamin seemed to be losing control – his mistress was clearly a bad influence.

His mistress. The thought made her stomach twist like a wrung-out rag. But she took a deep breath, smoothed down her dress, and finished clearing up the mess of the dinner party.

Benjamin was hiding away in his study, as usual. Probably drinking again. The mood he was in, she couldn't be bothered to tell him that Heidi's last words to her had been to confess quietly that the downstairs loo wasn't flushing. It would probably send him over the edge. One more thing that was falling apart.

# CHAPTER 65

The amber liquid swirled around Benjamin's glass, hypnotically. He was in no hurry to drink it; he'd already had plenty and then some. The booze had slowed his thoughts from a raging waterfall of panic to a sluggish, silt-filled bayou.

Swirl, swirl, swirl. Round and round the whisky went. Round and round his thoughts. Disconnected. Slow. Vulnerable.

What... what was he listening to? The classical music was supposed to soothe him, but Benjamin didn't actually like the bloody stuff. He could never remember the names of it all, and had simply memorised the titles of some of the more popular tunes. Tunes? Was it right to call them tunes? Concertos, perhaps that was a better word? Screw Classic FM. He only listened to it so he could sound like he knew what he was talking about to other people. Cultured. It was all part of the persona he wanted to convey: a successful businessman, intelligent, savvy, sophisticated, with a beautiful family.

He took a sip of the whisky. Held the liquid in his mouth, savouring. He was drinking too much. That was what was causing those broken veins on his face. Making him old before his time.

What had he been thinking? Oh, yes...

Ruby. She had really buggered things up for him. What the hell had she done to herself? Wearing those weird black clothes like some sort of Marilyn Monroe... no, Manson, Marilyn Manson wannabe. Mutilating herself by piercing her nose. How was he supposed to introduce his family at opportune times when she looked like she might produce a knife and massacre everyone at any minute? It wasn't the message he wanted to convey, and he was going to have to come down on this behaviour hard.

The alcohol was gently burning his tongue. He swallowed. Another thought drifted around.

*Two million pounds owed.*

A sobering thought. So he finished his drink and had another. See, that's how cunning he was.

Sending Ruby to that £20,000-a-year private school had turned out to be a gigantic waste of money, too. She had shown him up by getting thrown out. She was always showing him up. Why couldn't she behave the way she was supposed to? It wasn't hard. He had. If he had spoken to his father the way Ruby spoke to him, he would have been given a thick ear for his trouble. But times had changed. Unfortunately.

Benjamin swirled his glass again. Faster.

The house, the cars, the business, the trappings of wealth.

Wife. Children. Lover. Friends.

Everything would soon be gone. Everyone would know what he had done. That he was a loser.

What slayed him more than anything was the thought of Dominique finding out. A balloon of panic inflated inside his chest as he imagined the day it would finally all come out. The look on her face. The colour draining away as if someone had slit her throat.

It would be easier if she died.

The relief he felt as the thought eddied around his mind shamed him for the coward he was. If Dom were in a car crash or something it would save him the ignominy of having to admit what a failure he was to the most important person in his life…

Actually, it would solve his problems, he realised suddenly. Both he and she had generous life insurance. If one of them died, the pay-out would be massive. Enough to wipe out his debts.

Ironic, really, that without Dominique, all his reasons for being afraid would disappear.

He stopped agitating his whisky. Knocked it back in one hit, wincing slightly as he swallowed. He had some tough decisions ahead of him.

# CHAPTER 66

Harry chuckled as Ruby told him how the evening had played out. He had to bite the pillow to keep from laughing too loud when she acted out her dad's reaction, scared of alerting people to his presence.

Tonight, she was only wearing one of his T-shirts to bed over her underwear – making him turn around and close his eyes before getting changed. It looked good on her. Big and baggy and oversized, and completely sexy. Even with striped bed socks. And with that new nose piercing, she looked fierce. Ruby was definitely the most amazing person he had ever met.

They cuddled up to watch a documentary on YouTube about Eric Harris and Dylan Klebold, the two lads who had won infamy during the Columbine school shooting. Harry didn't hear a word of it, too busy thinking about how close he was to Ruby. After a couple of minutes, she wrinkled her nose and turned it off.

'They sound kind of crazy,' she admitted. 'It doesn't even sound like revenge for being bullied, more like they just wanted to hurt people anyway. Besides, I can't be bothered to watch that while you're here.'

Her face looked even paler than normal, like she'd had a shock. As she turned the light off, Harry thought he saw her eyes look a little red with tears, but when she cuddled up to him, she seemed fine. He had to shift a bit, because he didn't want her to feel what was happening to him. Talk about embarrassing, man. But they kept on kissing, and his hand moved up her thigh.

'What's that?' he asked, pulling back. She scooted away but not before he rubbed his hand over her leg again, feeling the raised bump of a scab, all in a long neat line. It stood proud and rough against her petal soft skin. 'Has someone hurt you? Was it your dad?'

'No. It's fine, I'm fine,' she whispered back. They had the light off, he couldn't see her expression. He felt blindly for his phone and switched it on. In the illumination it threw, he could see her eyebrows were drawn together, worried.

Anger pulsed. He was on his feet before he realised it, flicked the big light on. Threw the duvet back. His girlfriend scuttled to the far corner of the bed, pulling her legs up as if to protect herself from his righteous indignation. What she didn't realise was that it gave him a view of how the cut snaked around her inner thigh so far that it could be seen from the back, too.

Her beautiful skin was puckered with the scab, the skin reddened on its edges as though angry. It broke his heart.

'No, man, no, that's a proper deep cut, Rubes. Who did it? Tell me right now, or I'm marching straight into your parents' bedroom and kicking the crap out of your dad.'

He was still whispering, even in his fury, but it was loud enough. Ruby flapped her hands.

'Look. It's not Dad. Okay, just calm down, sit next to me and bloody listen.'

He hesitated.

'Please, Harry. You're the only one who ever listens to me, and I need you to do that now, okay?'

He nodded. Flicked the light out and clambered into bed beside her. 'Figured it might be easier for you to 'fess up in the dark,' he said, gently.

'See? That's why you're brilliant – because you understand stuff like that. Thank you.' The mattress shifted as she moved towards him. Soft lips found his. 'Right, I know this is going to sound mental but… I did that cut myself.'

'What? You fell or something?' Harry scrunched his face up in the dark. She wasn't saying it like it was an accident, she was saying it like there was something way bigger going on.

'No, I did it, well, because sometimes the pain inside me gets so bad that the only way I can cope is if I make it physical. So, I cut myself. With scissors. And when the blood flows it's like the pain is flowing out with it. I don't do it often. I've only done it a few times since meeting you, which is amazing because things have been pretty intense lately with those messages and stuff. But you help me cope. You, and the cutting.'

She fell silent. Harry didn't fill it. He was trying to get his head around what she was saying. In a weird way, it made sense.

'You're hurting yourself to stop the hurt. But like, you're in control of this pain, and it's the being in control that helps… is that right?'

'Kind of. I suppose. I've never thought about the being in control bit, but it does sound right now you've said it. It just gets the pain out of me. I – I like it.'

She took his hand, guiding it in the dark. 'Here, can you feel that?'

He nodded. Realised she couldn't see, so said he could. A little bump of scar tissue under his fingertips. Then another and another. They criss-crossed her belly.

So many emotions choked him up. He cleared his throat, trying to unblock the feelings so he could speak.

'Rubes? I know it helps, but I don't think you should do it no more. I think next time you want to do it, you should call me and I'll be here, right away.'

And if anyone ever made her feel like crap about herself again, if anyone made her so desperately full of pain that she was overflowing with it, he was going to find them and hurt them. He was a Woolwich boy. Woolwich boys meant business.

'You know that saying about being a big fish in a little pond?' Ruby said suddenly.

'Yeah?'

'Well, I don't even feel like a little fish. I'm what the fish feed on. But maybe I need to do something about it to convince everyone I'm a shark. Like those lads Klebold and Harris. Maybe they had the right idea after all.'

'That way everyone leaves you alone once and for all.' He gave a slow nod.

Ruby lifted up his arm and stole beneath it. Wriggled against him until she found the perfect place to rest her head.

'I don't want to watch anything, but tell me more about Columbine,' she begged quietly.

In the soft, sing-song voice his mum had used back in the day when she was reading bedtime stories, before things had got so bad, he whispered tales of hatred, revenge, mass shootings, and bombs that hadn't gone off as planned.

His girlfriend's head grew heavier and heavier, but he only stopped talking once she was fast asleep. He listened to her breathing, and his own breaths grew slower, his lids heavier...

# CHAPTER 67

## CHRISTMAS DAY

Ogundele had seen all sorts over the years, as he rose through the ranks of the Met. But every time he thought he couldn't be surprised something happened that shocked him.

An entire family wiped out by an angry teenager.

He thought for a moment, taking the pieces of what he had seen and fitting them together. Creating a working theory, though he would wait for forensic reports to confirm them. Because he still didn't feel as if he was seeing the whole picture. Instincts honed over years of policing were making his skin itch in curiosity.

# CHAPTER 68

Mouse practically bounced down the stairs that morning, almost tripped over her slippers as she went.

Christmas was so close now, so very close.

She ran over to her advent calendars, carefully opening the flaps to discover what was inside. A bell, covered in snow and glitter; the baby Jesus in his manger; Rudolph with his bright red nose. And on the inside of each of the doors it proclaimed, 'two days to go'. Her stomach flipped in anticipation.

Two sleeps left. Eek.

She squeaked like her namesake and did a happy dance. She was going to burst. But no one else was up yet. She raced back up the stairs, slipping once in her haste, then stood on the landing looking at the two closed bedroom doors – her parents' and her sister's. Her head swivelled back and forth between them, trying to decide who to share her excitement with.

Ruby. Maybe it would make her smile.

In her excitement, Mouse knocked but didn't wait for a reply, just flung open the door, bounced inside, flipping the light on, leaped onto the bed.

And screamed.

And screamed.

And screamed.

There was a stranger in Ruby's bed.

The duvet beneath her bucked violently. She was thrown to the floor, banging her head against the bedside cabinet. Ow. The man was standing up, looming over her. That made her scream even more. The piercing sound made her ears ring, but she couldn't stop.

Ruby bent in front of her, face level with hers, saying something. But Mouse couldn't hear, not over her own screaming, and she had forgotten how to stop.

Then Mummy was there, scooping her into her arms, and she felt safe. Daddy was there, too. Shouting at the man, making him leave.

Mouse buried her head into Mummy's neck and watched everything, eyes wide, as the world started to scream with her.

# CHAPTER 69

Amber burrowed into her mum. She had stopped screaming as soon as Dominique took hold of her, but then Ruby had taken over, and Benjamin was doing a pretty good job of bawling everyone out.

Was this real? Was Dom trapped in one of her nightmares, and any second now she would wake?

Dom's ears were ringing, as she took in the scene. Trying to drink in every detail to work out if she was awake or asleep.

That boyfriend of Ruby's, Harry Porter, was standing bold as brass in his jeans and socked feet. Hands out as if trying to calm everything down. Who was he trying to fool? He wasn't wearing a top and Dominique could see that although he was scrawny, he was strong, dark skin rippling over ripped physique.

Fiona's comments leaped into Dom's mind. Harry was from a rough area. He'd been raised surrounded by drugs, theft, violence; fighting was probably second nature to him. He could lash out, hurt them. He might have a knife – hadn't Fiona mentioned something about knife crimes being rife? Dom pulled Mouse that little bit tighter against her, protecting her child.

Benjamin stepped right up to him, shoving his nose against Harry's, every muscle clenched. Dom didn't think she'd ever seen him so furious. A vein in his temple stood out, and his face was red. Benjamin had once been a powerhouse of solid muscle and he was still impressive when he wanted to be, despite the barrel chest slipping down to his stomach.

'What the fuck are you doing in my house? If you've touched my daughter, I swear to God,' he growled.

'No, no! I swear—'

Ruby tugged at her dad's shoulders with both hands, virtually jumping on his back. Yelling and wailing incoherently, thin legs stamping furiously, fully on show because she was only wearing a T-shirt.

All hell was breaking loose.

Dominique put a hand down to the carpet and wiggled her fingers into the thick pile. Definitely real. She felt Mouse trembling beside her.

This was real.

'On three, we'll run out of here, yes?' she whispered into her youngest child's ear. A nod of agreement. She took tight hold of Mouse's hand, then…

'One, two, three.'

They jumped up and ran from the room, leaving the carnage behind them. In Mouse's room, Dom snatched up her daughter's bear and passed him over.

'I want you to stay here and look after Ted, okay? He'll be worried by all the shouting, so you keep him safe and let him know there's nothing to be scared of. Can you do that?'

Mouse nodded, eyes like saucers. She clutched Ted to her, as if her life depended on it.

'I'm going to go back into Ruby's room and calm things down, okay? But don't forget, there's nothing to be afraid of. Sit tight.'

The last thing Dom wanted to do was abandon her little girl, but the shouting was getting worse; incomprehensible insults punctuated by swearing and scuffling.

Ruby was between her dad and her boyfriend. Jaw jutting forward in stubborn fury. Harry held her back. Benjamin had five lines of red across his face where she had clearly slapped him. He looked about ready to explode. Dominique mustered all her calm, all her ice queen persona, to glide into the middle of the spectacle.

'Could everyone stop right now, please?'

To her surprise – and by the look of it, theirs – everyone did. Harry broke the spell first.

'Mrs Thomas, I know it looks dodgy, but I swear—'

'Put your clothes on and leave,' she said. 'Now.'

He scrabbled around, while Benjamin made rumbles of protest and Ruby started to whine that it wasn't fair. With a quick backwards glance at Ruby, Harry hurried away.

'It wasn't what it looked like,' her daughter began. 'Nothing happened. He just fell asleep, that's all.'

'He just fell asleep? When you're both virtually naked?' Benjamin bellowed.

'What was he doing here in the first place, Ruby? You're not even supposed to be speaking, let alone…' Dominique trailed off and waved a hand uncertainly. 'We're not stupid. This is completely inappropriate behaviour.'

'I should have torn him apart. You're grounded for so long you will never see the light of day.' Benjamin was working himself up from red to puce.

'You've both got dirty minds,' Ruby shouted.

Dom held her hands out. 'Stop. You are going to stay here and think about what you've done. Your father and I are going to discuss what will happen next.'

Ruby didn't protest. Instead, she folded her arms and slumped onto the bed, throwing murderous looks. Once upon a time Dom might have laughed at how melodramatic she could be, but now she felt a shiver of fear at her own daughter. There was no give to the glare; it was pure, unadulterated hatred.

Dom shook as she left the room, and did her best to hide it behind her usual façade. Harry might come across as polite, and he had left meekly enough, but Dominique wasn't willing to gamble on her little girl's future any longer. The time for understanding and waiting for Ruby's infatuation to burn itself out was over; she was far, far too young to be sharing a bed with someone.

⁂

She and her husband went to the kitchen and sat at the table. He looked as if he had been punched in the gut, his complexion fading from raging red to ashen. Dominique lay a gentle hand on his arm.

'I'll kill him.' His voice seemed barely a whisper.

'Not a good idea. But I do think we need to take action.'

'Too right. I'm going to—' he stood up again. Dominique's hand tightened, trying to pull him back.

'Benjamin, listen for a second.'

'What? Are you going to say that we should try to understand her? Give her a hug? We've been too soft on her for too long.'

'Actually, I was going to suggest we report him to the police. She's underage. It's statutory rape.'

Benjamin nodded slowly, the cogs of his brain turning almost visibly. 'No, that's a good idea. Better than me beating the crap out of him and getting arrested myself.'

'You agree with me?' Dominique was surprised by how good it felt. For the first time in a long time, they were working as a team towards a common goal.

'Definitely. Are you going to do the honours, or shall I?'

A quick but frustrating call to the local police station by Benjamin soon revealed that the powers that be weren't interested in pursuing the claim. Firstly, Ruby would turn sixteen in two months; secondly Harry was also underage; and, most importantly, there was no actual proof of any wrongdoing. Just as Benjamin started to change colour once more, Dominique had an idea.

'This could work to our advantage. Hear me out. We tell Ruby and Harry that we won't report him to the police – yet. But that if they contact one another ever again, we will. That way we get to look like we're not being heavy-handed, we're giving them the option to behave. They won't dare risk getting into trouble with the police, and that fear will keep them apart.'

Benjamin thought, then smiled. Took her hand and brought it to his lips. 'See, that's why I married you. You're so much cleverer than I am.'

'Don't you forget it.' Dominique smiled as she spoke, trapping the venom behind her perfect teeth.

'I'm going to keep the shotgun under our bed from now on, though. I want it on hand to put the fear of God in that boy if he ever does come here again.'

Typical Benjamin, always wanting to use a sledgehammer to crack a walnut.

# CHAPTER 70

How much worse could Ruby's life get? It was all Mouse's fault. She should never have come bursting into her room like that. Poor Harry. Now her parents thought the worst, of course, and her bitch of a mum had come up with some crappy punishment. If they'd just listened to her instead of jumping to their perverted conclusions, but no, of course they weren't going to do something as reasonable as that. They never listened to her. Instead, they accused her of all sorts, like she was no better than those people posting on the site believed she was.

She could never have anything to do with Harry again, or he'd be arrested.

Ruby's pain was baptised with yet more tears. Until the impossible happened: she ran out of tears. No one would ever make her cry again, she vowed. She would never again be so stupid as to feel hope.

She pulled out her 'Book of Hate' from its hiding place under the bed, and started to write a plan.

❖

Jazmine was pacing up and down in front of Benjamin as she spoke. She was off on one again. He rubbed his hands over his face and sighed.

'Sorry, am I boring you?' she snapped, pausing in front of him and tapping her foot.

'Yeah, actually. Listen, I've had a crap day. I discovered my daughter in bed with someone, spent the morning tearing down a trellis so the little pervert can't climb back into her bedroom, and now you're nagging me about being late. I'm your partner, not your employee. What exactly is the problem?'

'I want to know where the accounts are, Ben. Why aren't they on our server, so I can access them?'

'I don't know – I'm not in IT. Get someone to look into it.'

'You're sure you've not done something to them? Deleted them?' She didn't take her eyes off his.

He huffed, broke contact by rolling his eyes.

'That's right. I've hidden them away because I've been nicking from the business and don't want you to find out.' Now it was his turn to gaze at her. His mouth twitched. He turned it into a smile. 'Look, I'm sorry I'm late. Let me call a computer whizz I know, see if he can sort it.'

Her shoulders relaxed, whole demeanour changing. 'If you don't mind, that would be great.'

'Not a problem.'

'And Ben…'

Inside his trouser pocket, his hand tightened into a fist.

'I'm sorry to hear about your awful day. I hope things calm down at home soon.'

When she left the room, he twiddled his thumbs for fifteen minutes then stuck his head around her office door.

'Just to let you know, I've called my mate. He's snowed under until after Christmas, but will look at it then. I told him that was okay; it's only a few days away. But if you'd rather, I can try someone else.'

'No, no, it's fine. If you reckon he can fix it, I'm not in a massive hurry. Like you say, it's only a few days, really.'

A few days that might make all the difference between Benjamin and his family falling off the edge of a financial precipice, or living happily ever after.

# CHAPTER 71

The last time Dominique had seen Dr Madden she had been about to turn twenty, but in the intervening years the décor of the waiting room had remained the same soothing colours. It was sleek, clean, calming and all so fresh and spotlessly clean.

Dominique hadn't told anyone but Fiona about her two p.m. appointment. After the drama of Ruby that morning, she had thought about cancelling. Instead, she had told Ruby she was nipping out, not informing her where she was going or when she would be back, so that the teen would have no clue how long she would be left alone. If she had told Benjamin, he probably would have expected her to cancel, given the circumstances – there was no way he would have trusted their teenage daughter to be left home alone with Mouse. But he also wouldn't have changed his own work schedule to help Dom out.

She sat with her handbag resting on her lap. Every now and again she adjusted it slightly so it sat perfectly square, an even amount of thigh showing either side.

She had been so nervous the first time she had come here, aged nineteen, her mum sitting one side and Fiona on the other; Fiona insisting on coming despite Dom's shame at what she had done.

She hadn't meant it, though. She never would have hurt anyone when awake. It had been the screams that woke her, and there had been so much blood…

'Dominique Thomas?' The receptionist's call shocked her from her memories, and she hurried into Dr Madden's room.

His hair was a uniform snow white now, even though he must only have been in his early sixties, but his friendly face was surprisingly wrinkle free. Life must have been good for the doctor in the intervening years.

'Take a seat. How are you?' he smiled.

Now there was a loaded question. Dom knew better than to keep her mask on with Dr Madden. Instead, she offloaded everything. How she had discovered her husband was having an affair, how her daughter was causing her huge stress, and how Dom herself was struggling to cope. They discussed the dreams she had been having, and how the sleepwalking had now reared its ugly head once more.

'After what happened before, I'm scared,' explained Dom. 'What if I hurt my family? If anything happened to my kids because of me, I couldn't live with myself. I'd end it there and then.'

The doctor pressed his fingers together. 'Only one per cent of the adult population sleepwalk, and among them, those who have a violent episode are exceptionally rare.'

'Rare, but not unheard of,' she interrupted.

'True… Of course, you have already suffered such an episode, so you are at risk – which is why I've made time to speak with you now. But don't worry, this is extremely treatable; after all, you've been through it once with great success. We'll get back on top of things in no time.

'First things first: I'll contact the London Sleep Centre. They will book you in for a polysomnography – a series of tests to measure functions including brainwaves, muscle activity and breathing activity. You know the score.'

She did indeed. She remembered the centre of expertise well. Walking to the north end of Harley Street, as a teenager, to undergo a raft of tests, she'd been nervous as a kitten. After weeks of tests, where she had even had to sleep at the centre so she could be monitored, her sleepwalking had been confirmed. It had been terrifying to have it confirmed that she had had absolutely no control over her own body. When she got the news, she had walked around Regent's Park in a daze, trying to get her head around everything, because even to her the truth sounded crazy.

Like someone possessed, Dominique had indeed been sleep-walking at the time of the attack she had committed, in a state called automatism. With the help of the sleep experts, she had been found not guilty of the charges against her, due to non-insane automatism.

'I'm just so scared, doctor. I hate losing control. What if I hurt someone again? What if I kill them this time?' she asked now.

'Dominique, your stress is going to make your symptoms much worse. There have only been about sixty-eight recorded cases worldwide of murder in sleepwalking. See how rare it is? You have nothing to worry about.'

Nothing to worry about?

'Surely you could give me some sleeping tablets to knock me out, or some kind of medication?'

'Unfortunately, drug treatments for nightmares and sleepwalk-ing are not helpful. In fact, they are more likely to make them worse. But there are steps we can take to lessen the frequency of your nightmares, and the effect they are having on your life.'

'Such as?'

'While we're waiting for the appointment to come through with the London Sleep Centre, you and I can look at you making some behavioural changes.'

'What if that's not enough?'

He gave a small but reassuring smile. 'Let's not get ahead of ourselves. Imagery rehearsal treatment works something like seventy per cent of the time. We know it's worked on you once, so we have no reason at all to fear it won't this time.'

She sighed. Rearranged her handbag on her lap, knowing he was right but unwilling to concede the point.

'Talk me through the worst incident you've had so far this time.'

Dominique described holding a bloody Ruby in her arms. She vividly relived the feeling of knowing her daughter was dead, the gut-wrenching horror that had overwhelmed her. She trembled as she spoke.

'Okay, now imagine what changes you would make if you could. Run the dream through your head as if it were a film and you are the director. You rearrange the action, Dominique. You are in control.'

'There's a noise outside my bedroom door. A gurgling noise. It's... laughter. I open it, and lying on the hallway floor is... is...' Her voice faded. She forced herself to carry on. 'Is Ruby, and she's...' Not covered in blood. Not struggling to breath. Not clinging onto life by a thread. 'She's wearing a red dress, it's just a red dress, that's why she is red, it's not blood.'

Crying a river of tears that joined the scarlet puddle. Blood making her hands sticky, turned her fingernails into talons. Holding her daughter to her. Clinging to her rag doll body and holding it tight against her chest.

'And we hug. We put our arms around each other and we hug.'

It sounded so simple, but tears flowed unchecked down Dom's cheeks as she tried to manipulate the memory of the dream and work on inserting the new images into it.

She and Dr Madden went over and over it, talking through every sight and sound of the dream, every feeling she'd had. They then converted it to something related but positive. The rest of the session flew by as they practised the imagery rehearsal treatment.

If she drilled it enough, she would be able to take control of the dream and make those tweaks while asleep. It sounded crazy, but she knew from her own experience that it worked.

She simply had to calm down, trust in the process, and practice her imagery rehearsal therapy. And hope it worked really, really quickly – though in her experience it was a slow process getting a handle on changing dreams. Practice made perfect.

# CHAPTER 72

As soon as Mum shouted her goodbyes up the stairs and the front door clicked, Ruby picked up her phone. Held it. Didn't know what to do.

Should she call Harry?

The last thing her mum had done before she went out was to fix her with a long look.

'I'm trusting you, Ruby. I've deliberately not taken your phone away because you know what will happen if you have anything to do with Harry from now on.'

She certainly did. Her parents had stood shoulder to shoulder, earlier, united in destroying her life, if nothing else. Delivering the killer blow that if she had anything more to do with her boyfriend in any way, shape, or form, they would immediately have him charged with statutory rape. Ruby had offered to have a medical check done to prove she was still a virgin, but they weren't interested. Of course not.

She had not ranted and raved. She had not sworn and become explosive. The shock had been too much. Instead she had taken the news quietly, stunned that her own parents could sink so low. She had known they didn't understand her, didn't love her even. She'd known they took absolutely no interest in her. That had hurt enough to make her hate them.

What she felt now was way beyond that emotion, though. It was enmity hammered into something diamond hard and implacable.

That her own flesh and blood would blackmail her was despicable. They had sunk so low that they were threatening to destroy the only person in the entire world who loved her and who she loved.

And they knew it was all over a stupid lie. It would take minutes for an expert to assure them Ruby was untouched.

Ruby stared at her phone. The only good thing to happen today was that the messages seemed to have calmed down. Her phone was quiet for once. Perhaps it really was the season of goodwill. She gave a cynical snort at the thought.

She made a decision, and dialled Harry.

Without him, she had nothing to lose. Her parents had just taken away the only thing she had left to live for.

❖

While Mummy was out, Mouse decided to read the final book in the Narnia chronicles, *The Last Battle*. It always made her cry in the end, when everyone realised they were dead. But when they all went to heaven and were running around having fun, her tears went all funny as she read, because she was still crying but they were happy tears. Which was silly, really. How could anyone cry and be happy? But she could.

She wondered what it was like to be dead. Did it hurt? In the book, the pain was over quickly, then everyone was together and would never, ever hurt again. Mouse liked that. She was certain she was going to heaven – or Narnia, she wasn't sure which – and would meet Aslan.

She grabbed Ted, clambered into the wardrobe, and shut the door on the miserable afternoon weather outside and miserable atmosphere inside. Curled up in a corner with her torch, and opened her book.

❖

Kendra was still worried about the final stage of her plan to force Ben's hand. But she had tried everything else. Everything except…

There was one last desperate throw of the dice. Screw it, what did she have to lose except the love of her life?

She would do it.

She took her phone out and tapped out several messages. Her phone buzzed almost immediately with a reply from her neighbour, Dawn.

*'Come over now, the kids are about to go to bed.'*

Brilliant, she could always rely on Dawn, who was her only real friend any more. And goodness knows, she needed a pal to unburden herself on – well, to give an edited version of her life to, anyway. It was always an edited version, to ensure sympathy.

Ben took longer to reply to his text, finally confirming that he would come over at ten p.m., after dinner with a potential client.

She quickly sent him an emoticon of a smiley face and some love hearts, before grabbing her keys and heading across the hall to Dawn's place.

This was it: everything was in place to drive a wedge between Ben and his family once and for all. If only her courage held.

# CHAPTER 73

Harry held Ruby like he didn't want to ever let go. Fierce and protective. That was how she felt, too. They were both crammed into the downstairs loo, the only place they felt safe enough to meet. They couldn't go out because Ruby was grounded, and didn't dare go anywhere else in the house, in case they were discovered. At least in here there was a lock, and if her parents came home Harry could scramble through the window, and make a run for it with a good chance of not being spotted.

Mouse was squirrelled away in some hidey-hole or other, presumably reading. She and Ruby had not spoken since the morning.

'I'll never, ever forgive the squirt for bursting in and screaming the place down. She should have knocked. She should have waited. She should have quietly asked me what you were doing there, rather than totally overreacting,' Ruby fumed.

Harry nodded, then jerked is chin towards a carrier bag Ruby had chucked on the floor. 'What's in there?'

'Oh, it's a Christmas present for your mum. You know you mentioned the other day that she struggles with buttons so I've got her some nice tops, and a lovely pair of trousers from a posh shop – it's got an elasticated waist but you'd never know to look. They're smart.'

'Rubes, you're the best.'

'Nah. It's not like it's my money I'm spending.' But she felt her cheeks warming at the compliment. 'Think your mum will like them?'

'For sure. Hey, I can't believe your parents want to call the pigs on me over some trumped-up rubbish.'

Harry put the lid of the loo down and sank onto it. Patted his knee and Ruby sat on it so they could carry on cuddling.

'Why can't they just fuck off and die?' she huffed, anger igniting again.

'If we can't be together, I might as well be dead.'

She looked at him. Those big brown eyes of his, full of fire and love. 'That's how I feel, too.'

Without him all she had was pain. The constant insults were so deep-rooted in her now that they had tangled around her soul, choking off all the light, and stopping anything else from thriving within her.

The teenagers' fingers twined, no words needed. Ruby couldn't believe her parents thought she and Harry needed something so prosaic as sex, when they had this between them. Their love had been forged in a crucible of despair which made it unbreakable.

'I can't live without you,' she repeated. 'If my parents keep us apart, I'm going to kill myself.'

'You're the one good thing in my life, Rubes. Let's face it, my home life is shit – and school's worse. Don't leave me.'

'Maybe we should just kill everyone else instead. Blow up everyone who has ever crossed us, then we'd be free.' She started flippantly, but even before she reached the end of the sentence, the idea took hold. The same pain that had fed the darkness inside her now allowed this idea to take root and grow.

'Like Columbine? Great idea, except school is closed, I've no idea how to make a bomb, and it wouldn't get rid of your parents.'

'My dad's got a shotgun.' The words were out before the thought. 'We could shoot everyone and then run away, be free. Me and you and no one to interfere.'

'And if we got caught we could kill ourselves anyway.'

There was electricity in the air. Ruby's heart was beating fast, and she had never felt so alive. She should have been appalled by this talk; she knew that, somewhere in the back of her mind. But she wasn't. She was excited. The only other thing that made her feel like this usually was Harry – and the fact she felt so good as they talked now was confirmation for her that it must be right.

Harry seemed to feel it too. His eyes were fever bright, burning into hers. His pupils were huge, as if he had taken drugs.

His reaction fed her own fervour. Talking like this gave her an adrenaline rush even bigger than punching Jayne, or goading the police, or kissing Harry, all put together. It was wrong, horrifying – and that was the fun.

'We'd never get away with it. We'd last five seconds on the run with the police after us,' he said finally. 'Unless we planned things real careful, like. We'd need to fool the pigs into thinking it was nothing to do with us.'

'They'd need to think it's a break-in gone wrong or something.'

'Yeah, so, like, maybe I should bring knives with me, rather than using ones in the house. Like, I could nick some from home. Knives are better than guns because then no one would hear it.'

Good plan. And it was a plan, Ruby realised – both of them had slipped from saying what would happen were they to do it, to what they were going to do.

'How will we know when they're dead?' Ruby breathed.

'Well, it'll be bloody obvious from the blood – it'll be everywhere,' he laughed, then turned serious. 'But I know first aid, so I can check their pulses.'

'Just imagine thinking you've murdered everyone and then realising they're still alive,' she mock-shuddered. 'They could shout out for help.'

'I'll stab them in the throat first. Stop them from shouting out for anything ever again.'

There was such determination in his voice that Ruby shuddered again, for real.

'We could drug your dad,' he added. 'He's the only one who could really fight back and stand a chance of stopping us. Drug his food and he'd be taken out instantly. We can still slit his throat, even though he's out of it.'

'Yeah. I could slip something into his precious whisky. You could get like a roofie or something, couldn't you?'

Harry shrugged.

Ruby had never been the bad girl; she had spent her life trying to fit in around others. Only in the last few months had she given up – and discovered that being bad felt good. This was a great idea. Even if they did end up with the police after them, they could always go back to Plan A and kill themselves. At least they would first have dished out some punishment to those who had let them down.

# CHAPTER 74

Kendra's legs wrapped around Ben's hips as they pounded into her, breath hitching. Tearing at his skin trying to get closer to him, have even more of him. She'd claw her way to his heart if she could. Dragging her teeth against his chest, his heart thudded beneath her lips. Sweat pearled across his back as she pulled him closer, closer, closer. No holding back. She couldn't have done even if she had wanted to.

Yes, yes, yes!

Ben collapsed on top of her, then rolled to one side, breathing heavily. She snaked herself against him, throwing one leg over him possessively, running a hand over his chest. Sated for the time being.

He had set Kendra free. She had been shy before. But with him she felt free and fierce and capable of anything. He gave her confidence where she'd had none. She hadn't known it was possible to feel like that. Previously, the men in her life had been feeble fumblers, she realised now. As lacking in experience as she, but hiding it behind bravado. Ben turned her into a she-wolf.

'Did you scratch me?' he asked, breaking her reverie.

He sat up. Turned his back to her. She ran her fingertips over four straight, pink lines across his right shoulder.

'Oh, I did. I'm sorry.'

'Christ!'

Ben always told her off when she marked his skin. She knew why: he didn't want his wife to see. And that was another reason why she did it – Kendra wanted the world to know that Ben was hers and hers alone, and she saw no reason why she shouldn't mark her territory. Speaking of which…

'I'm pregnant,' she announced.

The blood drained from Ben's face. He looked like an uncooked piece of pastry.

'Fuck.'

It wasn't the reaction she had hoped for.

# CHAPTER 75

Harry lay in bed thinking about that afternoon. He and Ruby were going to carry on seeing each other, somehow, some way. He loved that they could talk so freely, get all their darkest fantasies out, and neither felt weirded out by it.

Death.

Revenge.

Freedom.

Murder.

Bottling it up was bad, so he was glad they could vent together. But it was all talk, neither of them would ever do something so horrific, it was just cathartic to get all that anger out.

❖

It was late. The house was quiet, kids in bed and Benjamin not yet returned from work or his mistress.

Illuminated by the glow of the Christmas tree fairy lights, Dominique opened up her tablet and typed 'sleepwalking killers' into the search engine.

There won't be any results. Oh, damn...

Her psychiatrist was correct; it was extremely rare for someone to commit murder in their sleep. But it wasn't unheard. Page after page of examples loaded.

A Manchester man who beat his father to death while asleep.

A chef who woke to discover he was hitting his wife with a claw hammer.

A New Zealand father who strangled his four-year-old son and killed the poor mite, before his shocked wife woke him as he attacked their other child.

Homicidal somnambulism was the technical term, apparently. Dominique hoovered up the facts, each case scaring her but also making her more determined. Her family would not suffer at her hands.

She put her tablet down and concentrated hard on her imagery rehearsal therapy.

The gurgling noise was laughter. The shotgun in her hand was a broomstick. Ruby was wearing a red dress.

Blood red.

# CHAPTER 76

Apart from the occasional bad dream, sleep had never caused Dominique any problems until Easter 1992. Back then, she had been such a different person, with a totally different life path mapped out. She was going to be on stage and screen, make it as a famous dancer. She was just coming to the end of her first year of studying dance at the University of Birmingham, and had loved every second of it.

One night during that Easter, a noise had woken Dominique. Her eyes felt gritty as she blinked them open, and she gave a sigh, not worried, only annoyed. She lived in a houseshare with five other students, so it was no big shock that someone was sneaking around.

Hang on…

Her sleep-addled brain took a moment to catch up. There wasn't anyone to make a noise. Everyone else had gone home for the long weekend, but she had decided to stay behind to get some extra practice done. A career as a professional dancer was all she had dreamed of since she was a child.

It had felt wonderfully indulgent to have the entire house to herself, and she had taken full advantage the previous night and day. Leaving the washing-up, knowing that there was no one to nag her. Buying a carrot cake as a treat and leaving it in the fridge in the knowledge it wouldn't have disappeared as if by magic the second her back was turned. She'd sung along with Bryan Adams to 'Everything I Do, I Do It For You' at the top of her voice. Later she'd gone to Blockbuster and hired a video, then spent an indulgent evening watching *Robin Hood, Prince of Thieves*, with no one to interrupt.

It had been wonderful having the large 1930s semi-detached house to herself.

Which begged the question: why could she hear someone moving around downstairs?

Someone must have broken in.

Her heart thumped in her throat, seeming to cut off her air supply. What should she do? The only phone in the house was downstairs. Only show-offs and rich businessmen had mobiles.

Maybe she should hide. In the dark, she ran blindly through all the possible places in her room. The wardrobe had a small mountain of shoes in the bottom; there was no way she could clamber on top of it without stumbling and making a noise. Under the bed would involve pulling out the random items she had shoved under there – her suitcase; the step for her exercises; a couple of boxes of jumpers that were too bulky to fit into the tiny chest of drawers.

No, hiding wasn't an option. The noise was getting closer. Soft footfalls on the carpet. The creak of the floorboard outside her bedroom door. Low voices.

She was trapped. To escape would mean running right past whoever was in the house. Thieves, rapists, murderers.

Scream. She should scream for help. She'd be lucky if anyone heard her. Unless she threw the window open, and then yelled. Yes, she'd do that. She grabbed the corner of the duvet to fling it back – and saw the door handle moving downwards.

Panic. She curled into a ball and hunkered under the duvet like a child. Felt sick with nerves. She was the mouse, quivering in fear of a cat, knowing that any second could bring death. Her back was against the cold of the wall, but she stayed still, holding her breath. Hoping, praying, that the intruders would not look closely at the heaped-up duvet.

The sound of the door opening. Time seemed to stretch out.

A rush of cold air. A feeling of exposure as the duvet no longer protected her. A loud expletive from somewhere in the darkened room.

Dominique stared up at two torches, unable to see behind the blinding yellow discs filling her vision.

'I thought you said this place was empty,' hissed one voice. A man's, with local accent.

'Shut up.' Another man. Older. More in control.

A torch's pool of light grew larger, heavy breathing closing in, bringing the smell of cigarettes and the faint whiff of beer.

'You're going to stay nice and quiet. Because if you make so much as a peep, I'll cut you. Understand?'

A whimper was her only reply.

She didn't think to scream. Didn't imagine for a second taking them by surprise by jumping up and bolting past them. Her mind was as frozen as her body.

*Please, don't hurt me.*

'You're going to count to 500, and then you'll be free, okay? Move before 500 and we'll be back, and we'll slice you from ear to ear. Tell me you understand.'

A finger ran light as a butterfly over her skin to demonstrate. She opened her mouth. All that came out was a croak.

Sliced from ear to ear. The agony. The blood pouring down her face. They'd laugh, enjoying her mutilation.

'Start counting when we get to the top of the stairs.'

The two men backed away. She could only guess from the difference in torch heights that one was taller than the other.

'One, two, three...'

Stairs creaking. Front door opening.

'... thirty-seven, thirty-eight...'

No sound of the front door closing. Had they really left? She imagined them downstairs, waiting for her to mess up, waiting for her to move before she reached 500.

'… one hundred and twenty, one hundred and nineteen…'

Wait, she'd messed up the counting, her mind so numb it refused to function properly.

*'Move before 500 and we'll be back, and we'll slice you from ear to ear.'*

She didn't dare make a mistake and move too early. She didn't want to die or be sliced. She'd have to start again.

Dominique didn't stop once she reached 500, continuing on to 1,000 in the darkness, using her shivers to keep time. Even then, she waited some more. Listening. Clutching at her hair to try to stop her head from bursting with terror.

When she crept downstairs, she didn't stop by the telephone. Instead, she bolted through the wide front door and finally let rip to the screaming fear inside her, hammering on the door of a neighbour until they opened up to find her a gibbering, sobbing wreck on their step.

❖

The police had been called. As she sat at her neighbour's kitchen table – a neighbour she had previously not even said hello to – she sipped over-sweet tea and gave her statement.

Only as they probed her did she realise – she hadn't even seen a knife. Had they really had one? Why hadn't she fought back? Why had she believed them? Why had she frozen instead of screaming for all she was worth?

The police told her she had done the right thing. Her parents, when they arrived pale and trembling-lipped, said she had done everything she could. Fiona came to visit her, leaving her own law studies, and gave her a stern talking to that obsessing over the past wasn't going to change the present – that she was alive and safe and should be bloody grateful.

But the guilt and anger at her own helplessness ate away at Dominique. She was furious, not with the burglars but with herself.

In her mind, the scene played over again and again. If only she had done this… If only she had done that… If only…

Even in sleep, she couldn't escape. Her dreams morphed into nightmare reruns. Over time they transformed into something even worse, as if the reality were not a scary enough scenario any more and her mind needed to really torture her. The men no longer left. They carried out their threat. Cold steel sliced across her flesh. Sometimes slow, sometimes fast, sometimes the blade forced into her mouth and tugged sideways to give her a 'smile'. Occasionally they held her down and raped her. She never fought back, frozen by her own abject terror.

She grew used first to waking up screaming, then to waking in the middle of her room, standing by her bed, arms raised as if warding off a blow, heart pounding. Sweat poured from her. This became her nightly routine. She hated to close her eyes, dreaded going to bed, did everything she could to avoid it. She felt as if she were going mad from lack of sleep, yet it was the very thing she dreaded more than anything – anything other than being left alone. Only leaden exhaustion drove her to close her eyes, and then it was generally in front of the television.

Her parents stayed with her at university, at first, then her friends offered to do shifts to make sure she was never left alone. It wasn't enough. Within a month of the attack she had quit her course, unable to face her old room or former life.

Weight dropped off Dominique. She became obsessed with being in control of everything, from researching what she bought, to the food she put in her mouth. Everything had to be perfect, because only then could she relax and know she and no one else ruled over her life.

Still the dreams haunted her. Dominique started to sleep with a knife under her pillow, her fear growing with every nightmare, the 'what ifs' looming larger each time she closed her eyes. If anyone got in again, she'd be ready.

❖

Two months after the attack, at the end of the semester, Fiona returned to her parents' home for the long summer break. She tried her best to encourage Dominique to get out of the house.

'Let's have a night out. Bit of dancing will cheer you up.'

'A dark room full of strangers and flashes of light. No way. I'm sorry.'

Just the thought made her tremble.

'Okay, well, how about a sleepover? I'll bring over a couple of bottles of wine, we'll have a night in, put the world to rights, maybe watch some films. Hmm?' She wiggled her eyebrows.

Dominique caved. 'Okay, that sounds good.'

They had a good time and for a few wonderful hours the teenager felt herself relax. There were entire sections of the evening where her mind didn't creep back to the time she had woken in the darkness.

The giggling pair went to bed merry, Dominique in her bed and Fiona on the floor beside her. They chatted until the words grew slower and heavier and both drifted into the land of nod.

❖

The dream that night had been horrific. In it, she could hear the noise outside coming towards her. The two men, their faces visible this time, features melted like something from a horror film, breath fetid. This time she wasn't going to go down without a fight. The confidence of seeing Fiona soared through her veins.

They grabbed hold of her arms, smashing her with promises of what they were going to do, the pain they would inflict with the huge hunting knife they pressed against her flesh. She fought with everything she'd got. Lashing out, kicking and screaming. The weight on her grew, but she was wild with adrenaline and terror. Kicking free, her hand slipped beneath the pillow and she slashed at the closest assailant.

A high-pitched scream rang out. Dominique's eyes flew open. She was transported back to reality. Only this time the blood hadn't disappeared like it usually did. It had stayed, running down her arms. Fiona was standing in front of her, wrestling with her as they stood in Dominique's bedroom at home. As truth sank in, Dominique realised she was holding something.

The carving knife she kept under her pillow for protection.

Shocked fingers sprang open. It dropped to the floor. Fiona, panting, glared into her eyes.

'Dominique. Are you awake? Are you okay?'

She nodded, slowly, as if still in a dream.

'What's happening?'

'It's okay… But we need to call an ambulance. You need to call an ambulance…'

Fiona sank heavily on the bed. Blood oozed from her side.

Dominique had stabbed Fiona.

The wound had turned out to look worse than it was. A few stitches and Fiona was fixed up. Dominique had needed some too – in the struggle to disarm her friend, Fiona had twisted the knife around and Dominique now sported two lines on her arm as a result.

The police had charged her with assault with a deadly weapon, but thanks to Fiona, along with expert testimony from Dr Madden and the London Sleep Clinic, she had been found not guilty.

The scars of both women had faded silver. What hadn't faded was Dominique's terror of knowing she had no control over her own body, and that she was capable of stabbing her best friend. She could so easily have killed Fiona.

After that, Dominique had retreated from the world, leaving behind her dreams of being famous and replacing them with a desire to stay at home and avoid stress. When she got together with Benjamin, it was perfect. A traditional man, he'd been happy she wanted to stay at home and raise children, and even in the years before she fell pregnant they had both been content for her to keep house.

❖

Now, though, Dominique's night terrors were back and she was scared of who she might hurt next. What if Dr Madden was wrong? What if she ended up like those poor people she'd discovered during her Internet search; people who had taken the lives of loved ones while they slept. The Christmas lights blinked at her, giving no answer as she wrapped her arms around her legs and tried to find the courage to go to bed.

What if, this time, she did kill?

# CHAPTER 77

No matter how hard he stared at the whisky in the tumbler, it refused to give Benjamin any magical solution to his problems. His jaw ached as if he had lockjaw, from it being permanently clenched. He opened it wide trying to crack some of the tension away.

He was in his study. Drinking. Again. Everyone else was in bed. He couldn't face joining Dominique there. Wasn't sure he could face her ever again. His grip on everything was slipping, and trying to keep hold of it all felt like trying to pin down water.

He sighed and stopped staring at the glass; instead, turning his attention to the ceiling.

A muscle in the far corner of his right eye twitched.

He was going to become a father again.

How could he even be sure it was his? It wasn't like Kendra didn't have plenty of time on her hands to have someone else on the go. Maybe she thought she was onto a good thing with him, that she'd struck gold. Over the years he had showered her with expensive presents, but only because he was trying to make himself feel vibrant by having a younger model on his arm and in his bed.

Now they were having a child. No, she was having a child. There was no 'they'. He should have ended things with her a long time ago, but he had become addicted to her, his hit of the elixir of youth. Both of them knew it wasn't a deep and meaningful relationship, though; he had explained to her as soon as he confessed about Dominique, four years earlier, that he would never leave his wife and children, and Kendra had accepted.

Still, he stared at the undeniably positive pregnancy test Kendra had gifted him, tied up with pink and blue ribbon. It sat on his desk, gazing back expectantly. Guilt stirred. He couldn't turn his back on a child of his.

Keeping it quiet from his family was going to be impossible. He was going to lose them, if not through this then because of his money woes.

In his mind's eye, he saw a huge countdown timer with red seconds of his life bringing him closer to zero. That was what he was going to be left with when all of this came out: a big fat zero.

If he was lucky.

For the first time in his life, Benjamin felt frozen with indecision and fear. He had always been the sort who acted on instinct, didn't need to think too much. He was a big believer in 'he who hesitates is lost'. Benjamin liked that attitude, it was one he could relate to. Usually. Not today though. He was on the ropes, no option but to throw in the towel.

Was there an obvious trick he was overlooking? A scam he could pull to buy some time? A deal he could land?

There were no options left.

All his hopes of where he would be by this age were shattered. As for the future, he would probably end up in prison, and be penniless when he finally got out. What would his kids – all three of them – think of him then?

Liquidating his assets by selling the house, flat, cars, jewellery, wouldn't happen fast enough. Plus, it would get him the money he needed for the taxman but not the rest of his debts, and wouldn't change the fact that he would now be arrested for fraud and embezzlement, and was facing prison time.

If he only had a bit longer, he was sure he could come up with something.

Someone was moving about upstairs. Creeping around. He chucked back the whisky he had been cradling, and swallowed hard as he stood, letting the fury at his situation leap to the source of the footsteps: that Harry boy. He must have come sneaking back here again. Benjamin would teach him a lesson he'd never forget.

⚜

Silent as death, he climbed the stairs without turning the light on. He cursed the fact he had moved the shotgun from his study to under his bed, but he didn't need it to deal with the skinny teenager. He couldn't wait to get his hands on the little scrote.

A figure was illuminated by the Tiffany lamp on the landing. But it wasn't the man-child Benjamin had been expecting. It was his wife, sobbing.

Her eyes were open but vacant. Poise, manner, expressions all seemed slightly altered, as though someone who looked identical to his wife had taken her place.

She was sleepwalking. Crying over some imaginary scene playing out in her head. Even as she looked at him, he knew it. It was nothing he could put his finger on, and yet he knew, as only someone who has known and loved that person for twenty-two years can know.

Benjamin's anger transformed into pity. He crept towards Dominique, as if she were a wild animal that might take fright any second and bolt away from him. She responded to the soothing sounds, her tears slowing. When she seemed ready, he gently led her back to bed. Curled up beside her, he murmured nonsense and stroked her hair until she closed her eyes and fell into regular sleep once more.

Sleep didn't come to Benjamin for a long time. He stared into the darkness, wondering what the hell he was going to do. There had to be an option he had overlooked.

# CHAPTER 78

What a waste. What an awful, tragic waste. What the hell had happened in the family to cause this? But Chief Inspector Ogundele knew there weren't always easy answers to such questions as why.

The team still worked to check the house for booby traps, other firearms and the like, then he could bring in the paramedics.

'We've another body out here,' came a shout.

The cop resisted the temptation to rub at his face in despair, but did heave a heavy sigh. He moved carefully but quickly to retrace his steps, then go through the house until he stood on the stone flags of the patio.

Only the closest of observers would have noticed his Adam's apple bobble momentarily. Even the most hardened officer couldn't help reacting to sights such as this, and Ogundele was experienced enough to neither beat himself up about it, nor show it too much to his more junior colleagues.

The body of a child, of around eight or nine lay, face up, eyes closed, as though in the middle of making a snow angel.

A firearms officer cautiously stooped over her, feeling for a pulse.

'Anything?' Ogundele asked. *Please, let her be alive. Please…*

A shake of the head. 'No, sir, nothing. She's gone.'

# CHAPTER 79

Jazmine had left her dodgy Dagenham roots behind many years ago, and worked bloody hard to do so. The only reminder was her accent. As such, it was easy to look at her delicate frame and forget her origins. But the fact was, Jazmine would never forget her childhood. She had learned hard but valuable lessons watching her family of criminals run the estate they lived on: who to trust and who not to when your life depends on it.

She had always had a soft spot for Benjamin. Beneath his cocky talk was a good man, with sound business sense. He pushed her to take chances; she kept his feet on the ground. They were close.

But she had a bad feeling. The instincts honed on the estate – which her family still controlled with patriarchal efficiency that sometimes required a spot of punishment – were screaming at her. Benjamin was hiding something.

He was twitchy and sweaty. He was getting brasher and cockier, and when men like that hid further and further behind bravado, it generally meant something catastrophic was on its way. Something they were terrified of.

And, of course, rather than acknowledge it, they went into total denial. Burying themselves further into the mire.

Problem was, if Benjamin went down he might take the business down with it. She wasn't going to let that happen.

Which was how she found herself in Benjamin's home, uninvited, at four a.m. on Christmas Eve. She didn't like that she had been reduced to breaking and entering, but if that was the only way to get to the truth, then so be it.

Benjamin's move into this house was what had really made her suspicious of her partner. Their business was doing well, yes, but the lifestyle he led was noticeably more opulent than her own. The watches, the car, now the house. Individually they could all be written off, but together they added up to a big fat pile of suspicion.

Benjamin was doing something dodgy.

For the past few months she had been trying to find proof to back up her instinct. She had checked his office, gone through everything with a fine-tooth comb. The more she had dug, the less she had discovered – which just went to prove that Benjamin was covering his tracks. Missing files, their own business accounts suspiciously unavailable for her to look at. She had started to dig deeper, and a fortnight ago she had finally discovered some discrepancies. Benjamin claiming money from HMRC on behalf of clients, but no evidence of it being passed on. The evidence dating back years – skilfully hidden but there nonetheless, if you knew what to look for and how Benjamin operated.

He was stealing. If he was doing that to the taxman, what was he doing to her?

She had a computer expert looking for files which had mysteriously 'disappeared'. Jaz was convinced Benjamin was up to his neck in do-do, and she was going to get covered in his stink. She had only asked Benjamin about the files that day to see if he had the cheek to lie to her face. He had.

Thanks to her dodgy past, Jaz knew a bit about breaking and entering. It had been a hobby her dad had encouraged until, aged twelve, she realised she wanted more to her life than being the next in line to a 'family business'. From that moment, she had trodden only on the side of the law, but now she was crossing a line by breaking into Benjamin's house. She had been ready to pick the locks, if necessary, but had discovered the latch on the downstairs loo's window was still broken – she had noticed it when she had come over back in July, and unsurprisingly, Benjamin still hadn't got round to having it fixed.

She crept through the house, to his study. No one stirred as she looked through paperwork, peered into drawers.

Finally, she found a crumpled piece of paper shoved into the back of the bottom drawer, hidden behind a bottle of expensive brandy. She smoothed out the letter and read it in the light of her torch.

Then crumpled it back up, nostrils flaring in anger

She was going to kill him. She was going to fucking kill him.

Jazmine realised she had taken a step towards the stairs, as if to confront him right there and then. He had completely screwed her over.

Now was not the time for confrontation, though. She needed to box clever.

As she slithered back through the window, she couldn't help thinking that her dad knew some exceptionally dodgy people; she could get someone else to kill Benjamin for a couple of grand, and her hands would be clean. No one would ever know.

Now that was a tempting thought.

❖

The duvet felt heavy and clammy on top of Ruby. The bedsheet beneath her was rumpled and damp. Shame flooded her as she wondered if she had wet herself. But the whole of her body was soaked, even the roots of her hair.

Sweat.

It was six a.m., and she knew she wouldn't get back to sleep. Fear stalked her constantly, but especially in dreams. There, she was naked of her mask of bravado and disdain, and terror's barbs cut all the deeper into her soul. Her nightmares were vivid, as though she had been flung into an alternative reality, or, even scarier, a future she had yet to live through, where her tormentors carried out their threats.

She needed Harry. Without him, the texts and bullying piled on top of her, suffocating her. The dreams overwhelmed her. She had to be with him, he was her lifeline.

But her parents had snatched him away from her, leaving her to sink.

She would make them pay for that.

She picked up her diary and wrote down everything she and Harry had spoken of the previous day. Putting the plan down in black and white made it feel more real.

Could she really go through with it? Scanning the notes gave her goosebumps. She did hate her family, she really did, but… But killing them was another matter. If they died in, like, a car crash or got run over or something, she wouldn't cry, she told herself. She wouldn't shed a single tear. She wiped at her face, removing the contrary evidence. No, if her parents just died it would be like fate stepping in to save her. But for her to actually murder them, and do the things she and Harry had discussed was a whole different level.

What about Mouse? She was so young. She hadn't meant to get Ruby into trouble. But there were more complicated things at stake with her. If Ruby were to end her little sister's life, hate would not be the driving force. In fact, out of everyone in her family, her baby sister was the one person she was most likely to murder.

If her courage held. She looked at the drawing of a lion Mouse had left under her doormat the other day. His slightly wonky, very sad face stared back at her. She kissed her fingers then touched them to his cheek.

Sometimes you have to be cruel to be kind, she told herself.

The sooner she and Harry went through with the plan, the sooner she would be free of fear and indecision at last.

Unable to resist, she picked up her phone and checked for alerts.

❖

The mattress moving beneath her woke Dominique. She opened her eyes just in time to see Benjamin disappearing into the bathroom.

He had four scratches across one shoulder. Clear as day even from across the bedroom.

The bastard was rubbing her nose in it now. She wanted to scratch his eyes out for what he'd done to his family. She could kill him.

Only for the sake of her children did she bite her tongue. All she had to do was get through Christmas, then she'd tell Benjamin exactly what she thought of him.

Exhaustion was making her feel crazy, though. Her eyeballs itched, and red threads draped themselves over the whites. There were so many things to worry about: Ruby's attitude, Benjamin's affair, his strange behaviour, and her own fears about what insane thing she might do next once the sandman took possession of her body. Sleep was hard to come by, not least because she was so afraid of it. When it did come, it wasn't restful.

Dominique pulled herself up until she sat on the edge of the bed. Her leg jiggled up and down, creating a judder reminiscent of a diesel engine ticking over.

# CHAPTER 80

Had he managed to sleep at all? Benjamin wasn't sure. There had seemed no difference between the darkness of his dreams and lying wide awake, staring into his unlit room.

Another of his hero, Ali's famous quotes sprang to mind. The one where he pointed out life was a gamble, and that people got hurt or killed every day in accidents – and winners simply had to believe it wouldn't happen to them. The boxer was absolutely right.

What a shame that someone so clever and sharp, such a great orator, had had to earn his living hitting people and getting hit. But what a gifted boxer he had been. And what an inspiration. That had been the only thing he and his father had ever agreed on.

The old man had never been satisfied with Benjamin; his son had never been good enough. Benjamin wondered what more he could have done. It wasn't as though his father's career had been that big a deal. He'd earned a good wage as a pilot, and it had always sounded impressive that he flew for British Airways, back in the day when that had been something to boast about. But he had never managed to make captain. Once, not long before he'd died, Benjamin had thrown that fact at his father's face, and realised first-hand what a very sore subject that was.

Just weeks later, he'd been dead. Everyone had thought Benjamin so generous when he had told Krystal and his mum to split his share of the inheritance between them. Kindness had been less of a motivation than the fact anything to do with his father sickened him. That was why his first flat with Dominique had been a freezing hovel. It hadn't taken long for Benjamin to work his way up, though; Dom deserved better than that.

Benjamin hadn't allowed himself to be defeated then, and he wouldn't now. He would keep on fighting.

The decision instantly birthed an idea. He knew exactly what he was going to do. With renewed vigour, Benjamin got out of bed, before even the magpie was up.

He hurried through breakfast, slurping down the dregs of his coffee as Dom came downstairs.

'Morning. Right, I'm off.' He gave her a peck on the cheek, looking at her only long enough to register she seemed in a bit of an odd mood. Presumably it was because of her weird sleepwalking.

❖

Confident and full of optimism, he drove to the tax office and got out of the car, eager to spot Bernard Bairden and get their little chat over and done with. In the freezing cold, his breath spilled out in front of him and filled the air like exhaust fumes. The street lamps were still bright, glowing in the gloom of the foggy morning.

Chalk figures hurried along the street towards the office Benjamin was staking out.

The atmosphere was erasing his confidence. The longer he waited, the more he stamped his feet not simply from cold but to stop himself from running. He slunk closer to the office and shrank into its shadow, suddenly ashamed of how low he was about to stoop.

Benjamin was about to throw himself on the mercy of a man whom he had baited for eighteen months.

Vehicles filled the car park. Finally, Bernard parked right in front of the building.

'Please,' Benjamin said, stepping from the fog.

The tax inspector fumbled his keys in shock and had to scoop them from a puddle. When he straightened up he was trying to keep the frown of annoyance from his face, and having only marginal success.

'Mr Thomas. This is a surprise. What can I do for you?'

'I've had your letter. Please, don't do this. Not yet. I've done nothing wrong, I swear.'

The look the inspector gave him made Benjamin squirm.

'Mr Thomas, I'm sorry, but you have had eighteen months to prove your innocence or comply. HMRC has no choice but to take action against you now.'

'You're making me sell my home. Think of my family, my kids – it's Christmas.'

'We have made careful calculations so that you and your family won't be left in dire straits. Obviously, you need to keep a roof over your head, and afford heating, food, all the necessities of life. But not an excess, I'm afraid. This is out of my hands now.'

'I could make it worth your while—'

'I'm going to pretend I didn't hear that. I'm going inside now. Goodbye.'

'You bastard, you're enjoying this,' Benjamin growled. Before he knew it, he'd stepped forward, fists clenched.

Mr Bairden's tone grew less reasonable. 'Abusive behaviour will not be tolerated. Bearing in mind you have spent money that isn't actually yours on the house and cars, I would say it is fair you have to get rid of them if needs must. And they must.'

'I don't have the money. My family will suffer for this.' Benjamin was begging again.

'I feel for them, I really do. However, it's out of my hands.'

A colleague walked over, hands in pockets, casual, but eyes sharp.

'Is everything okay here, Bernard?'

'It's fine. Mr Thomas here was just leaving. Weren't you, Mr Thomas?'

Benjamin gave a jerky nod that stuck here and there like a rusty piece of machinery. He had failed. As he walked away, his steps were heavier than lead.

'We could give him a bit of leeway, couldn't we? If he's a decent bloke,' whispered Bernard's colleague.

'If he's decent – but he's a complete arsehole. He's been arrogant, rude, and threatened me with a complaint a couple of times. I'm not inclined to bend the rules for someone like that.'

His colleague gave a huff that hung in the mist. 'In that case, call the bailiffs on him, they can clear his house out.'

❖

Bailiffs on Christmas Day, clearing the house out, snatching presents from the hands of his sobbing children. Dominique's expression one of complete disdain. Benjamin could see it all playing out in front of him.

Just a bit more time was all he needed. He could land a big deal, get the money, be a winner again. With just a bit more time.

But it had run out. What was he going to do now?

# CHAPTER 81

Another day, another text message. Or ten.

Ruby sat on her bed, gazing out of her window, trying to ignore the buzzing of alerts, but unable to. Each one was a piece of shrapnel she had to dig out of her soul, examine and discard. Some texts did put a smile on her face, though; the ones from Harry.

*'We can't surrender. If we surrender, we will never see each other again,'* he wrote.

It was them against the world, and Ruby had never felt happier.

*'We'll get rid of them all, then it will be just you and me,'* she texted back.

As she waited for his reply, she glanced out of the window, and spotted something strange under the sill. She got on her hands and knees, peered closer. It was a peacock butterfly hibernating.

She'd rip its wings off.

The teenager cradled the delicate insect in her hands. Felt its fragile wings flutter against her skin as it flashed its brilliant orange red display, and blue and black fake eye; there to strike terror into would-be predators. It barely tickled her skin, it was so light. Ruby braced herself, let the hatred and frustration fill her up and glared at the helpless creature. Gripped a wing between thumb and forefinger.

Let go.

Flicking her hand, she sent the beautiful insect flitting into the air, until it returned to its resting place.

She couldn't do it. She couldn't hurt something that hadn't hurt her.

Mum. Dad. Mouse.

The malevolence remained, though. The rage like a pounding drum inside her head. She would find another way to get rid of it. She might not be able to destroy something that hadn't hurt her, but she no such qualms about the people who had made her life a misery and brought her to this terrible point in her life.

As if in agreement, the phone chimed with a new message.

❖

Benjamin walked the streets in a daze. His heart palpitated; he was going to have a panic attack or a coronary.

Oh, no, it was his phone vibrating.

He pulled it out. Stared at the screen. Seven missed calls from Jaz. Ten from his PA.

They must have discovered the truth. Perhaps Bernard Bairden had made good on his idea, and sent the bailiffs around already. They would be stripping his office. His Montblanc pen would soon belong to someone else. Then they would arrive at his house and strip it like ravenous locusts.

❖

Jazmine put the phone down with a huff of frustration. She had tried Benjamin a dozen times or more and he wasn't picking up.

Stupid, really, to show him loyalty when he had shown her none, but she couldn't help it. She had wanted to speak with him one more time – to give him fair warning that she was going to call the police.

There was no other way.

Benjamin knew the law as well as she did. If one of the directors of a company ran off, leaving debts, the other directors would be chased for the outstanding money. She would, of course, argue she should only be responsible for paying half of the deficit at the very most, but it would be futile. HMRC would chase her for the payment in its entirety, even though she had not been involved in any way with the tax fiddle.

She would lose everything.

Unless, perhaps, she blew the whistle on Benjamin first. If she handed over the scant evidence she had gathered, conceivably, they would be a little more lenient with her and, hopefully, she wouldn't be prosecuted under criminal law.

Her hand hovered over the phone one more time, then moved away. She wouldn't call the police.

She pulled on her coat, and told her PA she was going out and wasn't sure how long she'd be. Her last thought as she left the building was that she could quite happily swing for her so-called partner.

# CHAPTER 82

Benjamin wasn't sure how long he had been walking. He realised with a start that he had left his car in the tax office car park. Well, it would be theirs soon enough, so there was no point going back to get it. He looked around, trying to get his bearings, but he didn't recognise the street or its name.

His phone rang again. He ignored it. When it stopped, he pulled it out and stared at it. Screwed up his courage and dialled voicemail. Instead of ranting messages about his secret shame, his PA and Jaz were worried about him.

'Just call me, Benjamin,' his partner begged.

Her concern made him feel like crap.

Even more like crap.

He still wasn't going to answer the phone, though, because he had absolutely no clue what to say. Pretending to be his usual, cocky self was impossible.

Benjamin hated being out of control. He needed to find a way to wrest it back somehow. How? Thoughts and fears whirled round his mind faster than a rotor blade. All his options had been closed down to him.

There was one person who might, just might, be able to help him out:

The Russian.

Benjamin thought of the dodgy rumours Jazmine had warned him about. He'd heard a load himself but reckless desperation had driven him to try to woo Vladimir Tarkovsky. Officially, the

Russian had refused the business proposition, but Benjamin had an alternative proposal.

Through the fog, he saw a familiar orange glow coming towards him and stuck his hand up to hail the black cab.

'Southwark Street,' he ordered.

Benjamin's destination was the Blue Fin Building, an edifice named after the 2,000 blue aluminium fins covering its outside. It stood at the back of Tate Modern, in the heart of London's South Bank, reaching to the sky like an eager child with all the answers. Renting office space there must have cost Vladimir an arm and a leg – or someone else their limbs, if rumours were to be believed. Benjamin tried not to be intimidated by the impressive double-height entrance, huge lobby, and floor-to-ceiling windows. He stood in the middle of the hangar-size lobby and looked up. The view was vertiginous. The architects had left a donut-like hole through the centre of the building, so he could see all the way up to the ceiling right at the top of the building. Surrounding him above were gleaming, glass-fronted balconies.

There was still time to change his mind.

Only, of course, there wasn't.

Up to the second floor the desperate man went, trying to slide on his mask of charming arrogance. There were so many cracks in it now that someone was bound to see the truth.

Shoulders back, head high, hands in pockets to add a casual air. He was as ready as he would ever be. Show time.

❖

The receptionist on the second floor looked wary when Benjamin tried to blag his way in, though.

'You don't have an appointment,' she kept insisting.

'He'll want to see me, just tell him who it is,' twinkled Benjamin. Nothing. 'You know what? Don't tell him. On your head be it.'

He started to walk away.

Smiled as he heard the PA pick up her phone and dial. A swift conversation later, and he was ushered inside. He tried not to look too smug as he walked past the secretary, but he couldn't resist tipping her a wink.

The Russian was gazing out of his window, but turned as soon as his unexpected guest walked in.

'Benjamin. What a pleasant surprise. Have you come to invite me shooting again?'

Benjamin shook Vladimir's hand; a two-hander of confidence that encased his new best friend's paw with both of his – and gave an all-important glimpse of that expensive watch. The one which helped Benjamin land deals and impress people.

'I'll cut straight to the chase,' Benjamin smiled. His successful business persona slid into gear as smooth as a sports car. Against all odds, he was in control again. 'I've got a great business opportunity for you. You have a finger in every business pie but accounting. Thomas & Bauer are expanding. Instead of us looking after your business concerns and you becoming one of our clients in the normal way… how about becoming a silent partner?

'It's a surprise, I know, Vladimir, but hear me out. We've got a lot of very exciting opportunities heading our way next year, and we would love you to be a part of that.

'I'll be honest, right now we need an investment of cash to make those dreams come true – but they are going to be stellar when they do. I thought I'd give you first refusal. You've an incredible reputation, and that precedes you in everything you do. I think this could be the start of a fascinating partnership that will be mutually beneficial.'

And breathe.

Benjamin held the Russian's gaze. Forced himself not to break eye contact.

'I'm not interested,' Vladimir said.

The words seemed to slip to the floor and shatter as Benjamin looked on, helpless.

'Have a think, get back to me in twenty-four hours. Business-men like us don't stop working just because it's Christmas,' he tried. He was met with a firm shake of the head.

'If that is all, Benjamin, I must be getting on.'

'Wait, wait, wait.' He wiped at a trickle of sweat running down his temple. Forced a smile. 'Wait. How about we come to a more personal arrangement then – a – a loan. I've heard you offer certain people loans, under certain conditions.'

A smile as wide as a shark's grew beneath Vladimir's porn star moustache. 'You have been listening to too many tall tales about me, my friend. Imagine for a moment they are true – do you think I am a fairy godmum who waves a magic wand to give people money? There has to be a chance of repayment, and you have the stench of desperation pouring from you.' He pointed at Benjamin's forehead, tracing the progress of the traitorous bead of perspiration.

The Russian leaned in. The men's faces were intimately close.

'I think you would find my terms of business a little… back-breaking. Particularly given the rumours I have heard about the taxman – yes, I do not contemplate giving someone my business without first doing a little digging. I suggest that tomorrow you hand back all the files you have on us, and you do not contact me again. Otherwise, I will not be a happy man.'

Benjamin swallowed and stepped away. Nodded quickly. 'Of course. Yes. Thank you for your time.'

# CHAPTER 83

'Yay! It's Christmas Eve; Santa's coming tomorrow!' Mouse eyed up her presents as she drew breath. 'Could I open one now? Please, Mummy? Pur-lease.'

Mummy carried on staring into the kitchen sink. She didn't even seem to realise Mouse was there.

Everyone was in such a stinky mood. It wasn't supposed to be like this. Everyone was meant to be happy, and make snowmen – although it wasn't snowing – and sing carols. Maybe if she sang some carols… She started to, but Mummy rubbed at her head and said she had a headache.

'You're so grouchy. I don't think Santa should bring you a present,' Mouse huffed.

She was sick of her family ruining her Christmas. Mummy probably had a headache because of all the shouting the day before. That was why Ruby was in a stinky mood, Mouse knew. She hadn't meant to get Ruby in trouble, but it had been such a surprise seeing Harry there that she hadn't even recognised him. Now her big sister wasn't speaking to her. She wasn't speaking to anyone, and had hidden herself away in the bedroom.

This was a rubbish Christmas.

It better not get any worse, or she'd start telling people exactly what she thought of them.

# CHAPTER 84

Every step up the garden path of his home took all of Benjamin's strength. The hordes of hell seemed to be hanging onto his limbs, trying to drag him down with them, he felt so heavy.

He was going to tell Dom everything. He had no choice. It was all going to come out anyway.

She was in the kitchen, arms up to her elbows in suds, hand-washing the delicate glass bowls which were a family heirloom she had inherited from her grandmother. Every year she used them on Christmas Day, in memory of the beloved gran she had been so close to.

Would she have to sell them?

It was all his fault.

The guilt wrapped itself around his petty heart and squeezed off the blood supply until it turned black. He cast his eyes around the kitchen, trying to find the words to explain what he had done, but all he found was more guilt, more anger, more failure.

He spied a pile of shopping bags. His blood pressure rose.

'You've been spending more money? It doesn't grow on trees, you know, Dom.'

She turned. Gave him a look full of disdain. She was trying to make him feel small. Bitch.

'Oh, hello, Benjamin. I didn't hear you come in.'

'More crackers?' He continued as if he hadn't heard her, pointing at the boxes of festive treats. 'Why do we have to have so many? Why do we have to have them at all? They're so pointless. The hats and the crackers are so clichéd, and nobody can honestly believe these things make people laugh. It's another piece of boredom.'

'They're for Mouse—'

'Amber—'

'She loves them. And I'm sorry if they bore you.' Her whole body seemed to stiffen, as if about to suffer some kind of seizure, before she spoke again. 'I know you're having an affair, Benjamin.'

She had said it. For all her good intentions of holding it in until after Christmas, for the children's sake, Dominique had failed.

She wasn't sure why she had chosen now to say those words. Perhaps because she liked the crackers and at that moment they seemed to symbolise every difference, large and small, that the couple had. Perhaps she was sick of being the hypocrite Ruby accused her of. Perhaps, simply because the washing-up gave her an excuse to look elsewhere, so she didn't have to meet Benjamin's eye as she exploded the lie their life had become.

She stared hard at the soap suds, fascinated by them, as she spoke the words again, to prove to herself that she had the courage.

'I know you're having an affair.'

'What on earth are you talking about?' he said, voice calm. 'Is this one of your funny dreams?'

The thump of hurt and resentment her heart gave made her flinch, but she carried on dabbing at the fragile glass bowl she was holding. It sparkled as she lifted it, the delicate carvings seeming to come to life for a moment as the light played across them.

She forced her voice to be as calm as his. She needed to bring the ice queen out.

'No, it's not one of my dreams, Benjamin. You aren't married to an idiot – unfortunately for you.'

'For goodness' sake, do you not think I have better things to do than discuss your vivid imaginings? I'm going out.'

'Back to work?' she spat. 'Poor you, having to work all those long hours.'

'You really don't appreciate anything that I do, do you? Eh? All the hard work I do to keep this family going, to buy you the perfect house, a decent car, and clothes, get your hair done every week. You and the kids have a bloody awesome lifestyle because of me, and not one of you ever shows any gratitude.'

What?

Usually, Dominique would be caught on the back foot by a comment like that. Not today. Today she lost the plot.

'How dare you? How bloody dare you accuse me of not appreciating what you do? I say thank you all the time to you, for all the hours you work, for providing for us. Do you ever listen to me, Benjamin? When was the last time you acknowledged the work I do holding this family together? Or thanked me for creating a comfortable home for you and the kids? You didn't acknowledge the Christmas decorations that took all day to put up; you completely failed to notice, and only grunted when I pointed it out to you. You certainly expressed no gratitude for me pulling out all the stops when you decided to invite Heidi and James here at the last minute. You hypocrite!'

Benjamin stood his ground but from the way he pulled his chin in, she could tell her words had knocked him for six. It wasn't enough. She beat her hands down in frustration, creating tidal waves of suds that slopped all over the counter.

'Is that your excuse for sleeping with someone else, Benjamin? Because I didn't say thank you enough?' She flung her arms up, jazz hands, mocking. Rivulets forming down her arms and dripping off her elbows as she turned to him full on, eyes blazing so hard he actually leaned back. 'Shall I dance my gratitude, Benjamin? Would that be enough? Ooh, I'm so very, very grateful to you for everything you've ever done for me. Thank you, thank you, thank you, for pretending to work long hours while actually having it away with someone else.'

'This is bollocks. I'm out of here. See you when you come to your senses.'

'When was the last time you showed me any love, Benjamin? When was the last time you put your arm around me?'

The recollection of him tenderly leading her to their bed when he found her on the landing, flashed in her mind.

She turned back to the sink, and her hands dived into the water, grateful of the escape from this awful scene. If only the rest of her body could follow, she wished. But she held onto the anger in order to stop guilt taking over.

'Once Christmas and New Year are over, I want you out. Until then we will keep up appearances for the children's sake. We'll sit them down together on New Year's Day and tell them we are splitting up.'

'Oh, happy bloody New Year. Are you kidding me? Get a grip, Dom, you've finally lost it. You're not taking my kids away from me. You're a wreck, you're dangerous around them. Who knows what you'll do in one of your crazy dreams. You know what? No one would blame me for having someone else on the go, not once they heard how deranged you are.'

Benjamin turned on his heel. Dominique heard his footsteps receding hurriedly.

She took a deep breath, then another and another until her heart slowed from painful thumping. There was no triumph at finally telling the truth; and victory over Benjamin was hollow because it signalled the break-up of her family. Her bare feet were soaked from the water that drip, drip, dripped over the counter edge still. Knowing no one else would take care of it but her, she whipped a couple of tea towels off the rail, got on her knees, and mopped up until the only trace of the argument was the slightest sheen on the terracotta tiles.

# CHAPTER 86

Mum had got the shakes again. Bad, man. Harry took the glass away from her before she chucked the whole drink down herself.

Harry's mum had Parkinson's, which doctors described as a progressive neurological condition, and he described as a total bastard. There was no cure, no magic bullet to make everything better.

His dad had apparently had a good job down on Angerstein Wharf, something to do with cement or whatever, but Harry wouldn't know as his dad had walked out on them when he was six – when his mum had given birth to his twin brothers, and she had started to exhibit the first signs of Parkinson's. She had worked at the big supermarket on the tills until she got too ill and had to leave. There had been complaints, because people thought she was drunk. Although the supermarket had stood by her and done their level best to keep her on, it had got too much for her.

Many people, Harry knew, managed to maintain a very good quality of life despite their Parkinson's. With her typical luck, his mum wasn't one of them, though. The condition had taken a brutal toll on her, and now she had trouble swallowing and slurred her words. She had barely any strength, was constantly knackered. Sometimes she'd sweat like a druggie going through withdrawal, but most of the time she was freezing, which was tough because they couldn't afford to have more than one bar of the useless electric fire on most of the time. Instead, Harry bundled her up with a duvet.

The days of her being able to cook, clean, or look after her family were behind her now. She tried hard not to let it get her down, Harry knew, but sometimes she was depressed. Like, proper depressed: staring at the walls and crying non-stop and saying everyone would be better off if she died. That she wanted to die. He hated it when she talked like that.

Harry did his level best to hold the family together, but it wasn't easy being Mum and Dad to his baby bros, and carer to his mum, when he hadn't even yet turned sixteen. Sometimes he felt like screaming, or running away, or both. Sometimes he wanted to die, too.

There was no time for friends, or homework, or anything else. He'd had nothing until he'd met Ruby. Then he had made time because when he was with her, the world felt different. Better. Even with all the crap that happened at school and those bitches making her life a misery, he felt happier.

But now her parents were threatening to call the Feds on him if he had anything to do with her. That was not cool. He didn't know what to do. Yeah, it was kind of fun blowing off steam about how great it'd be to kill the entire world, but what the hell were they really going to do? He didn't want to be without his girl. She was the only thing in his life where he felt free to be himself.

'Son, I – I need to get to the toilet. Can you help me? I'm so sorry.' His mum's face sagged with shame as she spoke. It ate him up inside that she was reduced to this. And it made him angry that he was the one who had to do everything for her.

He put her arms around his neck and carried her to the loo. Stayed outside, door open a crack, as she did her business. But all the time he thought about Rubes.

She really didn't mean it when she said she was going to kill her family and herself. Did she?

Maybe he should stop her.

Maybe he should join her.

# CHAPTER 87

In the fading light of the afternoon, Benjamin stalked to the Prince of Wales pub, overlooking Blackheath's open heath. The place was rammed with people celebrating. Spontaneous renditions of 'Merry Christmas Everybody' broke out every now and again. One set of blokes was particularly keen on doing a screaming Noddy Holder impression – to much eye-rolling from the bar staff.

He didn't want to spend his afternoon there, but where else could he go? There was nowhere left to run. All options exhausted. He settled at a table in a corner as far from the singers as possible, and sank into an armchair. He popped a couple of antacids: thought and crunched, crunched and thought.

The look on Dominique's face as she had told him about Kendra plagued him.

He didn't understand how she had found out. He thought he'd been so careful, with a separate SIM card for contacting his mistress. The paperwork for the flat he had bought and now 'rented' to Kendra was well hidden. Being an accountant, he took care of all the family's finances, so there was no way Dominique could have stumbled across anything. The pregnancy test lay in his pocket. So where had he slipped up?

He had intended to confess all as soon as he got home, of course. And the confrontation between him and his wife had been the perfect moment to tell Dominique everything. Instead, he had panicked and picked a fight, defaulting to his position of complete wanker. The knowledge made him hot with guilt and anger all over again.

It was Dom's fault, though. Taking him by surprise like that, he'd felt ambushed. After that there was no chance he could tell her about the financial storm heading their way.

Anyway, she had no right, no right at all, to lay down the law. Did she think she could take the house from him? The kids? If she thought she and her pal Fiona could clean him out in a divorce she'd be disappointed with the results – unless she wanted the shirt off his back.

His fingers drummed on the table, its surface tacky with drink spilled by a previous occupant.

He couldn't lose Dom. He couldn't cope.

What would people say? They would think he wasn't a real man; a real man could keep his family together.

The way she had looked at him as though he had let her down. It was her fault. If she had been a better wife he never would have looked elsewhere – he wouldn't have had to.

Dominique was still beautiful, had a great body, and was intelligent. She would find someone else. Take a new lover, fall in love, even. The thought of another man's hands on her made Benjamin furious. No way was he going to ever let that happen. He'd die before that happened.

She would die before he let it happen.

She was not going to steal his family from him. Why did she assume the children would be better off with her?

Because he was going to be in jail soon.

He shook his whole body free of the thought, dog-like.

No, he was not going to let anyone else take anything from him. He would not lose control of his family. He would do whatever it took to keep his family together. Dominique couldn't be trusted anyway, not with this weird sleepwalking business. She was dangerous. What if she hurt herself or the kids?

If she did, Benjamin's money worries would be over. There was that thought again. A lightning strike of selfishness. It was true, though. He and Dominique both had generous life insurance policies.

He barked a laugh. Just to show himself he was joking. A sick joke, but just a joke.

As if he'd ever hurt his family.

The family Dominique was going to steal from him.

She'd find someone else. She'd turn the children against him. He would be in jail and disgraced, unable to fight back.

He ordered a double whisky on the rocks and thought the unthinkable. The pub's walls seemed to be closing in. He couldn't lose his family, too. He needed to take back control. He needed to keep them with him. No matter what it took. If that meant them all being together in death, then so be it. He'd be showing the world, shouting from the grave: 'Look at me. Look how powerful I am.'

The thought was so strong that Benjamin found himself growing hard. He shifted to accommodate the growing erection, his hand lingering on himself for a little longer than necessary, marvelling at the reaction he had produced. Feel that. That was how strong he was. Proof positive that he was a real man. The Man.

A real man killing the people he loved.

It was ridiculous. Unthinkable. His penis curled up, a snail retreating into its shell of shame.

But he didn't mean it. It was purely an abstract to occupy his mind.

If he were going to do it – which he wasn't – he would get it over and done quickly. Like ripping off a plaster. He wouldn't want anyone to suffer. This was simply a way of them all being together and happy.

If he didn't do it then the kids would lose everything anyway. They'd be picked on, laughed at, face the humiliation of having a loser jailbird as a father. They'd have to live in some slum, owing rent to a dodgy landlord who'd rip them off. Barely enough money to afford to eat or heat the place. Every day a slog. He couldn't do that to them. It was kinder this way.

Not that he was actually going to do it.

He could use the shotgun. It would be quick. Painless. Relatively. Perhaps he could chloroform them all first, so they would have no idea what was coming, no chance to feel fear. He wasn't a monster, after all. He couldn't stand the thought of hurting them. No, he'd be sending them to a better place, where they could all be together for ever, and happy.

That was a nice thought, actually. All the worry and pain and arguments would be over. They would all be together, at peace.

What if the rifle was too long for him to be able to shoot himself?

Maybe he could take a load of tablets first, enough to kill him, but he'd have time while they worked to do what needed to be done with his wife and children. Then, if he couldn't shoot himself, he would simply drift away and join his family anyway.

The thought of going to sleep and never waking up comforted Benjamin.

Around him, another rousing chorus of 'Merry Christmas Everybody' started up.

# CHAPTER 88

Jazmine was exhausted. She sat in her office, head in her hands, trying to get her mind around everything. Her business partner's Christmas present to her had been to embezzle thousands, perhaps millions, from their partnership. Hers to him had been to go to the police and blow the whistle. She had given her statement and they had begun the process of investigating.

'It may be several days before anyone is ready to speak with Benjamin, as we need time to gather solid evidence before arresting and charging him,' warned the officer who took her statement.

It was four p.m. She had been back from the police station for over an hour and couldn't face going home. She just wanted to be alone for a while, and the office seemed as good a place as any, even though it was Christmas Eve.

She thought of their excitement when she and Benjamin had set up the business. They wanted to be more customer friendly, more dynamic than rival accountancy firms.

It had all turned to dust thanks to greed.

The door opened, making her jump. Three large men entered, all wearing suits. Behind them was an even larger man.

Vladimir Tarkovsky.

'Forgive my intrusion,' he said, not looking the least bit sorry. 'A very merry Christmas to you. I will keep this brief, so that you can return to your celebrations.'

If he noticed the lack of celebration and cheer, he didn't give any clue.

'Mr Tarkovsky, what an unexpected pleasure. I would prefer it if you made an appointment—'

'What I have to say is brief. I understand that you have been to the police regarding certain concerns you have.'

She recoiled. How the hell had he discovered that – and so quickly? He must be seriously connected.

'You understand that the last thing I would ever want, a man in my position, is to be linked to anything illegal. I am a good man, and the thought of something like that horrifies me. So, my men are going to take all of my files now, and everything that may connect me to your business.'

'I'm not sure—'

'Aren't you? I was sure you would be. I dread to think the repercussions of being caught up in such a scandal – and not only for your business… for family members also. Terrible.'

With the connections he clearly had, he could make anything happen – and make sure it was covered up. He was more powerful than her own family, by far.

She stepped back, nodded, and sat down. She knew better than to argue.

But inside, she was fuming. What the hell had Benjamin got her involved in? Dealing with corrupt Russians and thinly veiled threats; was her life now at risk as well as her business and reputation?

She let the men clear all traces of Vladimir Tarkovsky from the office, and prayed it was enough to save her skin.

# CHAPTER 89

Ruby was on the phone to Harry, trying not to shout. Keeping her voice to a whisper so no one would realise she was talking – which was pretty hard when they were having their first ever row.

'What do you mean, you can't go through with it? We planned it?' she hissed. 'You're just like everyone else, you're not there for me at all. I can't believe you've let me down.'

'Ruby—'

She ended the call and stared at the phone. Hurled it across the room. It fell into three parts, the front coming away from the back, and the battery flying loose. No great loss there. She let it sit where it was, broken in pieces, like her heart.

Fine, if Harry wouldn't help her then she would do it alone. Yes, she wasn't sure herself, but that wasn't the point – she felt betrayed. She wanted the world to open up at her feet and for her to slip through the cracks, leaving pain behind.

⚜

Kendra couldn't stop pacing. Ben had disappeared since she'd told him they were having a baby, the night before. It was Christmas Eve; she refused to spend another festive season alone. She grabbed up the bottle of cheap red wine that was sitting on the coffee table, already half empty, and the glugging noise of the liquid emptying into a goblet made her feel only slightly less tense. She took a swig, which turned into several, bitter tannins coating the back of her tongue. Better. Wiping her mouth with the back of her hand, she tried to talk herself down from the nervous energy buzzing around her body, urging her to take action, to do something, anything. She couldn't just sit around waiting patiently for Ben any more. She had started her plan and now she needed to finish it.

'*Where the hell are you? I need you!*' she texted.

But if he came around right now, he would smell she had been drinking. He'd realise she was lying about the pregnancy.

Dawn had been a real pal: stealing the positive test from the maternity ward where she worked, so that Kendra could give it to Benjamin. She'd told Dawn it was to test Benjamin's reaction, and her friend had gone along, saying better to find out his attitude now than when there really was a baby.

Stuff it, if he turned up she'd suck on a mint. As she finished the glass, she did exactly that, and sprayed freshener into the air, and perfume all over herself for good measure.

More pacing. Time passing. No reply from Ben.

She tried calling him but only got voicemail. She sent more texts. Some calm, some hysterical, some argumentative, trying every variation in desperation of getting some kind of response from him.

But there were no replies. Her grand plan to trick Ben into leaving his family was failing. She spent the whole afternoon texting as her impotent rage boiled over.

# CHAPTER 90

Dominique knocked on Ruby's door, trying not to feel intimidated by the *'Keep Out'* sign's beady-eyed glare.

'I've got food,' she called. 'It's almost half four, you've spent the whole day in your room. It's Christmas Eve, Ruby, don't you want to spend some time with your family?'

An indecipherable mutter was her only reply.

Dominique predicted her daughter would spend the rest of the day holed up in her bedroom, and not appear even to eat. She would leave some food outside the door and something to drink, but Ruby was renowned for her stubbornness and may not even take that much from her mother. Instead, she would lurk in her bedroom, filling the house with a mist of resentment so thick that Dominique could almost see it, could feel it filling up her lungs and choking her.

She wished she had the luxury of being able to throw a hissy fit and take to her room for a day. But there was too much to do; the cooking, the cleaning (yes, she had a cleaner, but it was amazing how untidy the place got with two children and two adults in the house), playing peacemaker. It was exhausting, draining. Quitting for a day was tempting.

She snorted a laugh, imagining everyone's reaction. Benjamin would be furious on principle, Ruby would...

Ruby would what? Probably be glad that her mum wasn't around to get in the way of her plans.

Even Mouse would probably just read for the day, if Dominique weren't around to look after her.

Her little girl wouldn't be little for much longer. Once Mouse reached the difficult teenage years, Dominique's role as a mum would lessen, she was sure. Ruby certainly wanted as little as possible to do with her these days, and Amber was bound to follow suit. The thought of missing a moment of her childhood by hiding in bed made Dom's heart sink.

Sometimes she felt like the only thing her family needed her for was to feed them. That, and stand between people in arguments, always trying to play the role of diplomat, always absorbing the insults and fury flung at herself or others.

She was going to have to step up, she realised. Her family was slipping away, but that was partly her own fault. Watching it happen and sighing in sadness about its inevitability served no positive purpose at all.

Time she stopped letting life happen to her, and started making some positive decisions. Time she took an active role in her own life.

Did that mean leaving Benjamin? That this would be their last Christmas together? The thought made her soar with lightness and shiver with fear all at once.

Benjamin's words from the argument haunted her.

'Is this one of your funny dreams?'

This wasn't one of her dreams. Was it? No, she was certain that she had truly experienced that awful moment on the street when her husband's mistress had confronted her.

When she and Benjamin had first got together she had been dazzled by him, had followed him like a flower follows the movement of the sun. He was strong and protective, but gave her space to flourish and build confidence in herself again.

Now she felt like a shrivelled-up bloom, parched and stunted.

She wondered if Benjamin's lover was thriving under his love now. Did this Kendra woman know Benjamin as well as she did?

That his confidence was a disguise? Did she realise that, for all his outward appearances, he wasn't materialistic at all?

What drove him to buy the latest gadgets, to have a big house, and good clothes was the need to look after and nurture his family. They were everything to him. This was the soft side he only showed to her and the children. He wanted to give them everything because he was a good man. A man who really did work long hours; she knew that much because she had seen it herself. She worried about his health, drinking too much, eating rich food, rarely having time to exercise. He gave that business everything he had – so that in turn he could give his family everything. He still had a chip on his shoulder about never quite measuring up to his own father's high standards, which made him constantly feel a failure in comparison.

The affair was a terrible betrayal. But intuition told her there was something else going on, too. Perhaps she should talk to him, try to find out what and see if she could help him.

Or she could leave him to his own stinking mess, because he had betrayed her and the children in the worst way possible.

The latter sounded a lot more appealing.

Even if she and Benjamin split, she wasn't the type to stop worrying about him, though. She had vowed to love him for life, and even now she knew she would never completely stop.

As she pondered, it hit her. The only thing that really, truly got to her husband was his business. Something must be wrong with it to be causing his volatile behaviour. Perhaps it was losing money.

If that was the case, she didn't care. So what? It was lovely to have a comfortable life but she wasn't bothered about trappings. As long as her family was together, it didn't matter if they had spare cash.

She realised what she was thinking. She was willing to fight for her marriage.

A roof over their heads was all they needed. They could downsize easily, and move to a far cheaper area that was still nice – they had paid £1.75 million for the house and that had been six months ago. Property prices had risen again since then. Benjamin could get a different car. Stop going to his gun club and golf club. Even if the kids only received half of what they had requested for Christmas, it would still be loads. And as long as they were all together, healthy and happy, that was enough.

If only she could get Benjamin to see that.

If only she were absolutely sure that the family she had in mind would include him now. Could she really forgive him for cheating on her for four long years?

It was a big question, and one she needed to take her time answering.

# CHAPTER 91

When Benjamin got home, he disappeared straight into his study, then came out and tramped around upstairs for a couple of minutes. Each creak of the floorboard filled Dominique with the urge to call him to her. They should set aside anger and denial, and talk; see if they really had anything left to save, see if Benjamin was even interested in trying. But she rolled her neck and vowed to keep a stoic silence until she stopped vacillating about her own feelings.

When Benjamin reappeared, he followed her lead, not saying a word. He made Dominique a cup of her favourite fruit tea. No mention was made of the argument. By either party. Dominique sipped the scalding lemon and ginger drink, lost in thought.

❖

After a frankly torturous half hour with Dominique, where she hadn't even bothered thanking him for the cup of tea he'd made, Benjamin retreated to his study. He had hoped he would find the courage to speak with her but, of course, he hadn't. He'd hoped she might have something further to say to him. He even would have welcomed another row. At least it would have shown she cared. But she hid in silence he had no courage to break.

What was he going to do without Dom?

She believed she knew everything. She had told him she was taking the children. If she was angry about Kendra, she'd be furious about the money. He really ought to tell her, but his courage was curled up and hiding alongside his shrivelled manhood.

Benjamin was filled with remorse for the impotent rage he had felt, blaming Dom for his shortcomings. How could he even for a second have thought that if she had been a better wife he wouldn't have looked elsewhere? She had always been patient and kind and honest. She had stayed true to him and put up with his temper, his endless hours at work, the fact he only paid her attention when it suited him.

Shame flooded him.

The truth was, he hadn't dared to tell her what a failure he was because he had never felt worthy of her. He had thought it from the first time he had ever properly spoken to her: that night when they got separated from their mates and his sister. He hadn't been able to believe he had managed to miss for so many years how amazing she was, but he had promised himself he would never take that for granted again.

But, like the complete idiot he was, he had done exactly that.

She was as faultless as a diamond, in his eyes. Unlike him. Over the years he had hidden his failings, first behind a veneer of confidence, then behind fancy watches and clothes, material things he hoped would detract from the man rotting behind them. The smaller his self-esteem shrank, the more impressive his window dressing had become. It had to be, to fool the world – and himself.

Even taking a mistress had been to shore up his sagging façade. He had needed to feel young and virile again. But he didn't love Kendra and never had; all he had done was use her for four years.

Now he risked losing Dominique and his children over his affair. What an idiot he was. Dom had been fooled for a while by him, but now she was starting to see him for what he really was. At last, his mask had slipped.

The children had never been taken in, though. Children lack guile, and seem able to strip it from others. Like animals can sense fear in someone, an infant can spot a liar. From the moment Ruby had been born, Benjamin had felt a rush of inadequacy and terror that he blamed her for, when it was really all his fault.

She would be better off with her mother, free from him. They all would.

Look what he had done to his poor eldest daughter. He had skint himself sending her to that school and expected her to grovel with gratitude. Growing up, he had learned the hard way that it was who you know not what you know that can often get you far in this life, and he wanted things to come easy to his children. He wanted Ruby to achieve without struggling. But he had never bothered telling her that, had simply expected her to realise, and fall in with his plans. He had utterly failed to take into account his own child might have hopes and fears of her own, or struggle to achieve everything he had mapped out for her.

He thought of his own father, and how he himself had railed against the plans his dad had for him, and how he constantly felt a failure as a result. It had been he who pushed Benjamin into accountancy. His dad had bullied him his whole life, told Benjamin that he wouldn't amount to anything, even hit him sometimes in the name of 'toughening him up' – 'boxing lessons' he had called them, telling his son to be more like Muhammad Ali.

He realised with horror that he was treating Ruby the same way. He had put impossible expectations on her, and told her to 'toughen up' when she tried to tell him she was struggling. The blows hadn't been physical, but it made them no less hurtful.

His selfishness took his breath away. For Ruby's entire life he had demanded everything be done his way, never bothering to think what she might want. Benjamin had always told himself that he knew better than them what they needed. They were ungrateful for not recognising all he had done for his children, he had thought. No more. Now he needed to put them first. It was a revelation to him. The thought left him feeling giddy and light-headed.

Finally, he knew exactly what he must do.

He would kill himself, sacrificing his life so that he could stop dragging his family down with him. The shame and money troubles would end with his death – he was worth far more dead than alive.

He wished he could tell Dominique that she was the love of his life. He longed to go back in time and never mess up. If only he could somehow win her and the children back. He really did want to be Ruby and Amber's best friend; to get to know them, and let them get to know a better him, rather than the self-absorbed, shallow idiot he had become.

But it was all too late now.

The only gift he could give his family was freedom.

# CHAPTER 92

Perhaps Harry was right. Perhaps Ruby needed to rethink.

She sat on her bed fiddling with the puzzle of her phone until the broken parts slotted together. The screen lit up, and she went to send a text to Harry.

But she couldn't help seeing how many alerts she had from social media.

She shouldn't open them. She should ignore. Stay strong.

Her thumb moved anyway. Like she had no control over it. Her eyes read. As if they had a life of their own. Her brain rebelled and screamed. But her body was silent as it absorbed the pain.

*'Slut. Whore. Smelly. Bitch. Fat. Stupid. Ugly. Freak.'*

These were her gifts. The texts were the worst. The messages from an unknown number that had become so familiar to her now that even when she closed her eyes it seemed tattooed on her lids. Blazing; goading her.

*'Everyone would celebrate if you fucked off & died. Even your family hate you.'*

Ruby tried to dam the tears with closed lids. Breathing slowly, until she had control. She knew what she had to do. She refused to suffer any more.

No more bullying. No more pain. She chose freedom. And when she went, she would make sure she was not alone.

There, the decision had been made.

Ruby felt strangely calm. For the first time in many years, she was peaceful. She brushed her hair free of knots. Pulled out her nose stud. Replaced her skull top with a plain jumper.

Went downstairs.

❖

'Merry Christmas, Ruby,' shouted Mouse, hugging her. 'Want to pull a cracker? Mummy says we can pull one today.'

'Why not?' she nodded.

Mouse won, eagerly putting on the paper crown. Her little sister, who would soon no longer be part of this world. She could be annoying, but she was so innocent and quirky. Could Ruby really hurt her, let alone take her life? Surely not.

'Why did the turkey join the pop group?' read Mouse.

'I don't know.'

'Because it was the only one with drumsticks.'

Even Dad laughed. He seemed more relaxed than he had in months. Ruby looked around and mentally said goodbye, feeling strangely fond of everyone when she had thought she would be filled with burning anger and hatred. She had learned in geography about how volcanoes are at their most dangerous and most likely to erupt when they have been dormant for years. The pressure building inside them, but the outside giving no clues, until one day the force could no longer be contained. A deadly explosion. That was how she felt now. This was the calm before carnage.

Tomorrow would not be a problem. Tomorrow she would no longer feel pain. Everything would be gone, and the peace she felt right now would last for ever. Not just for her, but for everyone. She couldn't wait.

✤

Mouse climbed into bed, cuddled Ted and screwed her eyes tight shut. She'd had such a lovely night, with all the family together exactly the way she had hoped. Tomorrow was going to be brilliant.

Now, she had to go to sleep, otherwise Santa wouldn't come. She hoped she'd been good enough to get her iPhone, and books.

She was too excited. No way was she going to ever sleep again.

But then she wouldn't get any presents.

A great big sigh of frustration shook her little body, and she turned on her bedside light. She would read for a while, even though it was almost ten o'clock.

She was a fast reader, the best in her class, and had already reached her favourite bit of *The Last Battle*. The bit where everyone was dead, but happy they were dead.

With each blink, her eyes took longer to open. The book fell to one side, but she didn't move. Mouse was fast asleep. In her dream, Aslan walked beside her, telling her to have courage. She wrapped her fingers in his golden mane and felt his courage tingling up her arm and filling her up.

'I'll try to be a brave girl,' she promised.

✤

Dom lay in bed, thinking. Thumped her pillow, turned it over to the cold side, and settled onto it once more, hoping sleep would come, but her thoughts refused to quiet.

What was she going to do?

Ruby had seemed better tonight, at least. There had been a glimmer of her old self; she was more relaxed, even smiled a couple of times. Hopefully, she was accepting that not seeing Harry was not the end of the world. She didn't need that boy.

But did Dom need Benjamin?

No.

She did want to save her marriage, though. For the sake of the children, and past good times, she was willing to try if Benjamin was. She thought of her family. Seeing Ruby smile for the first time in ages; the squeak Mouse always gave when excited or scared; even the desperation that had made Benjamin's voice hitch during their argument. She studied them all, and smiled. Perfect in its imperfection, it was worth fighting for. She had spent too long hiding away from reality.

Her marriage might still fail. If it did, she would walk away guilt-free, knowing she had done everything in her power to save it. The rest was up to Benjamin. Hopefully, he would put in the effort, too. If not, that was his decision.

But he had seemed different tonight, more like his old self. It gave her hope.

She would tell Benjamin in the morning. She would tackle everyone about their secrets and get them out in the open. She would fix her family.

She turned over, happier now, and went through the ritual of playing the dream through her head. Determined there would be no nightmare.

The noise was laughter. Ruby was wearing a red dress. The rifle was a broom…

# CHAPTER 93

Ruby tidied her bedroom. Silly, really, because it didn't matter and she certainly wasn't doing it to get out of yet another row with her parents. But it helped order her mind and make her feel more prepared for what lay ahead.

Clothes neatly folded. Keys left on her bedside cabinet, along with the 'Book of Hate'. A box stuffed with all the printouts was at the foot of her bed.

On her knees lay another box, this one filled with family photos of happier times. Drawings from Mouse of characters from her favourite books: Matilda, Oompa-Loompas, the Wicked Witch of the West, Aslan. Tickets to concerts her parents had taken her to. Birthday cards filled with meaningless messages, because words were so much easier than actions.

When had their love turned to disinterest?

Ruby felt like the most hated girl in London.

She had called Childline once. She had read on a poster at school that in the past year it had received almost 19,500 calls from children with suicidal thoughts. A mere 0.6 per cent of the NHS's budget was spent on children's mental health. It had made her burn with fury at the time, but now there was nothing left but ash and warm embers.

Did she have the strength to carry her plan through alone, she wondered. Or would this be one more failure to add to the list? She moved the shoebox of memorabilia from her lap and pulled something else onto it.

Dad's shotgun.

Everything was ready except her.

She sat without moving for a very long time. Long enough for her to grow stiff and uncomfortable.

Her phone buzzed like an angry wasp.

Finally, she moved.

❖

Imminent death focused Benjamin's mind. The whirling and panic had stopped. No need to reach inside the cabinet in his study, and have another drink. He felt lighter than he had for years, after shrugging off the mask that had been weighing him down.

He would write a letter apologising to Dom, Ruby, and Amber, and explaining everything. But what about Kendra, and his unborn child?

He kept forgetting about Kendra's pregnancy, thanks to everything else on his mind. That spoke volumes about his feelings for the young woman. But what of this third child of his – someone he would never meet if he went through with his plan to commit suicide.

Not if, when.

When he died, Kendra would lose her home, because he owned the property she lived in – or rather the bank did. She thought he paid her rent, had no idea he was actually her landlord. Just another lie of his to add to the mountain of untruths. Kendra would be left with nothing, like Dominique. The knowledge of what he had done to her made him hang his head in despair. He stared down at the leather of his antique desk and gave a shuddering sigh.

He didn't love Kendra, he never had. He had used her as a prop to shore up his ego. Soft young puppy flesh to make him feel less like the middle-aged sad act he'd become; she meant little more to him than his fancy watch or car, another appendage with which to impress people and prove what a winner he was in the game of life.

What a complete shit.

The pink and blue ribbons tied around the pregnancy test grew grubby from his repeated worrying at them. For a moment, he allowed himself to imagine the child: a mixture of Ruby and Amber. He wished he could stick around to see it, to find an alternative way. It wasn't an option. Instead, he had to explain to Kendra how sorry he was for leaving her literally holding the baby. This was his only option, though; the question was how he was going to make her realise it.

*'Dear Kendra,'* he wrote. *'By the time you read this, I will be dead.'*

His Biro paused over the paper. Was that too melodramatic? But there was no point beating about the bush, he might as well tell her immediately. He had no idea what else to say. Read the line again. A tear trickled down his nose, and he wiped it before it could splash the paper.

*'I'm not the man people think I am. I've done so many stupid things, and got myself into a lot of trouble. Despite the bravado, I'm a coward. I can't cope with the pressure. I'm so sorry for letting you and our child down.'*

This was not a time for holding back. Benjamin told his mistress everything, just like he would later confess to his wife. When the note was finished, he sat back and nodded. He felt better for getting it out. He was by no means doing the right thing by Kendra, he knew that, but at least he was leaving her an explanation. Now he only had to deliver it.

He listened, to check if anyone was awake, but no sounds came. The clock chimed midnight and he realised with a start that it was Christmas Day. No one heard the door click shut behind him.

# CHAPTER 94

Ruby shifted the shotgun across her lap and stretched towards her phone. It lit up like a festive decoration, there were so many new alerts arriving. She ignored those, and instead went to messages and started to type.

*'I'm sorry we argued. I love you always & 4ever. It feels good knowing you will go on living without me, cos the thought of you dead kills me. I wish things didn't have to be this way, but there's no other option. Goodbye oxoxox'*

She pressed send, knowing that by the time Harry read it in the morning, it would be too late.

Then she turned the phone off for good. Set it beside the 'Book of Hate'.

*Today's the day. I'm going to kill them all. I hate them. I hate them. I hate them,* she wrote.

She underlined the words, pressing so hard the pen almost shredded the paper. Did she really hate them, though? She wasn't sure any more. In fact, she felt like she was trying to persuade herself.

It was time to go through with the plan. So why couldn't she make herself move?

Drops of water splashed onto the shotgun's burnished grey muzzle. Ruby looked up at the ceiling to find the leak – then realised she was crying.

She turned the page of her book and scribbled something else. After a few minutes, she had said what had to be said.

Like it or not, she knew exactly what must be done, and lifted the rifle in readiness.

❖

Benjamin wiped at the tears. His dad would have told him he was pathetic, but finally Benjamin didn't care about him. Creeping up his driveway towards his home, the moon and the cold white streetlights silvered everything. The harsh illumination gave him the look of a cadaver, wrinkles etched deep on his face. He held his breath as he eased through his front door, wishing he could move as quietly as Santa Claus.

Mission accomplished. Well, half, at least.

There had been no sound of movement from Kendra's flat when Benjamin had slipped the note under her door. She would find it when she woke, by which time it would be too late. In his mind's eye, he could imagine her seeing it, becoming excited, thinking it was a present, opening it and being broken-hearted. He had done that to her and there was no shirking his responsibility. If he could go back in time and relive his life, he would have steered clear of Kendra, so that she could be free to find someone her own age, someone who would treat her well, love her properly, and settle down to give her a family. Those were things he could never give her. Not even if he lived.

Time was up. He had reached the zero hour. He had contemplated waiting until Christmas was over, for the sake of the children, but he didn't dare, in case he ran out of courage to act. The memory of their wonderful evening together of laughter and games burned bright, leading him towards his final destination. For them, he would find the strength to do what needed to be done.

In his study, he took off his Rolex and dropped it in the wastepaper basket. Then pulled out the old Sekonda his wife had bought him all those years ago, for their first Christmas. Turning it over, he read the inscription.

*Time for love*

Ran his thumb over the engraving, as if feeling it as well as reading it would help bridge the intervening years. He nodded as he fastened the strap. Paused for a moment and sniffed hard, then once again started writing; this time, to Dom. His hand shook.

❖

Harry stared at the message from Ruby, and his heart hurt it was beating so fast and so hard. He read it again, forcing himself to go slowly, in case his rush led to misinterpretation.

She was going to kill herself.

No way could he let this happen.

He checked on his brothers. They slept peacefully in their bunk beds, despite the excitement of Santa coming to bring them second-hand clothes and third-hand toys.

His mum was on the sofa, sleeping soundly, too. Her forehead smooth of worry, mouth free of the pinch of pain it so often wore.

No one would be disturbed by him sneaking out.

Harry pulled his coat on and hurried into the night, determined to save his girlfriend.

❖

Benjamin sat at the desk in his study. He had written and rewritten the letter to Dom and his children. It had taken hours. He'd had to abandon writing it by hand because the pen shaking with emotion made the words illegible. Using the laptop seemed cold and impersonal; yet another decision Benjamin regretted.

Finally, at around 2.30 a.m. he was ready to do what had to be done. He had spent the last hour tidying it, wanting things to be neat somehow, to order his mind. He didn't want to make things any worse for Dominique than it was going to be.

Really, he knew he was shuffling papers trying to put off the inevitable.

The first aid box was in the kitchen, on a top shelf out of habit, even though the children were too old now to be at risk of thinking any medication was sweets. Benjamin opened it up and took out the stash.

A full packet of ibuprofen. That should do the trick. Plus, four paracetamols, and a handful of sleeping tablets prescribed to Dominique a while back, but she'd never finished the course.

Carrying them back to his desk, he laid them out in front of him. The first pill felt abnormally large on his tongue. He gagged, body rebelling against intention, saliva filling his mouth. Forced himself to take a huge swallow of his favourite, ridiculously expensive whisky. Coughing and spluttering, the pill finally slid down. The next was easier. The third time, he grew bolder, swallowing a handful at once.

Every tablet in the house sat heavy in his stomach. All he needed to do now was wait. He hoped death would be peaceful, and that the sleeping tablets would mean he could drift off and never wake.

The study door was slightly ajar; he must remember to close it before his time was up. But for now, he wanted to sit down. Just for a moment. He'd get up in a minute.

His head lolled back, his breathing growing deeper and slower.

He was a selfish coward for taking this route. He knew that, and the knowledge only made him feel worse. Made him even less likely to swerve away from his destination. He wanted to die. At home. Surrounded by his family.

If only he could go back in time and change things, he would. If he could show his family how much he loved them, he would. If he could be given a reprieve, Scrooge-like, so he could live as a changed man, he would. But it was too late, he thought, as he stared at the ceiling, limbs growing heavier.

His fate was sealed. It was too late to turn back.

# CHAPTER 95

Something woke Dominique. A noise. She stared into the darkness, listening, instantly on high alert.

Benjamin wasn't beside her. Where was he? He was never here.

The noise came again. A strangled sob.

Was she awake? Was this a dream? Dominique wasn't sure. The clock read 3.45 a.m., but she didn't trust it. She tried to take control. To turn the noise into laughter, to turn her fear into hope.

It wouldn't happen.

She pulled the duvet back, felt cool air rushing over her body, making her shiver.

It felt real.

Planting her feet in the thick carpet, she concentrated on its texture. Warm, firm, authentic.

She rubbed at her eyes, then stood, pulled on a dressing gown. Heard the sound again, but still couldn't place it.

Was someone in the house? About to hurt her and the children?

She fell to her knees and felt under the bed. Her fingers didn't come into contact with cool metal. She bent down, peering. There was no sign of the shotgun.

By the door, she hesitated.

She didn't dare open it.

Ruby lying in a pool of blood. Someone had killed her. Who? Why?

But that was a dream, and this was reality. She was sure it was reality.

She stood straighter, threw her shoulders back. Nodded in determination. Then opened the door.

There was no one on the landing.

The noise seemed to be coming from Ruby's room. Had she got that boy with her again? Had he found a way to climb up to her room again, despite Benjamin ripping down the trellis?

Dominique pressed her ear to her daughter's door, unsure of what to do.

No, the noise was of crying. Heart-rending sobs.

Her poor little girl. What on earth was wrong?

Dominique rushed to hold her eldest tight and tell her everything was going to be okay. She threw the door open, not waiting to knock.

# CHAPTER 96

The door flung open, making Ruby jump up in shock, automatically gripping the shotgun, scared. Raised against her shoulder the way she had seen her father use it, the gun seemed to grow suddenly much heavier. One finger was on the trigger, the other steadied the barrel, which was wavering.

Her mum's eyes looked like they were about to bug out of her head in shock. Hands up in surrender.

'Ruby, what on earth…? Put that down right now.'

That familiar, imperious tone. Ruby had had enough of being ordered around.

'Shut up, and sit down. From now on, I'm in control. I mean it; it's loaded.'

Her mum blinked rapidly several times. The sight made Ruby feel stronger.

'Okay.' Her mum spoke slowly, and moved even slower. 'Shall I sit on the bed?'

Ruby nodded. Adrenaline had well and truly kicked in. She had the shakes; the length of the shotgun bouncing around. It was so bloody heavy.

'You're in control, Ruby. But I'd really like you to tell me what's brought all this on.'

She snorted her reply. Hilarious. 'You really are as utterly clueless as I suspected. You've no idea, have you? Here, read this, maybe it will give you a clue.'

With nothing to hide any more, Ruby shoved her diary at her mum, whose eyes ran over the black lettering.

'The "Book of Hate"?'

Ruby thought she could hear amusement in her tone. With some effort, she managed to balance the shotgun one-handed against her shoulder, leaning back slightly to hold it steady, while with the other she thumbed through to the entry she wanted.

'Careful,' her mum begged, but Ruby continued anyway.

'There.' She pointed at the underlined words screaming from the page.

'Today's the day. I'm going to kill them all. I hate them. I hate them. I hate them.'

Dominique's hand trembled as she held it over her mouth, as if trying to force back a scream.

*Not so funny now, is it, Mother?*

'Why?' The question was little more than an exhalation.

'Because my life is a living hell, and you haven't even noticed. This,' she tapped her finger on the page, sending the barrel of the shotgun jerking around again, 'is what I've been pushed to. I can't take any more.'

Her mother's eyebrows drew together sharply. Confused. 'Because of Harry?'

'No. For fuck's sake, keep up, Mum. Harry is the only decent thing in my life. He saved me.'

'Saved you? What…? I don't understand.'

'Saved me from this.' Ruby pushed the shoebox of printouts towards her mother with her foot.

Dominique lay the 'Book of Hate' down on the bedside cabinet again, open at the page she had been reading, then bent down. Ruby watched her leafing through bits of paper. Lingering at first. Then faster, faster, faster, shuffling them in disbelief, eyes growing wide.

Finally, she looked up. Ruby recoiled. Tears made a mirror of her mother's eyes, reflecting Ruby's own pain. Her mum cared? She hadn't expected that. Hadn't expected her mum's agony to open her own soul's wounds again, weakening her as her hurt bled out.

Ruby wouldn't allow herself to be taken in, though. Her mum was surely pretending, to save her skin. Wasn't she? Anger began to slide away, replaced by equally familiar companions: confusion, hurt and hopelessness.

Dom shook a handful of papers at her.

'I didn't know. I'm so sorry... How long? How long have you been dealing with this?'

She didn't wait for an answer, delved into the shoebox, searching for a date. She missed Ruby's shrug. Didn't notice her daughter sinking to the ground to sit cross-legged, the rifle still standing to attention against her shoulder. It was starting to sag, though. A wave of exhaustion washed over Ruby.

'It started years ago.'

'When you went to boarding school? You changed then...'

'No one would have anything to do with me. I thought it would stop if I moved schools. But then Harry and me were beaten up and one of the people filmed it – a girl from my old school, called Poppy.'

Dom's eyes narrowed. 'I remember Poppy.'

Ruby's laugh was short and wry. 'Yes, she's the sort of girl everyone remembers. Little Miss Popular.'

'Hang on, why did she beat you up? And when? I'd have noticed if you were wandering around with a fat lip.'

'You didn't. Most of my bruises were on my body; I wore long sleeves. A bruise on my cheek was hidden under make-up.'

A hand flew up. 'Wait – that's why you and Harry started wearing all that gothic stuff? Eyeliner and,' the hand waved, as her mother tried to think of a phrase, 'and everything.'

It must have been the only polite word she could think of. Ruby knew how her mother and father felt about her make-up. They had never bothered talking to her about it, though, just nagged and shouted.

'That's right; I didn't want anyone to see the bruises. It was something to hide behind.'

There was no point in trying to disguise the truth any more. Not now, when Ruby was so committed to death. And she was, she reminded herself. There was too much at stake for her to change her mind and choose cowardice. Let her mum know everything. It made no difference.

Mum gazed at her. 'I thought it was Harry leading you astray with the music and the weird make-up. I'm so sorry.'

There was that word again. Ruby's anger sparked and sputtered.

'You're only sorry now it's too late; now I have a gun.'

Her mum didn't even glance at the shotgun, continued to hold her daughter's eyes. Ruby looked away first.

'Why did you keep all of this? Was it to show me and your father? To give to the police?'

Ruby sighed, a huge sigh that shook her whole body. The shotgun's barrel sank to the carpet.

'At first, it was evidence compiled against everyone. I thought if I got enough to prove who was behind the comments, texts, calls, then I could show you and Dad, and it would stop. They'd be punished... But as time passed... well, it became evidence of something else.' She shook her head, trying to see through the tears. 'It's absolute proof that I'm a hateful, awful person. I must be, because everyone thinks it.'

'Love—'

'No, Mum; the constant insults from everyone would only happen if they were true. Every time someone new meets me, I let myself hope, but every time, they end up agreeing with the bullies. The printouts, they're to help me work out why I'm so awful. But

I can't figure out what's wrong with me, Mum. I'm broken and I – I can't be fixed. I've tried, but I can't do it.'

Ruby caught a movement. Jerked away as her mum tried to come towards her, arms open for a hug. She couldn't deal with that. With someone's fake sympathy.

Mum got the hint, settling back onto the bed but leaning forward as if trying to close the physical distance between them. That wouldn't change the emotional gap, though.

'Is it that Poppy girl? We can go to the police; they can find the proof to prosecute her.'

'No, Mum. It's everyone. Everyone hates me. What's the point of prosecuting Poppy or anyone else when they are always replaced by someone else who hates me just as much? For a few wonderful weeks, when I changed school, I was happy. Then people at my new school saw Poppy's video; she didn't need to do anything else. Someone else took over – a girl called Jayne is the worst. She made sure everyone at school saw the video. Now, she sends me texts and even set up a vile website about me. She doesn't use her proper phone, she uses a different one when she sends me texts. They're constant. I can't sleep because they're all night—'

'Jayne's the one you hit? Well, turn your phone off. Come off social media.'

'You don't understand.' Ruby's head and heart pounded. The shotgun snapped up with her temper. Hard and unforgiving, like she should be. 'I knew you wouldn't get it. Ignoring the messages doesn't make them go away, Mum. Ignoring it just means everyone is still slagging me off, but I have no idea what they're saying. It doesn't change the truth. I'm a freak – why deny it?'

'And so you… you want to kill us all? Really, Ruby? I know you don't mean that.'

'Keep reading the "Book of Hate", Mum. Read the last thing I wrote.'

# CHAPTER 97

Harry lifted the broken catch on the window in the downstairs toilet and eased himself through it. He stuck. His jeans pocket was snagged on the latch. Wiggling from side to side, he fought panic and rising claustrophobia. He mustn't get caught in this situation. He needed to reach Ruby and talk some sense into her. If anyone could get through to her, he could. Talking about slaughtering everyone they were angry with was all well and good, but actually doing it? No chance.

No one was dying tonight. Especially not Ruby.

On the way over he'd repeat dialled her. All he'd got was a message saying her phone was unavailable and to try again later.

He needed to get to her – fast.

Another frantic wiggle. He pulled and pulled and pulled and yes! It gave, making him lurch forward. He slithered onto the toilet. Good job he was skinny as a whippet because otherwise there was no way he would have got through. In a few years' time, he knew he would have broad shoulders like his deadbeat dad, but right now he was still slim from shoulder to hip, long-legged and a little gawky in his tight jeans.

Good job, too, that the loo seat was down and he was able to put his hands on it and twist around until he was standing right way up.

Tensing every muscle, he waited, not daring to breathe. Had anyone heard him? There were no telltale creaks of floorboards, no sound of footsteps.

❖

A maelstrom of emotions threatened to tear Ruby apart as she watched her mum reading the 'Book of Hate', full realisation hitting her. Ruby hadn't wanted this complication, not after she thought she'd found clarity and peace.

Before her mum had burst in, while sitting on her bed, crying, she had realised that, for all her anger at her parents, she couldn't hurt them. Ever. Truth was, she loved them to bits – even if they didn't love her. Ruby wanted only to die herself. To slip away quietly, peacefully, and have the pain finished once and for all.

That was the last thing she had written in the 'Book of Hate'. She had apologised for all the other terrible things written inside the notepad, and promised that she hadn't meant any of them. She had told her family how much they meant to her, and that the happiest moments of her life had been when she was with them, and with Harry.

*Please forgive me for being so difficult. I'm so sorry to have to say goodbye this way, because I know it will hurt you, but I've no choice. Goodbye.*

Now, watching her mother reach the end of the farewell note, and the pain it inflicted, Ruby was horrified. But she knew she couldn't face living another day.

'I'm a freak,' she repeated. 'I can't go on.'

'Let me help you, Ruby. Please. I have let you down so badly. But let me help you now. We can get through this, together.'

Her mum was begging her. The usual tone, the distance she always kept between herself and her daughter, had disappeared. Perhaps it was an act; after all, her mother had betrayed her before, had said she would be on her side against Dad and that Ruby would be able to leave the private school. She didn't know what to believe. Mum sounded so sincere.

Her mum's warmth melted her resolve. Ruby began to rock, cradling the gun now, the only solid, reliable thing she could cling to. She needed the pain to stop. She needed her mum to shut up! Ruby's thoughts were becoming a confusing whirl and she couldn't seem to grab onto a single one and hold it for more than a second.

'No, no, I don't trust you. And you'll send Mouse to that same school. You've got her a smartphone for Christmas, Mum. She's only eight, and you're opening her up to a world of hate. She's weird. She reads all the time and says odd things, and is way older than she should be, but way more childish, too. She'll get torn apart out there, cyber bullied non-stop. I – I've tried to toughen her up, for her sake, but she doesn't get it – she keeps drawing me bloody pictures to cheer me up, when I'm a total bitch to her. Think what the bullies will do with someone that soft.

'I love her to bits, and the thought of someone hurting her kills me. I have to protect her, no matter what. I have to save her from the same pain I've suffered. That's why I thought it would be better if... if she... if she died before the torture starts. But now I know the only way to save Mouse is if I kill myself. Then you'll take more care to protect her.'

❖

Harry crept through the house, hoping that no one was up yet and he would get to Ruby in time. Through the kitchen he went, the dining room, the living room, past the entrance of Ruby's dad's study...

Jeez! Her dad was in there.

Harry froze, giving a sharp intake of breath. Benjamin's own breath caught, then sighed out. Phew, he was fast asleep. His head slightly back, mouth open a tiny amount. He looked dead to the world, his breathing shallow. Despite the circumstance,

Harry couldn't help grinning when he thought of how shocked Benjamin would be if he woke and saw the teenager standing over him. The yell of surprise he'd give. He'd wet his pants, for sure. It was almost worth it for that.

But no, Harry had far more serious things to do than scare Mr Thomas. Moving even more cautiously now, Harry slipped through the darkness. It wouldn't be long until everyone started to stir to open their presents. He didn't have much time left. And this had to work. It had to. He and Ruby were soulmates, meant to be together. He couldn't let her hurt the people she loved. If she did it, the best-case scenario was she'd be locked up for life; in which case, his mum would probably never allow him to see her again.

The worst-case scenario was that Ruby would kill herself after the massacre. Harry couldn't live without his girl.

As he crept along the landing, he had a sudden thought. Mouse. She was always into everything, always hanging around. What if she heard something? He couldn't risk her overhearing what he was going to say to Ruby – and also, he couldn't risk the kid getting hurt if he couldn't stop his girlfriend from her killing spree.

He tiptoed over to the youngster's bedroom door, wondering how he could block it. It opened inwards, so putting anything against it was useless. He saw the nail poking out of the doorframe, pointing at him accusingly, and had an idea. Tugged the shoelace out of one of his boots, then wrapped it around the protruding nail and the doorknob. That should keep it secure.

⚜

Mouse's eyes flew open. She'd heard something. She was sure of it. Was someone sneaking around?

*Santa.*

Grabbing her teddy, she slipped her feet into her slippers, thought for a moment, then kicked them off again. She could move around more quietly if she had bare feet.

Hugging Ted tightly, she padded over to her door. Placed her ear against the cool wood and listened. Was that someone out there? She dropped to her knees and peered through the crack under the door, trying to see if she could make out a shadow moving.

There. She was certain she had seen something. She strained to listen and, yes, there it was, footsteps.

She waited for the person to move away, counted to ten to be certain, because she didn't want Father Christmas to know she was awake, then turned the door handle. But the door wouldn't budge.

Fear shivered through her. Until she remembered her dream, which had seemed so real. Aslan had wanted her to be brave.

So she would be.

# CHAPTER 98

Why hadn't Dominique known something was going on with Ruby? Why had she been so eager to write it off as simply her 'being a typical teenager'? The guilt weighed her down. Shock, too. She couldn't get past Ruby's words.

'The only way to save Mouse is if I kill myself.'

Dominique was a mum, it was her job to see what was happening, to realise. It was her job to look after her children. She hadn't, too busy getting her hair done and choosing the right carpet, ornament, top, whatever. Too busy worrying about dreams to see reality unravelling.

Dealing with something of this magnitude, though, left her utterly clueless.

She swallowed, trying to free the words that refused to come.

'Sweetheart,' she said, finally, 'I know you want to spare Amber the pain you've felt but, Ruby, darling, this isn't the way. There are other ways to end this torture – and protect you and your little sister.

'I know you believe that your father and I don't care, but think about it: what is the meaning of my life without my kids? When I'm on my deathbed, I won't be looking back on all the nice houses I've lived in, the clothes I've worn, the designer stuff I've owned. None of that matters. What matters is being able to look back on a life filled with love. What matters is you and Amber, and knowing that I have raised you well, loved you with all my heart and always done right by you. And if I have let you down then I am so, so sorry.'

Dominique felt with all her soul that she had just one shot at winning her daughter over. The words came out in a rush, straight from the heart.

'Let me make it up to you, Ruby. Please. I don't deserve any favours from you, I know, but give me the gift of a fresh start. Let me get to know you again. Help me to be a better mum, and protect you and Amber, and be there for you both. I want to, sweetheart, with all my heart. I'm devastated that my shortcomings as a mother have led to such unbelievable hurt for you. I will never forgive myself – but I'd like to spend the rest of my life trying to make up for it, and perhaps, one day, gaining your forgiveness.'

Ruby stared down the barrel of the quivering shotgun.

Dominique tried again. 'I know these are only words, but give me a chance to show you with deeds how sorry I am. Darling, together, we can all learn from this and protect Amber, and—'

'Mum, I just want you to love me…' Ruby broke down then. A vulnerable little girl, all the hard mask rinsed away by the tears.

Dominique couldn't hold back any longer. She threw the 'Book of Hate' onto the bedside table, where it fell open. Rushed forward, not caring about the gun, not caring about anything but that her eldest daughter was in pain. She gathered her into her arms and hugged her tight, kissing the top of her head. Ruby stiffened, then softened against her mother's body and let herself be loved for the first time in a very long time. Too long.

'I love you with all my heart, and all my soul – you must always believe that, Ruby Thomas. I will never, ever let anyone hurt you again. I'd rather die than let that happen.'

She whispered fiercely into Ruby's hair, stroking damp strands away from her daughter's face as she spoke.

'We'll find out who is at the bottom of this bullying. With all the evidence you've got, the police will find it easy to trace the perpetrators. They've got special officers for dealing with this kind of thing. We'll make it stop, and somehow, I will make it up to you for all the hurt I have inflicted on you by not listening, not being there. We'll find your smile again.'

Ruby sniffed and shook her head. 'No, I've got an ugly smile. Everyone tells me that. Except Harry. He thinks it's beautiful, but he's not all there.'

'Well, I agree with Harry. And in the morning, I'll call him myself and let him know that you and he can see as much of each other as you want.' As long as there really was no funny business, she added silently. But if Ruby told her there wasn't, then she believed her. From now on, she would be listening to her children.

Ruby's arms tightened around her.

'Y-you really don't believe those things then, Mum? That I'm evil and stupid and smelly and… You really love me?'

'Oh my God, Ruby, you are my life. There are no words to describe how much I love you.'

She put her hand under her daughter's chin and eased it up so she could look her in the eyes.

'Do you believe me, sweetheart?'

Ruby gave a wobbly smile, and tears started again. 'I do, Mum. And I love you, too. I'm so sorry for the horrible things I've said—'

'You've nothing to apologise for.' Dominique enfolded her once more in a hug.

❖

Benjamin was starting to feel sluggish and queasy. His stomach gurgled. He'd nip to the loo, then go back to his study, close the door for the final time. He should write another note, too, to pin to the door, warning everyone not to come in, but instead to call the police. He'd have to do that as soon as he got back. He didn't want his wife or children to have to deal with seeing that sight of him dead; it would stay with them for ever.

But first, he really must go to the loo; his stomach hurt and his head pounded. Maybe things were happening faster than he had anticipated. His stomach contracted again.

He walked towards the downstairs toilet, steadying one hand against the wall. Cursed, remembering that it wasn't flushing. Dom would have to call a plumber. Perhaps he should add a reminder to his note, but it sort of ruined the impact of what he wanted to write…

With a sigh, he tried to work out what was best to do as he made his way upstairs, trying to tread lightly so he wouldn't disturb anyone. The stairs wobbled in his vision. Lifting his feet was tiresome. Maybe he should sit down, just for a minute. He was almost at the top; only a few more steps…

Harry stood before him, his hand on the doorknob of Mouse's bedroom.

What the hell? Was he abusing her? Was he trying to burgle them? Murder them in their beds?

Fury punched adrenaline through Benjamin's body. He must protect his family. With a roar, he rushed forward.

# CHAPTER 99

Ruby felt as if she were melting. The hard shell of anger she had constructed was dissolving.

Her mum loved her. Her parents loved her. They were going to make everything better. And Mouse would be safe, too. All the anger and bad thoughts she had hidden behind, trying to convince herself that she was tough, drifted away from her like snowflakes in a breeze. She had never wanted to hurt anyone, let alone kill them, the planning had simply been acting out. The only life she'd wanted to take was her own, but now… now, perhaps, she could see a happy future.

The nightmare was going to be over soon – and she could even see Harry again. She wrapped her arms tighter around her mother, still gripping the shotgun awkwardly between them. Everything was going to be okay.

There was a shout outside. Her dad, roaring unintelligibly in anger.

Ruby leaped free of her mother's clutches, swinging the shotgun up and around on pure instinct.

❖

Harry fought with Ruby's dad for all he was worth. He didn't want to hurt him, so tried only to defend, not attack.

'Get out of my way!' he begged. 'You don't – ow! – understand—'

An elbow to block a blow. Raising his knee to ward off vicious kicks. Harry kept shouting, kept trying to explain that he was attempting to help. But the old git kept lashing out and he didn't have the chance to be heard.

He got Mr Thomas in a headlock. A jab to the kidneys made Harry yell, and loosen his grip. Kicked at the man in anger. His lace-less boot slid off his foot and flew through the air, hitting Ruby's dad on the shoulder with a soft thud then bouncing who knew where. It didn't slow Mr Thomas; he was huffing like a steam train, but didn't seem to be giving up.

If Harry didn't get past him soon, things were going to end in disaster.

'Listen—'

Another punch.

❖

Mouse stood in her bedroom, scared. She clung to Ted, hoping he would make her brave enough to know what to do.

Shouts came from outside her bedroom. Banging, crashing, and Daddy's voice raised in anger. He sounded furious. Her heart thundered. She scurried towards her wardrobe, flinging the door open and staring at one of her favourite hiding places.

No, she couldn't hide away. She had to warn Ruby that something bad was happening, even if Ruby used bad words at her like she usually did. Sometimes she really hated Ruby, but that was because she loved her so much, too.

Giving the hiding place one last longing look, she started to shut the door, then had a thought. Gave Ted a final hug and kiss before settling him in, and covering him with a blanket.

'You stay here, I'll be right back when it's safe. Don't make a sound,' she whispered.

Ted gave her a long hard stare of agreement. That made it easier for her to block out the shouts and icy fear. Feeling reassured that Ted would do as he was told, she closed the door on him, then opened her bedroom window wide. The early morning air made her shiver. She'd get cold feet, and then Mummy would tell her off. She slipped on her slippers once more, then sat on the windowsill and eased herself out, as she had so many times in summer.

⊹

Dom heard shouting and scuffling. Ruby looked terrified, reduced momentarily to the child she had been before she disappeared beneath the mask of warpaint. The shotgun bumping against Dom's side as Ruby jerked from her embrace.

'Ruby, please. Just hand me the gun.'

Myriad emotions flashed kaleidoscopically over the teenager's face.

'Mum, I think that might be Harry. He… he might be here to do what I can't.'

Dom's innards solidified with horror. Harry was going to kill them all. Just like the dreams she had been having.

'Give me the gun, Ruby. I've got to defend us.'

'You can't hurt him.'

'He's here to hurt us.'

'But I love him, Mum…'

The yells of the men were punctuated with grunts of pain.

'Please, sweetheart. Give me the gun.'

Dominique stepped towards Ruby, beseeching. For a moment, her daughter hesitated.

'Okay, here, I'll give it to you,' she said.

Her expression as she lifted the shotgun was unreadable.

⊹

Benjamin's limbs were heavy; it was like fighting in treacle. Every swift punch he tried to throw landed slow and ponderous. Harry dodged as a fast as a whippet. Wiry, though luckily not as strong yet as a full-grown man. Strong enough, though. Benjamin was scared.

Why had he taken those damn pills? He should have fought for his family the way he was now, not given in. So what if they had no money? So what if they lost everything, as long as they had each other? He'd been such a fool.

He didn't want to die.

Another punch cracked on his jaw. Dizzy. He tried to shake it away. Punched out again.

Two things kept him going. The first was the thought of saving his family. The second, that his blows must be having some impact on the kid, even in his weakened state, because he kept shouting: 'No. No. Listen to me.'

He wasn't falling for that trick. If he slowed the teen would use that moment to deal a killer blow.

Benjamin wasn't giving up when he was winning something for the first time in a long time.

All that mattered was being there for his family. He had to save them.

❖

'Okay, here, I'll give it to you,' Ruby said.

She stepped towards her mother, shotgun still at her shoulder. Lowered it. Started to remove her index finger from the trigger while twisting the whole rifle in her hands, inexpertly, trying to pass it butt first. Nerves making her fumble. It slipped from her grasp, tumbling to the floor, wrenching her finger. Down, to the side, bone going snap, crackle, pop.

Bang.

A shot rang out.

❖

Normally, Mouse did the climb along the ledge in summer, with bare feet, and it was easy. Especially with the trellis as a ladder.

But right now, Mouse was scared. The bottoms of her slippers were all shiny and slippery, which was great for doing big skids along the hall, but not good for climbing. Her feet kept slipping from beneath her, and she had to concentrate really, really hard as she edged along.

She could hear shouting, and she wanted to see Mummy and Daddy, and be safe with Ruby. She wanted to hide with Ted in the cupboard.

Her muscles trembled with the effort of holding herself in place. Almost there. Her foot slid from beneath her again, making her gasp, but finally she reached her big sister's window. Carefully, oh, so carefully, she wedged the fingers of one hand beneath the sill, then let go of the brickwork with the other hand and went to tap against the glass.

Screaming. A big bang. Deafening. Hurting her ears.

Mouse slipped in shock, slippered feet scrabbling at nothing but air. The trellis – Daddy had torn it down. One slipper fell, tumbling to the ground with a soft thump.

Mouse hung on to the ledge with one hand. Arm hurting, fingers burning and breaking.

'Mummy! Daddy!' she screamed.

Nails clawing at nothing as she fell.

The air shocked from her as she hit the stone slabs.

Pain.

Darkness.

# CHAPTER 100

Benjamin heard the shot. Heard the screaming. So did Harry. Both froze, glaring at the closed bedroom door. Benjamin recovered faster. Despite the drugs that were shutting down his system, the urge to get through that door and help his wife and children overwhelmed, pushing him on.

Muhammad Ali had a quote that would help. If only he could remember it. Something about only a man who has suffered defeat being capable of reaching right down into himself to find that extra ounce of strength to win an evenly matched bout.

Yes, that was Benjamin now.

For his wife, for his children, he dug deeper than he had known possible.

His body felt as wobbly as water, his vision swam. He lurched towards the Tiffany lamp. Raised it high. Brought it down with a sickening crunch onto Harry's head.

Harry didn't see it coming. He had his head turned and suddenly – wham. There were no stars, no ringing bells, only silence as the carpet rose to meet his face. His lips pursed, trying to form a single word. Ruby. After two blinks there was only darkness.

The man-child crumpled onto the lush carpet that Benjamin would never be able to pay off. Benjamin's strength had all but gone. That last blow took everything he had. He fell beside Harry, panting with effort.

Dying. He was dying. He knew that with certainty, even though he couldn't feel any pain. In fact, that was the most worrying thing, the total absence of agony; instead, he felt light as a feather, calm, and… what was the word? Serene, yes, serene.

He shook his head – why hadn't he been able to think of the word? Why was he even trying to think of words? He'd been doing something, going somewhere…

Ruby's bedroom. The shot.

With a huff of effort, he stood. Wobbled. Sank to his knees, crying in frustration. He tried to stand, tried to get his legs to do what his brain was saying. He went on all fours and tried to push up using his hands. They shook with effort. No strength in them. They felt strangely disconnected from the rest of him. It almost made him laugh – which was strange because his face was wet with tears.

Jelly legs. That's what he had. Like a drunken teenager. Try as he might, he couldn't stand, couldn't get his legs firm and strong. He remembered the Christmas he and Dom had got drunk and danced all night in their tiny flat. Then made love on the scratchy sofa. He remembered the terror and joy of Ruby's second Christmas, when she had taken her first steps and he had felt that already she was growing up and he would lose her. He'd run around their home putting cushions on every sharp corner, trying to protect her. He thought of reading bedtime stories to Amber, until she had got so good at reading that she had started reading them to him instead, until her eyes closed. He thought of the best days of his life, and not once did an expensive watch, or fancy pen enter his head.

He needed to reach his family now. He needed to protect them.

Benjamin blinked, eyes going in and out of focus. Sometimes everything seemed so sharp. As though he could see for the first time. Every lush fibre of the expensive carpet stood out clearly.

His face hit the floor. He let out a breath. Another. Softer than the last. Shallower, less substantial.

Fingers twitched, a mere reflex now. He had lost all control of his body. Mind skittering away.

Life was so short. It was over so quickly. And he had wasted it. Benjamin would never get old. He would never see his children grow up, or walk them down the aisle. He wouldn't get to become a better person with their help, and put right the wrongs he had done. He wouldn't be there for them in tough times, or share their triumphs and happiness.

Because he had put money before everything else.

What had he done?

❖

The last thing to go through Dominique's head, apart from the tight spray of shotgun pellets, was the image of her teenage daughter's face. Ruby's expression was so innocent as she stood before her mother. So young and wiped clean of the anger that had twisted it until so recently.

Ruby looked like Dominique's little girl again.

It had been a long time since she saw her daughter, truly saw her, and the mother's heart lifted.

Then she saw the shotgun slipping from Ruby's grasp, her finger snagging, and being twisted with a crack, pulling the trigger back, even as Dom pushed her out of the way with a warning shout.

She knew what would happen. Knew that she was putting herself into the line of fire. It was the only way to save her daughter. Dominique was going to do exactly what she had promised – step up, protect her family, save Ruby.

In the final fraction of a second before the shotgun pellets exploded from the muzzle, Dominique gazed at her daughter and felt joy. Ruby knew she was loved, at last. There was no more hurt and bitterness on her face. Dom's only regret in dying was that she wouldn't be able to share Ruby's bright future.

Then the pellets tore through her flesh and bone.

She died before the dusty, faintly sulphurous smell of shot wafted into the air.

❖

What happened played in a loop over and over in Ruby's mind. Accelerating with each viewing. Every time, she hoped it would stop. Normality restored. All one big, horrible mistake.

Faster, faster, faster.

'Ruby, move!' her mum screamed.

The teenager felt a blow to her side that sent her falling onto the bed, just as a deafening shot rang out. Mum's head snapped back. A mist of vermillion filled the air. Hung momentarily, before creating a constellation pattern on the wall and ceiling, as Ruby's mother slumped to the floor.

She was dead. Clearly. But Ruby couldn't believe it. She tried to untangle her ruined finger from the trigger, causing it to go off again, pellets embedding into the ceiling. With an agonised whimper of terror and denial, she broke free at last. Dropping it, she rushed towards her mother, screaming.

There had to have been a mistake.

Ruby tumbled to her knees, and hauled her mum's limp body into her arms. Held her, rocking, begging. So much blood, her skin sticky with it.

'Come back to me, Mum. I'm sorry. I didn't mean it…'

A dusty, metallic smell hung in the air. Coppery. Ruby's ears giving a tinnitus scream, eardrums damaged from the deafening blast. *eeeeEEEEEEeeeee.*

The shotgun stared at her. Hard. Cold. Unforgiving.

❖

Mouse lay very, very still. She didn't even breathe. It hurt to breathe. Finally, she stopped, and floated away on a cushion of blue, up, up and away, free as a bird. Like magic. Like all the best things she had read about.

Mummy was there, with Aslan. Waiting. Hugging her.

'You're no mouse, you've got the heart of a lion,' Mummy whispered.

She felt warm and snuggly. She never wanted to leave.

'I will always be here for you, sweetheart, watching. Even if you can't see me, I'm there.'

What was Mummy talking about?

She wanted to hug her back, but couldn't make her arms move. Mouse felt like she did when she swam underwater. The water made sounds all muffled and funny. And when she looked around everything seemed wiggly, and the colours weren't right because she was looking through the waves. That's how everything was now.

Mummy stopped hugging and pressed on the side of Mouse's neck, firm. But when she spoke, her voice was like a man's.

'No, sir, nothing. She's gone.'

Sir? Was she at school?

Everything around her started to fade. Like Mummy wasn't real. Mouse managed to lift her hands up, trying to hold onto her, but somehow Mouse was on the bottom of a swimming pool and Mummy's hands were on her chest, pushing down painfully as she counted.

'One, two, three...'

The man's voice joined in. Took over.

Mouse knew what she had to do now. She fought her way to the surface, kicking against the current that seemed to want to drag her back down, remembering Mummy's words that she had the heart of a lion. Mouse fought and fought and...

'Twenty-nine, thirty.'

A breath blew her upwards.

'Wait. There's a pulse,' shouted the man.

He sounded very happy, like he'd just opened the best Christmas present ever.

# CHAPTER 101

Chief Inspector Paul Ogundele did a dance of relief inside as he realised his CPR had done the trick. The child was alive! The only outward sign he gave, though, was a slight upturn of his mouth. An armed response officer hurried over to him.

'All clear, sir. We've checked the place and it's safe.'

A nod. 'Get the paramedics in, now,' he barked.

Florescent outfits overran the place in seconds. The little girl was taken away first, crying gently.

'Will she be okay?' Ogundele called.

'Hard to say, but she doesn't seem to have any broken bones. It's a miracle. The fact she's got the energy to cry is actually a good sign. I'm confident,' replied a paramedic as he rushed by.

The teenage boy left next. He needed an urgent CT scan, and possible blood transfusion.

'What about the father?' the chief inspector asked.

'Indications are he has overdosed, whether deliberately or not, we can't say. He'll have to have his stomach pumped, and until we ascertain what exactly he's taken, we can't be sure how to counteract the medication he's ingested,' a medic replied. 'If he's overdosed on paracetamol, there's probably nothing anyone can do to stop his organs shutting down.'

'Fingers crossed it's ibuprofen or sleeping tablets, then,' Ogundele replied. He was about to ask another question, but one of his officers sidled over.

'Guv, we've got a problem regarding the mother.'

The scene up in the bedroom hadn't changed at all. The teenager, Ruby Thomas, still lay prone over her mum. Blood still decorated the walls and ceiling. An officer stood nearby, looking lost and awkward.

A keening sound, so small and sad, drifted into the air.

Ogundele sighed, and a tiny part of his heart that still hadn't hardened after years of service broke a little more. He was going to have to somehow persuade her to leave her mum. He backed out, grabbed a protective forensic suit, overshoes and gloves, then returned. Bent over the girl, voice low.

'Hey, Ruby? My name's Paul. Would you mind if we had a look at you, to see if you're hurt?'

No movement. The only sound was sobbing.

Ogundele mouthed to the crime scene photographer, checking that everything had been recorded, then reached out and stroked the girl's hair. She was floppy, shock robbing her of her ability to move or speak. He had seen it before.

'Come on, Ruby. Your mum would want us to look after you. Can you look at me? That's it.'

It took a lot of slow coaxing to make the girl let go of her mother's body. He led Ruby down the stairs, away from the bloodbath, feeling her shaking as she leaned against him. At the moment, she couldn't speak to anyone, but Ogundele was keen to get her down the station for a statement. First, she would have to be checked over for injuries, and an appropriate adult found to sit in on the interview, as she was underage. A colleague was calling a family friend named Fiona who was down as an emergency contact.

Ogundele didn't make snap judgements, he had learned better than that over the years. He would let the scene tell its tale, allow the blood spatters to reveal what on earth had happened here. From his experienced eye, though, despite the diary condemning the teen, the blood and gore patterns did not add up to her standing in front of her mother and blasting her away. It looked like a terrible accident, particularly as Ruby's trigger finger was bent at a strange angle, clearly broken. As for what other tragic series of events had taken place in the house, the truth would come out, eventually. It always did.

❖

He watched the final ambulance pull away into the pre-dawn darkness and gave a sigh. The forensic team would be going over the house for hours before Dominique Thomas's remains could be removed. Detectives would arrive soon to start their investigation. But this would be a Christmas Day the chief inspector wouldn't forget in a hurry – and neither would the neighbours. He scanned the crowds of shocked faces at windows, rain tracking down the glass like tears. Those who had gathered soggily behind the cordon looked the same, too. Pale, open-mouthed, glassy-eyed beneath the street lamps and the twinkling fairy lights of neighbours' outdoor decorations.

A guttural staccato call of a bird rang out. That magpie again. It made Ogundele pause and look around once more.

Wait. One person's reaction looked different from everyone else's numb shock. A blonde woman, crying and shaking. She caught his eye and turned away, but not before Ogundele spotted something flit across her features. Panic and guilt.

Ogundele got that tingling sensation again; the one he relied on during all his years of policing. Sadly, hauling someone in for questioning required more than a tingle.

# CHAPTER 102

Black char chased an orange flame along the paper. Kendra watched, holding onto Ben's farewell note as long as she could before dropping it into the sink of her new flat in the New Town district of Edinburgh.

Kendra certainly had never imagined in her wildest dreams that she was putting so much pressure on Ben that he'd try to kill himself. Finding the note had been horrifying. She had only sleepily nipped to the loo that awful Christmas Eve, now seven weeks ago, and spotted it shoved under her door. Thinking it was a festive love message, she had ripped it open. The contents made her vomit. She had rushed straight to his house to try to stop him, but the police cordon was already in place.

Standing there in the rain, watching Ben and his family being carried out to ambulances, had been agonising. Rain had pattered on Kendra's head, creating a tattoo of guilt that trickled down her face and joined her tears as she waited, waited, waited to find out what was happening. Stretching her neck to see over the other onlookers, as rumours flew through the crowd.

As painful as it was, she had decided there and then to walk away.

Kendra had breathed a huge sigh of relief when she discovered Ben had pulled through, after several days in intensive care.

It was a shame Dominique had lost her life. Even more of a shame that Ben, now free of his wife, was on bail facing all kinds of embezzlement and fraud charges. It looked as though he'd be going down for a few years, even with his guilty plea and mitigating circumstances. From what she had gathered from the newspapers, he was staying with his sister, while the children were looked after by that best friend of Dom's, Fiona someone or other – the lawyer woman. Apparently, she was now their legal guardian, and they were getting counselling alone, and also as a family with Ben. According to the papers, anyway.

Kendra truly hoped they sorted themselves out. What had she done? All she had wanted was to force Ben's hand. To make life at home so miserable that he would willingly run into her open arms. They loved each other, they should have been together. Why couldn't he have seen that? Why had he clung to his family?

Why had she pushed Ruby so hard?

When Kendra had discovered Jayne went to the same school as Ruby, it had seemed the perfect way to find out more about Ben's kids. But Ruby had sounded such a pain. Jayne had confessed to Kendra that she couldn't stand the stuck-up teenager. She sounded a nightmare. Kendra worried she and Ben's eldest might not get on. Ruby sounded the type to act up and potentially make Kendra's perfect new life a misery.

One day Jayne had broken down in front of Kendra.

'I – I've done something awful. I'm so ashamed. What should I do, should I tell my mum?' she begged, those muddy brown eyes piggy pink with tears.

'What on earth is it?'

'That girl I told you about… Ruby. She got beaten up and someone filmed it. I got hold of the video and…' She sniffled incoherently.

'Take your time.'

'I've shared it with everyone I know. Got them to share it all over, too. It was just stupid jealousy. I can't believe I've been so mean. And now, she looks totally miserable. We all feel bad about it. Should I tell Mum? Should I apologise to Ruby?'

It had taken a lot to persuade the girl to leave things be, and not even apologise. But Kendra had managed it, buying her conscience with soothing words and a lot of impromptu presents such as lipsticks and eye make-up. Why? Because the mistress had realised Ruby was the key to Kendra's own dreams coming true.

If Ruby continued to play up, then it would put Ben under increasing pressure at home. At the same time, Kendra would show him what a safe haven her own place was for him. Eventually, he would leap at the chance to leave his miserable marriage and nightmare kids, and begin again with the young lover. Before you could say 'Bob's your uncle, Ben's my husband' he'd have proposed.

That was her Big Plan.

So, Kendra copied Ruby's number from Ben's phone one night. Next day she sent a couple of text messages to the teen, mentioning the fight, to throw the kid off the scent and make her believe it was her peers picking on her. The messages contained nothing bad, just intimating that she wasn't the most popular person in the world. She wanted Ruby to be miserable and cause trouble at home. It wasn't something Kendra was proud of, but all is fair in love and war, right, and she'd make it up to the teen once she became her stepmother.

Like Ben always said, you had to bet big to win big. And sometimes there was collateral damage.

As time had gone on, though, Kendra's texts had become more extreme, more bullying. She had often taken her frustrations with Ben out on the girl.

*'You stink.'*

*'You're ugly.'*

*'Why don't you do everyone a favour and die?'*

It had seemed fairly innocent at the time; after all, how bad could a few text messages be? Kendra had felt a bit guilty when Jayne got thumped by Ruby, who had mistakenly blamed her for the messages. But, as Jayne herself had admitted, she'd deserved the punch for sharing the video in the first place. Kendra couldn't help agreeing; as well as being grateful she herself wasn't sporting such awful bruising, when she always had to look her best for Ben. Still, after her chat with Jayne, she had gone food shopping and almost bumped into Ruby as she came out of one of the fast food places in the main shopping area of Charlton. It had seemed serendipitous, so Kendra had snatched the opportunity to send the teenager a text about her outfit, knowing the thought of being stalked would put the fear of God into her. That would teach her to pick on Jayne. Ruby needed to learn that violence solved nothing.

When she had seen how annoyed Ben was about the scuffle between his daughter and Jayne, Kendra had known she was on the right track, so continued to add pressure on him and Ruby. Clearly not enough, though, because he had still clung to his wife.

She'd confronted Dominique, bullied Ben's daughter, and desperation had even led her to pretend to be pregnant.

The website promoting Ruby as a prostitute had probably been a bridge too far, though.

But if Ben had only stopped mucking Kendra around and made a decision, things wouldn't have got so out of control. She'd never have acted this way if Ben had been a bit more reasonable. Kendra hadn't expected Ben to try to commit suicide – or that his daughter would get hold of a shotgun. The newspapers were at pains to paint the whole thing as a terrible accident; a domino chain of events that had tumbled to its tragic conclusion. Ruby faced no charge, and the police had even issued a statement explaining that forensic evidence had completely exonerated her. To accompany the article had been a photograph of her, leaning on her boyfriend, with her little sister, dad, and Fiona, them all gazing doe-eyed at Dominique's headstone. Thanks to Dominique's life insurance, those kids wouldn't have to worry about money.

So, on the whole, things hadn't worked out too badly for them, and the bad things weren't really Kendra's fault. But sometimes she did find herself feeling guilty for her part in everything.

Had Kendra pushed Ruby too far?

Just in case, she had thrown her old phone away and got a new one so she wasn't linked to Ruby's texts. But there was no reason why anyone would ever suspect her. She rubbed her hands over her face in relief as she thought, accidentally smearing ash over her cheeks. She turned the tap on, rinsing away the charred remains of Ben's note, then splashing her face.

After all that upset, she had done a midnight flit from her Charlton flat and moved back to Edinburgh. That business with her previous boyfriend had died down, finally, and his family wouldn't accuse her of being a stalker now if they bumped into her. Hopefully. She'd sold all of the jewellery Ben had given her, so she could afford a nice flat in the expensive New Town area, on the other side of the city from her family, and her ex. She had a plan to find herself a decent man, with some money, to settle down with. Someone who wouldn't mess her around.

In fact, she already had her eye on someone, which was why she finally felt ready to get rid of Ben's 'suicide' note.

She glanced at the clock – it was time to go. Her soon-to-be new man would be arriving at his favourite café soon, and she needed to 'accidently' bump into him.

She dried her face, then popped on a tiny bit of mascara and blusher. Perfect. Grabbing her coat, she sped towards the front door with a smile of excitement on her face. The future was looking rosy.

There was someone waiting on the other side of the door. His hand raised as though about to knock on the door.

Kendra's heart stuttered.

'Kendra Wilcox?' the police officer checked. 'I'm arresting you on charges of harassment against Ruby Thomas, contrary to section four of the Protection from Harassment Act 1997…'

# A LETTER FROM BARBARA

Thank you for taking the time to read *Her Last Secret*. If you did enjoy it, and want to keep up-to-date with all my latest releases, just sign up at the following link. Your email address will never be shared and you can unsubscribe at any time.

www.bookouture.com/barbara-copperthwaite

Poor, wounded Ruby, lashing out at those she loves, sprang into my mind whole, along with her dysfunctional family. They are not perfect, they are not likeable, but I love them for their imperfections. And in some ways that is what this story is about: loving people as much in spite of themselves as because of them. As the saying goes, you can choose your friends, but you can't choose your family.

I hope you have enjoyed reading *Her Last Secret* as much as I enjoyed writing it. I'd love to hear your thoughts on the book – and if you have the time to leave a review it would be very much appreciated.

If you want to get in touch, or find out the latest on what I'm up to, there are lots of ways: Facebook, Twitter, my blog, and website, as well as Goodreads. I'd love to hear from you!

Thank you for your continuing support and enthusiasm.
Barbara Copperthwaite

AuthorBarbaraCopperthwaite/

BCopperthwait

barbaracopperthwaite.wordpress.com

www.barbaracopperthwaite.com

# ACKNOWLEDGEMENTS

As *Her Last Secret* is about a family falling apart, it seems only right that my biggest thanks should go to my supportive family. While I'm busy writing, my partner, Paul, is running round keeping me and the house going. I couldn't do this without his practical and emotional help. My mum listens to me as I plot murder and mayhem. And my sisters, Rona and Ellen, and brother Rory, encourage me to keep going whenever they see me. I'm particularly grateful to Ellen, to whom this book is dedicated.

I'm no businesswoman, so I needed help when it came to plotting Benjamin's financial shenanigans. Without the incredible input of Peter, a former tax inspector who gave me brilliant insider knowledge, Benjamin would not have been anywhere near as artful.

Anne Henshaw, Dr Carol Cooper, and Kim Pocklington lent me their medical knowledge.

Anyone who would like to know more about Parkinson's can find information and support at www.parkinsons.org.uk

Massive thanks, too, to Facebook's THE Book Club, who put me in touch with Anne and Carol, and whose members are so enthusiastic about my work, along with Crime Book Club, Crime Fiction Addict, and UK Crime Book Club. Last but by no means least on Facebook is Book Connectors, which is so supportive and utterly brilliant.

Police expertise came in the form of fabulous consultant Stuart Gibbon, who was kind enough to share his thirty-two years of experience as a senior-level detective with me. Thank you, Stuart, for your patience even when I was asking the most basic of questions! You've been such a great help.

As always, the Bookouture team have been amazing, and I can't thank them enough. My editor, Keshini, is so talented and easy to work with, and I count my lucky stars to have her by my side. The tireless Kim also deserves special mention for all her incredible publicity work.

Finally, a big thank you to all of my readers for continuing to enjoy my books. One such reader, Margaret Dudgeon, won a competition to have her name in this book. Margaret, I hope you enjoyed seeing your name in print as Ruby's headteacher.

9 781786 812605